please forgive me

Also by Melissa Hill

Something You Should Know
Not What You Think
Never Say Never
All Because of You
Wishful Thinking
The Last to Know
Before I Forget

About the Author

Melissa Hill lives with her husband Kevin and their dog Homer in Dublin. Her previous books including *Before I Forget*, *Wishful Thinking* and *The Last to Know* have all been bestsellers and are widely translated.

For more information, visit her website at
www.melissahill.info

melissa hill
please forgive me

HODDER

First published in Great Britain in 2009 by Hodder & Stoughton
An Hachette UK company

First published in paperback in 2010

3

Copyright © Melissa Hill 2009

The right of Melissa Hill to be identified as the Author
of the Work has been asserted by her in accordance with the
Copyright, Designs and Patents Act 1988.

All rights reserved. No part of this publication may be
reproduced, stored in a retrieval system, or transmitted, in any form
or by any means without the prior written permission of the publisher,
nor be otherwise circulated in any form of binding or cover other
than that in which it is published and without a similar condition
being imposed on the subsequent purchaser.

All characters in this publication are fictitious and any resemblance
to real persons, living or dead is purely coincidental.

A CIP catalogue record for this title is available from the British Library

B format paperback ISBN 978 0 340 95295 5
A fomat paperback ISBN 978 0 340 95298 6

Typeset in Plantin Light by Ellipsis Books Limited, Glasgow

Printed and bound by Clays Ltd, St Ives plc;

Hodder & Stoughton policy is to use papers that are natural,
renewable and recyclable products and made from wood grown in
sustainable forests. The logging and manufacturing processes are expected
to conform to the environmental regulations of the country of origin.

Hodder & Stoughton Ltd
338 Euston Road
London NW1 3BH

www.hodder.co.uk

Massive thanks to the people who help make each book what it is: My magnificent agent and great friend Sheila Crowley, and all the team at Curtis Brown.

Everyone at Hodder, especially Auriol Bishop, a wonderful publisher and valued friend, fantastic editor Sara Kinsella, and all the team in the UK. Also to Breda, Jim, Ruth and everyone at Hachette Ireland for working so hard on my behalf.

Thanks to readers all over the world for your continued support and for sending so many kind messages through my website www.melissahill.info. I love hearing from you and treasure every message.

Dedicated to Luke
My favourite nephew

My love,

I know I'm probably the last person you want to hear from, but I just wanted to tell how sorry I am. You have to know that I would never do anything to hurt you, at least not intentionally, but I made a big mistake, a huge mistake this time.

I realise there's no going back, and I'm not asking for that; I just wanted to let you know how much I regret what happened, and how I wish from the bottom of my heart it never happened, or that I hadn't caused it. But it did, and it's all my fault, and I would do anything to get the chance to go back and undo it. But I can't.

I know I don't have any right to ask, but I hope you're OK?

I'm really not sure what else to say. Just know that I never meant to hurt you, and I'm so very, very sorry.

Please forgive me.

Chapter 1

Leonie Hayes looked around furtively as she joined the line of people in front of her. It was stupid but she was terrified of bumping into someone she knew from Dublin, someone who might recognise her and wonder what she was doing here. Well, she supposed it was obvious what she was doing here (weren't they all doing the same thing?) but she really didn't want to get into the hows and whys. Not that it was anyone else's business but still. Loosening the crocodile clip she was wearing, she let her long auburn hair fall further around her face.

'Move along . . . this way please . . . keep it moving,' a nearby official urged, as the long stream of people slowly shuffled ahead.

What *was* she doing here? Leonie asked herself, feeling a sudden flash of hesitation as she progressed along the queue. Was it too late now to turn around and go home, back to everything that was comfortable, normal and familiar? But just as quickly she remembered that things were different now, and home was no longer comfortable or indeed familiar – everything had changed.

The sharp tone of her mobile ringing from inside her handbag interrupted her thoughts and, rummaging briefly through her things, Leonie took out the phone and checked the number on the display.

Grace again.

Her heart quickened. It was the third call from her best friend in as many days and while she knew she should answer it, she really couldn't talk to anyone just now. There would be too many questions but Leonie could barely make sense of her own thoughts at the moment, let alone try and explain them to someone else. So no, she couldn't talk to Grace, not now anyway. Maybe when . . . when everything had settled down a bit more, and Leonie knew where she was, then she might be able to explain things to her better. Grace would be worried, she knew that, but wouldn't she be even more concerned if she found out where Leonie was or what she was doing now?

Yes, much better to wait rather than run the risk of worrying Grace even further, she decided, trying her best to ignore the shrill ring tone, which sounded even more urgent than normal.

Soon the ringing stopped, and the brief silence was quickly followed by the double beep signalling voicemail. Leonie listened to the message.

'Lee, it's me again,' Grace said, and Leonie could hear the twins shrieking in the background. 'Where are you? I've been trying to reach you for ages. I tried phoning your landline too, but there's no answer from there either,' she added, sounding disappointed. 'I just hope everything's OK, or more importantly that *you're* OK. I'm sure the weekend was tough but . . . look, will you just call me back when you get this? I'm here all day, as usual,' she added in a wry tone. 'Just please phone me back. Hope to talk to you soon, bye.'

Leonie snapped the phone shut. She should really have taken the call; by now it was understandable that Grace would be frantic. She hadn't anticipated her friend ringing the apartment though, and it was interesting (but no surprise) to hear that there was no answer from there either.

Well, there would be plenty of time to worry about that later. What she needed now was to stop thinking and just keep moving before she changed her mind. Although it was a bit late for that, wasn't it?

Of course she'd talk to Grace but only when she was ready. And, more importantly, when she knew it was safe to do so. Still, she mused, biting her lip, it really wasn't fair to have anyone worrying unnecessarily in the meantime. She flipped open the phone and dialled her friend's mailbox. The coward's way out, but it would do in the circumstances.

'Grace, hi, it's me, I'm so sorry I haven't been in touch before now, but things have been horrible . . .' Despite herself, her voice broke, and she felt a huge lump in her throat. Then she swallowed hard and took a deep breath before continuing. 'Just wanted to let you know that I'm OK and thanks for phoning. I promise I'll tell you all as soon as I can, but if you don't mind, I think I just need some time to myself at the moment. But please don't worry. I'm all right and I'll talk to you soon, OK?'

She took another deep breath before switching off the phone and putting it back in her pocket. That sounded all right, didn't it? And it was a truth of sorts. She *did* need some time to herself just now and she would tell Grace everything when the time was right.

After a few more minutes of waiting in line an official called Leonie forward and pointed her in the direction of a free booth. With some trepidation she approached the desk and smiled weakly at the serious-looking, heavyset man sitting behind it.

He didn't return the smile. 'Your documents please?' he asked and Leonie handed them over.

The man studied the details for what seemed like an age, looking from the paperwork to Leonie and back again, while almost instinctively she averted her eyes from his gaze. She wasn't sure why exactly, it was just what you did in these situations, wasn't it? She hated being made to feel so uncomfortable, in the same way she felt when going through the metal sensors earlier. Why did the set-up at these places always make you feel like you were up to no good?

'What do you do for a living, Miss Hayes?' he asked her, his tone neutral.

'I work for an event management company,' she replied, the half-truth tripping off her tongue easily. The official nodded, evidently satisfied with this answer.

'OK, now I'm going to ask you to please place your left index finger on the device here,' he told her, indicating the fingerprinting contraption positioned on top of the desk. When Leonie complied, he asked her to repeat the same process with her right hand. 'Thank you. Now please stand back and look up at the camera just here . . .'

Again Leonie did as she was bid, eager to get the whole thing over with as quickly as possible.

There was a brief delay as the man yet again checked her paperwork, and having inputted something into his computer, proceeded to double-stamp the documentation.

'OK, Miss Hayes,' he said his mouth breaking into a smile as he handed Leonie back her newly stamped passport and immigration documents, 'you're all set. Welcome to the United States.'

Chapter 2

Three Weeks Later

'I've got a confession to make.'

Leonie looked up, her heart sinking as she wondered what was coming. She supposed she should have known better than to assume it could be that simple, that *anything* could be simple these days. 'Oh?'

The real estate agent smiled. 'This place isn't strictly available right now. It will be soon which is why I'm showing it to you.'

'Oh, OK.' She looked around the apartment, trying her best not to look too interested, but the truth was she'd fallen in love with the place on sight. Nothing else she'd seen over the last two weeks had even come close.

The top floor of a converted Victorian house, the apartment was situated on Green Street, a pretty, tree-lined neighbourhood in the heart of San Francisco. The house was within walking distance of cafés, local restaurants, and myriad little boutiques and galleries that lined side streets nearby.

The apartment itself, with its oak ceiling carvings, ornate fireplace and huge bay windows, was warm, cosy and simply bursting with character. From the living-room window, Leonie could just about make out (if she moved to the right and stood high on her tiptoes) the Golden Gate Bridge straddling the waters of the bay, while the teeniest corner of Alcatraz Island was just visible from the left-hand side. Below, the roofs of neighbouring houses descended like stepping stones towards San Francisco Bay, where sailboats sparkled prettily beneath the sunlight.

But even without the gorgeous views, there was just something about these old houses that enchanted her. Outside, the house was chocolate box pretty; painted in white and eggshell blue, and elaborately embellished with decorative cornices and mouldings, angled bay windows, and a wooden arcade porch. Adding to the charm, the neighbouring houses were painted in various shades of pastels, pink, green and yellow, which made them look almost like a row of dolls' houses. It was a design that typified much of the architectural style in the city, and one of the reasons Leonie had so quickly fallen in love with San Francisco. She'd be over the moon to secure this apartment.

Granted the interior was dated and somewhat grubby but nothing that a little TLC couldn't cure. The oak parquet floor would scrub up nicely, and she could liven up the living room with some colourful rugs, find funky cushions for that drab-looking sofa and pick out some artwork for the walls. The kitchenette was small but practical, and the bedroom adjoining the living room was bright, roomy and had plenty of wardrobe space. Not that she'd need much of that, for the moment at least. But most importantly, it was a million times better than her shoebox room in the Holiday Inn, and wouldn't it be wonderful to find a place in the city she could call home?

'Well, I thought I'd give you a sneak preview seeing as nothing else I've shown you has fit the bill,' the agent said, putting an end to Leonie's day-dreaming. 'It's a great neighbourhood, very safe, and as you saw on the way in, you've got the bonus of a private access door too.'

From what Leonie could tell, the house was divided into three separate units, all of which had their own entrance. The ground-floor apartment looked to be accessed through a side-door alongside a garage at street level, while they'd entered 'her' apartment up some steps and through one of two adjacent doors beneath the porch, before taking the stairs to the top floor.

'You're right, it's absolutely perfect,' she agreed, unable to hide her enthusiasm. But wasn't it just her luck that it wasn't available! 'But you said there's someone still living here?'

Strange, it certainly didn't look or feel like that. Dust on the furniture and absence of any recent signs of inhabitation aside, there was an air of disuse and almost . . . abandonment about the place that was quite striking.

'That's right. Officially, I shouldn't be even showing you this,' the agent said with a mischievous gleam in his eye, 'because it isn't actually on the market until the end of this month. But . . .' He turned to face her. 'Personally I think it's kind of special. Green Street is a great neighbourhood, and these old Victorians don't come along every day either. If we put it on the open market, it'll be snapped up within the hour, so if you think you might be interested—'

'I'm interested,' Leonie said decisively, not needing to think about it for a single second longer. This place was perfect, and luckily for her she was the very first person to see it. It could be fate, or just blind luck, but either way, it certainly felt like finally something was going right. 'When can I move in?'

Later that day she phoned Grace with an update on her living situation.

When she first arrived, Leonie had contacted her friend to let her know where she was and unsurprisingly, Grace was dumbfounded to learn that she'd gone all the way to the States.

'You're really going through with this then?' she gasped, sounding crestfallen.

'What made you think I wouldn't? Grace, this wasn't just some mad notion on my part, you know.'

'OK, I can appreciate that you need to escape for a while, but why go so far? Why not just move down to Cork or some-where, at least then I could still see you now and again. I can barely pick San Francisco out on a map!'

She sounded hurt and Leonie felt a fresh pang of guilt. Clearly Grace was still upset that she'd left Dublin without saying a proper goodbye. But at the time, Leonie didn't have the courage to face her. Grace would almost certainly have tried to talk her out of it.

'I'm sorry,' she replied. 'It is hard not having you around to talk to, but at the same time I had to do this.'

'I know, but, well, it's just so extreme, Leonie. Running away from things never helps in the long run you know.'

Leonie felt a lump in her throat. 'Maybe, but at the moment, it's the only way I know how to deal with this.'

'But surely it's better to be here in Dublin with us, the people who love and care about you instead of all alone in some big city where nobody gives a damn?'

'It's not like that, people are nice here,' she replied, thinking of the helpful real estate guy who'd today found her the perfect apartment, and Carla the Holiday Inn receptionist with whom Leonie had struck up a friendship of sorts over the last couple of weeks. 'Everyone's been really friendly.'

Since her arrival three weeks before, she'd felt very much at ease in San Francisco. The gorgeous blue skies and bright Californian sunshine lifted her mood immediately, and although it was as busy and bustling as any other city, the place had a relaxed bohemian vibe about it too. So yes, of course she sometimes felt lonely and missed everything and everyone she'd left behind, but that was partly the point, wasn't it?

That afternoon, she'd signed the lease on the one-bed Victorian conversion and would be moving in at the end of the month.

'So how long are you thinking of staying?' Grace asked.

'Well, the lease on the apartment is for six months with a renewal option after that so I don't know, for as long as it takes, I suppose.'

'Six *months*?' Grace shrieked.

'Did you think I'd just stay here for a few weeks and then turn tail and come back? What would be the point of that?'

'Well, I know I couldn't just drop everything and abandon my whole life just like that. Now, don't get me wrong,' Grace added quickly, 'I know there's a very good reason but, look, it all seems so . . . drastic.' When Leonie said nothing, she went on. 'It's just, you're usually so calm and together about things; I guess I just didn't expect you to react like this.'

'Calm and together about other people's problems, maybe,' Leonie said wryly. But when it came to her own life she'd always been a total disaster, hadn't she? And yes, coming here might have been impulsive, but at the same time, it felt right.

'Well, OK, so now you've found a place to live, great – at least I'll know where you are for the next six months. But what are you going to do now? You can't just hide away on your own in some apartment.'

'Well, I suppose now that I have a base, I'm going to start looking for a new job.'

Right before she left Dublin, Leonie had resigned from her job at Xanadu Event Management and turned down her boss's kind offer of keeping a position open for when she returned, simply because she wasn't sure that she ever *would* be returning. And although she had a nice bit of savings to keep her going for a while, Leonie knew that if she really wanted to start afresh and settle in to the city properly, she needed to find some work.

'I just can't get my head around this,' Grace said mournfully and Leonie could almost picture her friend shaking her blond head in disbelief as she sat in her kitchen back home in Dublin surrounded by the toddlers' things. 'And *America* of all places . . .'

'Well, it is home too, in a way, isn't it?' Leonie replied, referring to the fact that she had actually been born in the States, although her Irish parents had moved back to Dublin soon after. Following their separation some time ago, they'd moved on yet again; her father now lived in Hong Kong and her mum was in South Africa with a new partner. She could have gone to her mum's of course, but she didn't want to be a burden, and more importantly she knew that in order to get through this, she needed to be on her own for a while.

'Look . . .' Grace said quietly, after a long pause, 'I suppose I might as well tell you, I bumped into Adam the other day.' Leonie's heart almost stopped. 'He doesn't know you've moved away.'

Leonie felt faint. 'You didn't . . . ?'

'Of *course* I didn't,' Grace replied quickly. 'I promised I wouldn't, didn't I? I'm not saying I agree with it, but a promise is a promise – even if it had to be made over the phone from across the Atlantic,' she added archly.

Leonie tried to digest what her friend had said but didn't really know why she felt so surprised that Grace had seen Adam; Dublin wasn't that big a city after all, was it?

'So, don't you want to know what we talked about or what

he said?' Grace prompted when Leonie stayed silent.

'No, I don't, actually,' she replied, swallowing hard. 'I'd rather not talk about him at all to be honest.'

'Well he looked absolutely terrible, and for what it's worth, I think he's really sorry that—'

'Grace, please,' Leonie interjected hoarsely. 'I just don't want to know, OK?'

'Well, I'm sorry but you're my best friend, and I'm really worried about you! Look, I know what happened was awful, but isn't there any chance you two could try and work things out? Forgive and forget, maybe?'

Leonie closed her eyes. 'I really don't think so, Grace,' she replied determinedly, knowing in her heart that some things just couldn't be forgiven.

Chapter 3

Two weeks later, Leonie got the keys to the apartment and moved out of the Holiday Inn into what would be her brand-new home – for the next six months at least. She'd told Grace the truth when she'd said she didn't know how long she'd be staying; all she knew was that escaping was what she'd always done when faced with any major decisions in her life.

OK, so her job required her to be cool, calm and decisive and she was usually pretty good at applying these same traits to other people's problems, but for some reason, she could never manage to call upon them when it came to her own.

In her teenage years, when all her classmates were worrying about exams and college places, Leonie decided to avoid the stress by taking a year out to go backpacking around Asia and Australia. While Grace and her other schoolfriends had been horrified (and more than a little envious), Leonie's parents had been fully supportive. In fact, the only major decision she'd given real consideration to recently was agreeing to marry Adam – and clearly, she should have thought even harder about *that*, she mused now as she dragged her rucksack up the steps to the front door of the house.

Entering her apartment, she was struck once again by the large angled bay window that dominated the living room, flooding it with light, and she guessed she'd while away many a day and evening sitting on the window seat and drinking in those amazing views across the bay. It was the perfect spot for curling up with a good book.

But while it was tempting to 'hide away' (as Grace put it) in a place so cosy and lovely, she knew there was no point. She'd end up dwelling even more on what had happened back home.

No, Leonie decided immediately, there would be no moping about here; she'd done enough of that already, hadn't she? Instead, she'd take a few days to settle in and then make it her business to explore the area properly. The city was so compact you could see most of it on foot, and if walking the hills got too difficult she could always hop on one of the cable cars (although they looked *very* scary going up and down those humongous hills on a single wire – what if it snapped?). It was lovely that her street was only a few blocks from Fisherman's Wharf; there was always plenty of activity down there what with tourist-thronged Pier 39 and the lively markets and street performers. It was hard not knowing anyone, but hopefully this would only be for a while and if she was seriously stuck for someone to talk to, she could always go down and chat to the sea lions!

But first things first Leonie decided, wrinkling her nose; this place needed a good spring clean. The previous occupant hadn't exactly left it in a pristine state. A sheen of dust lay on the coffee table and over the mantelpiece, and the adjoining kitchen (although it was more of a kitchenette really) looked decidedly grubby.

She dumped her rucksack in the bedroom, deciding to head straight back out to pick up some supplies. There was a mini-mart at the end of the street so she should be able to get enough cleaning paraphernalia there to keep her occupied for the afternoon at least. And while she was at it, she might as well stock up on a few essentials like milk and sugar. She'd do a full shop at one of the bigger supermarkets soon, but the place wouldn't really be home until she'd enjoyed a cuppa. An excited thrill ran along her spine as the reality of making her first cup of tea in her own little place in a city thousands of miles away from her normal life struck her.

Despite the problems that had led to her being here in the first place, she was already starting to feel much more positive. And if she had anything to do with it, she thought, putting her hands on her hips as she surveyed her new surroundings, Green Street would soon start to feel like home.

Having scrubbed the living room and the somewhat neglected kitchen, she eventually made her way to the bedroom, which to her relief didn't look like it needed too much work, apart from vacuuming the carpets and cleaning out the wardrobes – or closets as they called them here, she remembered with a smile.

Standing on a kitchen chair to give her enough height, Leonie set about dusting inside the wardrobe. It was a very old, practically antique piece made from dark redwood, and could very well be about the same age as the house itself, she thought, remembering that she'd read somewhere how a lot of Victorian houses had been constructed with the then easily available (and more importantly fire-resistant) native timber.

She reached inside and swept a duster along the shelf, intending to give it no more than a quick going over for the sake of it. Then she frowned, as her hand connected with something. She peered into the darkness and saw what looked to be a small wooden storage box hidden deep in the back. Great, she groaned inwardly, the last tenants had obviously left her a nice housewarming present of their unwanted rubbish!

Sighing, Leonie dragged the box across the shelf and lifted it out of the wardrobe, intending to place it on the floor and out of her way. But as she went to pick it up, Leonie suddenly lost her balance on the chair, and both she and the box went tumbling to the ground.

'Ah, look what you made me do!' she wailed rubbing the small of her back, which had taken the brunt of the fall. The little gold catch on the box had fallen open and its contents, a collection of envelopes loosely wrapped in cellophane, were strewn all over the floor.

So much for cleaning the place up, she grunted, deciding that it had to be a sign that she'd done enough for one afternoon. Not to mention a very good excuse for a cuppa . . .

Standing up, Leonie roughly gathered together the contents of the box. As she did she realised that, strangely, the envelopes were still sealed and unopened. She picked one up for closer examination. It was a letter, addressed to someone who must have previously lived here.

Helena Abbott.

In fact, each and every one was unopened and addressed to the same person.

Weird.

The box in her arms, Leonie went back out to the kitchen and switched on the kettle. While waiting for it to boil, she sat by the bay window and examined the envelopes one by one. The handwriting on each envelope was identical, she realised. Such beautiful handwriting too, almost like calligraphy.

Why hadn't the letters been opened? Assuming this Helena Abbott, whoever she was, had previously lived here and had intentionally stored the letters away in the box (and a very nice ornate one at that), then why hadn't she bothered to open them? Or taken them with her when she moved out? Had she just forgotten about them hidden away in the back of the wardrobe or . . . ?

The kettle boiled, and Leonie shook her head, telling herself that it was none of her business. Putting the letters aside, she went into the kitchen, took out a mug and made a fresh cup of tea.

But typically, her curiosity (or downright nosiness as Grace would call it) managed to get the better of her, and mug in hand, she returned to the windowsill and set the box on her lap and the tea alongside her.

Lifting the lid, she again took the envelopes out of the cellophane for a closer look. There seemed to be no return address on any of them so it was impossible to tell where they might have come from. She peered at the postmark, trying to see if this might yield anything, but it looked to be nothing more than an official-looking but pretty generic ink mark.

Oh well, she thought, putting them back in the box, she'd give the rental agency a call and see if they had a forwarding address.

Although, something told Leonie that Helena Abbott might not miss them.

'No, I'm afraid there isn't a forwarding address on file,' the man from the rental agency told her when Leonie called a few days later. She had since cleaned the apartment from top to bottom and found nothing else belonging to previous tenants other than the box.

'Oh. It's just, I've got a pile of post—'

'Post?'

'Sorry, I mean – mail,' she corrected quickly. 'She left it behind when she moved out, and it could be important.'

'I'm sorry but we've got nothing at all on file. In fact, we don't have a record of the name you mentioned as a customer of this office.'

Leonie frowned. 'What? But she only moved out a couple of weeks ago.'

'Perhaps so, but she wasn't a client of ours. The landlord obviously used another agency for previous lettings,' he explained.

'Well, maybe the landlord might have her address then. Could I have his number?'

'I'm afraid we can't give out that kind of information,' the man sighed.

'What?' Leonie cried, frustrated. 'So, what I am supposed to do about the letters? Surely there must be some way of contacting the landlord? I mean, what if something goes wrong with the apartment, if it burns down or something?'

'Ma'am, the agency is responsible for all aspects of the rental, but if you'd like to leave your name and number I can contact our client and pass on a message for him to call you.' He was sounding a little irritated now.

'OK then,' Leonie sighed. She supposed that would have to do. Chances were the landlord wouldn't give a fiddler's about some previous tenant's belongings but if nothing else at least she'd tried.

That much done, she started to prepare lunch, and thought about the next thing she needed to do; see about getting a job. She'd spent the last few days settling into the apartment and getting to know the neighbourhood a little better. The day after she moved in, she'd taken a cable car down to Union Square (which was *seriously* scary) where she'd spent a few hours picking up the various household items she needed to kit the place out completely. There was a gorgeous little art gallery nearby where she'd managed to pick up some funky pieces of wall art for an absolute song and which went a long way towards brightening up the living room, as did the pretty handmade candles from the craft shop she found a block away.

San Francisco was famous for its bohemian culture and hippy New Age roots, but she'd been taken aback by the number of small, independently run stores and eateries in the area instead of the ubiquitous chain stores she'd expected. That personal touch added to the lovely sense of community she'd felt in the neighbourhood right from the off, and many of the cheery café and deli owners were only too happy to chat and give her lots of helpful information on her surroundings.

In fact, the locals had been so friendly and open that they'd given Leonie the courage she needed to think about searching for a job. While she'd enjoyed spending her first few days in the apartment setting up home and alternating between watching (mesmerisingly addictive) American TV or reading by the window seat while gazing out at the sailboats on the bay, she was now starting to feel a bit restless.

Getting a job would hopefully focus her mind and help her settle in even further and even if it was just waitressing or working as a coffee barista, she'd prefer something that involved more interaction with people. Surely with all the bistros and delis in the area, (particularly on Columbus Avenue which boasted more Italian restaurants on a single street than Leonie had seen in any Italian city) she'd be able to pick up a job around here? Having finished lunch, she decided to bite the bullet and head in that direction for a look around.

Despite a little coastal fog it was another glorious sunny day, and as Leonie closed the front door behind her she caught a glimpse of someone entering the apartment downstairs. It was the first time since moving in that she'd heard a sound or noticed any activity from her neighbours, which was either a testament to solid Victorian construction, or a sign that the surrounding tenants were nice and quiet.

It was a pity she'd missed them though, she mused, deciding it would be nice to know her neighbours, at least enough to say hello to now and again.

Going down the steps, she slung her handbag over her shoulder and headed along the tree-lined street in the direction of Columbus Avenue.

On the way she spotted a gorgeous little Italian pottery shop just off one of the side streets; its colourful window display and vibrantly painted exterior attracting her like a magpie. Alongside this were a couple of pretty boutiques and even further along a dinky little bookstore, and before Leonie knew it, she'd wandered completely off course and ended up in an area she didn't recognise. But it didn't matter, she was in no rush, and this was merely another aspect of this city she loved; the notion of wandering around a neighbourhood and randomly uncovering some of its hidden treasures. She moseyed along window-shopping for a little while, occasionally stopping to browse in whatever shops took her fancy, when a sign in a nearby window caught her eye.

HELP WANTED.

From the extravagant flower displays in the window, it looked to be a florist. Leonie looked up at the sign over the door and gave a little laugh at the cheesy-as-you-can-get-name of the store. What else? Well, no time like the present, she thought pushing open the door of Flower Power and going inside.

'Hi there, I see you're looking for staff?'

A stern, heavyset woman, who looked nothing like the New

Age hippy-type Leonie expected gave her an appraising look. 'You know anything about flower arranging, sweetheart?'

Leonie gulped. 'Not a whole lot, to be honest. I mean, I don't have any training or anything.' Numbskull, she really should have thought of that. Leonie had no retail experience whatsoever, as she'd waitressed during her teenage years and on her travels, and from there went into event management. What had possessed her to think she could work in a place like this? 'Although, I used to deal a lot with florists in my last job,' she added quickly.

The woman shrugged. 'Doesn't matter, neither do I,' she said and Leonie was surprised at this given the lavish and highly stylised tropical arrangements that filled the room. 'Anyhow, I'm just looking for someone to work the till and the phones, and process the Internet orders. Do you know anything about the Internet?'

'I do, yes. Again, I haven't worked in this particular area before, I mean with flowers per se but I'm sure I can learn.' She went on to give the woman an account of her experience in event management, and how she'd only recently arrived in San Francisco and happened to be looking for work. 'I was just passing and I saw the sign so . . .'

'Where are you from, honey?' the woman asked, clearly thrown by the accent.

'Ireland. In Europe,' Leonie added helpfully, aware that not everyone would be familiar with her home country.

'I know where Ireland is, I've been there twice,' the other woman said, waving an arm dismissively. 'Guess that pretty hair should have been a giveaway.'

Yup, that and the translucent skin that burns so easily, Leonie thought wryly to herself.

'So have you got a social security number?'

'Well, no, I . . .' Stupidly, she hadn't thought about that

either and now she felt very foolish indeed. What had she been thinking, expecting to just walk into a job in a different country without the necessary documentation? Her resident's visa had obviously given her a false sense of security and—

'Doesn't matter. I guess we can work off the books until you get it.' The woman seemed very easy-going about it all, which made Leonie suspect that this kind of thing was (luckily for her) par for the course.

'You don't mind?'

'Well, let's see how the interview goes and then we can work out the details, OK?'

'Oh yes . . . of course.' Again Leonie felt foolish.

'So, what's your name?'

Introductions were made. The woman was called Marcy, and she owned and managed Flower Power.

'It's a great name for a flower shop, especially here,' Leonie smiled. 'I presume you were part of the hippy movement?'

Marcy looked insulted. 'Are you crazy? I'm a good Baptist girl from Mississippi! None of that "free love" stuff for me. Nah, I moved out West about ten years ago after my husband died.'

'Oh, I'm very sorry to hear that.' She was also horrified she'd raised the subject in the first place, but everyone else she'd met had been so friendly and forthcoming that she'd almost forgotten herself.

But Marcy was unperturbed. 'Look honey, here's the thing, my last girl left on Saturday, and we're heading into a real busy time here with Valentine's Day just around the corner. So I need someone who's smart, hard-working and most importantly doesn't need babysitting,' she added wryly. 'Though I might as well tell you upfront, the pay's not so hot.' She then quoted a weekly wage that was only a third of what Leonie had earned back home and would just about cover her rent. But she could live with that for the moment; she had some savings so all she really needed was enough to pay the rent and living expenses. Her lifestyle wasn't what you would call extravagant. 'There are tips on top of that too and some of our regulars can be very generous.'

Leonie nodded. 'Sounds fine.'

'You're sure?'

'Absolutely.' OK, so she knew very little about flowers (other than ordering them), but Marcy certainly didn't seem to find that a problem. Anyway, working in a place like this looked like it could be fun. Leonie had always loved the fuss surrounding big gift-giving occasions like Valentine's Day and birthdays, so it would be nice to be in the middle of that, and to be a part of an industry whose business was primarily helping other people to feel good. What's more, it meant she'd be involved in the local community, another plus.

They spent a few more minutes agreeing all the details and Leonie was struck again by the speed and ease at which she was settling in to her new life in San Francisco. What with the new apartment and a brand-new job, her old life had been left behind in no time. And that was the plan, wasn't it?

'OK then, Leonie,' her new boss said at last, 'see you Monday bright and early.'

Chapter 4

Alex Fletcher really thought she was going to scream at the pert little blonde standing in front of her.

'Hi, I'm Cyndi Dixon, live at the scene of—'

'Cyndi,' Alex interjected wearily, 'loosen up a little, will you? We're not live and this isn't CNN.'

'Don't I know it,' Cyndi grumbled, smoothing down her hair before turning to face the TV camera once again. 'Hi, I'm Cyndi Dixon and *Today by the Bay*, I'm here at the scene of this morning's rather, um . . . rather unusual life or death rescue,' she added, finally injecting the warmth into her voice that Alex wanted.

Five takes later, Alex nodded encouragingly. *Today by the Bay* – the two-minute entertainment/news slot Alex produced for San Francisco's local TV station SFTV – wasn't exactly *Live at Five* but it was her baby, and she wasn't going to let some jumped-up little Barbie make a mess of it. It was obvious that Cyndi was only using this as a springboard to the news studio, and good luck to her, but Alex had been running this show for close to two years now, so like it or not, Cyndi would have to do things her way.

OK, so telling her on the first day to lose the sorority-girl bangs and brighten up her wardrobe hadn't gone down particularly well, but *Today by the Bay* was a human interest segment and nobody warmed to a reporter that looked like she'd just been to a funeral.

Cyndi continued her commentary. 'It was right here behind me, that Jake Stephens risked life and most definitely limb,' she added, inserting a little chuckle into her voice, 'to carry out one of the most incredible water rescue operations the city has ever seen.'

'Cut!' Frustrated, Alex signalled to Dave the cameraman. 'A little too dramatic on the ending there maybe?' she said to the other woman, who rolled her eyes. 'Let's just go with "the most incredible water rescue operation" and continue from there, OK?'

'Sure,' Cyndi harrumphed, before filming began yet again. 'Yep folks, you *can* believe your eyes, because the footage you're seeing on your TV screens right now is of a man rescuing a *bear* from the fast-moving currents of the Bay. So how did a three-hundred-pound Californian black bear end up all the way down here in the city, let alone in the water? Well, how he got there didn't matter to Jake Stephens. Once our hero saw the bear was in trouble he leapt right in and helped get the animal to safety, without any thought for his own.'

'Cut. Great, Cyndi,' Alex enthused, knowing that this and the interview they'd already done with Stephens would most likely be enough.

Crazy bastard jumping into the water like that. Luckily the bear was too tired and weak from swimming to attack him; instead the animal had used the man as a flotation aid until help arrived. Like Cyndi mentioned, how the bear ended up down here in the bay was anyone's guess, but that part of the story didn't concern Alex; it was the drama of the rescue operation that would interest viewers the most, especially with the accompanying footage that they'd been lucky enough to get from a passing tourist. It was the kind of compelling, dramatic and often heart-warming news piece that *Today by the Bay* specialised in, and if Sylvester Knowles, the senior producer at the station didn't run this, Alex would eat her hat.

Sylvester had a very strict brief for *Today by the Bay* and this was right up his street. When Alex sometimes tried to veer off in other more interesting and newsworthy directions, she was quickly shot down. 'Come on, all that green stuff is totally snoozeworthy,' he'd protested, when she'd once pitched a piece about an airline who were using so-called environmental policies to sneak in new charges. The company were almost deliriously happy to be green if it meant extracting something even greener from their long-suffering passengers and had wanted to bring in a fee for toilet flushing under the 'water conservation' banner. Alex was sure such a story would interest the public but, as always, Sylvester ran a mile.

As much as she loved her little two-minute news slot and the variety it afforded her, sometimes she yearned to do a 'real' story, not necessarily about politics or current affairs, but something meaty that really got the average American fired up. She guessed she'd inherited this from her dad, who'd been a print journalist back in the day when stories, real stories, mattered.

'We're done now,' Cyndi said, in a tone that very much implied a statement rather than a question.

'Sure,' Alex replied easily. 'Do you need a lift back to the station? Dave and I are heading that way now.' Next it was straight into the editing suite to get the story ready for a slot on the evening news, and no doubt Sylvester would want a five-second teaser to run before all commercial breaks until then.

'I've got to be somewhere else, actually,' the other girl said, making it sound like she was due a meeting with the President.

'OK, well I'll give you a call if we need you for filming tomorrow. I think a voiceover might be enough though, I'm not sure.' Tomorrow's piece would be an interview with a sixty-nine-year-old guy who was the oldest cable car grip man in the city and shortly due to retire. Because (unlike most members of the public) the man had proven a lively and entertaining interviewee with lots of great anecdotes from his years on the job, they wouldn't need Cyndi's pretty face to hold viewer interest or fill screen time.

'Whatever.' Cyndi was already elsewhere and Alex made a mental note to ask Sylvester why he kept foisting these precious princesses on her. She knew he'd counter the argument by insisting that she should get in front of the camera herself but Alex wasn't interested. With her big brown eyes, high cheekbones and looks that people often described as 'exotic' (mostly down to her Mediterranean heritage), she suspected she could probably get away with looking the part, but she'd always felt much more comfortable behind a camera than in front of one. And, she mused, fiddling with a strand of long, dark hair, it meant she'd have to lose ten pounds and wear a ton of make-up every day, which just wasn't going to happen.

She made it back to her desk at the SFTV offices just before lunchtime. Checking her messages, she saw that mixed in with some other work-related stuff was a note to call her lawyer. Alex's heart automatically sped up.

It couldn't be, could it?

She wiped her hands that had suddenly become clammy on her jeans before picking up the phone to call him back.

'Doug, it's Alex,' she said trying to keep her voice even. 'You called?'

'Not good news I'm afraid,' Doug said without preamble. 'Same old story.'

'What?' Alex wasn't quite sure how to feel. She'd expected the news to be different this time. 'You didn't get him?'

'Well, according to our guy you were right; he *was* there at one time, but not any more.'

She honestly didn't know whether to feel relieved or disappointed. She knew what she *should* feel, of course, but when it came to this, Alex was never really on sure footing.

'So what do we do now?' she asked Doug. 'I mean, this needs to get done.'

'Not a lot I can do for you in the short term if we can't pin this guy down, Alex.' The lawyer was circumspect. 'Look, ask around some more and see what you can find out, or maybe think about getting a professional on the case. Otherwise, we'll need to consider an alternative route but it's probably too early for that just yet.'

'Too early . . . but it's been over a year!' she exclaimed, although in truth it was more than that since all this really began.

'Yes, but in the eyes of the law . . .' Doug began to repeat his usual mantra.

'I know, I know,' Alex said jadedly. 'I'll keep trying, see if I can find out anything new. I'm sorry about this; I was so sure this time.'

'You do that. And try not to worry, we'll get this guy nailed down eventually. We always do.'

'I hope so, Doug,' she said, trying to sound like she meant it when the truth was, she wasn't so sure. 'And I'm sorry your time got wasted on another wild goose chase.'

Although she knew there wasn't a chance in hell that the lawyer himself was doing the chasing; more likely some lackey the firm employed to do that kind of legwork.

'Not a problem. *I'm* sorry I didn't have good news so I

could wrap this thing up for you once and for all,' Doug finished before ringing off.

The conversation still buzzing in her head, Alex sat back in her chair and sighed deeply.

'Hey, what's with the long face?' Sylvester said, catching the tail end of the sigh. 'I hope that doctor of yours hasn't let you down, especially not with Valentine's Day so close.'

Thinking of Jon, Alex smiled. 'No, we're going out tonight, actually,' she told her boss.

'Good. Shit-hot surgeon or not, that guy's got *me* to deal with if he messes you around.'

'I'll be sure to tell him that,' she said with a grin.

She and Jon French, a surgeon from downtown Memorial had been seeing each other for a few months, and while things had been going great up to now, they were rapidly approaching a crossroads in the relationship, one that Alex knew she couldn't delay for much longer. He knew what was going on with her of course, had known from the very beginning and because of this, seemed happy enough to wait. But now, with their relationship coming up to four months and still nothing happening, well she supposed she couldn't really blame him for getting antsy.

Would she still be feeling this way if Doug's phone call had been different? she wondered. Would it have finally put everything to bed? Grimacing at her own choice of words, she tried to get a handle on her thoughts. There was no point in even going down that road. If anything she was lucky that Jon had come into her life when he had, and doubly lucky that he was so patient and understanding.

It was just her pragmatic side that wanted this dealt with, Alex reassured herself, and nothing else should come into it. Her relationship with Jon should move on and with any luck eventually she'd get the closure she needed.

But for the moment, Alex thought, checking the rest of her messages, it looked like that closure wasn't going to happen anytime soon.

'Wow, you look amazing!' Jon was full of compliments when Alex arrived at the restaurant that night, and she was pleased with her decision to wear the new one-shoulder Diane von Furstenberg blue silk dress she'd bought at Macy's the week before.

They were having dinner at the Cliff House restaurant, one of her favourites in the city, which as the name implied, was perched on the cliffs high above the Pacific Ocean. From their window table, the lights of Marin coastline glittered prettily in the distance, and below on the water, cruise ships sailed in and out of the bay beneath the Golden Gate. Jon looked pretty good tonight too, she noticed, dressed in a black Ralph Lauren shirt and tan Hugo Boss chinos. His dark hair looked freshly cut and his deep brown eyes sparkled in the low-level restaurant lighting. Man, he was sexy!

'So how was your week?' he asked, when the waiter had taken their order.

'Good, thanks.' Alex decided not to say anything about Doug's phone call earlier. Not that it made much of a difference (at least not to Jon) but she really didn't want to revisit that particular topic of conversation tonight. 'Although unlike you,' she joked, 'I didn't get to save any lives.'

'Hey, a job's a job,' he said with a modest smile and again Alex was impressed by his lack of arrogance or vanity. At thirty-six, he was one of Memorial's youngest but most senior surgeons, yet he always acted like it was no big deal. 'Course, the major downside is that I don't get to see you as often as I'd like.' He reached across the table and laced his fingers through hers. As he did Alex felt an involuntary shiver run down her spine.

31

'You've got some more nights coming up then?' She tried not to sound too disappointed.

'A whole week after Sunday. I'm sorry, honey, I'd really hoped we could do something special Thursday but it's just not working out.'

Alex was confused. 'Why Thursday?'

'Well, Valentine's Day of course,' he said as if it was the most obvious thing in the world and she had to smile. Another thing she loved about Jon was that there was no game-playing and none of the immature bravado and male posturing that often went hand in hand with dating. Instead, he was totally upfront and decisive about what he wanted, and to Alex this was deeply attractive. Clearly comfortable with his masculinity, he was also very attentive and quite romantic too (even though Alex was *way* past all that hearts and flowers stuff) and she was lucky to have found him. So why was she still holding back?

Well, there would be no more of that, she decided suddenly, drinking in his gorgeous face. No more delays or excuses; if after dinner Jon invited her back to his place on Nob Hill, this time she would go. And realistically, how much longer could she actually wait? There had been a real buzz between them right from the very beginning, so wasn't it about time she allowed herself to give in to that, and just go for it? And, come to think of it, why wait to be asked?

'Don't worry about that,' she said smiling coyly. 'Why don't we celebrate it tonight instead?'

Jon looked up and met her gaze, instantly catching her meaning. 'Sounds great to me. Wanna skip dessert?'

'Dessert?' Alex laughed. 'We haven't even had our entreés yet!'

'I guess I've just realised that I'm not really all that hungry,' he replied, with a mischievous smile.

Tonight, she and Jon would take their relationship to a whole other level and Alex would finally be able to cast aside the stupid, crazy guilt that resurfaced every time she'd thought about it up to now. And that was a joke, wasn't it? Why should she feel guilty about trying to move on with the rest of her life?

Jon picked up her hand and moved it to his mouth, tracing tiny kisses on the delicate skin inside her wrist, a small but effective preview of what was to come. Alex gulped. Tonight would *definitely* be the night, and she already knew it would be great.

Chapter 5

'You have a job – already?' Grace exclaimed. 'Gosh, you don't waste any time, do you?'

'It was just luck, I suppose,' Leonie said, explaining how she'd stumbled across Flower Power. That day, once she'd successfully navigated her way back to Green Street, she realised that Marcy's shop was only five blocks away from the apartment, a short ten-minute walk. It couldn't be handier and again, because everything now seemed to be slotting so easily into place, Leonie wondered if somebody up there might be giving her a helping hand. Today had been her first day on the job and while it had been hectic, she'd really enjoyed getting stuck in.

'But a florist's?' Grace continued disbelievingly down the other end of the line. 'Sure, you know feck all about flowers!'

'Well, I know a little bit from my time at Xanadu – but I'm picking things up as I go along.'

'Wow, you really are a gas, Leonie,' her friend went on, this time with obvious admiration in her tone. 'Only a few weeks there and already you're practically one of the natives! Me, I get lost in Dundrum Shopping Centre, never mind trying to find my way around a massive place like San Francisco.'

'It's easy to find your way around here though. It's a very compact city; you can pretty much walk to most places—'

'Well it wouldn't be me . . . oh, Rocky, stop, leave your sister alone!' Grace admonished her son, before smoothly continuing with the conversation, 'but I envy your confidence all the same. Probably comes from all the travelling you've done. Oh, and speaking of which, we're trying to plan our first family holiday at the moment,' she added excitedly.

'Really? Where are you thinking of going?' Leonie was surprised to hear this. Grace generally disliked travel and, three years old and full of beans, the twins would inevitably be a handful on any flight.

'Ray was talking about Tunisia. Apparently it won't be too hot over there around Easter, but it'll be warmer than Cyprus, which we were thinking of first. Now, don't ask me any more about it because he's supposed to be making all the arrangements and to be honest, I'm not even sure if it's one of the Greek Islands or the—'

'It's Africa,' Leonie told her smiling. 'Tunisia is in Africa.' Given her friend's wonky sense of geography, it was probably a good thing Grace didn't travel very much!

'Is it really? Now I didn't know that,' she said, sounding worried. 'Will it be a very long flight so? God almighty, I don't know why I let Ray organise these things; he just asked the travel agent for winter sun and that's what we got. Sure, he wouldn't have a clue either. Knowing him he probably thinks it's in Spain.'

Leonie smiled, trying to imagine *that* conversation in the travel agency.

'Oh, Rosie, will you give it a rest *please*!' Grace moaned.

'Are you sure you're still OK to talk?' she asked.

'Oh, don't mind them, they're just acting up cos they know my attention is elsewhere. God only knows what they'll be like on a plane! But thinking about it now, you'd be the right one to ask about where we should go really. Have you been there, to Tunisia, I mean?'

Leonie's heart skipped a beat. 'Yes,' she murmured. 'A while back, not long after the twins were born actually.'

'Really? I can't remember that at all but then again, that's no surprise – back then my brain was like mush! Africa, eh? So what's it like? Will it suit us because I really don't know if . . . oh!' she exclaimed, breaking off in mid-sentence, and Leonie knew she'd finally clicked. 'After the twins? Of course! Sure wasn't it there that you—'

'Yep,' Leonie finished, trying to keep her tone even. 'It's where Adam and I first met.'

'Oh Lee, I'm sorry, I completely forgot, and I didn't mean to bring all that up . . .'

'Hey, no need to apologise, I can't pretend he never existed, can I?'

'But isn't that sort of what you're doing now?' her friend pointed out and Leonie marvelled at how Grace, despite her scattiness, somehow always managed to zoom right to the heart of the matter.

'No,' she replied firmly. 'It's not. All I'm doing at the moment is trying to leave the bad stuff behind.'

'Oh, I don't bloody *believe* this . . .' Grace groaned again, and Leonie wondered what the kids were up to this time. 'Rocky! What on earth goes through that head of yours?' she said in obvious exasperation.

'Grace, honestly, you'd better go, it sounds like you really have your hands full there.'

'I suppose I'd better before they burn the house down around us,' her friend sighed. 'Typical, the one time I get to have a bit of adult conversation! Oh well, never mind, congratulations on the new job and I'll talk to you again soon, OK?'

'Sure,' Leonie replied. 'Give my love to the kids.'

Having said goodbye, she replaced the handset and walked over to the bay window, her thoughts still full of the conversation about Grace's holiday plans.

Tunisia of all places.

Well with any luck, she mused, her thoughts drifting back to her own experiences there, Grace would have as unforgettable a time as she had.

Three years earlier

The flight had been delayed in Dublin by a couple of hours, so by the time Leonie arrived at Tunis airport, she was jaded and irritable. The early evening heat and stuffy arrivals hall didn't do much to lift her spirits, and as she waited at the carousel for her luggage she was inclined to agree with what Grace had said before she left.

'I don't know what you get out of taking off abroad like this,' her friend chided when Leonie informed her she was heading away for a week's holiday. 'It'll hardly be much fun on your own. Maybe if you gave me a bit more notice, I might have been able to come along with you.'

Leonie knew that pigs would fly before Grace would leave her beloved newborns – and she wouldn't expect her to – not to mention the fact that these days her friend generally needed a few weeks' notice for something as simple as meeting up for coffee! No, Grace wasn't a fan of foreign travel, so in truth the thought of asking her to come along had never even crossed Leonie's mind. She'd been due a couple of weeks' annual leave from work, so she decided to make the most of them.

A quick search on the Internet for last-minute holidays in the sun had thrown up the usual packages in Spain, Portugal and such-like, which didn't particularly interest her. She was just about to abandon the plan altogether when she came across an option for Tunisia. It wasn't somewhere that had ever been high on her list of countries to visit, yet it did sound that little bit more interesting than the Costa del Golf.

A few days lounging by the pool combined with a taste of North African culture sounded good, and a bit of sunshine would definitely be welcome. Even though it was late April and almost summer, Leonie could barely remember what the sun looked like.

But now as she waited impatiently at the carousel, sweat rolling down her back and the reek of tobacco hanging heavily in the air, she wondered if this was such a good idea after all. She wouldn't mind but she'd only brought a teeny case, small enough to count as hand luggage on any other day, except for the old-school and restrictive rules of this particular airline. Hardly surprising when the ancient 737 that had flown them here had threadbare seats, an in-flight entertainment system that was out of order and looked to be held together with little more than duct tape!

A few minutes later Leonie finally spied her little case, a generic holdall, one of the few that wasn't festooned with brightly coloured ribbons and other identifiable markers. Outside the terminal she waved down a taxi, and much to her relief was soon en route to her hotel.

Almost immediately she felt her irritation subside and her body relax as she stared out the window of the cab and began to take in her new surroundings. There was always something wonderfully addictive about arriving somewhere new, and even though there wasn't a whole lot to see on the way in from the airport, it was still enthralling.

On her own or not, this was the main reason she had come here. It had been over a year since her last relationship, and she wasn't too hopeful of starting another any time soon. It was difficult being single in Dublin at thirty; the old cliché of all the good ones being taken was very true. And Leonie had tired of the merry-go-round of going with her friends to nightclubs and hoping to bump into Mr Right. It seemed like it was never going to happen and in all honesty, she no longer had the energy for that kind of thing. If she met someone, she met someone but she wasn't going to actively search for him.

Truthfully, she'd love what Grace had now; the lovely husband, gorgeous children and loads of extended family close by. But with her parents on opposite sides of the globe and ne'er a man in sight, it wasn't an option, was it? Oh well, Leonie thought, trying to shake any negative thoughts out of her head, and focus on the lovely week of sunshine and relaxation to come.

All the way in from the airport, the architecture had been very *Arabian Nights*, so she couldn't help but feel let down when the taxi eventually pulled up outside a well-maintained, but generic-looking tourist hotel. She'd been hoping for something a bit more exotic and interesting. But what the hell – after a few days she'd no doubt be glad of the home comforts!

Having checked in at the front desk, she went to her room and was delighted to see that her balcony overlooked a large and hugely enticing swimming pool. The room itself was basic but clean although, she realised, there was no air-conditioning! Rivulets of sweat were rolling down her back and Leonie seriously needed some cooling off. She stared again at the cerulean blue waters of the lighted pool. It was late evening so the pool itself was empty and there wasn't a soul to be seen in the surrounding area. A relaxing solitary dip would be just the thing to ease away the after-effects of the journey.

Leonie put her case on the bed and unzipped it, intending

to whip out her bikini and unpack the rest later. But instead of a familiar pile of colourful holiday clothes, to her astonishment (and immense dismay), she opened the case to find a selection of drab-looking stuff she didn't recognise.

'Blast you anyway!' she groaned, immediately realising she'd picked up the wrong bag. A man's bag too by the looks of things, and someone who would probably be just as pleased to find a load of rainbow-coloured shorts, sun-dresses, and bikinis when he opened hers. Not to mention her underwear, she moaned.

Leonie couldn't believe it. In all the places she'd been and all the flights she'd taken this had never happened to her.

But how *had* it happened, she wondered now. OK so she'd obviously picked up the wrong bag, but had the owner of this one – she began examining it for a name and hopefully an address – picked up her bag long before it even reached her at the carousel? That would have caused her to assume this one was hers. She flipped back the lid of the case and took a closer look at the front. Nope, there was absolutely no reason for her to think that it wasn't hers, as it looked exactly the same – except of course, she thought, kicking herself, she hadn't bothered to check the nametag. While she always included a forwarding address on her luggage tag this person hadn't bothered, which meant that the task of getting her stuff back anytime soon was going to be even harder.

But maybe something inside might provide a clue?

Leonie began searching through the packed clothes, the stifling humidity heightening her irritation even further. Whoever this guy was, he was pretty anal, she mused, taking note of the meticulously folded shirts, T-shirts and trousers and – ugh! She quickly avoided a few pairs of nasty Y-fronts.

Or maybe his wife was? Everything was neatly laid out

alongside shoes and toiletries as well as a couple of paper-
backs with literary-looking covers and titles she didn't recognise. OK, so he fancies himself as a bit of intellectual, Leonie
figured, rather enjoying building up a mental picture of the
owner in this way. She wondered if he was doing the same
in return with her things. She hoped not as this sure was a
stark contrast to her hastily thrown together selection of
mismatched shorts, T-shirts and dresses. And he'd almost
certainly turn his nose up at her unashamedly pink-jacketed
choice of reading material!

Having checked through one pile of clothes, Leonie shoved
them aside and went to start on the other, hoping to find
something that would help identify the owner (and therefore
the whereabouts) of the bag. But as she did, she spotted a
small navy box hidden in the centre of the two piles.

Her eyes widened and, as much as she knew she shouldn't
be doing it, she had the box out and open in her hand before
she could even think properly about the rights and wrongs.
Why would anyone carry a ring in a suitcase and not keep
it on them? Hmm. And a *very* nice ring at that. Expensive
too, she mused, lifting it out to study in more detail the delicate cluster setting.

Whoever this guy was, he was obviously planning on
popping the question throughout the course of this holiday
and . . . It suddenly dawned on Leonie that unlike herself, the
owner of this bag wouldn't just be inconvenienced, but was
by now probably up the walls about the mix-up. And here
she was merrily nosing through his things!

A sudden sharp knock at the door interrupted her thoughts
and caused her to jump almost ten feet in the air.

'Mademoiselle! Mademoiselle!' an urgent-sounding voice
called out from the hallway.

'Coming!' The voice was so insistent that Leonie didn't

stop to think before opening the door to find the hotel porter standing outside.

Alongside him was a tall, frazzled-looking man who held a bag identical to the one lying open on the bed behind her. And unlike the one in her possession, which had half its contents in a heap, this bag looked completely untouched.

She wished with all her heart that the ground would open up and swallow her when the man's disbelieving gaze moved from the messy pile of clothes on the bed, back to Leonie and the box she was still holding in her hand.

'What the hell do you think you're doing?' the man gasped, snatching the ring out of Leonie's tentatively outstretched paw. 'This isn't yours!'

'I'm sorry, I . . .' Leonie was mortified. Small wonder the guy was upset, she would be too if she happened upon some stranger rooting through her personal belongings!

'Look, it's not how it looks, I was just looking through the bag for a name, or an address . . .'

She cursed herself for her stupidity and downright nosiness. In truth, all her notions of trying to find the owner had gone right out the window once she'd started prodding and poking around in his suitcase. Why couldn't she just have left well enough alone?

'Looking for an address! What, did you think it would be inscribed on the inside of the ring, is that it?'

'No, it just appeared and—' She looked helplessly at the hotel porter, who was standing there looking equally appalled at her behaviour. 'It's really all very innocent, honestly.' God, the hotel wouldn't turn her over to the police, would they? She knew that in some of these countries the punishment for stealing was jail or sometimes even worse – like getting a hand chopped off. Oh God, imagine being locked up in the Tunisian equivalent of the Bangkok Hilton for sheer nosiness!

'And to think that I went out of my way, and came all the way over here to return *your* bag to you . . .' He paused from flinging his things back into the bag to run a hand through his hair in frustration, and despite the mortifying circumstances, Leonie couldn't help but notice how incredibly well-toned his arms were and how his eyes were the deepest darkest blue, almost violet. The image she'd built up of the guy from his stuff was so at odds with the reality it was almost startling.

'I'm so sorry,' Leonie repeated, so ashamed of herself that she could no longer even try to defend her actions. 'I really didn't mean to pry. Thank you for bringing my case back, I really appreciate it and hope you didn't have to go too far out of your way.'

'Well, I'm only glad I got here when I did, otherwise who knows where this stuff would have ended up,' he grunted.

Despite herself Leonie felt her hackles rise. Wasn't he the one who'd caused all this in the first place?

'Now, hold on a second, who do you think you are, barging in here and accusing me of all sorts?' she retorted, the heat once again stirring her irritation. Under normal circumstances she wouldn't *dream* of answering back like this. 'I was at the airport minding my own business and waiting for my stuff when *you* were the bright spark who made off with a bag without bothering to check it first! So think about who's *really* at fault here before you start accusing me of stealing your precious bloody . . . Y-fronts!' Then, she winced inwardly, wishing she'd chosen to refer to something other than his underwear.

The man turned back to her, his jaw twitching but, Leonie realised with some relief, there was also a faint twinkle in his eye.

'Y-fronts,' he repeated, his mouth tightening, and though

she couldn't be sure, it looked like he was trying his best not to smile. 'Well, don't you worry,' he continued, zipping up the case and heading for the doorway, where the hotel porter still hovered uncomfortably, 'I won't trouble you with them any longer.'

Once the luggage problem had been resolved, Leonie quickly began to settle into her holiday. She was so aghast to have been caught red-handed rummaging through a stranger's things on the first night, that ever since she'd been avoiding the hotel porter, horrified by what he might think of this unprincipled foreigner. But days later, she was restless and fed-up of lounging around the pool on her own, so she decided to book one of the excursions offered by the holiday rep – a trip to the Sahara desert. The two-day round trip would be a great way to see more of the countryside and get a better flavour of the real Tunisia, something that was difficult in a purpose-built, modern resort town.

The bus was scheduled to pick her up from the hotel at 5 a.m., and still half-asleep, Leonie waited out front until it trundled up the driveway. Getting onboard, she was dismayed to see that it was packed with other tourists and many of the seats were already taken. So much for a window seat, she thought ruefully, making her way along the aisle, hoping that she wouldn't end up stuck alongside some chatterbox for the next few hours.

Eventually she spied a free seat – the last one onboard. Stowing her bag overhead with the others, she'd only just sat down when she heard a male voice call out nearby. 'Sure you'll remember which one's yours?'

Leonie looked to her right, and realised to her horror that the guy from the other night was in the seat directly across the aisle and looking mightily pleased with himself. Caught off guard she reddened, unsure what to say, but then just as quickly found her voice. 'It should be fine,' she replied, 'as long as someone else doesn't make off with it first.'

'Yep, you have to be very careful with stuff these days, don't you?' he replied in a mocking tone, stretching a long limb out into the aisle between them. 'You never know what might happen or who it might end up with. Of course, most people are fine – very trustworthy – but there's always one or two . . .'

Leonie could tell that he was enjoying riling her, but refusing to indulge him she picked up her book and pretended to read.

Undeterred he went on. 'I mean, you'd think that the majority of people would be *appalled* to find they'd picked up someone else's things, and would go out of their way to—'

'But I didn't make the mistake,' Leonie retorted, blushing furiously. 'Someone took off with *my* bag, leaving me no choice but to—'

'Root around in their underwear?'

Her gaze darted around, mortified that someone would overhear. 'I told you, I was only trying to find out who *owned* the stuff,' she muttered out of the corner of her mouth. 'I couldn't care less what was in there, and I certainly wasn't trying to root around in your underwear . . .'

'You should be so lucky,' he chortled, and despite herself, she couldn't resist a grin. She looked sideways at him, deciding yet again that he really was quite cute, even cuter than she remembered from the other night. His sandy-coloured hair was still damp from his morning shower, his skin already lightly tanned. The white T-shirt he wore nicely set off his defined biceps. And there was no denying the pair of equally defined legs in those shorts, Leonie thought, swallowing hard.

Quickly remembering the engagement ring, she gave a surreptitious glance across the way to see if his girlfriend (or now fiancée) was sitting next to him, but there was only another man dozing against the window.

Exhaling heavily, she turned to look at him properly. Well he might be cute, but the existence of the ring rendered such observations pointless, didn't it?

'Look, I'm sorry about what happened with your bag. You're right; I shouldn't have gone through your stuff and I'm especially sorry about the ring – but I really did happen upon it by accident,' she continued, aware that she was babbling. 'I was just about to put it back when you knocked on the door. I mean I wasn't going to steal it or anything like that. I wouldn't *dream* of it.'

'Could have been a major catastrophe losing that ring,' he replied with a shake of his head. 'When you consider all the planning that went into it, all the trying to keep things quiet and keep it a surprise . . . not to mention the stress of having to propose in the first place.'

She nodded. 'I can imagine.' Leonie couldn't help but wonder if he had proposed yet. If he had, where was his fiancée?

'Mick nearly had a heart attack he was so worried. Poor fella wasn't even able to *see* straight, let alone try and get it back.'

'Mick?' she frowned. 'Who's Mick?'

'And of course he couldn't very well let on to Sophie what he was so wired about,' he continued as if she hadn't spoken. 'I mean, he could hardly tell her that he'd misplaced a two-grand engagement ring, not when she hadn't a clue he had one in the first place . . .'

'Oh my goodness,' she gasped, wide-eyed as realisation dawned. 'You mean it wasn't *your* bag at all?'

'Whatever made you think it was?' he said in all innocence.

'Well, your theatrics for one!' Leonie wasn't sure whether to feel relieved or annoyed. 'All that flinging stuff around and getting on your high horse. You were so riled up, I didn't think for a *second* the bag might not be yours!'

'Hey, I'd just come off a four-hour flight after a two-hour delay in Dublin, remember? And then having got to my hotel, I had to go back out in this heat and take a taxi *another* hour out of my way to try and get the bloody bag back. The luggage was my responsibility and I felt terrible that I'd picked up the wrong one and lost Mick's stuff, and even worse that I'd—'

'So it *was* you who caused all this in the first place,' Leonie interjected. 'And to think you had the cheek to blame *me* for . . .'

He winced, realising he'd caught himself out. 'Yikes! OK, I'm busted,' he said sighing. 'And yeah, you're right. I shouldn't have got so upset that night. I suppose it was all my fault really.'

'You *suppose*?' Leonie spluttered. 'And not only that, but then you had the cheek to start picking on me again today! I don't believe it!'

Now he was grinning. 'I know, I know, I'm sorry. I'm well and truly caught out now. But when I saw you get on, I just couldn't resist, and it was only a bit of fun . . .'

'Ha bloody ha,' was all she could say, but a smile tried to fight its way across her lips. There was a brief silence while Leonie tried her best to pretend she was annoyed. The truth was she was actually quite gratified that the bag wasn't his. For more reasons than one.

Eventually, he leaned further across the aisle. 'You didn't *really* think I wore that kind of stuff did you?' he muttered. 'Y-fronts? Come on . . .'

Leonie grinned broadly, refusing to look at him. 'To be honest, I didn't really give it a second thought.'

The day-long journey seemed to pass in no time at all, not when Leonie was able to share it with such a chatty companion. His name was Adam, he lived in Dublin, and worked as an engineer for a large multinational in Kildare.

And although Leonie didn't ask outright (she wouldn't dream of it after their misunderstanding about the engagement ring!) she also concluded that he was single. 'Mick dragged a few of us along on this holiday so Sophie wouldn't suspect anything out of the ordinary,' he told her.

'Which was why he put the ring in the bag and not the carry-on luggage,' Leonie said. 'I did wonder about that.'

'Yep. He couldn't take a chance on security blowing the surprise. Bit of a risk, I thought. Turns out I was right, although we were very lucky that someone as honest as yourself found it,' he added, mockingly.

Leonie ignored the remark. 'And has he done it yet? Proposed, I mean.'

'Nope, he's still working up the courage and from what I can tell, he hasn't had her to himself at all yet. Reason enough not to bring a busload of mates along with you,' he added wryly.

'How many of you came?'

'Nine of us altogether. Four loved-up couples and little old me. I think things got a little bit out of hand to be honest,' he continued with a shake of his head. 'It started off as just Mick and Sophie and one or two of us, and then all of a sudden the whole gang was coming. We've all been mates for donkey's years, so once word got round, nobody wanted to be left out.'

'I must say it doesn't sound very romantic to me.' Leonie grimaced thinking she'd hate having so many people around for what should really be a private thing.

'I know, but that's just Mick's way. Although, things certainly haven't gone smoothly for him so far.' Then he grinned. 'I just hope to God that when he does get the chance to ask her that she doesn't turn him down.'

Leonie smiled. 'Having seen that ring, I really don't think so.'

'So what about you?' Adam asked then. 'Are you here on your own?'

She nodded, hoping he wouldn't think she was some sad sack who had no friends. 'It was a last-minute thing and most of my friends have other commitments,' she explained. 'I don't mind though, I actually quite like travelling on my own.'

'Well, if that's the case, don't be afraid to tell me to push off and leave you alone. I only came on this tour because I haven't been to Tunisia before and wanted to do something different. And I needed a break from coupledom,' he added. 'Don't get me wrong, they're my friends and they're great, but—'

'Too much lovey-dovey business?' Leonie said.

'The opposite actually, they never stop snapping at each other. The married ones are the worst, but even Sophie and Mick are a disaster already so who knows what they'll be like once they're hitched! Sometimes I wonder why anyone bothers.'

But by Adam's tone and slight smile she was sure that his friends were just bickering in that good-natured way that couples do, though it must be hard for him as the only single person on the trip to have to listen to it.

'So as I said, don't be worried about me getting in your hair or anything. I'm just as happy to sit here staring out the window, and listening to yer man there snoring. Delighted in fact,' he added with a gleam in his eye.

But after that there was little chance of Leonie asking him to leave her be, and they continued chatting easily throughout the journey.

As they travelled further away from the main tourist areas, the vegetation gradually became sparser, and in the distance wild camels roamed, occasionally crossing the road in front of the bus.

Passing through towns and villages, they saw nomadic shepherds bringing their sheep and goats to roadside markets to sell or exchange, while village children waved at the bus as it passed by.

'It's tempting to stay by the pool, but I'm always glad when I do these things,' Adam commented when they stopped for lunch in a place called Nefta, a pretty little village of sand-coloured houses on the edge of a spectacular oasis overlooking thousands of date palms, pomegranate and apricot trees.

'Me too,' Leonie agreed, for more reasons than one.

On the way, the tour stopped off at the desert village of Matmata, a series of subterranean cave dwellings hidden amongst a lunar-like landscape. The area was used as a film set for the home of young Luke Skywalker in the first *Star Wars* movies and as Adam was a big fan, this was an absolute must-see. It was fascinating to walk through the various homes, almost like stepping into another era, if you overlooked the various TV aerials sticking out of the ground.

When the bus stopped at their final destination at the edge of the Sahara sand dunes, Leonie felt the arduous journey simply melt away. Immense waves of the finest golden sand undulated into the distance for what seemed like thousands of miles, while above was the clearest, bluest sky she had ever seen.

Exiting the bus, she and Adam eagerly approached the

camels that lined up on the edge of the dunes, waiting to show them the desert as it was meant to be seen. Once everyone was fully geared up with burkas to protect from the sand and sun, Leonie took the herder's lead and positioned herself upon a kneeling camel. She sat astride the animal, patiently waiting for it to stand up and move off nice and slowly when all of a sudden the camel buckled forward and knocked her headfirst to the ground.

'Ow!' she groaned, shell-shocked. 'What was that for?'

Perched nearby atop his own perfectly behaved charge, Adam guffawed. 'Making friends?' he grinned as Leonie dusted herself off and reluctantly tried to get back on again. This time the camel, seemingly content at showing her who was boss, stood up and moved off without complaint. She tensed a little, taken aback by how far above ground they were, as well as the strange bumpy motion of the camel trundling along in the sand. 'Getting off on the wrong foot seems to be a bit of a thing with you, doesn't it?' Adam went on, as their respective camels made their way further out to the dunes.

'Very funny,' she said unsmilingly.

Within a few minutes of the trek it was as though they'd landed on another planet. Leonie couldn't get over the immensity of the dunes that seemed to go on forever. The sheer tranquillity of the place took her breath away. And as the small group watched the sun go down, and saw the golden sand gradually deepen to an intense shade of orange, she looked at Adam and knew that he was as much in awe of this as she was.

'Pretty cool, isn't it?' he said eventually.

'Incredible,' she gasped, but her trance was quickly broken when her camel decided that now might be a good time to take a little break. 'Whoa!' she yelled, as the animal flopped to its knees, and once again deposited her on the ground like a ton of bricks.

Again Adam seemed to find the whole thing hilarious, and couldn't contain his laughter when Leonie had to dust herself off once more. She hadn't wanted to get back on the narky brute after that as they clearly weren't getting along, but had little choice, unless she wanted to trudge home on foot.

So by the time they got back on firm ground and reached the hotel, she was sore, bruised and covered in sand. Adam, on the other hand, was just hungry.

'How about you go and shower off all that sand and we'll meet back down here for dinner?' he suggested, the invitation so casual and easy it was as if they'd known each other for years.

Leonie was pleased. 'Sure, see you in an hour?'

'Perfect.'

And back in her hotel room, as she stood beneath the cold, but very welcome shower in a strange hotel on the edge of the Sahara, Leonie smiled, getting the distinct feeling that this could be the beginning of something great.

Chapter 6

It was the day before Valentine's Day and one of the busiest at Flower Power Leonie had experienced so far. She and Marcy had worked like demons all day long, frantically taking in and getting orders ready to go out first thing the following morning, as well as preparing bouquets for the wave of walk-in customers that they would undoubtedly have tomorrow. Valentine's Day mania really was something else; it felt like she'd been swimming in a sea of pink and red all day. Granted it was probably just as crazy back home, but as Leonie had never experienced it from the retailer side, she'd never really given it a second thought.

'I can't believe how *un*romantic this is!' she complained to her boss, after taking a telephone order from yet another man who asked that she put 'anything you like' on the gift card. And so many guys were just popping in on spec and ordering pre-made bouquets for their other half, which wasn't exactly in the spirit of the day. 'These guys don't seem to put any thought whatsoever into this.' She indicated the pile of generic orders and bland message cards.

'Welcome to the gifts industry, sweetheart,' Marcy said drily. 'What did you expect – Shakespeare?'

'Well, no, but I thought some of them could at least come

up with something sweeter or more meaningful than just the bog standard "Happy Valentine's Day".'

'Oh my, I think we've got a real live romantic on our hands here!' her boss teased. 'That sure won't last long around here, I can tell you. You know, most guys don't really think about this kind of stuff; they just do it because it's expected of them.'

'I suppose,' Leonie said glumly, the scales having well and truly fallen from her eyes today. She wasn't sure what she had been expecting exactly but it certainly wasn't this frantic, almost assembly line, frenzy. Back home, Adam had always sent her a bouquet of red roses at work and took her out for dinner that evening – kind of mundane and unimaginative now that she thought about it, but she'd always enjoyed the fuss and attention surrounding the occasion.

Looking at it from the other side, it felt very different.

'You didn't *really* expect them all to declare undying love, did you?' Marcy asked, putting the finishing touches to yet another red-rose bouquet, one of hundreds she'd already completed. 'Are they like that in Ireland? Poetic, I mean?'

'Well no, but—'

'But clearly *some*body was,' her boss interjected with a knowing smile and Leonie wished she hadn't brought the subject up. So far Marcy had been great fun to work for and so easy to chat to, but she wasn't yet ready to discuss with her the reasons for being here. She knew the older woman suspected it had something to do with a man back home, hence the teasing, but to her credit she didn't pry. 'Well, poetic or not,' Marcy continued, much to Leonie's relief, 'we've got a hell of a lot of lovin' to get through today, so we'd better stop yackin' and get crackin'.'

'Sounds good to me,' Leonie replied, answering the ringing telephone for what felt like the thousandth time that day.

When they finally finished at 7 p.m., having worked a full ten hours, Leonie was relieved to get back to the peace and quiet of Green Street. She put her key in the lock, deciding that a long soak in the bath, followed by some good TV sounded like just the thing, as no doubt they'd be even busier tomorrow and . . .

Leonie paused mid-thought, as opening her door, she spotted a couple of letters lying at her feet in the hallway. Her eyes widened. Wow, her very first post! This really made the apartment feel like home. But who on earth would be writing to her?

Then she smiled as she reached down to pick it up. That last time they'd spoken, Grace had asked for her address so she could send a housewarming card, so this was probably it. Phew, for a moment there she'd wondered if maybe Adam had found out where she was, but then again he would hardly . . .

Oh, there were two envelopes.

On the way upstairs to her apartment, Leonie tore open the first one to find, as expected, a lovely housewarming card from her friend. Despite herself, tears pricked at the corner of her eyes when she read the short message.

Happy housewarming. Hope you're happy in your new place, but not too much! We miss you and hope you'll come back to us very soon.
Lots of love, Grace, Ray, Rocky and Rosie. XX

She absently ripped opened the second envelope, the card having made her feel lonely and a little bit sad. That wouldn't have been Grace's intention of course, but she couldn't help it. It was almost as if . . . Leonie paused mid-thought as she unfolded a single piece of paper.

Dear Helena,

I'm not sure if you even live here any more, probably not, and I know it's been a while, but I just wanted to let you know how sorry I am . . .

Leonie frowned. What the hell? But then all at once, a thought struck her and she picked up the ripped envelope and turned it over.

'Oh you eejit,' she grunted, cursing herself for being so brainless. In her haste, she hadn't bothered checking the name on the front of the letter, automatically assuming it was for her. But the letter was addressed to Helena Abbott – the tenant who had lived here previously.

Feeling very stupid indeed, and also a little guilty for opening someone else's private correspondence, Leonie quickly stuffed the letter back in the envelope, as if to try and undo her mistake. But there was no way of re-sealing it, as she'd been so careless when opening the thing she'd practically torn the envelope to smithereens. She bit her lip, trying to decide what to do. The woman was still getting post here, yet the rental agency had no forwarding address for her so what was she supposed to do with it?

Turning the piece of paper over once more, she studied it properly. It was a very short letter – only a few scrawled lines, barely a note really – from a person called Nathan. Leonie scanned the text, looking for an address or something that might indicate where it had come from, when a particular sentence caught her eye.

Just wondering if you ever got those other letters I sent you? You never replied (which I guess is understandable) but I hope they went a way towards explaining some things.

Other letters? Leonie cast her mind back to that box of envelopes hidden away in the back of wardrobe. Was he by any chance referring to those? She peered at the handwriting, trying to make a comparison. Difficult to tell, but it certainly looked very similar to the elegant, cursive script she'd seen before. Intrigued, she headed in to the bedroom to get the box.

Sitting down on the bed, she unwrapped the cellophane and lifted out a single envelope for comparison. Yes, the hand-writing on this was *definitely* the same as the one that arrived today and, she realised, flicking through the others, it also appeared on the other ten or so envelopes in this box – the ones he was referring to in today's letter. Yet, all these remained unopened so clearly Helena Abbott *hadn't* read them, despite the sender's – what was his name again – Nathan's hopes that she had. Not only that, but she'd left them behind when she moved. So what was going on here?

Just then Leonie's stomach rumbled, reminding her that she hadn't yet eaten. And bringing her back to the fact none of this had anything to do with her. But still, she couldn't resist reading through the short note again. He sounded quite nice, this Nathan guy. And clearly he was anxious to hear from Helena Abbott and to find out if his letters had explained . . . whatever it was that needed explaining.

Leonie felt bad. She supposed she should let him know that Helena had moved and that his letters hadn't been received. But then, there was no bloody return address on the envelopes, was there?

So what was she supposed to do now? she wondered going back outside to the kitchen to make dinner. Chances were she was going to keep getting letters for Helena Abbott at this address, which was a bit of a pain. And seeing as there was no fear of Nathan getting the reply he sought, she certainly didn't want to run the risk of him turning up at her door one day and demanding to speak to Helena. Who knew what had gone on between them? No, she thought, her mind racing, as she flung a ready-meal into the microwave, she'd better nip this in the bud and soon.

So maybe after dinner, she reasoned, she should open one of the other letters and take a teeny peek at it to see if there was a return address. Then if she found something, Leonie could try and make contact with the guy and explain what had happened. OK, so it probably wasn't the most straightforward way of doing things, but as there were so many unknowns, she really didn't have much of a choice, did she?

My darling Helena,

It's been some time since my last letter and while I guess I didn't really expect a reply, I hope it helped you understand why I did what I did. I'm sure you must hate me for it, but if it's any consolation I hate myself even more.

I was selfish, stupid and blinkered . . . all those things you accused me of, and although at the time I didn't want to hear it, I know now that you were absolutely right. Is it too late to say I'm sorry?

Please believe me when I tell you that I love you more than anything else in this world. No matter what happens, and despite what you might think of me still, I just hope you realise that.

Please forgive me,
Nathan

Setting the letter down alongside her on the sofa, Leonie stared into space, her thoughts going a mile a minute. After dinner, she'd taken the box into the living room and carefully opened the first letter on the pile.

And once she'd read the first couple of lines, she couldn't bring herself to stop. OK so she really shouldn't have read it all the way through, particularly when she was only supposed to be looking for a return address, but she just couldn't help herself.

Anyway, it was such a short letter that she'd had it read before she knew it, and it wasn't as if it revealed all that much really.

But this all seemed pretty ominous now, didn't it? Who was this guy? Clearly he was Helena Abbott's other half – or had been once – and was trying to get back into her good books after something he'd done.

Please forgive me.

Leonie couldn't help but be intrigued. Had the couple split up, same as her and Adam? If so, then it seemed like Nathan was the one at fault and whatever he'd done, clearly he was very sorry for it. Why else would he be looking for forgiveness? And clearly he wasn't aware that Helena had since moved out, given that he was still sending stuff to this address.

Anyway, whatever he had done, Helena *couldn't* have forgiven him, could she? she pondered. Not if she hadn't read any of the letters in this box. And chances were this was why there were so many letters, and possibly why they were unopened in the first place! Leonie's mind was racing now. Helena hadn't opened any of the guy's letters because whatever he'd done must have been bad enough for her to ignore him, and leave them all behind when she moved.

Leonie's curiosity soared, not least because this situation had a few parallels with her own. The guy was obviously determined to get Helena back but clearly had no idea that she hadn't even read his previous letters, let alone forgiven him. Picking up the letter again, she reread Nathan's words.

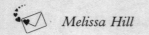

I'm sure you must hate me for what I did, but if it's any conso-lation I hate myself even more.

What on earth had he done? Far from coming across as a faithless love-rat type, Nathan actually sounded quite sweet, and was obviously still very much in love with Helena. But the poor guy had no idea that his letters would continue to be unanswered and he was wasting his time.

Well, however intriguing this particular letter might be, Leonie sighed, it was certainly no help in finding its sender or recipient, given that there was no return address.

Wasn't it odd not to include this? Although maybe not so much for a personal letter, she realised then. After all, chances were if Helena was the love of Nathan's life then she'd know where to reach him anyway, wouldn't she?

Yes, that had to be it; unless . . . Leonie mused, her mind galloping again as she came up with yet another possibility; perhaps he hadn't included a return address because he didn't want Helena to know where he was?

But then, why would he have mentioned something about her sending him a reply to an earlier letter he'd sent? *I guess I didn't really expect a reply.*

She rummaged through the pile of letters, hoping to find the other letter he referred to, the letter, which supposedly 'went a way towards explaining some things'. They'd got all mixed up when she'd knocked them over that first day and some of the dates were hard to read so impossible to tell what order they were in.

Maybe she should just open another one? She bit her lip, feeling guilty about reading someone else's correspondence, and especially something so personal . . .

'Leave it alone, you nosy wagon!' she berated herself, leaving aside the box of letters and turning on the TV. It was late and she was tired, and she really should know better than to let something like this preoccupy her. Goodness knows her snooping had got her into enough trouble in the past!

She really should make the effort to get out and about a bit more; maybe join a club or something – anything that would help occupy her time and stop her poking her nose into other people's business. Yes, that's what she'd do, she decided, flicking through the channels to try and find something interesting to watch.

But no matter how hard she tried to concentrate on the TV and forget about the letters, Leonie just couldn't stop thinking about Helena and Nathan and what might have gone amiss in their relationship.

My darling,

How are you? Still missing you like crazy but more than anything else, I guess I just hope you're happy. I still can't tell you enough how sorry I am, and I hope that someday you'll understand, and maybe some time in the future, if it's not too much to ask, you might be able to forgive me.

I can't stop thinking about you and how much I miss being with you. I miss your smile, your laugh, the scent of your skin, and it's driving me crazy not being able to hold you close and tell you how much I love you.

As I write this, I can just picture you sitting in your favourite place on the windowsill gazing out at the bridge. Maybe the morning fog is slowly cascading over the towers and sweeping into the bay in that way that you love. You've always adored the bridge and although I've never been able to share your fascination with it, how could it not be special to me too, when it's where we first met?

I still remember how you looked on that day, your long

hair blowing in the breeze, your beautiful green eyes screwed up in intensity as you tried to find the perfect angle for the perfect shot. Your camera was pretty much an extension of you back then.

I can still remember how amazing the weather was that morning, the flaming orange of the towers contrasting against the deep blue sky. You were aiming the lens upwards, trying to capture that image when this goofball crashed into you and ruined it all . . .

Lying in bed, the letter open in her hand, Leonie felt a lump in her throat. He sounded so lovely!

It was one o'clock and despite herself, all that evening she couldn't stop thinking about the letters and hadn't been able to resist opening another one to see if she could find something that might help her restore them to their rightful owner. And blast it; she was just *dying* to find out what had happened to the couple!

Clearly this letter wasn't going to enlighten her, but from his writing, Nathan really did sound like a lovely, gentle, romantic guy. His heartfelt words and account of how he and Helena had met on the bridge made her feel as if she was personally acquainted with them both, and discovering that Helena too liked to sit by the bay window and stare out at the bridge, Leonie had felt an odd sense of kinship towards her.

I miss your smile, your laugh, the scent of your skin, and it's driving me crazy not being able to hold you close and tell you how much I love you.

Where it had all gone wrong? He and Helena had clearly been madly in love right from the off, so what on earth had happened? What was so bad that she couldn't forgive him?

Please Forgive Me.

What on earth had this guy done?

Chapter 7

The following morning, she decided to confide in Marcy about opening the letters. 'I know I shouldn't have done it, but I just couldn't help it,' she said.

It was just before eight, and she and her boss were out back loading the first Valentine's Day deliveries into the van before the store opened and the mania began.

'You do know that opening someone else's mail is a felony, right?' her boss said dubiously.

'Well, yes, but . . .' Leonie felt panicked. She was so caught up in the contents of the letters that she hadn't really considered these implications. 'But the first one was completely unintentional as I really thought it was for me.'

'Doesn't quite explain the other two though, does it?' Marcy said, checking the load against the delivery sheet before heading back inside.

'Well, no.' Leonie reddened, following her. 'But I'd really like to find some way of getting them back to him.'

'Why? They're just a bunch of letters.'

'Oh no, you should read them, Marcy, he seems really sorry and so genuine—'

'I'm sure he is, sweetheart, but unfortunately he isn't one of our customers, whereas those guys,' she said, pointing to the burgeoning queue of men out front, 'are.'

In her fixation with Nathan's plight, Leonie had almost forgotten that today there were plenty of men who needed assistance in keeping their loved ones happy – most of them now waiting outside the store and looking very impatient indeed.

'Bloody hell,' she gasped, taken aback at the length of the queue. 'Those guys look like they really mean business, don't they?'

'Yep,' Marcy grinned, as she opened the door to let in the first wave of eager customers. 'If you thought yesterday was bad – you ain't seen nothing yet.'

At around midday, Leonie was double-checking the afternoon deliveries when something on the delivery sheet caught her eye.

'Look at this,' she said, pointing out one particular recipient to Marcy. 'That's my address.' The bouquet was addressed to someone in the downstairs apartment of the Green Street house, one of the neighbours that Leonie still hadn't met. 'I could drop it in on my way home later, save the guys a journey,' she offered, knowing that the delivery vans would be working like crazy trying to get everything out on time today.

Marcy seemed to like the idea. 'You don't mind?'

'Of course not, I'm literally passing the door. Anyway, if nothing else it would be a good excuse to meet one of my own neighbours, wouldn't it?'

'Ah, so you have an ulterior motive,' her boss teased, studying the list of recipients. 'Alex Fletcher,' she read out loud. 'With a name like that it's hard to tell if that's male or female, but for your sake, honey, here's hoping it's a good-looking Romeo with buckets of cash.'

'That's *not* why I'm offering to drop them off!' Leonie assured her. 'Believe me, that kind of complication is the *last* thing I need.'

'Well, let's take a look at the card and see if we can find out – just in case,' the older woman added mischievously, before going cut back to seek out the relevant bouquet. 'I think I wrote this one out myself . . . aha . . . here it is.' She picked up the card from an especially lavish arrangement of red roses. 'It just reads "Guess who?"' she said, shrugging in disappointment. 'Huh. Not very romantic, and it doesn't tell us much either.'

'And anonymously sent.' Leonie read over her boss's shoulder. 'I don't remember this being phoned in, do you?'

'Can't say I recall it from the thousand or so we've had this week,' Marcy said wryly, putting the card back in the envelope and fixing it to the bouquet. 'Well, whether it's a he or a she, I guess all this Alex needs to know is they're getting the best bunch of Valentine roses in the Bay Area.'

'I'll be sure to tell them that,' Leonie said with a grin.

'You do that. So, are you expecting any deliveries yourself today?' Marcy asked, trying to sound offhand. 'From back home, maybe?'

'Nope, and even if I was, I'd be tempted to send them back.'

'Really? Why's that?'

Leonie smiled inwardly, knowing Marcy's mind was probably working overtime by now. 'Because now I know that today has nothing to do with romance and is more of a money-making exercise,' she teased.

Marcy shook her head. 'Whatever you say, sweetheart,' she winked, before they both went back to work.

Much later that evening, as promised, Leonie took the bouquet of roses back home to Green Street to deliver it to the occupant of the downstairs apartment.

It had been a crazy day and she was almost dead on her

feet, although Marcy had very kindly ordered a takeaway to be delivered to the store immediately after closing so at least she didn't have to worry about cooking dinner tonight. It was great after such a long day to be able to relax and take it easy without having to rush straight home, but at the same time, Leonie was keenly aware that she had one last job to do.

Now, knocking lightly on the entrance door adjacent to her own, she gave a quick flick of her hair to try and make herself look some way presentable. After today she probably looked like she'd been dragged through a hedge backwards so God only knows what her neighbour – male or female – would think of some wild redhead calling to the door!

She was decidedly taken aback when a girl looking non-too-presentable herself opened the door. She was tall, reed thin, and Leonie suspected, normally very beautiful, but at that moment, her eyes were red-rimmed and puffy.

'You've got to be kidding me,' the girl gulped, looking aghast at the flowers. 'Not another one!'

'Erm, delivery for Alex Fletcher?' Leonie announced timidly, wondering if this had been the best idea. Far from being delighted at the surprise, at that moment the girl couldn't have looked any more upset than if someone had arrived bearing a stick of dynamite!

'Just take them away, please,' she insisted, moving backwards into the hallway as if she'd been burned.

Leonie wasn't sure what to think. The girl was holding a tissue in one hand and her eyes looked red-raw, as if she'd been crying. God, maybe the flowers weren't for Valentine's Day like she and Marcy had automatically assumed?

'I'm very sorry to bother you,' she said apologetically, 'but I work for Flower Power, the florist down by Van Ness, and these were ordered for an Alex Fletcher who—'

'I'm sorry, I really can't take them,' the girl insisted yet again. 'Can you take them back, please? I don't want any more flowers. I hate flowers! Or more accurately they hate me. Damn hay fever,' she added with a sniff, and only then did Leonie understand the cause of the watery eyes.

'This is the *third* delivery today, and it's not friggin' funny anymore. Not that it was ever funny, but you know what I mean. Anyway, I can't take these either. And let me guess, they're anonymous too?'

'But . . .' Leonie wasn't sure what to do, but when Alex sneezed again she decided it was probably best not to force it. 'I'm sorry,' she told her, turning to leave, 'I'll take them back to the shop tomorrow and just tell the sender we couldn't make the delivery. We can refund his credit card.'

'Wait a minute,' Alex said, her tone stopping Leonie in her tracks.

'Yes?'

'You said you'd refund "his" credit card. Which means you must know who sent them, right?'

Again Leonie wasn't sure what to say. 'Well . . .'

'It's anonymous, but they had to leave a name when placing the order, didn't they? Especially when using a credit card.'

'Well, yes, but I'm not sure if we can give out that kind of information . . .'

'Listen, honey, this is no joke, I'm dying here.' Alex indicated her watering eyes as if to push home the point. 'I have no idea who's been sending me all these flowers – well, maybe I do have an idea – but I need to find out for sure. So tomorrow, why don't I call to your store . . . what's it called again?'

'Flower Power. It's just a few blocks away, off Van Ness.'

'Flower Power,' Alex repeated with a faint smile, and even with the red-rimmed eyes and blotchy face Leonie could tell that she was very beautiful. 'Let me guess, the florist is an ex-hippy?'

She smiled back. 'That's what I thought too, but nope, just someone with an ironic sense of humour.'

'Oh, OK. So how about you guys tell me who placed the order, and then I'll go and wring his neck – hey, just kidding,' she added quickly, seeing Leonie's horrified look.

Now she wished she hadn't so willingly offered to drop off the bouquet this evening. This was more than a little weird. She'd have to talk to Marcy about whether or not they could give out a sender's details though; it wasn't as simple as just handing over the information. Still, something told her that this Alex Fletcher wasn't the sort of person who'd take no for an answer.

'Well, I'd better go,' she told her, turning again to leave, the bouquet still in her hand. 'I'll take these back to the shop tomorrow and see what I can do about helping you find out who sent them.'

'Off Van Ness, you said?' Alex repeated.

'That's right. I've just come from there.' She paused then, trying to decide whether or not to tell her they were actually neighbours. Well, she supposed Alex would find out sooner or later. 'I don't normally do deliveries actually; it's just, well I live upstairs and today was really busy with Valentine's Day and everything, so I thought, seeing as it was on my way . . .'

'So someone *has* moved in then,' Alex said, nodding sagely to herself. 'I knew I wasn't hearing things.'

Leonie was mortified. 'I hope I'm not being too noisy . . .'

'No, no, I guess I only noticed because it's been a while since anyone's lived up there. Well, welcome to Green Street,' she continued, a smile quickly lighting up her face. 'Good meeting you . . . ?'

'Leonie,' she supplied, shaking Alex's hand while at the

same time trying to keep the flowers at arm's length.

'Well, with that accent, I'm guessing you're not from the Bay Area?'

'No, I'm Irish – from Dublin,' Leonie told her.

'Great country. Well, I've never actually been there, but it certainly sounds great.'

She smiled again and Leonie was struck by how utterly stunning she was. Her huge brown eyes gave her features a delicate almost fragile appearance, which seemed completely at odds with her self-assured demeanour and rapid-fire chatter.

'So, as I said, welcome to Green Street. This is a great neighbourhood and I hope you'll be really happy here.'

'Thanks.'

There was a short pause, as neither woman seemed to know what to say or do next.

'So hey, do you want to come inside for a coffee or something?' Alex asked eventually.

Leonie was delighted. 'You don't mind? I don't want to intrude or anything.'

'Not a problem. I was just making myself a cup and some company would be nice. And I guess I kind of owe you one, for all that shouting and stuff. Sorry about that.'

'Not at all. I'd love to, but I suppose I'd better get rid of these first,' she said, indicating the flowers. 'I'll drop them up to my place, and then come back down OK?'

'Sure.'

Pleased by the prospect of getting to know her neighbour, Leonie hurried up the stairs to her own apartment. Setting the flowers down on floor beside the sofa, she tried to dust any stray pollen off her clothes and was just about to go back out again when the box of letters lying open on the window seat caught her eye.

Hmm, she thought, closing the apartment door behind her.

Seeing as Alex had lived in this building for a while, getting to know her might be a good idea for more reasons than one.

'Wow, this place is really nice,' she said, stepping inside Alex's apartment.

Although it was similar in size and layout, it looked a lot more homely and lived in than Leonie's. Colourful cushions of various shapes and sizes were strewn across an old but very comfy-looking sofa, and the walls were dotted with funky contemporary art canvases. An open laptop computer lay on the carpeted floor, its cursor blinking where Alex must have left off typing when Leonie disturbed her with the flowers. A half-used packet of hay fever tablets on the coffee table further confirmed her allergies, which in the absence of the flowers, Leonie noticed, seemed to have subsided a little.

'Make yourself comfortable,' Alex urged, taking a sheaf of papers from the sofa. 'I'm sorry about the mess, but the hay fever was so bad earlier I needed to try and catch up. I refused this morning's delivery but then I got another one at work,' she added with a shake of her head.

'And you have no idea who sent them? Why would anyone do that when you suffer from hay fever?'

'Oh, I could think of one in particular,' she replied cryptically. 'Which is why I'd appreciate taking a look at your records tomorrow.'

'Well, as I said, I'll see what I can do.' Leonie wondered if Marcy would allow this. 'So how long have you been living here?' she asked while Alex made coffee.

'A few years now,' the other girl replied. Which meant she must have known Helena, Leonie thought. 'It's close to where I work and the rent's pretty good, although as you can see it's a little bit on the small side for all my stuff.'

Leonie smiled. There was indeed plenty of stuff.

'What about you?' Alex asked, handing her a cup of coffee and taking a seat on the armchair across from her. 'When did you move in upstairs?'

'Just a few weeks ago. It took me a while to find somewhere I liked, but I must admit I fell in love with this place on sight. I just adore these Victorian houses.'

'Yeah, the "painted ladies" are great,' Alex agreed, using the same term Marcy had to describe this type of house. 'Hell on the heating bills, but better than some of those ugly old tower blocks down by the wharf.'

'Or the Holiday Inn,' Leonie grinned, filling her in on her previous living arrangements.

They chatted for a while about their respective lives, and Alex told Leonie about her job at the TV news station.

'*Today by the Bay*? Wait a minute, I think I've seen that!' she gasped. 'Wasn't there something on recently about a bear being rescued from the water?'

Alex smiled proudly. 'Yep, that's us.'

'Wow, what a fantastic job!'

Although Alex was at pains to point out that she never actually appeared on camera, Leonie still felt a little starstruck. Imagine meeting a real live TV person . . . Grace would be goggle-eyed when she heard!

'So what's your story?' Alex asked. 'What brings you all the way to the West Coast?'

Leonie stiffened a little, unwilling to get into that. 'I just needed a change of scenery,' she told her airily. 'Ireland's great, but I find it hard to stay in one place for long. And the weather's a bit of a drawback too,' she added, forcing a smile.

Alex looked directly at her, and for a second, Leonie thought that the other girl sensed that there was a lot more to it than what she was saying. But just as quickly, she smiled too. 'So I've heard,' she said with a roll of her eyes. 'Green fields are all very well but give me blue skies and sunshine any day of the week.'

'Exactly,' Leonie agreed, feeling stupid for even thinking that a complete stranger, someone she'd only just met, would have any clue about her life. But in any case, she thought it best to change the subject. 'Tell me something,' she said, deciding now was a good time to ask. 'The tenant who lived upstairs before me, would you by any chance happen to have a forwarding address for her?'

'You mean that couple?' Alex frowned. 'To be honest, I didn't really know them, just enough to say hi to really.'

Oh, so they'd *both* lived there, Leonie realised. That was interesting!

'What were they like?'

Alex shrugged. 'Hard to say. Nice enough, I suppose. Why do you ask?'

'I'm still getting mail for them – well, for her actually, and I wanted to forward it on.'

Leonie didn't want to admit that she also knew who the mail was from. For one thing, she didn't want Alex to think she was a nosy old so-and-so and for another, as Marcy had pointed out earlier, opening someone else's post was a felony.

'Can't help you there, I'm afraid, but I'm sure the agency would know.'

'I already tried that,' Leonie said despondently. 'The agency had no forwarding address so they told me I should just throw the letters away.'

'Well, then maybe you should. I mean if they didn't bother leaving an address then they probably don't . . .' Alex paused frowning. 'No, hold on, wasn't there something . . . ? I remember hearing something about it at the time and as I said I didn't really know them, but I think there was some kind of . . . situation.'

Situation? Almost unknown to herself, Leonie leaned closer, all ears now. 'What kind of situation?'

'As I said, I'm not really sure and it was a while ago now, but I remember there was a lot of activity going on around the time they moved out.' She shook her head. 'I can't remember what exactly, but I got the impression that things didn't end so good.'

'Between Nathan and Helena, you mean?' In her eagerness to find out more about the couple, Leonie had forgotten that she wasn't supposed to know anything about them. 'That was their names, wasn't it?' she added quickly. 'That's what's on the letters anyway.'

'I couldn't say. Again, it was some time ago.'

'When did they move out?' Leonie realised she didn't know this. 'When I first came to see the apartment, the agency told me someone was still living there.'

'I don't think so,' Alex said with a shake of her head. 'By my reckoning, nobody's lived there for a few months.'

That was odd. 'But there was stuff still there, all the furniture and the letters . . .'

'Well, as I said something was going on around the time they left, so maybe they only moved their stuff out when the lease was up?'

'They must have broken up then,' Leonie said, knowing that this was exactly what had happened.

Alex sipped her coffee. 'Well I've got to say *that* wouldn't surprise me in the least, the noises that used to come from up there.'

'Really?' Leonie sat forward again. 'You heard them arguing?'

She nodded. 'And then some. I think she was kinda partial to flinging plates at his head.'

'Oh.' Now, Leonie couldn't help but feel sorry for Nathan.

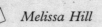

From his letters he seemed to have adored the ground Helena walked on, so to think that she was cruel to him . . . but then again, maybe she had every reason to be?

'You're sure you can't remember when they moved out?' she asked Alex again. Hearing such little snippets about the couple now made her even more eager to find out what had happened to them. 'And you have no idea where they might be now?'

'Not a clue.' Alex shook her head. 'They could be in Timbuktu for all I know.'

Chapter 8

'So . . . ?'

'So?' Alex repeated, confused. It was the following morning and she was just about to leave for work when she got a call from Jon.

'You didn't get them?' he replied dejectedly, and instantly the penny dropped.

Alex flushed from head to toe, horrified at her stupidity. Of *course* it had been Jon who'd sent the flowers, why on earth hadn't she even considered him . . .

'You mean the roses?' she replied, not sure what to feel. 'I did get them and yes they were beautiful, thank you, but the thing is—'

'I really hope they were beautiful, Alex,' he laughed. 'Some florists can be a bit careless on those busy days, so I used three different places just to be sure.'

Immediately she felt guilty, and more than a little stupid.

She wasn't sure why she'd jumped to the wrong conclusion, and really, the *least* likely conclusion, considering.

It was the message 'Guess who?' that had caused her to suspect something else was going on. So much so that she hadn't even considered that all three bouquets might have been sent by Jon. Even though it was exactly the kind of thing he would do given how apologetic he'd been about not seeing her on Valentine's Day. And *especially* stupid given what had happened that very same night, Alex recalled, smiling at the memory.

'Jon, they were amazing, honestly and I really appreciate it, but, well . . . I'm sorry but I had to send them all back,' she told him sheepishly. 'It's my fault, I should have told you before, but I suffer from really bad hay fever.'

Jon sounded horrified. 'I'm sorry, sweetheart, I had no idea.'

'Hey, no need to be sorry, you couldn't have known. But thank you all the same, it was really sweet of you.'

'I guess you didn't appreciate three separate deliveries then,' he said, sounding shamefaced. 'But I felt kinda guilty about not being able to see you yesterday, especially after the other night . . .'

'I know.' Alex's face flushed at the memory. That night, all her previous hesitation had gone straight out the window once they made it back to Jon's house. No, strike that, once they'd left the restaurant and made it into the *cab*.

'So I thought a roomful of red roses might make up for it.' Jon was still talking. 'Guess, I read that one wrong.'

'Honestly, it's fine,' Alex assured him. 'And no need to feel guilty about working the late shifts this week. We'll see each other again soon.'

'I can't wait,' he said, and Alex smiled at the promise in his tone. 'Listen, gotta go, things are crazy here. I'll call you at the weekend, OK? We'll do something nice.'

'Sure.'

'And sorry again about the hay fever. Some doctor I am, huh?'

Alex chuckled. 'It's fine – honestly.'

Saying goodbye to Jon, she hung up the phone and again remonstrated with herself for being so quick to jump to conclusions – the wrong conclusions. The new girl from upstairs,

Leonie, probably thought she was a right whacko, what with her behaving like a crazy woman and demanding information from the flower store.

Alex sighed. She guessed she'd better let her know that she no longer needed it, and that her so-called 'mystery' had turned out to be nothing of the sort.

Leonie had thoroughly enjoyed spending time with her neighbour. Alex was good fun, chatty and open in a way that reminded her a little bit of Grace. Last night, they'd talked so much it had been well after ten when she'd left her neighbour's place and gone back upstairs to her own. Thinking of Grace, she felt a pang of guilt. She really should phone her, it had been over a week since they'd last spoken.

Not that she wanted too many reminders from home, but Leonie knew that no doubt her friend would still be worried about her. Well, she needn't worry too much. Wasn't she getting on grand in her new life in the city, what with her nice apartment, easy-going job and new friends in Marcy and now, hopefully, Alex?

Her neighbour had arranged to call in today to try and find out more about the mysterious sender of her flowers.

'We can't give out that kind of information,' Marcy said when Leonie outlined what had happened. Her boss was sweeping bits of broken greenery off the floor. 'If a bouquet's sent anonymously then we have to abide by the sender's wishes.'

'I know but Alex is a TV personality, what if she has a stalker or something?' She skimmed through the store's database, trying to find the relevant order.

Marcy stopped and frowned. 'Didn't you say she was just a producer? Not sure if stalkers are all that interested in the ones behind the scenes.'

'Maybe. But I'd like to help her if I could. She seems really nice *and* she was able to tell me a couple of things about my predecessor in the apartment,' she added pointedly.

'Really? Did she know her?'

'Not just her – *them*. And no, she didn't know much about them other than the fact that there *was* a them, which I thought was interesting.'

'So I guess the guy used to live there too.'

'And there's more.' She then went on to tell Marcy what Alex had said about there being some kind of incident around the time the couple moved out.

Her boss raised an eyebrow. 'Curiouser and curiouser, huh?'

'That's what I thought. But I was thinking that he must have left before she did, seeing as he's still sending her letters and doesn't know she's moved out.'

'All very interesting but what are you going to do? Are you still thinking about trying to get the letters back to them?'

'I'd certainly like to at least try. I know one thing for sure, if I was Helena I'd want to be given the opportunity to read them. And it breaks my heart to think that he still doesn't know that she *hasn't* seen them.'

'My, you really are an old softie, aren't you?'

She shrugged. 'Not really. I just think that sometimes people deserve a second chance.'

'Hmm, sounds like there's more to this than meets the eye,' Marcy replied, giving her a sideways glance.

Leonie coloured. 'What do you mean?' she asked warily, her insides jumping.

'Well, I hope you're not doing a *Sleepless in Seattle* and have gone and fallen for this guy. Fancy words are one thing but sweetheart you don't know the first thing about—'

'No, it's nothing like that!' Leonie laughed, relieved. 'I don't know, I just think that maybe I owe it to these people to try and get the letters back to them, especially when I know they're so personal. I think it's important to at least try.'

The problem was that Leonie really didn't know how to even start going about this.

'Well, it wouldn't be me, but I think it's very honourable of you to take it upon yourself to do that for a couple of strangers.'

Yet for some reason Leonie didn't quite see it like that. Since she'd read those letters and had that small glimpse of the couple's relationship, they no longer felt like strangers to her. Especially Nathan. How could she not try and intervene in this situation especially when he'd been trying so hard (in more ways than one) to reach the woman he loved? Maybe she was a bit of a softie like Marcy said, or maybe she was just downright inquisitive, but either way she felt like she had to do something.

So what next? She'd tried finding a forwarding address for Helena Abbott, and there was no return address for Nathan. So how else could she go about this?

Leonie sighed, deciding that now wasn't really the time to think about it, as there was still plenty of cleaning up to do after the craziness of yesterday.

'And speaking of strangers,' Marcy said, 'I just can't give out customer information to anyone who asks for it. So while I'd like to help, I think your friend Alex will just have to trace her secret admirer some other way.'

Leonie knew by her boss's firm tone that there was no point in arguing, so while she fretted for most of the day about not being able to help Alex when she called, it seemed there was no need, as by the end of her shift that evening there had been no sign of the other girl at all.

Maybe she'd already found out who sent them?

Leonie hoped so, and as she said goodbye to Marcy and

made her way home, she wondered if there was something about the Green Street house, what with all the mysteries that were happening there lately! First those unopened letters and then Alex and her anonymous flowers.

She'd only just turned on to her street when she saw Alex approaching in the other direction.

'Hey there!' the other girl greeted warmly. 'I was hoping I might bump into you this evening. Turns out there was no need for me to call and see you today.'

'So you found out who sent the flowers?'

'Yep,' she replied, explaining that it had been Jon, the guy she was seeing. She rolled her eyes. 'I'm such an idiot, I should have guessed, as it's exactly the kind of thing he'd do,' she said fondly.

Leonie couldn't help but wonder why this was such a good thing when she was actually allergic to flowers.

'We've only been together a couple of months and he didn't know about my hay fever,' Alex explained as if reading her thoughts, 'but thanks for taking them back and thanks too for offering to help. I appreciate it.'

'No problem. I'm glad you didn't need it in the end.'

'Me too,' Alex laughed. Then she looked at her watch. 'So hey, have you had dinner yet? I'm just heading out for a bite to eat, so if you'd like to join me . . . ?'

'No, I haven't eaten and yes, that would be brilliant.' Leonie was more than happy to accept Alex's invitation, she had nothing planned for that evening other than a ready-meal and a night in front of the telly. As she hadn't really ventured out anywhere in the evenings since she got here, it would be nice to do something different, and especially nice to get to know Alex more.

'Fancy grabbing some seafood then?' Alex asked. 'I know a great place a couple of blocks from here, a million miles away from that tourist crap you get down by Fisherman's Wharf. They do the best clam chowder.'

'Sounds good.' Steaming, creamy seafood chowder served in a bowl made entirely from crusty sourdough sounded absolutely perfect. Boudin's sourdough bread was a San Francisco institution, and Leonie was already a convert of what was a huge favourite with city natives and tourists alike. And something to warm the cockles would be nice! When she'd left the house in short-sleeves that morning the sky was clear and the sun was beaming down, in sharp contrast to the chilly Pacific fog that had since enveloped the city.

'Mark Twain was spot on, you know,' she said shivering and rubbing her arms as she and Alex headed off down the street.

'"The coldest winter I ever spent was a summer in San Francisco",' right?' Alex quoted with a smile. 'He sure got that right. Don't worry you'll get used to it, just never forget to bring a sweater,' she advised, eyeing Leonie's goose-pimpled arms. 'Anyway, what's the big deal, I thought it was always cold in Ireland?'

'It is, but at least the weather doesn't mess with your head like this!'

Leonie was relieved when eventually at the bottom of the hill towards the wharf, they reached a small, innocuous-looking seafood place that looked much more sedate than the glitzy tourist-themed restaurants further along the pier. They went inside and almost immediately one of the waiters greeted Alex. 'Well, well, well – if it isn't Miss Today by the Bay!'

'Hey, Dan, long time no see,' she replied easily, taking a seat at a vacant table by the window.

'You know, I was only saying to Phil the other day that we hadn't seen you in here for a while,' he said, coming across to the table. 'We were afraid all this TV success had gone to your head. I loved that bear story, by the way. Do you guys make that stuff up, or what?'

'You're hilarious, you know that?' Alex replied archly.

'And when are you going do something about that oil scoop I gave you? If you're not careful someone else will steal it from right under your nose . . .'

'I'm working on it, Dan,' Alex said, in a tone that implied anything but.

Introductions were made, and Leonie learned that Dan and his partner Phil owned and ran the Crab Shack.

Dan cocked his head at Alex. 'I'd be careful around this one if I were you,' he warned Leonie jokingly, but there was a fondness in his voice that made her suspect this kind of teasing was par for the course. 'She might look cute on the outside but underneath lies a heart of pure steel.'

'Do you mind?' Alex cried, feigning annoyance. 'Leonie's new here and I told her I'd show her the best seafood place in town. Do you want me to take her to Joe's instead?'

'OK, OK.' Dan put his hands up in surrender. 'I'll leave you guys to it then. Leonie, great to meet you, and you're welcome here anytime.'

'Thanks, nice to meet you too.' He seemed lovely and despite their banter Alex seemed very fond of him also.

'Don't mind him, he can be full of it but he's good fun,' the other girl said when Dan had taken their order. 'I've been coming here for years and I meant what I said, just *wait* until you taste Phil's chowder. I promise you it's out of this world.'

Alex hadn't been exaggerating. The food quickly arrived, and Leonie lifted off the top of the sourdough bread bowl and dipped the crust into the creamy seafood mixture discovering that it tasted just as good as it looked; much better than the stuff she'd been getting from street sellers up to now.

'I don't mean to be nosy but what did Dan mean by that oil story he wanted you to do?' she asked.

Alex rolled her eyes. 'OK, I guess I should tell you, Dan and Phil are conspiracy theorists. You name it: aliens, fake moon landings, dodgy presidential elections . . .' She shook her head. 'Hell, they even spend their summer vacations down in Roswell.'

Leonie smiled indulgently. 'And what kind of piece did he want you to do?'

'Well, you know this whole oil crisis thing that's going on now? According to Dan and Phil it's all just another government smokescreen to keep us in line and there's no shortage at all – just lots of stuff that hasn't been tapped yet. *And* they want me to uncover this so-called "conspiracy" and broadcast it to the whole world. As if,' she said, taking a chunk out of her sourdough. 'But even if I did want to do it, my producer wouldn't touch it.'

Leonie loved hearing this kind of thing. Only in America. 'So is there any truth in it?'

'Probably,' Alex replied matter-of-factly. 'I've heard there's something like a trillion barrels in the Rockies.'

'Really?'

'Sure. Anyway, better change the subject,' she murmured, lowering her voice as Dan approached again. 'If he hears me talking to you about this, he'll never leave it alone and we could be here till midnight!'

'No problem.'

'So hey, I'm sorry for being so full-on yesterday – about the whole flowers thing, I mean,' Alex said.

'That's no problem. I'm glad you didn't need my help in the end – not that I don't think I could have helped much anyway as my boss won't give out customer information,' she added apologetically. 'And it turns out the order came in through the Internet.'

Alex shrugged. 'That would have been more than enough to figure it out.'

'Really? How? There was no name or address on the order . . .'

'Doesn't matter. We could have traced it thorough the IP address.'

At Leonie's blank look, she went on. 'It's kind of like a unique computer address. It tells you where the sender is located, or at least, where his *computer* is located. And if you know that much then you have a very good chance of tracking the person down.'

Leonie was amazed. 'You can actually do that? Find someone through their computer, I mean?'

'Hey, I was trained as an investigative reporter, I do this kind of thing all the time,' Alex said, with a knowing smile. 'Seriously, it's no big deal,' she continued, scooping up some more chowder. 'You can pretty much find anyone, once you know where to look.'

Really? Well in that case . . . Leonie thought, immediately spotting the opportunity.

'Alex?' she began, 'I think I might have a favour of my own to ask.'

Chapter 9

'You read somebody else's mail? You know that's a felony, right?'

'So I heard,' Leonie replied. Bloody hell, they were all so conscientious around here, weren't they?

It was later that evening and after they'd finished having dinner, they went back to Green Street where Leonie showed Alex the letters. Earlier, she'd told her she could do with her help in trying to locate someone, seeing as she seemed to be a bit of an expert on that kind of thing.

Apparently well up for a challenge, Alex instantly agreed and while Leonie didn't at first tell her that she had opened and read the older letters, she did tell her about the one she'd opened by mistake.

But now, with the pile of Nathan's letters laid out on the table and two of them open, she really had no choice but to come clean with Alex about what she'd done.

'I was hoping to find a return address for him, so I could return them to sender but then I sort of got sidetracked. Honestly, when I read the first letter, I couldn't bring myself to stop.'

'So how many have you read?' Alex asked, sifting through the envelopes.

'Just two, and I couldn't help it,' she reiterated again. 'I suppose I was intrigued by the fact that she and Nathan lived here in this apartment. And of course that he seems so desperate for forgiveness.'

'It's a bit of a mystery for sure,' Alex said, 'although I'm not convinced that opening the letters was such a good idea.'

'As I said I needed to try and find an address.' Now she was almost sorry she'd taken Alex into her confidence, especially as she'd been certain the other girl would be just as intrigued as she was about this. Not to mention the fact that Alex had lived in close proximity to the couple in question, so surely she would be able to shed light on a couple of things? 'So what do you think I should do with them?' she asked.

Alex shrugged, evidently not sharing Leonie's sense of urgency. 'Nothing you can do, I guess. Although wait, have you checked the postmark?' she asked, peering at the front of one of the envelopes.

'I've already tried that and look, it tells us nothing other than the letters originate in California. There's no specific town or area mentioned and the date's illegible but at the same time it looks a bit . . . official, doesn't it?'

'It is kind of weird,' Alex went on, studying the postmark. 'Looks like it could be some kind of crest . . . federal maybe?'

Leonie's eyes widened with amazement. 'You mean from the FBI?'

Alex laughed. 'Oh boy, TV sure has a lot to answer for! No, no, federal simply means it could have something to do with a central government department rather than a state one.'

'Oh.' Leonie felt very gauche indeed. But then again what would she know about the different types of US government?

'Even so, that still doesn't give us a whole lot to go on in terms of where they're coming from.'

'Exactly. Which is why I *had* to try opening up another one, to see if there was anything else that would help identify this.' Leonie felt a strong need to justify herself. 'I mean think about it. All these letters and none of them have been opened. The guy is probably going out of his mind wondering why she hasn't responded.'

'Yet he doesn't include a return address . . .' Alex seemed to be thinking it over.

'I know. That seemed strange to me too at first, but perhaps not when you're writing informally to someone who already knows where you live?'

'I guess. Beautiful handwriting though, isn't it? Kind of . . . artistic, almost?'

'Like calligraphy, I thought.'

The elegant handwriting also fit the mental picture of Nathan that Leonie had built up. The man had taken a lot of time over these letters, and it looked like he'd written them with an expensive ink pen instead of your standard ballpoint.

'Hmm.' Now Alex was scanning the contents of the first letter Leonie had read. 'Please forgive me,' she said, repeating his words out loud. 'Something's definitely up there. I wonder what he did?'

Leonie shrugged. 'I wish I knew. Chances are we'll never find out, but seeing as it's all so personal, I really thought I should at least try and let him know that Helena Abbott doesn't live here anymore.'

'Kinda hard to do when he doesn't leave any contact details though, isn't it?' Alex sat back on her haunches. 'OK, well if you really want to find these people, have you thought about maybe doing a search for either one on the Internet?'

'God, I never thought of that,' Leonie admitted, feeling like a right idiot.

It was the obvious thing to do, wasn't it? And definitely

more preferable than just opening up people's post and poking around inside?

'Well, wait here,' Alex said, getting up. 'I'll just pop downstairs and get my laptop. I bet Google will have these two located in no time.'

'That'd be brilliant,' Leonie enthused, feeling much more positive about getting somewhere now that Alex was on the case and they could buzz ideas off one another.

A few minutes later her neighbour returned with her laptop, and the two of them sat side by side on the sofa in front of it.

'OK, let's try her first,' Alex said, keying in Helena's name and almost instantly, pages upon pages of Helena Abbotts appeared.

Leonie groaned. 'Oh God, where do we even start?'

'Not so fast, just give me a second.' Alex narrowed the scope of the search by adding the words 'San Francisco'.

'But there's still loads,' Leonie said, crestfallen when another long list appeared.

'Well, at least it's a start,' Alex pointed out, scrolling through the hits. There were a couple of entries they could discount immediately, like those related to high school sports results, as they knew from the letters that Helena couldn't be a teenager. But even so, there were still a hell of a lot of Helena Abbotts listed in the San Francisco area.

'Let's try and narrow it down some more. What else do we know about her from the letters, besides the fact that she was in a relationship with this Nathan guy?'

'Well,' Leonie thought, 'they lived here at this apartment, and she loved sitting over there by the window and looking out at the bridge . . .'

Alex looked up from the computer screen. 'I'm talking about *useful* information, Leonie,' she said pointedly. 'Was there anything mentioned about what she did for a living, maybe somewhere she worked . . .'

'Oh, she's into photography,' Leonie recalled. 'Although I'm not sure if it's as a job or a hobby, the letters didn't say. It's how she and Nathan first met,' she told her.

'Hmm, doesn't really give me that much to go on . . .' Her brow furrowing, Alex typed something else into the computer. 'Nope, nothing at all here in relation to any Helena Abbott about photography. And I've already tried searching using this address and it's given me squat too. Chances are they leased the apartment same as you and me, so wouldn't be listed as owners.' Her fingers raced over the keyboard once again.

'Do you know who actually *does* own this place?'

Alex shrugged. 'I have no idea. I've always dealt with an agency, and as the rent stays reasonable and the landlord stays out of the way, I can't say I've ever really thought about who it belongs to. Either way that won't help us, because if these two were here before you, then I'm guessing they were leasing too.'

'Isn't there anything you can remember about them?' Leonie probed. 'Anything that might help with the search?'

'Like I said, they kept to themselves pretty much, and so did I. I bumped into him a couple of times on the way out the door, but I can't recall seeing her at all.'

'So what did he look like?' From the couple of letters she'd read, Leonie had built up a picture of Nathan as being a typical romantic hero: tall, handsome and brooding, irrespective of the fact that he had never once made reference to his appearance.

'Pretty ordinary-looking,' Alex said, bursting her bubble. 'Medium height and build, although a bit on the chubby side – I'd say he liked his beer,' she added, wrinkling her nose.

Leonie was almost sorry she'd asked. What had started out as a vision of George Clooney was very quickly morphing into Homer Simpson!

'But now that I think about it, there was also something a bit . . . I don't know, something kind of *intense* about him.'

'Intense in what way?'

'Well,' Alex screwed up her eyes as she thought back, 'I remember one day we were both heading out to work at the same time. I presume he was heading to work, because he was wearing a suit and carrying a briefcase,' she added in an aside. 'So I said hi, and right before he replied he gave me this . . . odd look, kind of like he was sizing me up or something.'

'Sizing you up,' Leonie repeated flatly.

'Yes, you know the way guys in clubs sometimes run their eyes over your body as if giving you marks out of ten? Well, it was kind of like that.'

'Oh.' This was completely at odds with what Leonie had imagined. The way Alex was talking, he sounded almost sleazy!

'I'm only telling you what I remember. Like I said, I didn't really get to know them while they were here. It was only for a year at the most.'

'But you said you heard them argue sometimes?' Leonie said.

'Yes. But the floorboards are ancient here, so that really wasn't too difficult.' Alex grinned. 'I guess you should keep that in mind in case you're thinking of bringing any guys back.'

'Well, you needn't worry about *that*,' Leonie said tightly.

Alex looked back at the computer screen. 'So yeah, I guess he was a bit sleazy, the way a certain type of married guy can be—'

'They were *married*?' Leonie gasped. Suddenly, the

circumstances surrounding the couple's separation had become a lot more interesting. 'How do you know that?'

'Sorry, I thought you already knew,' Alex said off-handedly. 'I noticed he was wearing a wedding band.'

'Wow, this is even more serious then, isn't it?' Leonie said, her mind racing. 'I don't know; for some reason I'd just assumed they were boyfriend and girlfriend. I didn't think for a second it might be more than that.'

And seeing as it *was* more than that, then she had to do whatever it took to get those letters back to either one of them, didn't she? Especially when there was so much more at stake. She picked up one of the opened letters and again read the last line.

Please forgive me.

Alex seemed to read Leonie's thoughts. 'Well, seeing as he definitely had an eye for the ladies, I think we can probably guess what went wrong, can't we?'

'Oh, I hope not,' she said despondently. From these letters, Nathan certainly didn't sound like your typical cheat, but then again, what would she know?

'Anyway,' Alex continued, turning back to the laptop. 'I really don't know what else to tell you about them that could help us find Helena. You don't know what she did for a living, and I can't tell you what she looked like. So maybe we should try searching for him instead?'

'Good idea.'

She watched while Alex typed in another Google search, this time for Nathan Abbott, and again within the relevant parameters. And almost immediately her friend's eyes widened. 'Aha! Now *this* looks promising,' she declared, as Leonie leaned forward for a better look.

'What?' she asked, staring at the screen. 'What am I supposed to be looking at?'

'See this here?' Alex pointed at one of the listings. 'It's a website for a stockbroker firm that lists a Nathan Abbott as one of its senior employees.' She turned to look at Leonie, her eyes shining with anticipation. 'It certainly fits with the suit and the briefcase, doesn't it?'

'I suppose so.'

'And maybe I was wrong about the federal-type postmark, but if he's sending the letters from the office, they would almost *certainly* be franked,' Alex continued enthusiastically. 'Granted, there's no photo here, but he's the only Nathan Abbott listed in the search that fits. All the others are too young or way too old. But the biggest thing,' she said, her excitement growing, 'is that the firm is based downtown, right across from the TransAmerica building.'

Barely a mile away, Leonie realised, her heart beginning to race with excitement.

'You should give him a call tomorrow and ask a few questions,' Alex said, clicking on the firm's contact page.

Leonie felt a strange mixture of nervousness and excitement. Could this really be the Nathan whose letters she'd been reading? The one who'd been declaring undying love to his wife and asking for forgiveness? And if it was, what would she say to him or more importantly how on earth would she explain how she'd come about finding him, let alone the letters?

'So yes, I think we might just have found our man,' Alex grinned triumphantly at Leonie, before saving the relevant page to her PC. 'See – not hard at all!'

Chapter 10

'Hello, stranger.' Although Grace's tone was warm, Leonie still sensed that her friend was a little put out that she hadn't been keeping in touch as often as she had initially. 'Sorry for phoning so early, but with the time difference it's hard to know when to catch you.'

'No problem and it's great to hear from you!' Leonie replied smiling. It was just after eight in the morning, so by her reckoning, it had to be teatime back home. 'I'm sorry I haven't phoned myself – it's just been really busy, and work has been crazy . . .' Even as she said the words she knew they sounded weak. She supposed she wasn't phoning as much now because she was trying to leave most of her old life behind, for the short term at least.

'The job's going well, then?' Grace asked.

'Yes, I'm really enjoying it. Marcy's lovely – you'd like her and she's really helped me settle in here. I've started making a few friends too.'

There was a short pause. 'Oh. Well that's good, I suppose.'

'So listen, how are you and the twins?'

'Oh, don't talk to me about those two,' Grace groaned, sounding much more like herself. '*Wait* till I tell you what they did last week . . .'

Leonie listened while her poor friend described the terrible twosome's latest exploits. She and Ray were mortified after recently discovering that Rocky and Rosie had been pocketing chocolate on shopping trips to Tesco. They were only made aware of it when Grace was gently taken aside by a security guard and informed as to what was going on. 'I nearly died!' she said still horrified. 'Imagine, they're barely three years old and already they're carrying on like little hooligans! What in God's name will they be like when they're teenagers?'

Despite herself Leonie had to laugh at the idea of Rocky and Rosie as mini versions of Bonnie and Clyde. 'What did Ray say when you found out?'

'He said what he always says, Lee – absolutely bugger all! No, as usual it's up to mummy to dole out punishment and be the bad guy.' Leonie knew that Ray wasn't exactly a hands-on dad, and was such a soft touch he probably wouldn't be able to carry out any punishment anyway.

'Ah, you poor thing. But listen, how are the holiday plans going? The last time we spoke you were in the process of booking something.'

Grace harrumphed. 'I think that's definitely on the long finger now. Sure, you couldn't bring those two out of the country; they'd probably get arrested for terrorism or something!'

'That's a pity – it sounded like you were really looking forward to it.'

'I was more looking forward to the break to be honest, but I don't think *that's* likely anytime soon.'

'Well look, try not to stress about it too much, I'm sure it's just a phase they're going through.'

'I sincerely hope so.' Grace gave a deep sigh.

'So how are things otherwise?' Leonie asked, changing the subject. 'Anything strange at home?' Then she winced, hoping that this didn't sound like she was fishing for news of Adam.

Because she really wasn't.

Still Grace was no fool. 'Well, seeing as you asked . . . he's been in touch again.'

'Who has?' Leonie asked, trying to sound innocent, but inside her heart was racing.

'Who do you think? Adam phoned again looking to find out where you were. And look, I know you're my friend and my first loyalty is to you, but you have to realise what a terrible position all this is putting me in. Even though I've told him upside down and inside out that I don't know, I think he knows full well that I do.'

'I know, and I'm sorry . . .' Now she felt terrible. It wasn't fair to Grace but at the same time she prayed with all her heart that her friend hadn't betrayed her confidence and told Adam where she was.

'I haven't told him anything and I'm not planning to either, but it's difficult. He's being very insistent. And to be honest, Lee, I think he's worried. As far as he's concerned, six weeks ago you just disappeared off the face of the earth.'

'Yes, but with good reason,' Leonie countered, not knowing what to make of this. She wasn't sure whether to feel worried or relieved that Adam was still anxious to know her where-abouts.

'Maybe, but you know I think you should at least have given things a chance to settle down before making such a rash choice.'

Now Leonie remembered why she'd been reluctant to phone Grace recently. She knew they'd end up having the same argument over and over again about her decision to leave.

'It wasn't a rash choice, Grace – it was the *only* choice. And it looks like it was also the best one. Things are great here, I'm feeling much better and best of all I'm miles away from . . . everything.'

'Well, I wouldn't be so sure it was the best choice, Leonie,' Grace interjected softly. Then she sighed. 'I suppose I might as well tell you.'

Leonie's heart skipped a beat. 'Tell me what?'

Grace hesitated for a moment before continuing. 'Well, Adam mentioned it the last time we spoke, and I wasn't sure whether to say anything, but . . . Suzanne's moved in.'

Dublin – Three years earlier

Leonie had understood right from the very beginning that Suzanne could be a problem. Well, perhaps not *right* from the beginning, but definitely within a few weeks of her and Adam's return from Tunisia when they started seeing one another seriously, mostly because he never stopped talking about how brilliantly she and Suzanne would get along.

'She's going to just *love* you,' he'd say, and every time he did it made Leonie more and more uncertain that she would. 'You're going to get along great.'

She was incredibly nervous when Adam told her he'd arranged for them to meet for the first time.

He organised for them all to go out for dinner in town, and Leonie hoped he'd book somewhere informal and easy-going, like Cactus Jack's or TGI Friday. But then he informed her that Suzanne was 'a little particular' about the places she liked to frequent.

'Particular in what way?' Leonie queried, concerned that maybe Suzanne was a fussy eater, or was she perhaps shy?

'Shy?' Adam guffawed. 'Not a chance!'

So all she knew about Suzanne so far was that she was 'amazing', not in the least bit shy, but at the same time 'a little particular'. And of course there was the tiny detail of her being the most important person in Adam's life up to now.

Not that Leonie was claiming any greater importance, but given that their relationship was rapidly becoming more serious, she'd like to think she took at least second place in his affections.

'I've booked a table at Bang,' he said, referring to one of the city's trendiest restaurants. A bit of a celeb hangout, it wasn't the kind of place Leonie would have chosen for a first meeting. 'She's been there a few times, so I know she likes it.'

'Great, well I haven't ever been there, but I'm sure it'll be lovely,' Leonie said, agreeing to meet him and Suzanne at the restaurant at seven the following Friday night. It would be handy for her, as it was close to the office and she'd be coming directly from work.

For the entire week leading up to the dinner, Leonie just couldn't dispel her nerves. She couldn't quite understand why. She knew that Suzanne would hardly be an ogre, but right up to the very moment she arrived at the restaurant she couldn't help but have a bad feeling about the evening ahead. Although, she reasoned, the fact that Suzanne seemed very eager to meet her should have given her some comfort.

'She has me driven demented, wanting to hear all about you, what you look like, the kind of clothes you wear – everything!' Adam had informed Leonie. 'And I told her that you were a wonderful person who makes me very happy,' he had added, kissing her on the nose. 'Which is the truth.'

That evening, Leonie was led to their table by the maître d' and found she was first to arrive, which at least gave her time to gather her thoughts and calm her nerves. What the hell was wrong with her? This was going to be fine; no doubt she and Suzanne would click on sight and end up being firm friends from here on in.

'Hey, you're here!' Adam boomed. With a start, Leonie

looked up to see that her dinner companions had arrived. Adam looked handsome as usual in light-coloured Levi's and a navy Fred Perry shirt. Alongside him stood the famous Suzanne.

Leonie gulped. Tall and blonde, she was wearing a daringly low-cut top, *very* short miniskirt, vertiginous heels and an expression that could only be described as sullen.

'Hi,' Leonie said, standing up from the table as Adam handed their coats to the maître d'. 'Hello, Suzanne, it's really nice to meet you.'

'Hi.' Patently ignoring Leonie's outstretched hand Suzanne gave a flick of her expensively styled blond hair.

'The traffic was just crazy, wasn't it, Suze?' Adam said, missing the snub. He took the seat alongside Suzanne, leaving Leonie facing the two of them. 'And I thought we'd never get a parking space. Were you here long, Lee?'

'Just in before you,' she replied easily, trying to hide her discomfort at the fact that Suzanne had steadfastly blanked her. She was quite beautiful though, she thought, trying not to stare at the other girl who now had her nose buried in the menu. A perfect little button nose.

'So, what's good here?' Adam said, after the waiter had taken their drinks order. 'Suze, you've been here before, is there anything you'd recommend?'

'Yes, I was thinking about having the lamb, have you tried that?' Leonie asked her, eager to open a safe topic of conversation.

Suzanne looked up from her menu and gave Leonie a look that would cut diamonds. 'I wouldn't know.'

'Suzanne is a vegetarian,' Adam interjected easily, completely unaware of the atmosphere. 'Has been for ages now, haven't you?'

Well, what on earth are we doing here then? Leonie

wondered, her eyes raking over the menu. It was heavy on meat dishes with few vegetarian options. And according to Adam she was a regular?

Suzanne sighed and put down her menu. 'I don't feel well,' she exclaimed theatrically and Adam turned to look at her, frowning.

'What is it? Not another headache, I hope.'

Leonie reached for her handbag. 'I have some aspirin here if you want . . .'

'I already took some,' Suzanne interjected curtly. Leonie was taken aback by her tone; Adam was looking at her with an exasperated expression, while Suzanne was sporting a pout that would make a three-year-old proud.

'Are you feeling faint, is that it?' Adam asked. 'Here, drink some water; it might help cool you down.'

'I don't want any damn water,' Suzanne snapped. 'I think I want to go home.'

'But Suze, we just got here, and Leonie really wanted to meet you.'

Huh? Leonie thought puzzled. Wasn't it supposed to be the other way round?

'But I don't *feel* well!' Suzanne whined again.

'I'm really sorry, Lee,' Adam said hesitantly, and Leonie looked at him. He wasn't giving in to this kind of behaviour, surely? 'Suzanne hasn't been very well lately so it might be best if we just head away.'

Leonie couldn't believe it. Talk about being twisted around someone's little finger! The girl looked up, an expression of intense relief on her face – or was it triumph? But in fairness to Adam, he looked mortified, so Leonie decided to make it easy for him.

'Hey, it's no problem – go and look after her,' she insisted. 'We can always do this another time.'

'Are you sure?' He looked away uncomfortably. 'I'm really very sorry about this, and I don't like abandoning you . . .'

'Honestly, go. I'm fine. I've got some work that needs doing back at the office so I might pop back there,' she said forcing a smile. 'It's no problem, honestly.'

'Well, as long as you're sure.' With that, he reached down to kiss her on the cheek, while his companion had left the table and stood idly by, fiddling with her hair. 'Again, I'm really sorry,' he whispered softly, 'she's not normally like this. I'll call you tomorrow, OK?'

'Sure,' Leonie smiled at them both, trying her best to ease Adam's embarrassment. 'Nice meeting you, Suzanne. I hope you feel better soon.'

There was a deep sigh. 'Whatever.'

And Adam's daughter fixed Leonie with a look of disdain that only a thirteen-year-old could perfect.

Having thanked Grace for the heads up on Suzanne and saying goodbye, Leonie gave a wan smile thinking about that first meeting, and how naive she'd been to expect that Adam's teenage daughter would accept the new woman in his life at the drop of a hat, especially when father and daughter had such a close relationship. She'd known from the outset that he had a daughter; he'd told her all about Suzanne in Tunisia.

After that trip to the desert, they'd been pretty much inseparable and one night over a couple of cocktails at Leonie's hotel, he'd told her the details. Unwilling to pry, she hadn't forced the subject, but Adam had no problems with putting her in the picture.

'It was a bit of a shock to the system,' he explained. 'I was only twenty when it happened, can you believe it?' he grinned. Leonie had to admit that it was indeed hard to believe as Adam looked a very youthful thirty-three.

'Suzanne's mother and I hadn't been together all that long when she became pregnant, so needless to say it was a bolt from the blue for both of us. Naturally our folks weren't too impressed – poor Andrea's parents went apoplectic – but right from the start I told them that I'd stand by her, no matter what. We were so young there was no question of marriage – not for me, anyway,' he added ominously. 'I'd just finished college and had already gone off to work in London so to say the timing was bad would be an understatement. Still, even though we didn't raise her together, we raised her well, so I'd like to think I stood by that promise.'

Even though we didn't raise her together. Leonie didn't want to admit that she had already been wondering about Adam's relationship with Suzanne's mother.

'So you and Andrea never married?'

Adam shook his head. 'Don't get me wrong, Andrea's great and I was mad about her at the time, but in reality we were only kids ourselves. So I moved back from London when Suze was born, and while we tried to give it a go for a few months afterwards, in the end we couldn't just stay together for the sake of the baby.'

'It must have been very difficult.'

He nodded. 'It was but especially so for Andrea. She took the break up pretty badly.'

'I can imagine.'

'Still, that was ages ago, and we're grand now. I've made sure she doesn't want for anything as far as Suzanne's concerned,' he continued easily but Leonie couldn't help but feel sorry for the other woman. Was it more likely that Andrea had taken the break up badly not because of money worries but because she was in love with Adam and didn't want him to leave? And he'd either failed to notice this or convinced himself otherwise. It seemed a bit too tidy and straightforward to her. Then again, she only knew half the story and Adam certainly seemed very much at ease with it.

'So, do you and Andrea get on OK now?' she probed.

Adam grimaced. 'Most of the time,' he said meaningfully. 'There's no bad blood though and she's since had another child.' He explained how Suzanne had a five-year-old half-brother called Hugo.

Again Leonie couldn't help but wonder if there was more to this than he was letting on.

'Good that you've managed to get through it, for your own sakes as well as Suzanne's,' she said.

'Well, we're getting there, I suppose. Suze was always such a sweet little thing and relatively easy to manage growing up. It's only now that she's that bit older and somewhat more . . . headstrong,' he continued with a roll of his eyes. 'Well, let's just say that these days Andrea and I have different ideas about how to handle her.'

Recalling that conversation word for word as she set out on the short walk to Flower Power, Leonie was struck by how much of an understatement that had been, and how neither she nor Adam had any idea of what was to come.

Chapter 11

Alex frowned as she studied her reflection in her bedroom mirror. She wasn't sure if the dress she was wearing – a strapless pale cream and gold evening gown – was quite right for the occasion, a fundraiser she and Jon were attending that night. The event, which was in aid of the hospital, was taking place outdoors at the very beautiful setting of the Palace of Fine Arts. Guests would be dining by candlelight at the edge of the lagoon and beneath the soaring dome of the famous neoclassical rotunda.

It was a stunning location and certain to be a very elegant affair, which was why Alex wasn't entirely confident that her choice of attire would fit the bill. Maybe a cocktail dress was more suitable for an outdoor event?

Man, she hated feeling so unsure of herself like this! Normally she was fine about this kind of stuff, but this was different, because tonight she would be meeting Jon's friends for the first time.

And these guys were no ordinary friends; they were bankers, consultants, doctors . . . in other words the kind of rich, high-society types that were all part of Jon's circle and which went hand-in-hand with his career. In her line of work Alex came across people from all walks of life and could easily hold her own, but mixing with high-fliers generally left her cold. Yet if she and Jon were to have a serious future together, which Alex really hoped they would, she guessed she'd just have to get used to it.

She smiled, thinking of her friend Jen, who the year before had moved to the East Coast to take up a job on Capitol Hill. Jen would have been able to tell Alex in an instant whether or not the dress was right. Her dark eyes narrowed. Hmm, thinking about it now, maybe another opinion was *exactly* what she needed, she decided. Quickly throwing a sweater over her bare shoulders she went outside to ring the upstairs buzzer.

'I *love* it!' Leonie gushed. They had gone back into Alex's flat so she could finish getting ready. 'The cream is gorgeous against your skin tone, and with your hair swept up like that you look so . . . I don't know . . . very Greek goddess – kind of like Angelina Jolie in that *Alexander* film.'

'Thanks – I think,' Alex self-consciously put a hand up to her recently styled French twist. She wasn't sure if the 'Greek goddess' look was a good thing, but she was pleased with Leonie's reaction nonetheless. As someone who generally preferred to live in jeans and a T-shirt, it was good to know that she looked the part, for tonight at least.

Hopefully Jon and his friends would think so too.

'It sounds like it'll be an amazing night,' Leonie said dreamily when Alex told her where the fundraiser was being held. 'What a fantastic location. The rotunda will look even more atmospheric lit up at night and . . . sorry,' she said breaking off suddenly. 'I used to work in event management back home, and old habits die hard.'

Interesting, that was the first time Leonie had voluntarily mentioned anything about her life in Ireland, Alex realised. Up to now, she'd seemed quite reticent about it.

'Sounds like a fun job,' she said, applying a coat of mascara.

'How long did you—' But the rest of her question was cut off by the loud buzz of the intercom.

'Damn,' Alex cursed, looking at her watch. 'That's got to be Jon, and I'm nowhere near ready yet.'

'Take your time; I'm sure he won't mind waiting a couple of minutes,' Leonie assured her. 'Do you want me to let him in? I can always chat to him while you finish getting ready.'

Alex looked at her gratefully. 'Do you mind? I don't want you to feel like you have to make small-talk with some guy you don't even . . .'

'Are you mad? I'm only dying to get a look at him!' Leonie grinned, before heading out to answer the door.

She really was fun to be around, Alex thought, smiling as she quickly rushed through applying the rest of her make-up. It was nice having another girl to talk to, something Alex had really missed recently. She and Jen spoke on the phone whenever they could but it just wasn't the same. Her best friend had helped her get through one of the most difficult times of her life so while Alex knew she'd miss Jen terribly when she left, she really hadn't anticipated just how much, or how adrift she'd feel without her.

It was kind of strange how life worked though, wasn't it? While two hugely important people had disappeared from her life at almost the same time, now, waiting for her in the next room, were two others who a few months ago had been complete strangers. Speaking of complete strangers, Alex thought she'd better get on out there and save poor Leonie from having to make small-talk to someone she'd never met.

Taking a final appraising glance at her reflection, she picked up a matching gold clutch and headed out front. Although, judging from the sound of laughter emanating from the living room, she needn't have worried too much about leaving her neighbour to entertain Jon.

'Hey there, sorry for keeping you waiting,' Alex said, entering the room to find Leonie and Jon, looking especially handsome in a crisp, black tuxedo, engaged in easy-going banter.

'Don't worry, my fault for being early, and Leonie here has been keeping me . . . wow!' Turning to look at her, Jon stopped in mid-sentence. 'Oh honey, you look incredible,' he continued. 'That dress really is something else.'

Leonie was nodding. 'Isn't it?'

'Glad you like it,' Alex said modestly. 'I take it you two have introduced yourselves?'

'We certainly have.' Jon smiled at Leonie, and Alex could tell by the other girl's expression that he'd already made a good impression. And all of a sudden she felt hugely gratified and incredibly lucky that she'd managed to find someone like him.

It was crazy to be so concerned about meeting his friends; hell, if they were anything like Jon, there was nothing to worry about, was there? Although it was definitely a relief to know she'd got the dress code right.

'Have a great night,' Leonie said when they were ready to leave. Outside in the hallway she gave Alex a mischievous wink. 'I can't wait to hear all about it.'

Alex smiled. 'Don't wait up,' she joked, following Jon outside and down the steps towards a waiting limousine.

What struck Alex when they arrived at the Palace of Fine Arts was how magnificent the huge rotunda and towering decorative colonnade looked mirrored in the calm black waters of the lagoon. To Alex's eye, the colonnade had always been distinctly Greek and thinking of Leonie's 'Greek goddess' comment about her dress, she grimaced, wondering if the other guests would spot it.

'Thanks for coming with me tonight, Alex,' Jon said, as they walked towards a crowd of partygoers enjoying cocktails by the lagoon, their faces lit up by the low-level candlelight. 'I know this kind of stuff isn't really your thing.' He made a face. 'To be honest, it's not mine either, but seeing as it's in aid of the hospital . . .'

'Hey, no need to apologise. I'm happy to be here.'

'Really?' he said, with a disbelieving eyebrow. 'You don't mind listening to stockbrokers and venture capitalists boasting about their golf handicaps? And hell, that's just the women,' he added wickedly.

Alex had to smile. 'Well, OK, maybe it wouldn't be my *first* choice for a fun night out . . .'

'I'll make it up to you, I swear,' he said under his breath, as one of the guests approached, closely followed by a waiter bearing a tray of champagne. Alex sipped her drink quietly as one after another a selection of expensively dressed and clearly moneyed people bore down on Jon like a flock of pigeons. Eventually, when all the back patting and hand-shaking was over, he managed to introduce her.

'Ah, so you're the famous Alex,' one of the men said.

'Famous?' she said with a light laugh. 'I don't think so.'

'Close enough,' Jon quipped. 'Alex is a producer at SFTV News,' he told them proudly.

'A producer – really?' another man replied, his eyes widening with interest. 'So I guess the economy has been keeping you guys on your toes.'

'It has, but I don't actually produce in-studio,' Alex told him, explaining how *Today by the Bay* covered lighter, more localised news pieces.

'Oh,' a woman said in that sniffy tone that was often all too familiar to Alex, 'I didn't realise it was *that* kind of news.'

'A damn sight harder than just taking the story of the day from the nationals,' Jon said, immediately rushing to her defence. 'Alex's team brings us the kind of stuff we might otherwise never see.' Although, pleased that he was standing up for her, Alex knew there was no getting away from the patronising looks the others were giving her. 'Take the report she did on this place for instance,' Jon continued, indicating the recently renovated interior of the rotunda. 'Until then, I had no idea that without maintenance these amazing buildings would subside into the bottom of the lagoon, did you?'

The others nodded politely, but she could tell that they were convinced the work she did for the station produced nothing but fluffy, idle entertainment for the masses. And she couldn't help wonder once more what the hell she was doing in the middle of all these shallow, self-obsessed assholes, most of whom she'd be quite happy to see ending up at the bottom of the lagoon!

Well, let them look down their noses at her, Alex thought, she worked hard at her job, harder than the in-studio producers sometimes, and didn't feel the need to justify herself. But if they weren't careful, maybe in the future she'd think about doing an exposé on the inner workings of the stock market or Silicon Valley, or whatever unscrupulous means these guys used for making money!

Things improved a little when dinner was served, and Alex was pleased to find she was seated alongside a warm elderly woman from Berkeley who confessed she and her husband didn't normally attend such events, but had been given the ticket for free.

'Memorial were brilliant to Abe when he was there last year, so I couldn't waste it,' she told Alex. 'Although I feel a bit of a fish out of water here, I can tell you.'

'You and me both,' she agreed conspiratorially and the two women spent much of the evening chatting and enjoying one another's company, while Alex was happy to let Jon mingle with the hospital's more influential patrons.

Sometime after midnight, much to Alex's relief, they made their excuses and left.

'I guess I'm not much of a society girlfriend,' she apologised quietly in the car, as they made their way towards Nob Hill.

Jon frowned. 'What are you talking about? Everyone *loved* you.'

'Thanks, but you really don't need to make me feel better. I did try for a while, but I got the feeling they'd much rather talk to you.'

He took her hand. 'Alex, do you think I give a damn about what these people think of either of us? Tonight was work for me – and for you too by the sound of things,' he added wryly. 'I'm sorry that I wasn't more attentive.'

'Don't be silly, tonight was important and I was fine.' Man, he was great! To think that she'd spent practically the entire evening sitting in a corner chatting to a 'regular' person – someone who would have no influence whatsoever on the future of the hospital – and here he was apologising to *her*! 'I enjoyed it,' she assured him, feeling like a heel for not making more of an effort. 'It's not often I get to be wined and dined like that.'

Jon shook his head. 'Well, it's not all its cracked up to be. Believe me, if I had my way, we'd have been home tucked up in bed hours ago. And speaking of which,' he added, nuzzling her neck suggestively, 'I hope you're staying over?'

Alex smiled. She had been convinced that tonight would be the night Jon would come to realise that they were two completely different people, that she wouldn't fit in with his friends, and ultimately was all wrong for him. But he seemed totally cool about her lack of effort at the fundraiser, and equally cool about his friends' lukewarm response to her.

He really was a guy in a million, and the more she knew

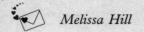

of him, the more convinced she felt that this relationship really looked like it was going somewhere. Alex bit her lip.

All the more reason to get her situation sorted once and for all.

Chapter 12

The following morning, Leonie finally plucked up the courage to call Jones Cantor, the stockbroker firm where (hopefully) Nathan worked.

She'd been putting it off until she'd worked out exactly what she was going to say, and how she was going to explain how she – a complete stranger – had somehow managed to get caught up in his domestic problems.

'Well, if it is your guy, just tell him the truth,' Marcy shrugged as if it was all very straightforward. '*You're* the one going out of your way here, remember.'

'I suppose. Do you mind if I do it here?'

'Sure, knock yourself out. Go out back if you like, and I'll hold the fort here.'

'Thanks.' Leonie took the cordless phone into the store's small back office and dialled the number.

'Hi, I was wondering if I could speak to Nathan Abbott,' she asked when the call was answered.

The receptionist was polite but friendly. 'Ma'am, I'm afraid Mr Abbott no longer works here.'

'Oh,' Leonie said, her heart sinking. 'Well, do you have any idea where I might be able to reach him? A phone number or anything.'

'I'm afraid not.'

'Well, did he move to another company?'

'I'm sorry but I'm afraid I can't help you. Mr Abbott no longer works here,' she repeated, but there was a firmness about the woman's tone that made Leonie feel like she was missing something.

'I see. It's just . . . well, I have some important correspondence I need to get to him and I'd really like to know where I could send it.'

'We did try to notify all existing clients . . .'

'No, it's nothing like that. I wasn't a client, I mean, I didn't even know . . .' For some reason Leonie couldn't stop babbling. 'Can I just ask . . . I know this is a strange question, but how old is Mr Abbott?'

'How old?'

'Yes, it's just that I'm not quite sure if he is the man I'm looking for.' God, the woman must think she was a right idiot gabbing on like this! 'Was he in his twenties, thirties or perhaps fifties?'

Now the receptionist sounded a little impatient. 'I'm sorry, ma'am, once again I'm afraid I can't help you. We don't give out personal information about our employees, current or otherwise.'

'OK, well can you just tell me when he left the company then?' she asked quickly.

The woman sighed. 'Nathan Abbott was no longer an employee of Jones Cantor as of January first this year.'

'Thank you, I appreciate that,' she said.

'My pleasure,' the receptionist replied.

Leonie hung up the phone, trying to get a handle on her thoughts. That woman had seemed oddly tight-lipped about it all, hadn't she? Which made her wonder if Nathan might have been sacked or made to leave in disgrace. Who knew with these stockbroker types? With all the scandals going on these days anything could have happened. Although Leonie couldn't imagine someone who sounded as sweet and nice as Nathan being involved in anything untoward. Maybe he was the fall guy or something? She'd ask Alex if she knew anything and . . . oh hell, Leonie scolded herself, the man probably just changed jobs, and that was all there was to it!

'You have the most overactive imagination of anyone I know,' Adam used to tease her. A bit of a joker himself, he'd always got great mileage out of Leonie's tendency to over-analyse.

Although, there were a few times she hadn't minded all that much, Leonie thought sadly, her thoughts drifting back to one particular joke Adam had played on her a couple of years before.

Dublin: Two years earlier

It was a year to the day since she and Adam first met and Leonie was looking forward to celebrating. The year had gone by in a whirl, the relationship was going great, and a couple of months before, much to Leonie's delight, Adam had asked her to move in with him.

She could still hardly believe her luck. This time last year she'd been single and holidaying on her own in Tunisia, and now here she was shacked up with an amazing guy who made her insanely happy and who probably knew her better than she knew herself.

The only fly in the ointment was the difficulties Leonie was still having in getting to know Suzanne. It was tricky but she was sure the teenager just needed more time to get used to the fact that her beloved father had someone else in his life. With any luck, she'd come round eventually but in the meantime, for Adam's sake, all Leonie could do was keep trying.

He doted on his daughter and the more Leonie learned about the situation the more impressed she was with how he handled everything. Although she hadn't yet met Suzanne's mother, she'd gathered from a number of frantic phone calls to Adam's mobile that Andrea could be a bit of a handful. Moreover, she got the sense that Andrea was not at all impressed by the fact that Adam had a serious girlfriend, which made Leonie all the more convinced that the woman still held a candle for him.

While initially, this had made her feel a little bit sorry for Andrea, the demands she continually made on Adam gradually changed Leonie's mind. In addition to maintenance, he paid for pretty much every other expense Suzanne incurred, like hobbies, holidays and pocket money. He was incredibly dedicated to his daughter and always so generous and willing to keep his relationship with Andrea on an even keel that Leonie really had to admire him.

Tonight, for their anniversary, he'd booked a table at a Lebanese restaurant in town. 'It's the closest I could get to Tunisian food,' he'd told her and Leonie couldn't wait. As they were living together now it wasn't as though they needed time alone together, but it would be lovely to celebrate the occasion in some small way.

Halfway through the day she got a call from Adam at work.

'Lee, something's come up here which means I'll be back later than usual this evening, so probably best for me to go straight to the restaurant and meet you there. Is that OK?'

'Of course. How late do you think you'll be?'

'Not too late, but not early enough to get home and change either. And speaking of which, do you think you could bring a change of clothes for me to the restaurant? My Ben Sherman shirt – the khaki one, not the blue one – and maybe those new Levi's you bought me for my birthday.'

'Sure. Anything else?'

'Nope, that'll do fine. Just make sure it's not the blue shirt, OK? I don't want that one. Sorry about this, Lee, but there's nothing I can do.'

He sounded flustered. 'Look, it's really no problem,' Leonie reassured him, 'and no need to rush. Just be careful driving, won't you?'

'I will. See you there sometime after seven then?'

'Perfect.'

Later that evening, before leaving for the restaurant, Leonie went to the wardrobe to get a change of clothes for Adam.

She flicked through his shirts, trying to locate the khaki one and finding it easily she plucked it off the rail. Then she paused, recalling how adamant he'd been on the phone that it should be this one and not the blue one. What was wrong with the blue one? Was it that it needed a wash or . . .

It really wasn't like Adam to be that bothered about what he was going to wear. Flicking again through the hangers, Leonie spotted the offending blue shirt and lifted it out for a better look.

And as she did, she noticed a bulge in the front right pocket, a bulge that on closer inspection looked suspiciously like . . .

No! Leonie quickly put both shirts back on the rail as she tried to take this in. There was a little box in the pocket, a red, velvet covered box, which could only be . . .

No, no, this wasn't what she thought it was, Leonie told herself, but still she couldn't help taking out the blue shirt again for a closer look. Then, before she knew it, her hand was inside the pocket, and the ring box in the palm of her hand.

Wow.

Was Adam going to . . . was he planning to . . . surely he couldn't *seriously* have been planning to propose to her tonight? He must be though – why else had he sounded so flustered on the phone and so adamant about the shirt she should (or more to the point *shouldn't*) bring?

Leonie gulped and her heart thudded a mile a minute. She almost wished she hadn't spotted the box now. Clearly his plans had changed, so what should she do – just play dumb and wait until he got another opportunity? But Leonie knew she wouldn't be able to do that; the suspense would kill her and who knew when Adam would eventually decide to do it?

She stared at the closed box, wondering what the ring was like. God, this was so weird, to think that this time last year, she'd been in almost the exact same situation, except this time the ring in the box could very possibly be hers . . .

Damn it, she had to sneak a peak; knowing Adam it was bound to be gorgeous but if it wasn't then at least she'd know, and would be well prepared if he presented her with something horrible . . .

Trying her best to stop her hand from shaking, Leonie opened the little box, and was dismayed to find not the stunning diamond ring she'd anticipated but a tiny piece of folded up paper. What the . . . ?

'Gotcha!' was the one-word message inside, and Leonie turned the note over, her mind doing cartwheels as she frantically tried to work out what was going on.

'I'd have thought you'd have learned your lesson by now,' Adam said from where he stood in the doorway, a broad grin on his face. Leonie nearly jumped out of her skin.

'How long have you been there . . . I didn't hear you come in. Adam, what's going on?' she said perplexed.

'Didn't I tell you to go for the khaki shirt?' he replied, his eyes twinkling as he moved across the room towards her. 'But of course, you couldn't resist checking out the blue one that I specifically said not to, could you?'

'I . . .' Leonie was lost for words.

'Lucky for me that I know you so well, isn't it?'

By his mischievous tone (and the fact that he obviously hadn't been working late at all), Leonie now understood that Adam had planned this whole ruse as some kind of jokey re-enactment of their meeting last year.

And she'd played right into his hands.

'I can't believe you did all this just to trick me!' she gasped, feeling unbelievably stupid.

'Not just to trick you,' Adam said, his voice becoming more serious. He nodded again towards the khaki shirt. 'So are you going to check out that one too, or do I need to do everything myself?'

Leonie could only watch in amazement as he reached inside the pocket of the other shirt and produced another box, one that she in her curiosity about the blue one had completely failed to notice.

'Leonie Hayes,' Adam said, opening the box before getting down on one knee, 'will you and that inquisitive mind and overactive imagination of your marry me?'

The following Friday after work, Alex called upstairs to Leonie's place, her laptop under her arm. She was going to be tickled pink by this! she thought knocking on her door.

Truthfully, Alex was still a bit bemused at how much time the two of them were spending together lately, she'd never been big on the whole neighbourly relations thing. However, Leonie was good fun to be around, and had this sweet guileless way about her that made Alex almost protective of her.

Jon had confessed he liked her too, and from the way Leonie had gushed about him after the other night, she knew the feeling was mutual.

But all that aside, Alex was loving trying to unravel this thing with the letters! To her, such a mystery was an itch that needed to be scratched, and following Leonie's recent report that the stockbroker firm had turned out to be a dead end, she'd spent a couple more hours at work searching online for any other information on the couple. OK, so they might have hit a blind alley with Nathan, but with regard to his wife . . . well they just might be getting somewhere . . .

'Hi,' Leonie said, somewhat surprised to see her. 'What's up?'

'I think I found something,' Alex said, waving the sheet of paper she held in her other hand and when Leonie looked confused she went on, 'something else that might help us find our couple. Sorry, is this is a bad time?' she asked, realising that her neighbour looked a bit frazzled.

'No, no, I was just about to start dinner,' Leonie replied. 'Would you like me to make you some too?'

'Well if you're sure, sounds great, I'd love that.' Alex wasn't a great cook; in fact, sometimes she got so caught up in researching a story that she forgot to eat. So yep, having Leonie around was definitely good for her!

'Don't get too excited, it's nothing fancy – just some tomato pasta and a salad.'

'Well, count me in!'

Leonie returned to the kitchen to boil up some pasta before rejoining Alex in the living room. 'So, tell me what's going on?' she asked then. 'You said you found something on the Abbotts?'

Alex handed her the sheet of paper. 'A photographer's studio in Monterey.'

'OK.' Leonie seemed dubious. 'How exactly does that help us?'

'Well.' Alex set her laptop down on the coffee table and powered it up. 'When you got nowhere with finding Nathan, I did another couple of searches associating Helena's name with photography. And look at this, some of the photographs on this particular studio's website are credited to none other than . . . Helena Abbott!' she finished with no little trace of pride.

'Really?'

'Yep. I remember you mentioning something about her photographing the bridge. So instead of just restricting the search with her name and the photography references to the city, I widened it to the entire state. This popped up.'

Leonie sat down alongside her in front of the laptop as the studio's website filled the screen. 'Wow, you really *are* good at this. Do you actually think it could be her?'

'Only one way to find out. Says here they're open till nine, so do you want to phone them, or will I?'

'You!' Leonie said quickly. 'You'd be much better at that kind of thing than me. I told you what I was like with your woman from the stockbrokers. It was like getting blood out of a stone.'

'No problem,' Alex said easily. 'Can I use this phone?'

'Of course, go ahead. But what are you going to say?'

She shrugged. 'I guess I'll just ask to speak to Helena and take it from there.' Picking up the receiver, she dialled the number listed on the website. The phone was answered after three rings.

'Cannery Row Photography, Mark speaking, how can I help you?'

'Hey there, Mark,' Alex greeted, while Leonie watched her, an eager expression on her face. 'Could I speak to Helena Abbott please?'

'I'm afraid Helena's on vacation at the moment,' Mark replied. Alex grimaced and made a thumbs-down sign to Leonie.

'She's on vacation? Oh, well perhaps you can help me in any case,' she continued, thinking on her feet. 'I'm calling from San Francisco, and I'm wondering if Helena happened to work in the Bay Area at any time? The reason I ask is that I've got some really great shots of the Golden Gate Bridge credited to a Helena Abbott, and I'm hoping it's the same person.'

Mark hesitated. 'I'm not sure, she may well have worked in San Francisco one time, but I can't be certain. I've only been with the studio a couple of months.'

'But your photographers do that kind of work, right?'

'Well, we mostly specialise in portrait and event photography. And wildlife too of course.'

'Of course,' Alex agreed, thinking this made perfect sense for Monterey. 'OK, Mark, thank you very much for your time. Maybe I'll call back when Helena returns from vacation and talk to her then. When will that be?' she added casually.

'Let me check.' There was some shuffling for a moment before Mark spoke again. 'She's back one week from Saturday.'

'Great. Will I be able to catch her at this number then, or does she have a cell I could try?' Alex asked, and Leonie grinned approvingly.

'Well, according to the schedule she's got some portraits slotted in for Saturday afternoon, so assuming there are no changes, she should be at the studio then.'

'Thank you again, Mark, you've been very helpful.'

'You're very welcome. Have a great evening.'

'You too.' Alex hung up the phone and smiled triumphantly at Leonie.

'Well?' her friend demanded, obviously dying to know the other side of the conversation.

Alex filled her in.

'Isn't it just typical that she's away on holiday?' Leonie said, frowning. 'So we still can't tell if it's her.'

'Yeah, but if it is, great that she's not so far away either.'

'Really? I'm not sure where Monterey is . . .'

'It's only a couple of hours' drive south from here. Beautiful place, the most gorgeous bay with all this amazing wildlife, you'd love it. I haven't been there for years, which is a shame as it's really great, and . . . hey,' she said, her brain moving into gear. 'Why don't we drive down there? I know you'd love it and while we're there we could always think about paying Ms Abbott a casual visit . . .'

'You mean calling in to see her face to face?' By Leonie's expression, Alex could tell that the prospect worried her. Small wonder, seeing as she'd opened the woman's mail! 'Oh God, no, I couldn't do that. Couldn't we just post the letters on to her?'

'We could, but I guess we'd need to make sure it *is* her first. Anyway, if it is, we can always just play dumb and tell her those first two letters were already opened and . . . what?' she asked then, seeing Leonie redden furiously. 'Oh, you're kidding me, right?' she asked, immediately realising why her friend had seemed so flustered earlier. 'You opened another one?'

'Oh, I know I shouldn't but I just couldn't help it,' Leonie admitted guiltily. 'I just thought there might be something else . . . something that might—'

'It's somebody else's mail, remember.'

'I know.' Leonie bit her lip. 'And I really didn't mean to, but when I couldn't find Nathan at the stockbrokers I just thought there might be something else. I can't really explain it, I just felt like I had to read more.'

'This has really gotten under your skin, hasn't it?' Alex said, faintly amused, but more curious as to why her new friend was being so dogged about finding this couple. 'So what did this one say?'

'Not a whole lot. Just some more about how sorry he is, and how much he misses her. He just sounds so apologetic, Alex, and the way he talks about her . . . it's obvious that he still really loves her.'

OK, so there was clearly a lot more going on with this girl than she was letting on, Alex pondered, it seemed that she hadn't moved here just for the weather.

'Well then, we'll do what we can to find them, but let's just work with what we've got for the moment, OK? This woman down in Monterey could very well be the person we're looking for, and I don't know about you, but I certainly don't want to have to explain why we're passing on a box of opened mail.'

'I won't read any more, I promise.'

'So what do you think about taking a trip down there? We could take the coast road, and I could show you some of the real California.'

'It does sound lovely.'

Alex could tell that despite her misgivings about meeting Helena, Leonie was sorely tempted by the prospect.

'I'm seeing Jon again this weekend, so probably best to wait for when Ms Abbott's back from vacation. It could very well just be another dead end, but if it is, so what? It'd still be fun, wouldn't it?'

Leonie nodded enthusiastically. 'OK then, you're on,' she said with a grin.

Chapter 13

My love,

You must be getting tired of these letters by now, but I guess I just can't help myself. Things can get kind of lonely around here, and it's good to have somebody to . . . well, not to talk to exactly, but someone who is better able to understand. The other guys are nice enough and I've made one or two friends, but in reality, I guess all we have in common is that we're in this together. And, somehow that makes us friends. It doesn't stop me missing you though, and wishing that I'd made a different choice. I know I should have listened to you, should have understood what you were trying to tell me. But I know there's no point in saying that now . . .

Nathan opened his eyes and stared at the ceiling. Today was his birthday, he realised suddenly.

Not that it mattered. He wouldn't be celebrating it; hadn't celebrated it in years. What was there to celebrate? Birthday or not, there hadn't been a whole lot to get excited about in a very long time, and it was difficult to differentiate this birthday from any other.

He smiled. Even more difficult to differentiate one day from the next.

He wondered if anyone would notice the date and realise

its significance. Unlikely. Most people had long since forgotten about him; that was for sure.

Helena would have remembered of course. Nathan smiled. She used to make such a fuss over him, especially on days like today.

Well, they always made a fuss of each other on special occasions. Crazy old romantics, the two of them. At least they were back in the good old days, each going to so much trouble to make things special on big occasions like birthdays or Christmas or any occasion at all.

Nathan's mouth tightened as these happy memories wormed their way back into his consciousness. He shouldn't allow himself to think about these things. No good ever came of it, he should know that by now. But yet he couldn't help it. That last birthday they'd spent together had definitely been the best, the one just before everything went crazy. Nathan shook his head wistfully.

He wondered if she'd got the note he'd sent her recently, and if so, what she'd thought about it. He wasn't sure why he'd done that really, it wasn't as if—

'Breakfast, rise and shine!' A voice calling out in the distance brought him back to the here and now.

Hearing stirring noises nearby he realised that the others were already up and raring to go so he'd better get a move on too. He stretched languidly before getting up, Helena still on his mind.

And although he thought about her all the time these days, Nathan knew that – birthday or no birthday – it was pointless reminiscing about his beloved Helena and the life they'd had, a life they'd hoped would always include the other.

How stupid they'd been.

Leonie was so excited she could hardly contain herself. Since

Alex's call to Cannery Row Photographers over a week ago she had barely been able to keep her mind on her work at Flower Power, and had been counting down the days until the trip to Monterey – and meeting, perhaps, Helena Abbott. It was now Saturday morning and she and Alex were inside the house's dusty garage readying the car for their trip down the coast.

Monterey was a couple of hours' drive from San Francisco, so to make the most of their time there they'd decided to stay overnight and travel back to the city the following afternoon.

'So, what do you think?' Alex asked, caressing the car's hood. Leonie wasn't really into cars but she couldn't help but be impressed by this one, a sleek black vehicle that looked to be some kind of American sports car.

'It's very cool,' she replied. 'What kind of car is it?'

'What kind of car?' Alex looked insulted. 'This, my friend, is a '78 King Cobra Mustang.'

'O-K.' Predictably this went right over Leonie's head. Strange, she hadn't pegged Alex as the petrol-head type.

'Beautiful, isn't she?' her friend said, running her hand admiringly along the doorframe. 'You wouldn't *believe* how long it took us to find her – or get her back to her former glory.'

'Us?' Leonie queried but Alex had already sat inside and was revving the engine. Well, Leonie thought, getting in beside her, however long the car took to restore, she hoped to God it was up to scratch, because it had just hit her that in order to get out of San Francisco, they would have to negotiate its scarily vertiginous hills.

'Um, when was the last time you took this out?' she asked Alex nervously, as the car rattled along Green Street.

'Relax, just give her a chance to warm up,' her friend admonished, as she crossed Union Street before taking a very tight left on to Van Ness Avenue. There, and much to Leonie's horror, they were immediately faced with one of those impossibly steep and absolutely terrifying downward slopes.

Leonie gulped as they made their way down, and her knuckles whitened as gravity took over and the car began to zoom wildly down the seemingly unending hill. The height and distance from the bottom made it feel very much like riding a roller coaster, except for the fact that there was a series of four-way intersections all the way down. And as they approached the first one, she prayed with all her heart that the Mustang's brakes were sound, otherwise . . .

'Arggh!' she cried, covering her eyes when it looked like the car was about to career straight through the crossing without stopping.

But at the very last millisecond, Alex jammed on the brakes. 'Don't you trust me?' she teased wickedly as they waited their turn at the bottom of the hill. Then briefly checking that the way was clear she whizzed down the next slope in similar hair-raising style. Clearly, she was a fan of Steve McQueen.

'Oh . . . my . . . God.' By now, Leonie was almost expecting her life to start flashing in front of her eyes. Why in the name of all things holy had she agreed to get in a car with the likes of Alex, who clearly had some kind of death wish?

But a couple of blocks later, the Mustang veered right and the torment was finally over. And when Leonie's heart rate had returned to a relatively normal pace, she turned to look at Alex. 'Please tell me that we won't be driving on any more hills on the way,' she begged. 'I don't think my heart can take it.'

Alex was still grinning. 'What, you didn't like that? Come on, it was great! I'd forgotten how much fun it was actually, but going *up* is even better, so maybe on the way back we'll—'

'OK, I definitely think I want to get out now!' Leonie exclaimed, only half-joking. 'Or else you'll have to drop me off at the hospital to be defibrillated.'

'Don't worry, it's all plain sailing from here,' Alex reassured her as they left the city behind and headed south on to Route One, the fabled coastal highway that led along the cliffs to Monterey Bay.

Alex was right: the views were amazing, and although visibility out to sea was partly obscured by the intermittent fog rolling ethereally along the shoulders of the cliffs, it simply made the scenery all the more spectacular.

After a half hour or so into the journey, Alex switched on the radio and immediately began singing along to an old Johnny Cash number, while Leonie sat back in silence and thought again about how much her life had changed – and in such a short space of time. She couldn't help but wonder what Adam was doing at that moment and what he'd think if he could see her now, zooming along the highway in an old Mustang with a girl she'd only just met. The two of them had clicked right from the beginning but already it felt like they were on the way to being very good friends. She bit her lip, wondering what Alex would think about what had happened back in Ireland. And although she was sure she would confide in her sometime in the future, there was no way she was ready to talk about it just yet.

In truth, she was still flabbergasted at Grace's news that Suzanne had moved in with him. What did that mean? And perhaps even more importantly, where did Andrea come into it? Well, it didn't matter now, Leonie thought, stopping herself from thinking about it any further. All that was no longer any of her business, was it?

Over an hour into their drive along the coast, the Mustang passed through a stunning area of marshland and hills. Then, later, ahead in the distance, Leonie spotted a spectacularly beautiful circular bay nestled in the crook of an enormous peninsula. The reflection of the clear midday sun glittered on the water, while sailboats dotted the length of the coast. 'Monterey Bay,' Alex told her. 'It's stunning, isn't it?'

'Amazing.' Leonie was mesmerised.

'You know, I'd almost forgotten how beautiful it is,' her friend continued, 'I haven't been down here for a long time.'

As they headed further along the gentle curve of the coastline and rounded the bay, Leonie began to make out countless seabirds offshore, some diving down into the surf to catch their prey, others drifting majestically in the breeze.

'So, what are we going to do when we call into the studio?' she asked Alex when they took the exit off the highway into the town. 'I mean, what will happen if we do find Helena?'

There was a side of Leonie that desperately hoped the woman at the studio was the Helena they were looking for, yet another side of her hoped it wasn't, as then she wouldn't have to explain the open letters. Who knew how the woman would react to that? With all the talk about felonies, what if she called the cops?

But Alex seemed very easy-going about the whole thing. 'I guess first we'll just have to see if it *is* her, then we can think about what happens after that.'

Leonie definitely didn't like the idea of just rolling up to the studio with no real plan in mind, but as Alex seemed to think it was the most effective way of doing things, she couldn't really argue. It had been a lovely idea, and very generous of Alex to drive down here and show her around, and while Leonie was looking forward to seeing more of this beautiful place, the prospect of having to explain herself to Helena was nerve-racking.

They parked the car in a public car park in town and

decided to break for lunch in a shrimp place nearby before heading to the studio.

Monterey's Fisherman's Wharf was full of seafood shacks and markets and looked to Leonie to be a sort of miniature version of the one in San Francisco.

Having shared a basket of delicious fresh shrimp served with lime juice and followed by a leisurely coffee, they got back in the car and headed for the photography studio, which was right in the heart of Cannery Row.

The now-defunct sardine canning street in Monterey had become a tourist destination, and as she and Alex made their way along the narrow streets, Leonie couldn't help but admire the old historic canning factories, charming Victorian-type inns, and pretty shop fronts everywhere. As they walked, she kept stopping to gaze into the windows of the little cafés, chocolate shops and art galleries that were dotted along the street.

Eventually they came to a stop in front of Cannery Row Photography.

'Oh God,' Leonie grimaced nervously once again. 'I'm really not sure if this is a good idea at all. I mean, what are we going to do, and how are we going to know if it's the real Helena. I just don't think I can . . .'

'Relax, you don't have to do anything,' Alex reassured her. 'You wait here and I'll go in and ask a couple of questions, and then come back out and let you know what I think. Then, once we're sure it's her, we can decide where to go from there, OK?'

'Right, sounds good.' Leonie's stomach lurched. 'You'll know if it's her straightaway, though, won't you? Seeing as you were neighbours and everything.'

Alex sighed. 'I wouldn't count on it. I never really met her properly, and it was some time ago. Who knows, maybe the face will ring a bell?' she said before going into the studio.

After a few minutes waiting outside, Leonie decided to find a shadier spot. The streets were busy and the afternoon sun hot and punishing, and she could do with some cooling down. She headed a little way down the street, the light sea breeze giving her instant relief. She couldn't help but be drawn towards the waterfront, where the water sparkled prettily in the sun. Much to her delight, Leonie spotted what looked like a couple of seals basking lazily in the water. The sight of them lying on their backs, lolling in the sunshine was wonderful to behold. Adam would have loved this; she mused, the thoughts of her ex drifting into her consciousness yet again.

'Cute little guys, aren't they?'

A male voice lifted her out of her skin and Leonie quickly discovered that she wasn't alone. A little further along, someone else was watching the seals. A surfer, perhaps? He was barefoot and wearing a wetsuit, and with his hair slicked back from a sun-kissed and rather weather-beaten face, he looked as though he himself had just stepped out of the ocean.

'They're amazing,' she replied, shaking her head in wonderment. The sea creatures had now disappeared from view back beneath the water, but she was still keeping her eyes peeled in the hope of a repeat performance.

'You think that's something, you should see what's going on underwater,' he said in the manner of someone who knew exactly what he was talking about, and Leonie realised that she'd been wrong in thinking he was a surfer. A scuba diver more like.

'I can imagine,' she said, wishing she could have the opportunity to dive here. She and Alex wouldn't have time on this visit.

'Have you been to the aquarium?' he asked in a slightly accented drawl that Leonie couldn't place.

'Nope, I'm just on a flying visit, I'm afraid,' she told him, explaining how she and Alex had just got here.

'And how long are you guys staying?'

'Just the one night, although we haven't found anywhere to stay yet,' she added, just for something to say.

'Well, ain't that a shame,' he replied, and Leonie couldn't be sure, but she thought she heard a hint of mischievousness in his tone. Was this guy *flirting* with her?

Suddenly non-plussed, she reddened, unsure how to react. He was tall, very tanned and possibly blond although it was difficult to tell when his hair was so wet. There was no denying he was *extremely* attractive, she noted, blushing even more.

'I can recommend a couple of places if you like,' he said.

'Um, thanks but I'd better go back and find my friend,' she muttered uneasily, moving away. 'Oh . . . there she is now.' To her immense relief, she spotted Alex heading towards them, looking distracted. 'Alex, over here!' she called out, and as her friend approached, she noticed the guy stop suddenly in his tracks.

As did Alex.

'Well, how did it go? Was she there or . . .' The rest of Leonie's sentence trailed off, as she realised that her friend was staring hard at the wetsuit guy, an unfathomable expression on her face.

'Seth,' she said, her tone measured.

'Hey, Alex,' the guy said quietly. 'It's been a while.'

Chapter 14

OK, get a grip, Alex told herself. So Seth – of all people – had just materialised out of the blue.

'How are you doing, Alex?' he drawled easily, as if it was only yesterday since they'd last seen one another. And, judging by poor Leonie's flushed cheeks, clearly he hadn't changed a bit!

'I'm doing just fine,' she replied in a breezy tone, determined to match his relaxed attitude.

Leonie looked from Alex to Seth, as comprehension dawned. 'Oh, you two know each other.'

'Yep,' Seth replied, while Alex tried to figure the quickest way out of this.

'So, how was Florida?' she found herself asking. 'I heard you were down that way recently.'

But according to her lawyer, not for some time.

'OK.' He shrugged his bare shoulders in that careless offhand way that had always driven her nuts. But damn it, he looked good and she couldn't blame Leonie for getting flustered.

All that time spent out on the ocean leading diving expeditions had lightened his hair and darkened his complexion, while the wetsuit defined his lean and rangy frame. 'I missed the West Coast though,' he added, eyeing her directly.

'Yeah, well I'm sure you made the most of your time down there – you always do,' she added, unable to resist the barb. 'So how long have you been back?'

'Just a couple of weeks. There's a guy with a dive-shop here I promised I'd help out for a little while.' Now he looked a bit shame-faced. 'I was going to call—'

'Sure you were,' Alex smiled tightly, unwilling to even entertain the idea. 'Anyway, we'd better get going,' she said, turning to Leonie.

'Wait – I hear you guys are looking for somewhere to stay?'

'We're just fine, thanks,' Alex interjected, but maddeningly still found herself unable to take her eyes off him.

He held his hands out wide in supplication. 'Hey, you know I'd be only too happy to help you ladies in any way I can.'

'I'm sure you would,' she replied sardonically, with a pointed glance at Leonie, 'but we're doing just fine as we are.'

'But I know this place like the back of my hand . . .'

'It's fine, Seth, honestly,' Alex said her tone firm, and Leonie gave her a questioning look. 'As I said, we'd better go.'

'Come on, Alex, don't be mad at me,' Seth pleaded. 'I was going to call, I swear I was. It's just, I kind of got side-tracked and—'

Alex whirled around. 'Side-tracked – for a whole year?' she retorted, and immediately wished she hadn't. 'Not that I give a damn,' she added quickly, 'but the very least you could have done was told me where you were.'

So I could have got you out of my hair once and for all, she added silently.

'Yeah, well, maybe I didn't want to,' he shot back, not in the least bit apologetic now. 'Maybe I wanted—'

'You just wanted to suit yourself, and to hell with everyone else, right?' Alex argued, shaking her head in disgust. 'Wow, you really haven't changed a bit, have you? I guess I thought you might have grown up by now.'

'You thought *I'd* have grown up?' he snapped, eyes flashing.

'Um, I think I might go and do a bit of shopping . . .' Leonie began meekly.

'It's OK, Leonie, you don't need to go anywhere,' Alex replied. 'We're done here.' With a final stony glare at Seth, she went to walk away again.

'OK, you're right, you're right, it was wrong of me,' he conceded, his voice somewhat gentler this time. 'I should have told you where I was.'

'Damn right you should,' she reproved, refusing to grant even an inch in return. But that had been part of the problem, hadn't it?

'Actually, yes, I think I will go shopping!' Leonie interjected brightly. 'There's a lovely little toffee-apple shop back there I liked the look of, so how about I meet you back here in say . . . half an hour?' she said, quickly heading off before Alex even had a chance to reply.

Now the two of them faced each other again, and this time neither seemed to know what to say.

Eventually Seth spoke up. 'So, how have you been?' he asked his tone softer this time.

'Fine, no thanks to you.'

'I know, and I'm sorry things got left that way, but everything was so crazy and I couldn't think of any other way to—'

'To hurt me? I thought you'd already done that,' she said, folding her arms across her chest.

'Don't be like that, Alex.'

'How the hell do you expect me to be, Seth? You just walk away like nothing happened . . .' She shook her head, annoyed with herself that even after all this time he still managed to get under her skin. It was the sheepish, hangdog face that did it, that and those slate grey eyes and lopsided smile . . . not to mention the fact that his sheer proximity seemed to send every nerve ending in her body on full alert.

'I guess I hoped we'd have put all that behind us by now,' he said gently. When she said nothing, he continued. 'Anyway, I'm here now and . . .' He moved to approach her and Alex quickly stepped back.

'You've got no right, Seth,' she reproached him, snapping back out of her reverie. 'Not after what you've put me through.'

'Hey, why does it always have to be my fault?' he said, getting angry again. 'You were the one who decided to—'

'Well, what did you think I was going to do?' Alex answered hotly. 'Just stand by and do nothing? What kind of an idiot do you think I am?'

Seth took a deep breath and sighed. 'Look, there's no sense in going over all this again, is there? Can't we talk about it some other time?'

Alex didn't particularly want to get into it now either; there was hardly any point and besides it was ancient history. 'You're right, this really isn't the time or the place,' she agreed. 'Believe me, the last thing I expected was to bump into you today.'

'What are you doing down here anyway? That girl, she said you guys were here on a flying visit?'

'It's a long story.' Alex sighed, feeling jaded all of a sudden.

Strangely, Seth seemed to sense this. 'Look, she probably won't be back for a while, so why don't we go and catch a beer somewhere while we're waiting. We can keep an eye out for her.'

Alex didn't really trust herself to be anywhere near him, and it was hard enough coming face to face with him today, let alone sitting down and sharing a drink. Yet somehow, she found herself agreeing. 'Fine, but don't think you're off the hook that easily,' she warned him, in a weak attempt at keeping her composure.

But as was always the case with Seth, this was damn nigh impossible.

He led her along the street to a bar with outdoor seating, and they sat facing each other on opposite sides of the table, neither of them making eye contact while they waited for Leonie's return. The afternoon was sweltering and due to this, and also in no small way the shock of bumping into him, Alex drank the majority of her Corona down in one long gulp.

Seth raised an amused eyebrow. 'That's my girl. Good to see you haven't lost it,' he grinned, his eyes crinkling up in that familiar mischievous way.

'Don't push your luck, Seth,' she warned, fiddling with the neck of the bottle. It had been a long time since she'd heard him call her that, and damn it, the casually intimate way he'd said it still got to her. Avoiding his gaze, she fished out the lime quarter and began to chew on it, while staring unseeingly out across the bay.

'You still do that too, huh? Guess you haven't changed at all.'

Alex gave a short laugh. 'Don't be fooled. I've changed a hell of a lot, unlike some people.'

He set down his drink. 'Meaning?'

'*Meaning* I saw you with Leonie earlier. You were hitting on her before I came along, weren't you?' She looked up, and saw that he was trying his utmost to maintain a solemn expression.

'Hey now, I don't know what you're talking about.'

'You might as well admit it. It's not as though I give a damn either way.'

'I was only being friendly . . .' Seth insisted, but failed to contain the impish smile working its way along his lips.

Alex shook her head, recognising that look all too well. 'You really just can't help yourself, can you?'

'Well, maybe I was – just a little bit,' he admitted, a twinkle in his eye. 'She is kind of cute, but not really my type.'

'Not your type . . .' Alex rolled her eyes in disbelief and no small measure of amusement. 'I didn't think there was such a thing.'

'Of course there is,' he declared. 'Why – are you jealous?'

'Give me a break.' She'd very nearly forgotten how damned infuriating he could be; almost like a five-year-old kid trying to get out of trouble, she mused, taking a sip of what was left of her beer. 'You are really incredible sometimes, you know that?'

There was another flash of those blindingly white teeth. 'Why, thank you, darlin',' he said, exaggerating his Texan drawl, before nodding at her empty bottle. 'Another?' He was already out of his seat before Alex could reply, and in his absence she sat alone at the table, trying to work out how she should be feeling.

A whole year . . .

And yet it still felt like it was only yesterday, no, she corrected herself quickly, Seth was *making* it feel like it was only yesterday, as if everything that had happened in the meantime was insignificant. But that was him all over, wasn't it?

Seth returned to the table with another two Coronas.

'So, do you still live at Green Street? Hey, only making conversation,' he added innocently, when Alex gave him a look that suggested this was absolutely none of his business. 'I do know you're still with the station, though. I caught a couple of your shows lately. They're good.'

'Thanks.' She felt weird, almost exposed, at the idea of him keeping an eye on her work. Again, her gaze met his, but this time she didn't look away.

'Alex, I . . .'

'Leonie, over here!' Suddenly spotting her friend across the street, Alex stood up and waved at her. Just in the nick of time too, she thought. Things were getting way too uncomfortable for her liking and she didn't want to be alone with him for any longer than she needed to be.

Leonie approached the table, smiling. 'Oh great, I was afraid I might miss you or get lost, or something. It's lovely here but everything looks a bit samey and my sense of direction is just brutal and . . . well, I've found you now.' She looked from Alex to Seth as if trying to determine in what direction the wind was blowing.

'Can I get you something to drink?' Seth stood up and held out a seat for her, all polite and solicitous now, apparently forgetting that he'd been flirting shamelessly with the same girl not an hour earlier.

'I'd love a beer too, thanks.' Leonie, on the other hand, hadn't forgotten this, Alex noticed with some amusement, her friend reddening again in his presence.

'Coming right up.' Seth headed towards the bar once more.

'Buy anything nice?' Alex asked, eyeing Leonie's shopping bags.

'Just a couple of fiddly little things I thought might be nice for the apartment.' Sitting down, she leaned forward conspiratorially and cocked a sideways glance at Seth. 'I hope you don't mind me just abandoning you like that, but I got the impression you needed some privacy.'

Alex waved her away. 'Not a problem, it's fine.'

'I got a bit of a fright when the two of you just started sniping at each other; I mean, I had no idea you actually *knew* him. He seems nice though. While I was waiting for you he just came up and started talking to me right out of the blue! I couldn't believe it.'

'Yep, that would be Seth,' Alex said wryly.

'I have to admit I didn't exactly mind though, I mean, it's not every day that this gorgeous hunk comes up and starts talking to you, is it? And wow, he just has this way, I don't know . . . this *incredibly* sexy way of looking at you. It sort of like, turns your legs to jelly.'

'*Definitely* Seth.' Alex took another sip of her beer, trying to keep from smiling.

'Well, he had that effect on me – still does a bit, actually.'

Leonie giggled, throwing another glance in the direction of the bar, where Seth stood waiting to be served. 'So who is he?' she asked casually. 'Some old boyfriend or something?'

Alex looked at her, deciding she'd better come clean. 'Actually,' she said, with a weary sigh, 'he's my husband.'

Chapter 15

Leonie's mouth was still agape when Seth returned, she was so floored by what she'd heard. Alex felt kind of bad, her poor friend was probably embarrassed at admitting the effect he'd had on her, but what else was new? The guy had that effect on everyone.

The questions began when the girls left Seth and headed back into Monterey to find a place for the night.

'But you never said anything about being *married*!' Leonie was so taken aback, it was like she'd forgotten the real reason they were here at all. When Alex explained that Helena wasn't at the studio when she called, and wouldn't be until the following day, it almost didn't register with Leonie – she seemed much more interested in finding out the story with her and Seth.

Although it was the last thing Alex wanted, he'd somehow coerced them into meeting up again for dinner later that evening.

'I know this great Mexican place, it's got the best margaritas in the state,' he'd assured them, and while she was reluctant to indulge him, there was no avoiding the fact that the two of them had issues to sort out. Issues Alex was determined to resolve, especially while she knew where Seth was, which couldn't be said for the last year.

Now, having found a motel and unpacking their things, Leonie was still full of questions. 'How come you never said anything? Especially with Jon and everything . . . I presume he knows?' She shook her head, incredulous. 'I still can't believe you never told me you were—'

'Well, that's because I'm not, as far as I'm concerned,' Alex shrugged. 'Yes, we're married, but only on paper, and of course Jon knows. I haven't seen Seth since he took off about a year ago.'

'Oh.' It no longer sounded quite so dramatic to Leonie. 'So you're separated then,' she said, sounding faintly crestfallen.

'Well, if I had my way, we'd be divorced by now, but because Seth refused to tell me where he was, I could never have him served.'

And it wasn't for the lack of trying. In the early days, once she realised he had gone, Alex had searched high and low for Seth's whereabouts, an address, a place of work, even a beach – anywhere he could be served the damn divorce papers. But until today her errant husband had remained as slippery as the conger eels he regularly swam alongside on his ocean dives.

'Now I understand why you were so angry when we bumped into him earlier,' Leonie said. 'But what happened? Did he disappear after you two split up or . . .'

'Leonie, you've seen him. That roguish smile and the hangdog expression? Not to mention all the flirting he was doing with you beforehand. Do you *really* need to ask me what happened?'

She looked uncomfortable. 'Right. He wasn't exactly the faithful type then.'

Alex snorted. 'I'll say! Ever heard of the seven-year-itch? Well, with Seth it only took seven months.'

'God, Alex, I'm sorry for bringing it up, I have no right to ask and it's really none of my business . . .'

'Hey, it's not a problem, I'm way over it,' she assured her. 'I think I knew deep down from the very beginning that he wasn't the marrying kind. But I was besotted and very stupid and I took a chance.'

Not to mention that she'd been completely bowled over by Seth. It had been a whirlwind romance in every sense of the word.

They'd met in this new club down by the Marina District in San Francisco and sparks had flown. Alex was ordering drinks at the bar when he'd started hitting on her, and while she was instantly attracted by his rugged good looks and Southern charm – any woman with a pulse would be – it was obvious he was a player. But Alex relished the challenge of keeping his interest, and for the best part of the next year, she did. The sex was as explosive as their never-ending arguments, but Seth's boundless energy and lust for life was like nothing she'd ever experienced.

'He was born and bred in North Texas, about as far away as you can get from the ocean, and he ends up a scuba diving instructor – which just about sums him up, I guess,' she told Leonie, emphasising Seth's contradictory nature. 'A few months into the relationship, he took me down there to meet his family. I didn't think too much about it; he'd been driving me crazy talking about his horses and how much he missed them, and so on. His family are cattle-breeders and the loveliest people you could meet,' she said with a wistful smile, thinking of his mother with her gentle Southern mannerisms and his dad – a greyer and more rugged version of his son, but who shared the same devilish twinkle in the eye.

'The same weekend we went to a local rodeo a few miles outside Dallas. I don't know if you've ever been to one of those things, probably not, but it's like nothing you'll get anywhere else in America. Maybe it's just a Texan thing but there's this great community spirit, you know?' Alex was seriously reminiscing now, but she couldn't help it.

It had been an amazing evening. Seth had bought her a cowboy hat so she blended in nicely with the locals, who all strutted around in full rodeo garb. Everyone – young and old – wore cowboy boots beneath jeans or skirts, and even the kids looked like miniature cowboys in their little checked shirts and hats. Alex could easily imagine Seth at that age, racing around like crazy beneath the bleachers while waiting for the show to begin.

'He'd told me he was taking part that night, but I figured he'd just be parading around on his horse. I mean, I had no idea . . .'

The rodeo officially kicked off with everyone singing along to 'The Star-Spangled Banner' and while the crowd was still standing in the bleachers, Alex and Seth's mom Sally among them, Seth suddenly appeared in the middle of the ring.

'You should have seen him, Leonie,' she laughed, shaking her head. 'You think he looked good today – well in those cowboy boots, denims, and that hat . . .' she smiled again at the memory. 'He took the microphone and bantered a little bit with the announcer, a guy he knew well – Seth knew *everybody* well. Anyway, like I said, there he was in the middle of a dusty rodeo ring, microphone in hand, when he dropped to one knee and . . .' She shook her head, now almost sorry she'd started this story. 'And he turned to where I was sitting in the bleachers and in front of half the state of Texas, asked me to marry him.'

'Oh wow,' Leonie swooned.

'I know.' And even though she'd had her doubts, mostly about the short length of their relationship, how could she have said no? Besides, the crowd had turned its gaze on her, waiting for her answer. Alex had been completely blown away by the grandeur of it all and caught up in the excitement of the whole event. Stuff like that only happened in the movies, didn't it?

'Then, when the whooping and hollering had died down, and I'd given him his answer, which of course was yes, guess what he did next?' she asked Leonie.

'Raced over and gathered you in his arms?' the other girl said dreamily.

'Nope.' This was what Alex had expected too, but instead Seth had grinned, winked, and against a background of thunderous applause, said 'Wish me luck, darlin'.'

'And with that, he disappeared back in the direction of the holding pens. I was so dumbstruck by what had happened I didn't have a clue what was going on. Then, two minutes later, there was a burst of loud country music, and my future husband,' Alex said shaking her head in renewed bewilderment, 'reappeared in the ring – bucking around like a rag doll on the top of a freaking *bull*!'

'You're kidding!' Leonie's eyes were wide.

'Nope. He asks me to marry him and then proceeds to almost get himself killed. *That's* the kind of guy we're dealing with here,' she said finally. 'I should have known there and then that it was never going to last.'

They married shortly afterwards. It was a crazy, impulsive time and Alex couldn't resist being carried along on the ride. Unfortunately, what attracted her to Seth – his wild energy and boundless passion – was the same thing that ultimately rang the death knell for their relationship. He craved novelty and excitement, and the ring on his finger quickly put an end to that. They hadn't even reached their first anniversary when Alex caught him out on the town with some bimbo, when he'd told her he was going out with the crew on a night dive.

She and Jen had gone to a popular place in North Beach for a few drinks when they came across Alex's new husband wrapped around this blonde lollipop in a manner that was far from innocent. Seth's face was still buried in the girl's neck when Alex walked right up and asked him what kind of 'night dive' he'd actually meant.

'You *didn't*!' Leonie gasped, gobsmacked.

'You bet I did.'

Despite Seth's pleas afterwards that nothing was going to happen, that he was just 'fooling around and being stupid' it was more than enough for Alex, and within a few weeks of kicking him out, she contacted a lawyer about filing for divorce.

Maybe he did love her, but a guy like Seth, one who possessed such an undeniably sexual magnetism and was incredibly flirtatious by nature, could never restrict himself to just one woman. She might have been stupid enough to marry him but Alex wasn't so stupid that she didn't realise this, nor could she even consider asking him to change. Seth was Seth and he would never be any different, despite his protests.

He'd tried to reason with her, tried to convince her that of course he'd stay faithful, but Alex wouldn't hear any of it. So he moved out and a few weeks later, she contacted her lawyer and told Seth to expect the papers.

'You're serious about divorcing me?' he'd said, flabbergasted that she'd made good on her word.

'Of course. What's the point in wasting any more of each other's time?'

'But this is crazy! You're crazy! This isn't what marriage is supposed to be about, you can't just give up on me after one stupid—'

'It's *supposed* to be about love and respect and most of all, trust! And I just don't trust you, Seth, in fact, I'm not sure I ever have.'

'Honey, let's not jump into something like this so quickly,' he pleaded. 'Let's give ourselves some time to think about what we're doing here. Divorce . . . it just seems so drastic.'

'I'm not your honey, and soon I won't be your wife either,' Alex countered, unmoved.

She couldn't take him back, couldn't even contemplate it. She didn't want to be one of those women who forgave and then watched the same thing happen over and over again until every last shred of self-respect had disappeared. That was no life. As much as she still loved Seth, she couldn't be that woman. No, it was now or never. And today, watching him in action with Leonie, Alex was more convinced than ever that she'd made the right decision.

'I wasn't going to be made a fool of again,' she said finally. 'And thinking back on it, I was the bigger fool for getting into that situation in the first place. What was I thinking, getting hitched to a guy like that? It was always going to end in tears.'

'Well, I'm no expert,' Leonie said, 'but from what you're telling me, it sounds like Seth didn't want to get divorced at all. Maybe – and I'm not condoning what he did – but maybe he really did love you?'

Alex had to smile at Leonie's romantic little heart. 'That's not it. A guy like Seth will always find it difficult to face up to his responsibilities, and I think he just hated the idea of having to sign the paperwork, the finality of it. He hated having to legally undo what had seemed like such a good idea at the time.'

'Well, that doesn't make much sense to me,' Leonie said, frowning. 'Disappearing for the best part of a year is a hell of a length to go to just to avoid signing some paperwork.'

'Well, you don't know Seth. But I'll tell you this much,' she said grimly, making a mental note to ring her lawyer first thing Monday, 'he's not going to get away so lightly this time.'

That evening at eight, the girls met up with Seth back at Cannery Row, despite Leonie's protests that she didn't want to get in the way.

'The last thing you need is me stuck in the middle like a big gooseberry,' she insisted. 'I'll just stay here and watch the telly, maybe order in a pizza or something.'

'No, you won't.' Alex practically frog-marched her outside and into a cab. 'We came here to try and find Helena Abbott and that's exactly what we're going to do. Don't you worry about Seth Rogers, I'll deal with him.'

But despite her determination not to let her ex get to her, Alex's insides gave an involuntary flip when she saw Seth waiting for them outside the restaurant. Dressed in camel chinos and a stark white linen shirt that set off his tanned skin, he wore a row of wooden beads around his neck. His hair was freshly washed but slicked back with gel. He looked the epitome of laid-back, bohemian masculinity and, Alex had to admit, sexier than ever. Damn . . .

The Mexican place was located on the edge of the coast high above the ocean. Its immense floor-to-ceiling windows, and the dual level seating arrangements, ensured that every table in the room had a magnificent unobstructed view out over Monterey Bay.

Seth sat on the banquette seat beside Leonie, directly opposite Alex. While she wasn't happy about having to circumvent his gaze all evening, it was a damn sight better than them sitting side by side.

Full of enthusiasm, Seth instantly ordered a round of frozen margaritas for the table.

'You've got to try the guacamole here,' he said, as they studied the menus. 'They make it fresh at the table and I guarantee it's the best you'll taste outside of Mexico.'

And he would know, Alex mused, knowing how much he adored that kind of stuff. It was funny, but Mexican food almost summed up Seth: fiery, exuberant and extraordinarily delicious, yet very messy and often difficult to grapple with.

She recalled now how their very first proper date had been in some Mexican place on Castro Street, and how inherently sensuous the simple act of eating it had been; or at least how Seth had *made* it seem. The way they needed to use their hands instead of utensils, wrapping warm tortillas with spices and jalapeños, sprinkling grated cheese, and licking off the runny cream and spicy salsa that dripped on to their hands and fingers. And then there was this other time back home, when Seth had got particularly imaginative with some chillies and half a piece of lime . . .

She looked up to see him watching her with a knowing smile, almost as if he could read her mind, and Alex made a mental note to order a mild and mess-free burrito.

'I've never tasted guacamole,' Leonie admitted.

'You haven't?' Seth turned to look at her. 'Well, boy, are you in for a treat.'

'This is great!' Leonie grinned at Alex when their margaritas arrived in huge glasses the size of hot tubs. 'First, the Crab Shack and now this, I'd never have come across places like this on my own.'

'You've been to the Crab Shack?' Seth said enviously. Alex remembered that it had been he who'd originally introduced her to the place. 'How are Dan and Phil? Still chasing UFOs?'

She finished drinking from her straw. 'Yep. Same as always.'

'Man, those guys do the best clam chowder! Did they ask about me?'

Alex looked at him. 'People stopped asking about you a long time ago, Seth.'

Before he could reply, the waitress appeared at their table and, laying down an enormous basket of fresh tortilla chips, she pulled up a trolley and set to making the guacamole they'd ordered. The three of them watched as she scooped out avocados, added fresh tomatoes, chillies and sour cream and the juice of three freshly squeezed limes, before including a hefty dose of coriander and mashing it all together. 'Have fun, guys.' Job done, she put the bowl on the table and left them to it.

'Mmm, this *is* delicious.' Leonie licked her lips and went to load another tortilla chip.

'Here, try it with some salsa too,' Seth suggested, pushing the bowl towards her.

'Be careful, Leonie, he likes it really hot and if you're not used to it . . .' Alex stopped short, only just realising the double-entendre. By his grin, she knew Seth had spotted it too but to her relief, he let it go. 'The green stuff isn't as spicy,' she added softly.

But her warning came too late, just as Leonie gaily put a chip with piquant salsa in her mouth. Alex winced, waiting for the inevitable, and she and Seth both watched as first the poor girl's eyes widened like saucers before she immediately leapt on the nearest glass of water.

'No, water won't help, use the margarita!' Seth chuckled, as Leonie practically buried her face into the crushed ice.

'That was mean,' Alex berated him, but she too couldn't resist a giggle. Poor Leonie looked like she was going to burst into flames.

'Oh my God!' she gasped, when she'd downed close to half the liquid in the glass. 'That stuff is unreal!'

'I did try to warn you, but you wouldn't listen.'

'I didn't expect it to be that hot. God, Seth, I don't know how you can stomach that, or anyone can to be honest. I'm surprised it's not used as a form of punishment.'

'It has a few uses,' he said, not taking his eyes off Alex, who immediately looked away and fixated on a flock of seabirds swooping down on the water.

The bay looked completely different at this time of night, when dusk had set in and the light was fading. It was as if all the wildlife had come out to hunt, feed and play, oblivious to the audience high above them. She spotted a group of seals frolicking in the surf, leaping and diving with happy abandon, and was struck again by the delicate beauty of the place, and the calming effect it had on her. Ironic, then, that it was here she'd bump into the person who exemplified the very opposite of calm.

'So, tell me again why you guys are down here,' Seth asked Leonie, who had just about recovered from her run-in with the salsa, and had since returned to the tamer guacamole. 'You said before you were trying to find someone?'

Leonie looked at Alex, as if asking permission to tell him.

'Who knows, maybe you can help,' she said to Seth, before the two of them in turn went on to explain all about the letters and how they believed Helena might now be working in the Cannery Row studio.

Seth seemed shocked. 'You read someone's else's mail? You know that's a—'

'Yes, I know it's a felony!' Leonie groaned in exasperation, before going on to tell him the hows and whys of opening the letters in the first place. 'Then the more I read them, the more the need to find her took on a life of its own.' She shook her head. 'I don't know, it just seems so sad that she hasn't read them and he seems so nice.'

'Well, if he was that nice, he shouldn't need to look for

forgiveness in the first place, should he?' Alex pointed out, again wondering why Leonie seemed so fixated with this. 'Maybe she's much better off without him.'

'You know, I don't believe that,' Leonie argued. 'But at least, if she got a chance to read them she could make up her own mind.'

'I agree,' Seth said, with feeling. 'Whatever the guy did, he's her husband and for that I still think he deserves a second chance.'

'Oh, come on!' Alex gasped, while Leonie looked like she wanted to crawl under the table. 'He could have been screwing around the whole time for all we know. What makes you think he *deserves* a second chance?'

Taken aback by her own vehemence on the subject, now Alex wanted to kick herself. Was she talking about Nathan, or Seth? A bit of both probably. Alex knew she needed to get those papers served soon. Having Seth around was clouding her judgement, making her feel on edge and uncomfortable.

And when a couple of minutes into their main course, Leonie got up to use the bathroom, she decided to tell it to him straight.

'I'm not taking this any longer, Seth. I've been waiting long enough. You need to sign those papers and I need to know exactly where you are so I can get them to you.'

When he said nothing, she reached for her handbag and took out a notepad and pen. 'Here, write down the address of the place you're staying, and the dive shop address too. I'm not taking any chances this time.'

'OK.' Oddly compliant, Seth took the pen and did as he was told. For some reason, this seemed to annoy her even more.

'Why couldn't you have done that before now?' she said shortly. 'Why keep me hanging on all this time?'

He shrugged, but this time his body language held none of the insolence of earlier. 'I just thought we shouldn't make any hasty decisions. You were so angry and—'

'I've had to keep my life on hold for the last year, trying to find you, wondering if I'll ever be free. It might not be a big deal to you but it is to me, and as long as I stay married to you, I can't move on with my own life.'

'You can't?' he said, giving her a penetrating look. 'Why?'

Alex gritted her teeth. 'Don't flatter yourself – for all sorts of reasons, mature adult things, things that you wouldn't have the faintest idea about.'

'Hey, are those seals leaping around out there?' Leonie said reappearing at the table, and as she and Seth looked out the window, Alex tried to compose herself again. Why did she get so out of control like that? She couldn't allow him to get under her skin again, it had been difficult enough getting to the place she was in now without him coming along and messing things up even more. No, she'd talk to her lawyer first thing Monday morning and with any luck Seth would be out of her hair soon.

Seth was chatting to Leonie as if nothing at all was amiss, which was of course absolutely typical. 'So tell me, how does an Irish girl end up living all the way out here in California? And how do you guys know each other?'

'Well, I work in a flower shop in the city and ended up delivering flowers to her for Valentine's Day.'

'Flowers?' he repeated, raising an eyebrow. 'Who from?'

Leonie grimaced, realising she may have made a faux pas.

'From the guy I'm seeing,' Alex said with a determined slice through her burrito before adding archly, 'not that it's any of your business.'

'A guy you're seeing . . . and he sent you *flowers*?' Seth's worlds dripped with scorn.

'What kind of *moron* sends someone who has hay fever flowers?'

Alex put the fork in her mouth. 'He didn't know.'

'He didn't *know*? How long have you known this guy?'

'Long enough to know that he treats me well and makes me happy.'

'By sending you flowers that could potentially kill you? Sounds like a *complete* moron to me.'

'Well, you don't know anything about him.' Alex gave Seth a level stare. 'And now that I know where to find you, you won't need to, either.'

Chapter 16

Alex and Leonie spent the following morning down at Monterey Bay wharf lazing in the sunshine while they waited for Helena Abbott's shift to start in the photography studio at midday.

'Even though I know what he did was awful, I have to say I really like Seth,' Leonie admitted.

Alex groaned and shook her head. 'Everyone does, that's part of the problem,' she said. 'But behind that handsome face and winning smile, he's nothing but trouble.'

'Oh no, I didn't mean . . .' Leonie was horrified that Alex was getting the wrong end of the stick. 'I don't *fancy* him or anything, although he is very attractive. I just meant that I really warmed to him, as a person.' She looked steadily at her friend. 'And from the way he was behaving around you yesterday, I think he's genuinely sorry for what he did.'

'Don't be taken in by the charm overdose, Leonie, that's classic Seth. The puppy-dog eyes and cheesy smile are all part of his "please forgive me" routine.' She gave a short laugh. 'Maybe he and this Nathan should get together some-time and swap stories.'

'Well, I'm sure it was very hard on you at the time, but try not to be so cynical. I saw his expression when he came face to face with you yesterday, and you'd have to be a fool not to notice how he was looking at you last night. I think he still loves you.'

'Oh, Leonie, come on, don't be so gullible,' Alex laughed. 'You seem to have conveniently forgotten that right before I came along, he was hitting on *you*!'

'No, no, he was just being friendly. You should have seen the state of me, blushing like an eejit in front of him.'

Alex wasn't convinced. 'Seth rarely needs an excuse.'

'Are you sure it's not just a front, though?' Leonie persisted. Although the atmosphere at last night's dinner had been strained, anyone with half a brain could see that there was still a spark between Alex and her husband, and although she did like Seth, at the same time Leonie really couldn't condone what he had done . . .

Alex rolled her eyes. 'Good old Seth does it again. Seriously, Leonie, I know what I'm talking about. Don't get me wrong, I know better than anyone how easy it is to be taken in by him, but that was a long time ago and I've learned my lesson since. He's not to be trusted, simple as that. Anyway, I've moved on now and I'm very happy.'

'So what does Jon think – about Seth, I mean?'

'He's cool about it, but I think like me, he'd rather things were straightened out.'

'I can imagine. So you're definitely going to have Seth served then.'

'Of course. Why wouldn't I?'

'What if he refuses to sign the papers again?'

'He never refused to sign them, Leonie, I just never managed to find out where he was to send them.'

'And you never wondered why that was?'

Alex frowned. 'I'm not following you.'

'Well, maybe he didn't tell you where he was all this time because he didn't want to get a divorce.' That was Leonie's thinking on it anyway, because even though she'd only learned a little about their relationship, it was clear to her that Alex and Seth still had unfinished business.

'Are you crazy? Getting married was the worst thing that ever happened to him, because it put an end to his woman-ising. Or at least it was supposed to,' Alex added sardonically. 'So please don't give me any more of this sentimental stuff; we have enough of that to be dealing with already. And speaking of which,' she added, checking her watch, 'Helena should be starting her shift soon so we'd better get going.'

'OK.' Leonie picked up her bag, deciding not to push the Seth thing any longer. Alex was right, maybe he had worked his magic on her in the same way that Nathan's letters had. God, she was a disgrace to the female population, so willing to forgive and give both of these guys the benefit of the doubt!

She and Alex hopped in the Mustang and made their way back to Cannery Row. Leonie still had mixed feelings about meeting Helena, now that she was so close. What if this really was the woman they were looking for? Would she be grateful to them for letting her know about the letters, or would she take Leonie's head off for reading her private correspon-dence? No, she'd surely understand that she'd only done it because she had no other choice, and if this whole thing ended up with her reuniting with her husband perhaps she might even be grateful?

Upon entering Cannery Row Photography, she and Alex were greeted by a pleasant woman sitting behind a reception desk.

'Hi there,' Alex said confidently. They'd already agreed that, it would be she who'd do most of the talking, as she was used to questioning people whereas Leonie knew she'd only get tongue-tied. 'One thing we also should consider is the possibility that she might not want to know about the letters,' Alex suggested on the way there. 'She didn't take them with her remember?'

But Leonie couldn't see this somehow. Their romance came across as very passionate and enduring and despite whatever it was he'd done, she couldn't imagine any woman not wanting to read such an amazing outpouring of devotion.

But that was her.

'Can I help you?' the woman behind the desk asked.

'Yes, we were wondering if Helena Abbott was free?' Alex asked. 'I called yesterday and was told she'd be here today.'

'Sure. Are you guys here for the portraits? You're a little early and she's just setting up, but I'll check if—'

'We don't have an appointment actually. We were just hoping to have a quick word about some other stuff of hers.'

Well, that could be true in a way, Leonie thought, once again impressed at Alex's ingenuity.

'OK, well I'll just check if she's free.' The girl stood up and went through a doorway to the right of the reception area, and a minute or so later they heard voices and the approaching footsteps of two people.

Alex looked at Leonie and winked as if to say 'here we go' and when the door opened, the receptionist reappeared, followed by a slim and elegant, dark-haired woman who looked to be in her mid-thirties. Instantly weighing this against the description she'd read of her in the letters, Leonie's heart pounded in excitement. This could be her!

Alex stood up while Leonie stayed rooted to her chair. 'Helena Abbott?' she asked.

The woman nodded. 'Can I help you?'

'I'm sure you're very busy, but I wonder if we could just have a minute of your time.'

Helena smiled amiably. 'I have an appointment at two so I guess I have a couple of minutes. What can I do for you?'

'Well, I hope you don't think this strange, but are you from San Francisco or did you live there recently?'

'I am from the Bay Area as it happens,' she replied. 'Why do you ask?'

'Did you happen to work as a photographer there at any time?'

'Yes, as a freelance before I moved here a few months ago.'

'Specialising in photographs of the Golden Gate by any chance?'

'Not particularly, but I think every photographer worth his or her salt photographs the bridge once in a while,' she joked. 'Again, why do you ask?'

Alex looked at Leonie. 'Well, it's just me and my friend here are trying to locate a former resident who lived in our building and her name was Helena Abbott. You didn't happen to live on Green Street?'

Leonie couldn't be absolutely certain, but as soon as Alex said this, she thought she saw the woman's green eyes grow wary. It could very well have been her imagination though because her breezy tone didn't waver. 'I'm afraid not,' she replied with an apologetic smile. 'You must have the wrong Helena Abbott.'

'That's a real shame,' Alex went on. 'Thing is, she's still getting a lot of mail – some of it looks pretty urgent. We just wanted to make sure she wasn't missing out on anything important.'

Again the woman shook her head. 'Can't help you, I'm afraid,' she said. 'But I'm sure the landlord would have a forwarding address for any previous tenants, wouldn't he?'

Although Helena's voice still sounded easy-going and unaffected, Leonie was pretty certain she was now thinking there was plenty more to this than met the eye. Why else would anyone come all the way down here just to send on some stranger's mail? Alex must have come to the same conclusion.

'Unfortunately no, but me and my friend were here for the weekend, and when we heard by chance there was a Helena Abbott working here, we thought why not just ask and see if it's the same one?' she said, sounding as if it was all completely casual.

'Well, I'm really sorry I can't help you,' the woman said with a smile.

'No, we're very sorry for bothering you,' Alex said apologetically, moving towards the door. She cast a surreptitious glance at Leonie before adding with a light laugh, 'I guess all those love letters will just have to be returned to sender.'

Helena Abbott nodded again, an unreadable expression on her face. 'I guess so.'

'So what do you make of that?' Alex asked when they went outside. 'Is she our girl or not? Can't say I recognised her myself, but as I said I couldn't really say what she looked like back then.'

'I'm not really sure what to think either,' Leonie said truthfully. 'She's probably the right age and fits the description in the letters, so much so that when I saw her first I really thought we were on to something. But while she *says* she didn't live in Green Street, I think something in her expression changed when you mentioned it, and that was odd.'

'That's why I threw in that bit at the end about them being love letters, but she didn't really react, did she? At least, not how you'd expect.' She exhaled. 'I don't know, Leonie, we could very well be seeing odd signs where there are none. On the face of it, if that woman in there was the right Helena

Abbott, there's no reason for her to pretend otherwise, is there?'

'Well, none that we know of anyway.'

'No.' She made a face. 'Well, I never thought I'd say this, but I reckon we need to find out more about those two.'

'Helena and Nathan you mean?'

'No, freakin' Laurel and Hardy, who do you think I mean?'

Leonie grinned. 'So you're saying we should open up some more letters, and see if there's anything else we can go on?' she asked expectedly.

'Why not? We've read three already. So let's go nuts.'

Leonie was delighted. She was dying to read more of the letters but because everyone had practically made her feel like a criminal for doing so, she'd so far resisted the urge. 'You're right – I suppose we might as well be hung for a sheep as a lamb.'

Alex looked puzzled. 'Whatever you say.'

Might as well be hung for a sheep as a lamb . . .

The expression, which had been a favourite of Adam's, kept repeating itself in Leonie's mind on the drive back to San Francisco. Interestingly, she thought – her mind again drifting back to events leading up to her departure from Dublin – it probably just about summed things up when it came to how she'd approached the situation with his ex.

Dublin: Eighteen months earlier

In preparation for their forthcoming wedding, Leonie and Adam had opened up a joint account and redirected their wages and respective debits and standing orders into the new one.

The first statement arrived in the post one morning, and

to say that Leonie was gob-smacked at her future husband's obligations was an understatement. While she'd known that he contributed a significant amount to Andrea's housekeeping expenses, it seemed he also gave his a daughter a very generous weekly bonus too.

'A hundred a *week*?' Leonie gasped at Adam, shocked. 'What does a fourteen-year-old need that kind of money for?'

OK, so it hadn't really been anything to do with her up to now, but seeing that they now had joint finances, and she was trying to cut down in order to save for the wedding, she felt that it was now very much her business.

He looked up from the newspaper he was reading. 'You mean Suzanne's pocket money?' he said with a shrug. 'It's only a couple of quid.'

'Adam,' Leonie replied, somewhat concerned at his flippancy, 'four hundred a month is a lot of money for a girl her age.'

Especially when Andrea seemed to have the hand out every other day for a contribution to their daughter's exam grinds, dentist fees, and anything she could think of. Adam had already agreed to pay close to a thousand for an upcoming school trip, and only last week Andrea had sent them a bill for some redecorating she'd had done to the girl's room.

'She's a young woman now so she can't be expected to put up with all that "pretty little princess" stuff you did before,' Suzanne's mother had argued, and at the time, Leonie couldn't help but think that such an environment sounded just about right for the pampered little madam who had been harder work than ever since the engagement. So to find that on top of all of this there was also a generous weekly allowance . . .

'Do you think so?' Adam replied, looking surprised. 'Andrea suggested it, as I really wasn't sure. She reckons teenagers really need their independence at that age.'

'Getting handouts from Daddy is hardly independent,' Leonie said, the words out of her mouth before she could stop them.

She knew she shouldn't be needling Adam about this, especially when it looked like he was just being led by the nose, but she couldn't hold back any longer from saying something. It was plain to see that Andrea was taking advantage, and while Suzanne was merely taking her mother's lead, Leonie felt the teenager should be taught that money doesn't grow on trees.

Although, picturing Suzanne in her fashionista-in-training uniform of pricey Ugg boots, Abercrombie and Fitch leisurewear, and Juicy Couture handbag (not to mention her penchant for high-end shopping centres), she figured this was unlikely.

Adam put down the newspaper. 'I suppose it might be a bit much now that I think of it,' he said. 'But then again it is only pocket money, and as her father, I don't begrudge her it.'

'Of course you don't,' Leonie said, recalling how up to now she'd always viewed Adam's dedication to his daughter as incredibly admirable. And she still did, except that it was now clearly obvious this dedication was being taken advantage of. 'It's just that sometimes I wonder if your kindness is really being appreciated,' she went on, treading carefully. 'You've always worked so hard to keep the two of them going, yet Andrea has never had to work a day in her life. I just think that maybe some of the time she should take responsibility for Suzanne's expenses too.'

'Never had to work a day in her life? Leonie, what about that very important job of being Suzanne's mother? Of nurturing and raising her into the lovely young woman she's become?'

Leonie thought about it. Was he right? Was she discounting the immense effort and sacrifice that went into raising a child? Perhaps so, but she still couldn't see why this entitled Andrea to be a lady of leisure while the fathers of her children picked up the bills. It didn't seem fair, and worse, she wasn't sure how this would work out when she and Adam got married and perhaps had a family of their own. Would they as a couple have to contribute to two households? If this were the case then Leonie knew that unlike Andrea, she wouldn't have the luxury of being a stay-at-home mum; their combined wages couldn't cover that – especially not when almost a third of Adam's pay went straight to Andrea as it was.

No, she and Adam would have to get this straightened out and soon. OK, so she knew coming into this that it would be slightly more challenging than a relationship with someone with no other commitments, but she loved Adam with all her heart, and wanted to spend the rest of her life with him.

'I understand that Andrea made a lot of sacrifices in raising Suzanne,' she conceded. 'But Adam, I think you forget sometimes that you did too, and whereas you're still making them – financially and otherwise – Suzanne is no longer such a burden on her mother's time. She's now old enough for Andrea to live her life pretty much how she likes. Don't you feel that it's perhaps time for her to contribute in other ways too? Especially when you've always done so much for her . . .'

'Lee, what I did was ruin her chances of having a normal life, or any semblance of a carefree youth,' Adam interjected, and she could see in his eyes that he absolutely believed this. 'Andrea could have done anything she wanted, gone to any college in the country, walked into any job. But, thanks to me, she was robbed of that bright future and ended up chained to the kitchen sink with a baby in tow.'

While he painted a very convincing picture of Andrea as the innocent victim, Leonie couldn't help thinking that surely there were two of them in it back then – unless there was something he wasn't telling her, she thought, worried now. Perhaps something more sinister?

'Of course, I'll admit that I was taken aback when I found out she wasn't on the Pill like I'd thought,' he went on, looked a bit uncomfortable then, as if suddenly realising the discussion might be a little bit too intimate for Leonie. 'But it doesn't really matter how or why it happened, does it? Suzanne was the end result and that's something I've never regretted, not for a single second. She's my daughter and I love her, so how can I begrudge her a bit of pocket money?'

Now Leonie felt that by raising the issue it was *she* who was begrudging the girl her dues, and by the way Adam was talking she knew she was fighting a losing battle.

The mother of his daughter had a very firm hold on her fiancé, one that Leonie knew she'd be an absolute fool to try and loosen.

Chapter 17

My darling Helena,

I just wanted to let you know I'm still thinking about you and hope you're OK. I hope too that you don't mind me writing to you still; if you do, I'll stop. To be honest, I'm not sure why I keep writing these letters, although I guess it's because it helps to get things off my chest. And I've always been able to talk to you about things I could never share with anyone else and it's a hard habit to break. There are things happening here that I wish I could share with you too, but I won't. You just don't need to know.

Besides, time just seems to pass by so slowly these days. In this place, sometimes time almost seems to stand still. Well, it does for me anyway, I guess it might be a little bit different for you.

So how is everything? As I say, I hope you're OK and I especially hope that husband of yours is treating you well. I know I said at the beginning that you deserved someone better, someone who would give you the world and for a while, I thought I might have been that person.

I guess I was wrong about that too.

Please Forgive Me.
Nathan

Leonie raced down to Alex's place, excitedly waving the letter over her head. 'You're not going to believe this!' she said when the other girl opened the door.

'What?' she asked, standing back to let her inside.

'Helena was *married*!'

Alex was unmoved 'So what?' she shrugged, going back into the kitchen to resume making a tuna sandwich. 'We already figured they were married.'

'But not, according to this, to Nathan.'

That got Alex's attention. 'What?' she repeated. 'You're kidding me.'

'Nope.' Leonie perched on the stool in front of Alex's breakfast bar. 'It's all here in this letter. I don't know why I always assumed that they were married to one *another*; I never for one second thought that they were having an affair!' She looked at Alex. 'So now we know we've been wasting our time. There was never any point in looking for Nathan Abbott because Abbott has to be *Helena's* name. And before you ask, I have no idea what her husband's first name is, he's just referred to in the letter as "that husband of yours".'

Alex cut the sandwich in half. 'Well, I guess that's it then, isn't it?' she said airily. 'Mystery solved.'

'What do you mean?'

'I guess that's what Nathan's so sorry about. Sorry for making her cheat on her husband.'

'No, no, that can't be it.' Leonie shook her head defiantly. 'Here, read the letter yourself.'

Alex picked up the page and quickly scanned the text, while Leonie waited.

'Well, he doesn't seem to think much of the husband, does he?'

'I'd say neither of them do,' Leonie said confidently. 'Now, *I* think the marriage was in trouble even before Nathan came on the scene, because it doesn't sound as though Helena felt any way guilty about it . . .'

'Leonie, remember we're only hearing all this from Nathan's point of view,' Alex pointed out. 'And whatever way you look at it, I think we can both agree that the guy seems pretty infatuated. So maybe he just wants to believe that Helena didn't care about her husband?'

'I know that, but something tells me she didn't care about him as much as she did about Nathan – at least up until it all went wrong.' Leonie was convinced this was the case. 'Why else would he want her forgiveness so badly?' She set the letter down on the countertop. 'So here's what I think. The couple who lived upstairs weren't Helena and Nathan but Helena and her husband. And he was the creepy guy who looked you up and down.' Leonie was much happier with this explanation; she had never been able to visualise Nathan as that kind of man, so to think it was the husband made a hell of a lot more sense.

Alex nodded. 'OK, that's certainly a possibility. And if they weren't getting on it would certainly account for all the shouting,' she added.

'Exactly. So now we know we've been barking up the wrong tree entirely. Problem is we're still nowhere nearer to finding out how to reach either of them. That woman from Monterey didn't call yet, did she?' They were hoping that the Helena from the photography studio – if she was the one they were looking for – might have had a chance to think and would contact them out of curiosity about the letters. But the weekend had been and gone and they'd heard nothing, which could only mean that it wasn't the right Helena after all.

'Nope, not a sound. It's hasn't been long though and I'm sure she's still a little taken aback by two complete strangers turning up out of nowhere and asking all those questions.'

'I suppose we'll just have to wait and see.' Leonie wasn't convinced. What woman wouldn't be curious about a pile of letters in her name? Especially when Alex had made a point of mentioning they were love letters. No, if this was the right Helena they would have heard from her, no question.

She picked up the new letter again and showed Alex something else she'd noticed. 'Look at the bit where he says "there are things happening here that I wish I could share with you". What things? And where is here? Sounds to me like he's moved away from this area or—'

'Oh, Leonie, I don't know,' Alex interjected tiredly with a shake of her head. 'I wonder if this is getting kind of out of hand.'

'What do you mean?'

'Well, we really don't know *anything* about these people other than what we can try and guess from the letters, and we made one major wrong assumption already – Nathan's surname. Who's to say that we're not just reaching here?'

'I still don't understand . . .'

'If you ask me, there's probably a very good reason Helena hasn't answered those letters. Who knows, this guy could be some kind of psycho stalker, and she had to move to get away from him.'

Leonie's face fell. 'I seriously doubt that. From his letters, you can tell that he really loves her and more than anything else, wants to make things right between them. And how could he possibly be some random stalker when they spent time together in that apartment? She must have loved him just as much as he loved her, Alex.'

Alex gave her a sympathetic look. 'Look, I know you're only trying to help, but maybe we should just stay out of this. Who knows what kind of stuff we could be getting mixed up in here? Things aren't always what they seem. Yes, I agree

Nathan's letters are romantic and charming, but that doesn't mean they're genuine. Take Seth, for instance,' she said, with a roll of her eyes. 'That guy could convince Satan he's as innocent as pie, when the reality is he'd do anything to turn a situation to his advantage.'

'It's not the same, I know it's not.' Leonie felt almost injured on Nathan's behalf. Clearly Alex's recent run-in with her ex was colouring her thinking.

Alex looked at her. 'Seriously, Leonie, what are you really hoping to achieve here? You don't know these people, and let's face it, if anyone other than you had found those letters they would have dumped them weeks ago. Why are you taking it upon yourself to be this guy's saviour when you're not even sure of the circumstances?'

'I don't know.' Marcy had asked her pretty much the same question, and Leonie still couldn't truly explain to herself, much less to them the real reason she was so interested in reuniting this couple.

There was just something about Nathan's words that resonated with her. Something in his voice and the way he sounded so heartfelt and honest in his attempts to atone for what he'd done had really captured her imagination. Yes, Alex was right; none of them had any idea why he was so desperate for forgiveness or why.

But more than anything, Leonie wanted to help him get a second chance. Everyone deserved that, didn't they?

Chapter 18

Dublin: One year earlier

It was only six months till the big day and Leonie was feeling on top of the world. She'd since pretty much learned to put her early misgivings about Suzanne aside and tried to ignore what sometimes felt like the girl's continuous drain on her and Adam's finances. At the end of the day, she was Adam's daughter and Leonie's soon-to-be stepdaughter, so she'd just have to try and get over it.

And in fairness, it wasn't entirely the teenager's fault; her mother had nurtured in her such an innate sense of entitlement that she just didn't know any different.

So Leonie was fine with Suzanne these days and apparently realising that Leonie wasn't going anywhere, the teenager also seemed to have softened her behaviour towards her father's fiancée.

But it was a different story altogether when it came to Andrea.

In all the time that she and Adam had been together, the two women had never met, and as far as Leonie was concerned this was absolutely fine. She could quite happily live her entire life without meeting Andrea; it was bad enough having to listen to her whiny (but for Adam's benefit, studiedly sugar-coated) tones over the phone. So when one morning over breakfast, Adam casually suggested they should pay Andrea a visit, she tried not to spit out her coffee.

'I know she'd really like to meet you,' he said, and Leonie wondered when exactly Andrea had expressed such an interest. Was it when she'd phoned wanting Adam to cough up for Suzanne's guitar lessons, or one of those times she needed an 'emergency' donation to her household expenses? It never failed to amaze her how Adam didn't stop to question why a woman whose lifestyle he'd chosen to support was (according to Suzanne) swanning around in the latest designer labels, while his own fiancée generally made do with the sale rail.

'You should see her handbag collection,' the younger girl gushed. 'Marc Jacobs, Miu Miu, Zagliani – you know the snakeskin ones they inject with Botox?' she continued, while Leonie tried to figure out if such a thing was included in the 'essentials' Andrea insisted she needed. Suzanne held up her own 'beginner' designer Juicy Couture handbag for examination. 'I'm a long way off having a collection like that, but Dad's promised to get me a Balenciaga for my birthday so I'm sure I'll catch up.'

When Leonie had picked her jaw up off the floor, she made a mental note to discuss with Adam the wisdom of encouraging a designer handbag fetish in a fourteen-year-old girl. At this rate, Suzanne would be expecting head-to-toe Chanel at sixteen! But even worse was the fact that by virtue of their engagement, Leonie had little choice but to contribute to this extravagance, despite the fact that she and Adam really couldn't afford it.

So to say that she wasn't exactly chomping at the bit to meet the woman at the root of all these frustrations was an understatement.

'Yes, she was only talking about it the other day,' Adam went on, and Leonie couldn't help but recall how insistent he'd been too in the beginning about Suzanne dying to meet her. That hadn't turned out so well, had it? And not for the first time, she was forced to wonder that for such a bright and mature guy, sometimes Adam seemed oblivious to the simplest of things.

'I can't really imagine why Andrea would want to meet me,' she replied, taking a bite out of her toast. 'I mean, what do we have in common, apart from you – and Suzanne, of course.'

'Well, I think it's only natural that she'd want to meet Suzanne's future stepmother, don't you? Obviously Suze would have been telling her all about you so . . .'

Leonie could only imagine what the teenager had been saying to her mother about her. 'I guess she's sort of OK-looking but in a dowdy kind of way. She badly needs a makeover . . . and could do with losing a few pounds but honestly, can you believe she doesn't own even *one* pair of Choos!'

Although on second thoughts, perhaps this was unfair. She'd come to realise that Suzanne could be sweet in her own way and although it had taken a while, Leonie would like to think that she and Adam's daughter were slowly but surely becoming, well, if not exactly friends then at least getting along as well as stepmother and stepdaughter could.

'OK, so when do you want to do it?' she asked, trying her best to conceal her lack of enthusiasm.

'I was thinking maybe next weekend? Neither of us has anything on, and as it's not our week to take Suzanne, I thought it might be nice to pay her a visit instead. We could all go out to dinner and maybe I could take in a round of golf the following day and—'

'You want us to go down there overnight?' she exclaimed, her reluctance all too clear from her surprised expression and the disbelieving tone of her voice.

'What do you mean, "down there"?' he laughed good-naturedly. 'It's only Wicklow, not Outer Mongolia.'

'I know.' Leonie was relieved he didn't seem to notice her reticence. 'It's just well . . . I'm not really sure it's a good idea.'

'Why not?' he said looking at her quizzically.

'Well, maybe Andrea might not be too happy with us landing in on top of her at such short notice—'

'Not at all,' Adam interjected with a casual wave. 'She's grand about it.'

'You mean you've already asked her?'

'I mentioned that we were thinking about it, yes. What?' he asked catching sight of her expression.

'I think you might have asked me first, don't you think?' she said in a wounded tone.

He shrugged. 'I suppose I thought you'd be OK with it – what's the big deal?' After a beat, when she didn't reply, he looked at her. 'Seriously, Lee, what's going on? Is there some kind of problem here?'

'No, I mean . . . it's just . . .' Leonie wasn't sure how to tell her fiancé that she'd rather have her teeth removed one by one with pliers than spend time with the dreaded Andrea!

But Adam seemed to have realised this anyway. 'Look, it's no problem, if you don't want to go down there; we can always do it some other time,' he said gently, but his disappointment was palpable.

And all of a sudden Leonie was struck by how awkward this whole thing must be for him too. Clearly it was important to Adam that his future wife and the mother of his child got on reasonably well, particularly where Suzanne was concerned. So maybe she should just bite the bullet and get the meeting over and done with. It wasn't fair to her fiancé who had enough on his plate dealing with Andrea, without her trying to make things awkward for him as well.

'No, no, it's fine,' she insisted. 'I was just wondering if you wanted me to book a hotel, or will we be staying at Andrea's or . . .' She didn't know if this was even a possibility, as she had no idea if the other woman's house was big or small. Although knowing Andrea, Leonie thought uncharitably, she'd probably got Adam to stump up for a stately castle.

Her fiancé reached for her hand. 'Look, I realise it'll probably be a bit weird for you and I'm sorry for asking. It's just, well I know us getting engaged was a big deal for everyone, and I suppose I want to make sure that we all know where we stand. Don't get me wrong, I know Andrea is delighted that I've found happiness with you, and for that reason alone I'd really like you two to meet. Also, I suppose I'd like to reassure her that our getting married doesn't mean that I'm planning on leaving my responsibilities behind. Suzanne is as much of a priority now as she ever was and that's not going to change.'

'I know that. And I'd be happy to meet her too,' she said, trying to sound convincing, for his sake at least.

But as she and Adam continued to make arrangements to travel down to Wicklow to meet his ex, Leonie couldn't ignore an overwhelmingly strong sense of foreboding.

They went to Wicklow the following weekend. As they pulled into the driveway of Andrea's house near Ashford, she realised that the place wasn't quite a stately castle – but goodness, it wasn't far off!

Now Leonie understood why the woman's household bills were always so high. If she lived in a two-and-a-half thousand square foot mansion, hers would be too! She wondered again if five-year-old Hugo's father brought as much to the table as Adam did. If so, did his partner feel as envious and it had to be said, bitter as Leonie sometimes did about the sacrifices they needed to make to keep another family going? Nobody would deny that Adam and Andrea's other ex shouldn't contribute to their offspring's rearing, but compared to the cosy two-bed apartment she and Adam were currently in the process of buying in Dublin, this place was something else entirely! And when a tall, curvy and beautifully dressed woman appeared at the doorway with long, blond hair and exuding such sexuality that Leonie almost felt she had to grab hold of Adam, she finally began to understand what kind of woman they were dealing with.

Andrea was the type men just couldn't say no to. Never mind that she and Adam had broken up well over a decade ago and there was little need for Leonie to feel insecure, in front of this Venus, how could any woman not? She understood now where Suzanne had inherited her watchful, almost cat-like eyes, which bore no resemblance at all to Adam's bright, open gaze.

'Hey there,' Andrea addressed Adam in that childish, sugary-sweet tone that always grated with Leonie no end on the phone. 'You're early.'

No 'Hello, you must be Leonie, the one whose fiancé every month donates the debt of a small country to my bank account, so nice to meet you' or even as much as a brief hi! Instead, and much to Leonie's chagrin, Andrea reached forward and held Adam in an embrace that was way too intimate for her liking. Not to mention obvious.

'Good to see you, Andi,' Adam said, stepping back, and to his credit looking embarrassed. 'Yeah, we are a bit early – the traffic was a lot lighter than we expected so . . . Anyway,' he said, introducing Leonie with a grin that immediately made her feel a whole lot better, 'this is Leonie.'

'*This* is the famous Leonie?' Andrea trilled in a falsetto voice that sounded like nails scraping across a blackboard.

Finally deigning to look at her, Andrea's derisive gaze travelled from head to toe. 'I've heard so much about you, although I must admit you look a hell of a lot younger than Suzanne described you. Typical teenagers, always so prone to exaggeration!' she added with a childish and equally irritating giggle, leaving Leonie wondering what on earth Suzanne had been saying.

'Nice to meet you too,' she replied automatically, as if Andrea had expressed any such sentiment. Then, having also failed to utter a word of congratulations or any mention at all of the reason Leonie and Adam were actually here, Andrea motioned them into the hallway.

And as she picked up her overnight bag and followed Adam and his ex inside, Leonie felt like she was entering the dragon's den.

The inside of the house was amazing. Decorated in chic, contemporary style; all cream walls, walnut floors and leather sofas, the place looked like it could have come straight from the pages of an interior design magazine.

Andrea had a good eye for interiors that was for sure, Leonie mused, going through to the large, open-plan kitchen at the rear of the house. Sitting at the kitchen table was Suzanne, alongside a small child doing crayon drawings, who had to be her younger brother Hugo. Well, half-brother that was, she corrected herself and when the little boy looked up, she realised that Hugo shared Suzanne's (and Andrea's) looks, possessing the same fair hair and green eyes.

Suzanne jumped up at their arrival. 'Dad, there's a disco on at the community centre tomorrow night and I really want to go but Mum says I have to ask you,' she said without preamble. Leonie couldn't help but wonder why Andrea had suddenly shifted this decision on to Adam, when usually he only ever had the tiniest say in what his daughter should or shouldn't do.

'Honey, Leonie and I just got here,' Adam replied brusquely. 'Let's talk about it later, OK?'

'Fine!' Giving her dad one of her vintage 'looks', Suzanne turned on her heel and stormed out of the room.

Andrea seemed to be having difficulty in keeping the smirk from her face. 'Would anyone like coffee?'

'I'd love one, thanks, Andi,' Adam replied, dropping their bags on the ground.

'Tea for me, please, if you don't mind,' Leonie said pleasantly.

'I'm afraid we don't drink that in this house,' Andrea replied in a grave tone that made Leonie feel like she'd asked for a line of coke.

'No problem,' she said shrugging, 'coffee is fine.'

'Hey, Hugo my man – how are you doing?' Adam greeted, sitting down at the kitchen table alongside Suzanne's half-brother. 'You've got so big since the last time I saw you. How's school?'

'Fine,' the little boy said, eyeing Adam rather warily. As Suzanne usually went to his place, Adam didn't visit the house very often so the child probably didn't know him very well, Leonie mused. He was a cute little thing, she thought watching him continue with his drawing, his tongue sticking out of the side of his mouth.

'Hello there,' she said, going over to join them. She sat down at the table and picked up one of the drawings. 'Wow, these are really great drawings, is this you?'

'Yep,' the little boy nodded happily, before pointing out another stick-thin character, this one with bizarre pink-coloured hair, and a sullen-looking face. 'This is Thuzanne.'

Leonie tried to stifle a chuckle. 'That's a lovely one of your sister,' she told him. 'You're very good at drawing, aren't you?'

Hugo nodded again and smiled shyly.

'He's going to be a world-famous artist when he grows up, aren't you, darling?' Andrea cooed, coming over with a tray of coffee and biscuits.

'Speaking of world famous, how's Suzanne getting on with those guitar lessons?' Adam asked her.

'Oh, she gave that up yonks ago,' she replied airily. 'You know Suze, can't get her to do anything she doesn't want to.'

I sure do, Leonie thought inwardly but just as quickly she remembered something. 'But the full course of lessons was paid for upfront, wasn't it?' she queried, recalling the exact amount very well, as the cheque had put her and Adam's account temporarily in the red.

'Yes, but what can you do?' Andrea replied with a casual shrug. 'These things happen.'

These things happen? Her blatantly dismissive manner made Leonie's blood boil. The cheek of it, when those lessons had cost an absolute fortune! As did the dance classes and the tennis coaching and any other random hobby that Suzanne got it into her head she wanted to try!

Beneath the table Adam laid a gentle hand on her thigh, hoping to calm her down. She'd really had enough of this woman's bloodsucking attitude and was sick to the teeth of her bleeding Adam dry. God knows she didn't begrudge Suzanne her child support but this was taking the mickey. But whatever her feelings towards Andrea, she wouldn't dream of expressing them here and especially not in front of the child.

'Well, we might have to see about getting some of that money back then, Andrea,' Adam said diplomatically, much to Leonie's relief, 'or at least try and get our money's worth by getting Suzanne to finish the course.'

'Be my guest,' Andrea replied with a self-satisfied smile, her tone implying that there wasn't a snowball's chance in hell of this happening. Leonie couldn't be sure but it almost seemed like the woman was pleased the subject of the wasted lessons had come up. Was she aware that Leonie had a problem with all this, and so was only too happy to rub her nose in it? Surely not, as she'd never expressed these feelings to anyone other than Adam, and he certainly wouldn't want to rock the boat by reporting this to Suzanne's mother.

In person, she found Andrea even more infuriating than she had imagined she would and wondered how on earth she was going to get through the rest of this visit. At least it was for only one night, although she really would have preferred to stay in a B & B, rather than under Andrea's roof.

'But there's loads of room at the house and she'd really like to have us stay with her,' Adam had argued beforehand. 'And I know Suzanne would really love that too,' he added, so how could Leonie *not* agree?

She looked again at Hugo's scribbling. 'You really are very good at this, you know,' she said, hoping to relieve some of the tension by changing the subject. She picked up one he'd drawn of just three people; two adults holding hands with a child. 'This one is lovely, is this you?' she asked, and again Hugo nodded. 'This must be your mum, and who's this?'

'That's Billy,' Hugo said.

'Oh? Who's Billy?'

'I think that's enough drawing for today, darling,' Andrea said, and before the little boy knew what was happening, she quickly proceeded to tidy his things away. 'Adam, I suppose you'd better show Leonie to your room.'

'Sure – the usual?' he said, and she felt somewhat relieved to learn that he did indeed stay in a separate room when he

visited. Not that she had any reason to believe otherwise
but . . .

'So, who is Billy then?' she asked Adam when they were
alone upstairs.

'He's an old friend of Andrea's. They had a bit of an on/off
thing going for years so maybe he's back on the scene.'

'Well, whoever he is, she certainly seemed reluctant to have
Hugo talk about him, didn't she?'

'Do you think so?' Adam, typically, hadn't picked up on
anything out of the ordinary.

'You didn't notice her clearing his colouring things away
in lightning speed?' she prompted.

Adam shrugged. 'I just assumed she wanted to start getting
things organised for dinner.'

But Leonie wasn't convinced. Andrea had been the epitome
of cool calm and collected all throughout the visit until Billy's
name was mentioned.

Then she'd changed completely.

A half hour or so later, Leonie and Adam came downstairs
for dinner. Suzanne, who they hadn't seen since their arrival
earlier, was sitting at the dining-room table, a dour expression on her face.

'Hey,' Leonie said, taking the seat alongside her. 'How's it
going?'

Adam was in the kitchen assisting Andrea; the other woman
having already politely refused Leonie's offers to help. 'I've
got everything under control, thank you, you just take a seat
and relax,' she said, before adding archly, 'besides, I understand that cooking isn't exactly your forte.'

Having decided not to please Andrea by letting her get
under her skin, she ignored the barb and did as she was
told.

'Did you get a chance to talk to your dad about that disco?' she asked Suzanne.

A loud sigh. 'There's no point; he won't let me go. He never, like, lets me do *anything*.'

'Oh, come on now, you know that's not true,' Leonie thought, deciding not to mention the Caribbean trip, school tour and countless other hobbies that Adam had paid for. 'What about your mum? Does she think it's OK for you to go?'

Suzanne crossed her arms. 'She doesn't care *what* I do as long as I keep out of her way,' she sulked. 'And when Billy's around, me and Hugo, like, might as well not even exist.'

At this Leonie's ears pricked up. 'Who is Billy? Your little brother was talking about him earlier too, but I've never heard you mention him before.'

Suzanne rolled her eyes. 'He's Mum's *boyfriend*.'

Leonie's ears immediately pricked up. Boyfriend? Well, this was interesting . . .

'But they're always, like, fighting,' the girl went on, flicking an imaginary piece of lint off the table.

'I see. Well, adults do that sometimes you know.' Leonie knew better than anyone that Suzanne was often prone to exaggeration. 'Hugo seems to like him,' she went on. 'What about you – do you get on well with him?'

Suzanne shrugged. 'I suppose, but he like, doesn't really talk to me much. I think he likes Hugo more because he's a boy and everything.'

'That's probably it all right,' Leonie agreed sagely. 'So is he coming round for dinner tonight or . . .'

'Who – Billy?' The younger girl made a face. 'No way. He like, never comes round when Dad's here, so I don't think he likes him much either.'

Even more interesting, Leonie thought, her brain working overtime. Adam had mentioned earlier that he knew Billy too, hadn't he? Had there been some kind of falling out or some-thing since? Well, whatever Billy's problem might be, it certainly didn't seem to bother Adam anyway as Leonie had never heard mention of the man before today. Might he resent Adam still being involved in Andrea's life? If so, then she and Billy would probably have plenty to talk about if they ever met, Leonie thought wryly, wondering if she might have some sort of ally in Andrea's boyfriend.

So if Billy did indeed resent Adam's involvement, what did he make of Hugo's dad being around too?

'What about Hugo's dad?' she asked, unable to resist probing further. 'Does he come to see you guys very often?'

Suzanne looked at her as though she was the stupidest person in the world. She rolled her eyes. 'Leonie, Billy *is* Hugo's dad.'

Chapter 19

Alex returned to the office after a morning's filming to find a message from her lawyer. Guessing that it had something to do with the divorce papers they'd dispatched to Seth earlier in the week, she immediately called him back.

'Doug, it's Alex. You called?'

The lawyer was once again straight to point. 'Hate to have to tell you this, Alex, but that husband of yours has taken off again.'

'*What?*' she practically screeched down the phone. 'What do you mean he's taken off?'

'Well, apparently he no longer resides at that Monterey address you gave me.'

'But that's just not possible!' Alex argued. 'I only spoke to him last weekend and he promised, he *swore* he lived there . . .' Now she wondered if Seth had even given her the correct address in the first place. Of all the crafty, dishonest . . .

'Well, not anymore. Our process server talked to some other guy who said that he moved out a few days before.'

'I don't friggin' *believe* this!' Alex couldn't restrain her frustration. 'That no-good, good-for-nothing, lying *toad!*'

She'd really believed Seth when he said he'd do the right thing by agreeing to be served this time, but as usual he'd been lying through his teeth. At that moment, more than any other time in their history together, Alex really wanted to strangle him!

Doug was still talking. 'Well, we could probably look to file a motion to serve by publication, but like I said before, the judges don't tend to grant those too easily, so we could very well be wasting our time.'

If – as in Alex's case – a spouse couldn't be located for divorce papers to be served, a notice of the application for divorce proceedings could be published in a newspaper. When close to a year had passed and Seth still proved impossible to find, she'd asked her lawyer to investigate this option, but it was considered by the courts to be a last resort and was only allowed if it could be proven that all other avenues to locate him had been exhausted. Judges were generally reluctant to grant such motions, and it was difficult for Alex to prove that Seth couldn't be located, especially as his damned social security number was still registered to the Green Street address.

So Doug had advised against it and instead filed for more time, something he was in favour of doing yet again. 'It's a shame you didn't think to tell me you'd met him while you were there; we could have had our guy down there the same day.'

'I know, I know.' Alex was kicking herself now. But at the time Seth had seemed OK about it all, and up until Leonie mentioned it, she'd never even considered that he might have been avoiding her attempts to serve him on purpose. 'He swore he'd accept them, and like an idiot I believed him!'

'Well, I guess we're back to square one then, Alex. I'll apply for more time from the court, but in the meantime, as long that husband of yours keeps slipping through your fingers, this divorce just can't happen.'

'I can't believe he would do this to me again!' That evening after work, Alex spilled out her frustrations to Leonie. They were both sprawled on her sofa in front of the TV, waiting for the newest instalment of *Grey's Anatomy.*

'Told you he was avoiding all this on purpose. He doesn't want to get divorced, Alex, it's as simple as that.'

'It's not up to him to decide!' she grimaced, standing up. 'And he should have thought of that before he started screwing around.' Going into the kitchen, she switched off the heated cafetiere and poured fresh coffee into a couple of mugs. 'If I'd known he'd do this I would have wrestled him to the ground in Monterey and got him to sign the papers there and then. But of course I didn't have them with me, did I? Man, I just can't believe this!'

She handed a mug to Leonie.

'I don't understand – I thought you said he was happy enough to give you his address at the weekend.'

'He was! We talked about it that night at dinner when you'd gone to the restroom. He told me to send them on and it wouldn't be a problem.' She slumped back down on to the sofa. 'Clearly he was lying through his teeth.'

Leonie looked thoughtful as she sipped her coffee. 'Well, I didn't want to say anything, or more to the point, *you* didn't particularly want to talk about anything to do with Seth afterwards, but that night I did notice he seemed a bit put-out at the mention of Jon.'

'Put-out?' she queried blankly.

'A bit miffed . . . or annoyed?' Leonie tried to find the American equivalent.

Alex sat up straight. 'Do you really think so?' Her eyes narrowed. 'God, that's just so typical, he doesn't want me, but he doesn't want anyone else to have me either! Grr, I'd kill him with my bare hands if I ever got near him again, I swear I'd—'

The intercom buzzed loudly, startling them both, but before Alex could get up to answer it, they heard a key turn in the lock. Then she and Leonie both looked worriedly out towards the hallway at the distinct sound of someone trying to enter the apartment.

'Are you expecting someone?' Leonie asked nervously.

'No, and I'm the only one who has a key to this place. Well apart from . . .' But the rest of her sentence trailed off as Alex suddenly realised exactly what was going on, or more importantly *who* had just come in.

A familiar head popped around the living-room door. 'Guess who?' Seth called out merrily, that trademark mischievous grin written all over his face.

Alex leapt out of her seat. 'What the hell are you doing here? How come you still have a key? And who do you think you are just waltzing back in here like you own the place?' The questions came as thick and fast as Alex's rising blood pressure. The cheek of the guy! How *dare* he?

'Well, that's a nice homecoming,' Seth said, setting his bag down and giving Leonie a little wink that infuriated Alex even more.

'Homecoming . . . What the hell are you talking about? This isn't your *home*!'

'Um, speaking of which, I think I might head back upstairs,' Leonie mumbled, smiling awkwardly. 'I'll talk to you tomorrow.'

'You don't need to go anywhere, Leonie,' Alex said firmly, looking daggers at Seth.

'No, honestly, I have a few things to do, um thanks for the coffee,' she insisted meekly, before slipping out the door as fast as she could.

'Well?' Alex urged, when she and Seth were alone. 'Would you like to explain to me what the hell you think you're doing here?'

He looked as though butter wouldn't melt in his mouth. 'I miss you,' he said simply.

'*What?*' Alex couldn't believe what she was hearing. 'You *miss* me? When exactly over the last year did you figure that one out, Seth? Was it while you were partying down in Miami? Or was it when you found out that I was no longer sitting here pining over you?'

'You pined over me?' he asked in feigned surprise, and Alex wanted to punch him.

'You know what I mean,' she said through gritted teeth. 'And I asked you a question.'

Seth sighed, and his playful tone suddenly grew more serious. 'I mean it, Alex, I really do miss you. When I bumped into you guys in Monterey last week, I realised exactly how much.'

'Oh please!' she groaned. 'Come off it, Seth, what's really going on here?'

He spread his hands wide as if to say 'give me a break'. 'Look, I've been thinking a lot about what's happened with us and I know you don't believe me, but I really meant it when I said I was going to call you. I'd planned to come back to the city, but I had to carry out that favour down south first.'

'The job in the dive shop?'

'Yes. I met the guy in Miami. He was on vacation there and we got talking and he mentioned he had a place on the West Coast. I thought it was the perfect excuse to come back, maybe work there for a couple of weeks while I plucked up the courage to call you.'

Alex eyeballed him, not believing a word. Once a player always a player. There was something else going on here, and thanks to what Leonie had said earlier she was now pretty certain she knew what that something was.

Jon.

It made sense actually. In the past Seth had always been hugely possessive of her, and at the time she hadn't minded all that much, almost viewing it as a compliment. But it was just a demonstration of Seth's humongous ego.

'The perfect excuse,' she repeated flatly. 'But if you were that sure about coming back then why would you need an excuse?'

He gave her his best soulful look. 'I guess I still wasn't quite ready to face you. Things ended so badly with us back then . . . I guess I didn't know how you'd react.'

'You didn't know how I'd react to what? To you just rolling up here, not just to the doorstep but actually letting yourself in like you owned the place? Or to the fact that you lied yet *again* to my face last weekend about signing the divorce papers, not to mention avoiding them for the last twelve months,' she added bitterly.

That hangdog expression again. 'I'm sorry, but you caught me by surprise. I guess I never really thought you'd go through with that, I mean, not without us talking about it first.'

'You never thought I'd go through with the divorce?' she asked incredulous. 'Seth, you disappeared for the most part of a year! What did you think I'd do, just sit around and wait for you to return?'

'I don't know, I guess I thought we needed some space from each other, then we could try counselling or something . . .'

'I can't believe I'm hearing this! I just can't believe it . . . Seth, are you out of your mind? Although, no wait, I think it's me that must be out of *my* mind for even considering this bullshit when all you're doing is making it up as you go along so you can worm your way back as if none of this was your fault!'

'I never said none of it was my fault, but there were two of us—'

'Seth, I just don't want to know, OK? Your stupid excuses meant nothing then and they mean even less now. To think that after all that you just walked away and left me to deal with everything by myself . . .' She shook her head, determined not to let him get to her again. It was so long ago, and she was back on her feet now. 'So how dare you come back here and tell me that you miss me, when all you're worried about is . . . well to be honest, I don't know what in the hell you're worried about, but I'm guessing it has a lot to do with your ego.'

He looked hurt. 'My ego? How?'

'Because I'm over you – long over you and now I'm seeing someone else. You didn't expect that, did you? Nope, you expected me to just sit around broken-hearted for who the hell knows how long. And then, when you find out I didn't do that, you suddenly appear out of nowhere and start talking about how much you miss me! What kind of an idiot do you think I am?'

'I don't think you're an idiot at all. Yes, it was tough finding out that you're with someone else now, but I guess I didn't really expect anything else. Any guy would be lucky to have you.'

Alex put a hand on her hip, wondering how much more of this crap she'd have to take. 'Give it a rest, Seth, OK? I don't know the real reason you're here, but let's get one thing straight. I've been waiting to divorce your sorry ass for the last year and I don't intend on waiting any longer. So for once in your life, try and put your own selfishness aside and let me move on with the rest of *my* life, OK?'

For a long moment, Seth just stared at her, saying nothing. Eventually, he looked away. 'No,' he said in a low whisper.

'No? What do you mean "*no*"?' Alex gasped. 'What is *wrong* with you?'

'I don't want us to get divorced, Alex. I meant every word I said. This is nothing to do with jealousy or ego but everything to do with the fact that I still love you and I want to make this marriage work.'

'Make this marriage work?' she echoed yet again, wondering if she was seriously hearing things. Or if he seriously had a brain. 'Seth, there is no marriage, you cheated on me, remember?'

He shook his head defiantly and Alex couldn't believe that after all this time, he was still trying to deny it!

'Are you sleeping with this guy?' he asked after a pause, his jaw tightening.

'I can't believe you would even ask me that question.'

'Are you?'

'We've been seeing each other since before Christmas, Seth, what do you think?'

There was the oddest expression on his face. 'I see.'

'What – you think that makes us even, or something?' she said, trying to guess his thoughts. 'For Christ's sake, it's not the same thing at all!'

But the truth was, it was possibly part of the reason she'd hesitated for a time before sleeping with Jon. It had always felt . . . well, not quite dishonest but disloyal in some weird way because she was, on paper, still married to Seth. OK, so it had been pointless thinking that way when clearly their marriage vows hadn't meant a thing to him, but Alex couldn't help feeling like she was letting herself down by sleeping with another man while she was still married. The fact that she hadn't been able to end the marriage, through no fault of her own made things even worse.

But she'd got over that, hadn't she?

And then today, Seth turned up, making her feel like crap for being with someone else, as if *he* was some kind of injured party!

Seth sighed deeply. 'Look, Alex, back then, I'll admit I was stupid . . . even now I can't understand why I lied to you about where I was going that night. I guess for me flirting with other women was almost like a force of habit or something . . .' Even as he said the words, he seemed to realise how pathetic they sounded. 'All I can say is that I never for one second set out to hurt you. Never.'

Alex looked at him, and all the pain and sorrow she'd felt in the aftermath of that awful time came flooding back. Why should she feel guilty for being with Jon? He had no right to make her feel that way. 'Well, I'm sorry, Seth,' she said hoarsely, 'but you did.'

'I know. And I also know that I was stupid for taking off like I did. I guess I thought we could just work things out, but then you started talking about divorce. Look, all I'm saying is that I'm back now and I want to try to again. Don't you owe me that much at least?'

'I don't owe you anything,' she told him firmly. 'As far as I'm concerned you're no longer my husband and I don't want you in my life. This divorce is going to happen, Seth, whether you like it or not.'

Chapter 20

But over the week that followed, Alex found herself plagued by Seth and his great intentions 'to work things out'.

'He's driving me nuts!' she complained to Leonie, who maddeningly seemed to think it was actually quite romantic.

'Why are you so convinced he's not sincere?' she asked when they met up for one of their regular lunches in the Crab Shack.

'Because I *know* Seth, and I know damn well this isn't about us getting back together; it's about him trying to mark his territory! You were right, you know; the Jon thing really rattled his cage.'

'Poor you, and poor Jon too. What are you going to do?'

'What can I do, other than keep him at arm's length as much as I can, although not so much that he takes off again. I still need him to sign those papers.'

'I still can't believe he just let himself into your apartment like that,' Leonie exclaimed. 'And the innocent face on him too, like it was all perfectly normal and he'd just been away for a couple of days.' She grinned. 'You really should have seen your face.'

'I know!' Alex was still taken aback by his audacity. 'And even worse, having fed me this whole line about how we were "meant to be together",' she repeated with a roll of her eyes, 'I really think he thought he could move back in too – as if we could just take up where we left off! God, what is it with guys that they can be so damn clueless sometimes?'

At this Leonie smiled tightly. Not for the first time, Alex wondered what really had brought her here. Clearly Leonie was running away from something, that much was obvious, but what? Or more likely, who?

Her preoccupation with those letters and the story behind them seemed a little too intense to put down to just nosiness and Alex wondered if Helena and Nathan's romance had struck some kind of a chord with Leonie, something other than plain curiosity. Granted the letters were mysterious, and when Alex first learned about them she too was eager to figure things out, but only because she sensed a good story behind it. But there was a story behind Leonie too, and although she was interested in learning more about her new friend, she wasn't going to push it.

Leonie would spill her secrets in her own good time, and in the meantime, the poor girl had to put up with listening to her godawful situation with Seth.

'So where did he go afterwards?' Leonie asked her. 'I take it you didn't let him stay with—'

'Are you crazy? Of course I wasn't going to let him stay over! He was lucky I let him stay standing after talking so much bullshit! Ooh, I never meant to hurt you, Alex, I just couldn't help myself . . .' she mimicked. 'Did you ever hear such a load of cheesy crap in your entire life?'

But Leonie just smiled indulgently as if it was all very endearing, and again Alex wondered how Seth always managed to get on the right side of people – no, strike that – the right side of *women*.

'Well, I suppose he was right about one thing,' Leonie ventured sheepishly. 'By sleeping with Jon, you are sort of even, aren't you?'

'Come on, it's not the same thing, and you know it!' Alex was frustrated that this had come up again. 'I didn't go behind Seth's back . . . at least not intentionally, so it wasn't cheating.'

'I know, but from Seth's point of view it probably *is* the same thing. You know how pedantic men can be about these things.'

'When it suits them!' It annoyed Alex that Leonie was twisting things in this way. 'Anyway, I doubt that Seth's been lonely in the meantime so it's a pathetic argument as far as I'm concerned,' she grumbled, signalling Dan for the check.

Leonie seemed determined to play devil's advocate. 'Who knows? Maybe he did realise he messed up, and didn't know how to cope with the aftermath?'

'So he runs away? Very mature,' Alex said drily but in the same instant, realised she might have hit a nerve. Leonie's reaction left her in no doubt that she had done something all too similar in coming here.

But what had she run away from? Alex really wanted to ask but damn it, this probably wasn't the time or the place. 'I guess people do have different ways of dealing with stuff,' she said diplomatically, 'but you can't run away for ever. Things have a way of coming back and biting you in the ass sooner or later, as Seth's figuring out now.' She was particularly careful to make it sound like they were still discussing Seth, although by her face, she knew Leonie was mired in thought about whatever it was that had happened to her. Alex decided to risk it. Taking a deep breath, she tried to sound casual. 'Seems to me like you might have done a bit of running yourself,' she said gently. 'Do you want to talk about it?'

Leonie paled. 'What? I don't know what you mean.'

'Honey, I know we haven't known each other all that long,

but I think I know enough about you to see that you're hurting about something. You don't have to tell me what it is, but if you'd like to talk, you know I'm here, OK? Sometimes it helps. Hell, listen to me yakking on about Seth. I don't what I'd do if I didn't have you to complain to.'

Leonie smiled uncomfortably. 'Thanks, Alex, but there really isn't anything to talk about.' She sighed. 'I broke up with my fiancé recently, and I needed a change of scenery. That's about it, really.'

'I'm sorry to hear that; it must have been tough.' Clearly there was a *lot* more to it. 'Were you guys together long?'

'A few years, and we were engaged about a year when things ended.' Leonie's body language was screaming that she didn't want to discuss it, but Alex couldn't help but probe a little further.

'That's a long time. Are you guys still in touch?'

Leonie shook her head and looked away, trying her best to hide the tears brimming in her eyes. Alex got the message loud and clear, but she wondered whether the two of them had more in common than they'd thought. 'Goddamn men,' she joked grimly. 'I sometimes wonder why we even bother. It's not as though we actually *need* them for anything, is it?'

'I suppose not,' Leonie smiled, her eyes still suspiciously bright. 'But speaking of which, what does Jon think of all this stuff with Seth?'

'He doesn't know anything about it yet. Although I suppose I'd better say something, let him know what we're up against for the next few weeks.'

'Few weeks? Do you think Seth will give up that easily?'

'It's not a case of giving up, more a case of waiting until he gets bored, I think.' Alex pushed her plate away. 'Nah, he might have a bone to pick at the moment, but knowing Seth as I do, he'll soon get tired and move on to the next challenge.'

After lunch, Leonie returned to work and was out back getting the afternoon deliveries organised when she thought some more about her lunchtime conversation with Alex. It was tempting to confide in her. But the truth was, Leonie wouldn't even know where to start when it came to what had happened between her and Adam. It would undoubtedly be difficult for Alex to comprehend, in the same way that back then, it was difficult for Grace to understand too.

Dublin: One year earlier

After Leonie and Adam returned from their visit to Andrea's house in Wicklow, she went to see Grace to let her know how the visit went.

'It was so weird,' she told her friend over a cup of coffee. 'As far as I knew, Hugo's dad was also out of the picture. I'd never once heard mention of this Billy before now, but according to Suzanne, *he's* Hugo's dad.'

That night at Andrea's when they were getting ready for bed, Leonie had repeated to Adam what Suzanne had told her, but much to her frustration, he couldn't see what all the fuss was about.

'So what if Andrea is seeing Billy again?' he'd said shrugging. 'They've been on and off for as long as I can remember and as he's good to Suzanne, it's really none of my business.'

'But aren't you the slightest bit curious about it?'

Adam took off his shirt and hung it on the back of a chair. 'Nope, as I said, it's nothing to do with me.'

'But why did Andrea say Hugo's father was out of the picture?' Leonie urged, amazed that he didn't seem in the least bit perturbed about this. But then again, nothing Andrea *ever* did seemed to perturb Adam!

'Well, as I recall, she didn't actually tell me anything,' he said, getting into bed alongside her. 'I suppose I just put two and two together. As I said, I really don't keep track of who Andrea is or isn't seeing.'

'Oh.' For some reason Leonie felt deflated.

'Gosh you really are an imaginative little thing, aren't you?' he said, kissing her fondly on the nose. 'Always looking for big mysteries where there are none. If Andrea's seeing someone and he's making her happy, then that's good news for all of us surely?'

Now Grace seemed to be echoing Adam's sentiments.

'What does it matter?' her friend said. 'It doesn't have anything to do with you or Adam either way, does it?'

'I suppose.' For some reason, Leonie had expected her friend to be as intrigued about all of this as she was. 'But why did she react so strangely when Hugo mentioned him?'

'Chances were she was just annoyed about her fancy man being brought up in conversation, especially in front of you.'

'Maybe.'

In fact, once dinner had been served there was no mention of Billy for the rest of the night. Instead Andrea had spent much of the evening trying to undermine Leonie's clothes, hair, even her engagement ring.

'If Adam had ever even *thought* about presenting me with a crumb like that, I'd have run a mile,' she'd said, examining Leonie's small but delicately pretty solitaire while Adam was out of earshot.

But he *didn't* think about it, did he? she wanted to retort, but didn't want to bitch in front of the kids. Not that their mother seemed to have any problem with it.

'So, when's the wedding then?' Andrea asked during dessert. 'I presume Suzanne will be bridesmaid.'

Leonie in the hope of surprising Adam's daughter (and in truth, scoring some Brownie points) was planning on asking her to be *one* of the bridesmaids when the time was right. But trust bloody Andrea to go and blow the entire thing!

Adam was annoyed too. 'Uh, thanks for blowing the surprise,' he said, shaking his head in dismay.

Leonie turned to look at the teenager, hoping to rescue the situation. 'Well, I was going to wait for another time to ask but yes, I'd really like you to be one of my bridesmaids, Suzanne.'

The younger girl rolled her eyes; her mother's eagerness having now ruined any chance of her taking the idea seriously. 'As if I'd want to wear a tacky, frilly dress,' she groaned.

'Hey, mind your manners, young lady—' Adam began, before Andrea made a swift interjection.

'Oh, I'm sure Leonie wouldn't *dream* of choosing anything tacky,' she said archly, her sugary-sweet voice dripping with sarcasm. 'But speaking of which, where did you get that interesting dress you're wearing?'

For 'interesting' translate 'horrible', Leonie thought, livid at the woman's blatant nastiness. Still, she was also kind of glad she'd asked.

'I bought it in Tunisia last year,' she replied, and at this Adam met her gaze and smiled conspiratorially. It was the same dress she'd worn to dinner at the hotel in the Sahara that night, and while he wasn't a big one for compliments, she knew he liked it.

Spotting the look, Andrea harrumphed. 'At one of those tacky foreign markets I suppose. I don't know why people buy things in places like that. Give me Brown Thomas any day.'

'Well, I prefer a more individual look, to be honest,' Leonie replied. 'There's nothing worse than looking like a clone of every other woman in Dublin.'

'Absolutely,' Adam agreed, reaching for her hand. 'And to me, Leonie would look good in a paper bag.'

Now, listening to her recount the scene, Grace laughed. 'Yay, strike one for Leonie!' she said, putting up her hand for a high five. 'Good on you, she does sound like an awful cow. I don't know how you put up with her.'

'I really don't have much of a choice unfortunately.'

'As if that daughter of his wasn't enough trouble.' Grace, who had met Suzanne a couple of times when over for a visit, wasn't one of the girl's greatest fans.

'Suzanne I can handle, it's her mother I'm not so sure about.'

But that weekend, the battle lines had been well and truly drawn between Leonie and Andrea. The problem was, she thought mournfully, was that she wasn't sure she had it in her to fight such a battle, let alone try and win it.

Chapter 21

'What do you mean he wants to try again? I thought you guys were getting a divorce?'

As expected, Jon wasn't overjoyed to hear that Alex's husband was back in town.

It was Friday night and they were in North Beach sharing an al fresco pizza at Calzone's when she decided to broach the subject. But in retrospect, she probably should have picked a quieter spot because as usual, the whole area was buzzing. Sidewalk tables here were a premium and fought for space with the scores of people passing up and down the street.

'It's nothing to worry about,' she reassured him. 'He has no real intention of trying again, he's just being Seth. He heard about you and is acting like a little boy who doesn't want to share his toys, that's all.'

Jon didn't seem convinced. 'Are you sure? And how come he's back all of a sudden? I thought you said he couldn't be found.' He recoiled a little as an overgrown Dalmatian flopped beneath a neighbouring table. Jon was afraid of dogs – tough in San Francisco, where most places in the city welcomed them.

Alex smiled as the dog lay peacefully at its master's feet, unruffled by the hustle and bustle all round. 'He couldn't – up to now.' She went on to explain how she'd bumped into him while in Monterey with Leonie. 'Like I said, he'll be out of our hair soon, but in the meantime, I have no choice but to humour him – at least enough to get him to sign the papers.'

'I guess.' He sounded somewhat threatened, and at this Alex couldn't help but feel oddly gratified. Although it was obvious that things were becoming more serious and they were getting on brilliantly, it was still nice to know that Jon felt that strongly about her. Not that he had anything to worry about where Seth was concerned. Nope, once Alex had him served that would be the end of her husband, and with any luck, the end of her troubles. After that, she'd be free to move on with the rest of her life, and even further along with this relationship.

Not that Jon was putting undue pressure on her or anything. Thinking about it now, he was actually the opposite of Seth, really. And although he didn't possess her ex's irresistible magnetism (but who the hell did?), he was hugely attractive in his own way.

Anyway, Alex wondered, why had she started comparing him to Seth all of a sudden? Jon was who he was and such comparisons were completely immaterial.

'Alex, are you sure you're really over this guy?' Jon's voice broke into her thoughts, making her feel even guiltier about what she'd been thinking. Was he that perceptive or was she just easy to read?

'Absolutely sure. Honestly, Jon, you've got nothing to worry about!' She gave a light laugh. 'He's a part of my life that's very much in the past; unfortunately I can't get rid of him until . . . oh hell!' Stricken, she looked up at the figure approaching them on the sidewalk.

No *way*, this could not be happening. How on earth could he . . . ?

'Hey there, Mrs Rogers, fancy meeting you here!' Seth grinned, appearing alongside their table. As if out of the thousand-odd restaurants in the city, he'd just happened upon the same one. Alex groaned inwardly. He was doing this on purpose, she just knew it. Somehow, he'd found out that she and Jon were meeting here tonight and had decided to gatecrash.

Jon was looking from one to the other in surprise, much like Leonie had that time in Monterey, she thought.

'Mind if I join you guys? Seems pretty full here,' Seth said, pulling out the unoccupied chair alongside Jon, as if they were all old friends. Then as if to once again highlight to Alex the differences between the two men, he bent down and patted the Dalmatian with relaxed ease. 'Hey, big fella.'

'Um . . .' Jon looked at Alex, urging an explanation.

'So aren't you going to introduce me to your friend?' Seth was saying now, not even bothering to hide the smug amusement in his tone.

Alex glared at him through narrowed eyes. 'This is Jon, my boyfriend. Jon, this is Seth who, I think I might have mentioned before, is my ex-husband.'

'Ex-husband? I don't think so,' Seth corrected, shaking Jon's hand as if they were old friends but if they'd been dogs, his leg would have been well and truly cocked.

'Um, pleasure meeting you.' Jon's expression was dark and as Alex watched him squirm beneath Seth's grasp, she couldn't tell if it was with discomfort, or actual pain.

'Pleasure's all mine,' Seth replied, beaming mischievously at Alex.

Alex was furious. 'I cannot *believe* you gate-crashed my date like that!' When a few minutes later Jon excused himself to use the restroom, she let Seth have it with both barrels.

'Don't know what you're talking about,' he said, feigning innocence. 'I just happened to be passing by when I saw you guys sitting outside.'

'Don't give me that. It was no coincidence. How did you know?'

'Know what?' His amused and blatantly self-satisfied expression made her want to slap him.

'That I'd be here tonight. Don't bother trying to deny it, Seth, I *know* you did this on purpose.'

He shrugged offhandedly. 'I guess Leonie might have mentioned it.'

'What?' She was going to *kill* Leonie. 'When did she tell you that?'

'I called by your place earlier but you weren't in, so I went upstairs to see if she knew where you were.'

Alex couldn't understand why Leonie would have volunteered this information, but knowing Seth it was likely she hadn't *volunteered* anything, no doubt he'd managed to wrangle it out of her somehow!

When Jon returned to the table, she met his gaze and tried her utmost to convey an apology while they tried to finish the rest of their food in peace – impossible with Seth yakking on as if they all got together on a regular basis.

'So what do you do for a living then, Seth?' Jon asked eventually.

'Actually, I'm sort of between jobs right now–'

'Between jobs?' he repeated chuckling. 'You're kidding, right? Because I really don't think I've ever heard that from anyone over twenty-five.' Seth's face reddened with anger or embarrassment, Alex wasn't quite sure. Clearly Jon wasn't going to let him get away with hijacking their date so easily!

'So, would you like to share some of our food, seeing as things must be tight for you right now?' he continued gravely.

Seth shook his head. 'No thanks, doc, I find I generally don't have to rely on money to get what I want.' He might have been speaking to Jon but his gaze rested squarely on Alex.

'Right. Well, let me know how that works out for you.' Jon picked up a slice of pizza and took a bite out of it.

'OK, well, I guess we should order some dessert!' Alex blurted, unable to stand any more of this male swagger. For Christ's sake, they were like a couple of silverback gorillas squaring up to one another!

She and Jon finished their meal in silence, while Seth remained sitting across from them, his expression indolent.

Eventually, Jon pushed away his plate. 'I'm sorry, Alex, but I'd better be going,' he said, putting a hundred-dollar bill on the table – way more than the bill plus tip warranted. 'I'm on an early shift tomorrow morning.'

'So soon? But it's Friday night!' Seth exclaimed exaggeratedly.

'Yes, well, unfortunately brain surgery doesn't lend itself to sociable hours.' Jon's expression was tight.

Alex stood up. 'I'll come with you,' she said, only too eager to get away.

'Honey, the guy just said he has an early start tomorrow,' Seth protested, and Alex felt like she was going to explode, 'so I'm sure the last thing he needs is you keeping him up late. Right, doc?'

'Butt out, Seth,' she grunted, but because neither of them could really argue Seth's point, Jon simply nodded. 'I'll call you tomorrow?' he said, and when his gaze met hers Alex tried again to convey her own frustrations about it all.

She stood up from the table and gave him a long lingering (and very obvious) kiss on the lips. 'Thanks for dinner. I had a great time.'

Jon smiled. 'My pleasure. See you soon.'

'Nice meeting you, doc. Hope we bump into one another again sometime,' Seth called after him, which to Alex sounded ominously like a promise.

Once Jon had left she turned on Seth again. 'Who do you think you are, my father, or something? And don't think I didn't notice you trying to provoke Jon. He's a good guy.'

'A good guy? What about those cheap shots he laid on me just there? *And* he sent you flowers for Christ's sake!'

'Well, you deserved it and I told you, he didn't know about my hay fever. He'd hardly have done it on purpose. He's a doctor, remember?' Alex grabbed her purse and stood up to leave.

Seth got up too. 'Yeah, so I keep hearing.'

'And what's that supposed to mean?' she asked, marching down the street ahead of him.

'It means that I can't figure out why you're with this guy, Alex. He's about as interesting as watching paint dry. Come on, I bet he's never even been to a forty-niners game!'

'It's none of your business why I'm with him, and so what if he's never been to a stupid football game. Too busy saving people's lives maybe?'

'Of course, I forgot, he's a doctor,' Seth's voice was dripping with sarcasm. 'Let me guess, he's got a mansion in Pacific Heights and a boathouse in Sausalito, he drives a Hybrid and donates generously to charity. Come on, Alex, this guy isn't you!'

Alex whirled around to face him. 'And what the hell would you know about it?' she retorted hotly. 'For your information Jon is wonderful. He's kind, hugely considerate, treats me like a lady and, most importantly, doesn't jump into bed with every female in close radius.'

'Oh, so we're back to that now, are we?' Seth snapped. 'Alex, how many times do I have to tell you . . .' He shook his head. 'Hell, I don't even know why I'm bothering; you wouldn't believe me back then so why would you believe me now.'

'Because it doesn't add up, that's why!' He was right; Alex didn't believe him. And she couldn't understand why he still insisted on making a fool of her by refusing to admit the truth. 'You told me you were going out on the boat. What, so diving trips extended to Ruby Skye too?'

'I know I shouldn't have lied about going to the club, and you're right I was an asshole to do that. But me and the guys had a couple of beers and, well . . . I thought you'd get on my case for staying out late. Look, I know what you saw, but that's all there was too it and—'

'But you're *still* an asshole, Seth!' she cried, refusing to listen. 'And tonight is just another example of that! You knew I was meeting Jon here, so you decided to come along and make things difficult, just because you could. This is just a game to you, isn't it?' she said, running a hand through her hair in frustration.

It was becoming too much. First, there was the huge step of getting over Seth and involved with Jon, and just when she'd done that, just as she'd got her life back on an even keel, Seth had sent her emotions into turmoil when she met him in Monterey. And as if that wasn't enough, now there was all this talk about him supposedly wanting to 'try again', when deep down Alex knew he didn't mean a word of it. Why did he have to keep messing with her head like this? Small wonder she'd automatically assumed the Valentine flowers were from him when it was exactly the kind of thing he'd do!

She turned to look at him. 'Seth, up until two weeks ago

I didn't know if you were alive or dead because you didn't have the decency to let me know where you were. Then when we bump into each other, and you find out I'm seeing someone else, you appear at my doorstep and tell me you want to start over. Do you think I'm stupid? Do you think I can't see what you're doing here?'

'All I'm doing is—'

'All you're doing is the same thing you've always done, which is mess me around! I've moved on. Why can't you give me that at least?'

'I don't know what you mean.'

'I mean, why can't you just let me be happy? Before, as soon as things got crazy, you took off and left me to deal with everything on my own. And now to add insult to injury you can't even let me have closure.'

Seth was silent for a while and when he spoke again, his tone held none of his usual bravado. 'By that you mean the divorce.'

'Yes. This might be all a big game to you but it isn't to me,' she said, her tone wavering. 'I'm thirty-three years old, Seth, and I've already got baggage from a first marriage. I don't want to deal with it anymore and I'm tired of waiting around for it to be finished. I want to move on with my life. I need you to help me do that.'

'You really want to go through with this?'

She looked at him, willing him to take her seriously. It was the only way she could ever truly rid herself of the pain he'd caused. 'I've never been more serious about anything in my life. What, did you really think I went to all that trouble to find you for nothing?'

Seth seemed unmoved. 'So you can be free to marry the doc, I suppose.'

'It hasn't come to that, and I don't know if it will,' she said honestly. 'Anyway, it doesn't matter either way. For as long as I'm married to you, on paper or otherwise, I can't move on. I want a clean slate, Seth. And I can't have that until you agree to let me go.'

His gaze held firm and for a brief moment, she thought he was about to agree. But then his expression darkened. 'Well, I'm sorry but it's not that simple.'

'What?' she said, shocked.

'This might surprise you but I have a lawyer too, and according to him, that no-fault divorce application your lawyer just filed isn't valid.'

Alex's thoughts whirled. 'What are you talking about? Of course it's valid. California law states I don't have to prove you were unfaithful and we have no property, no children, no assets to dispute . . .'

'Well, that's where you're wrong,' he replied, eyeing her triumphantly. 'Actually, there is one asset we both share, and until we can come to agreement about that, the petition doesn't stand.'

'What asset . . . ?' But almost as soon as she said the words, Alex had figured it out. 'The Mustang,' she gasped.

'Yep. So until we come to some kind of agreement about ownership, officially our assets *are* in dispute.'

No way. He was *not* getting her beloved car. Not after all the sweat and effort she'd put into it – well truthfully what they'd both put into it, but that wasn't the point. Seth *knew* how much she adored that car – he wasn't seriously thinking of taking it from her?

'But you bought me that car for my birthday!' she cried, maddened beyond belief. How the hell did he come up with this stuff? 'So it's mine.'

'Actually, in the eyes of the law, it's a shared asset by way of our marriage,' he told her smugly. 'So I guess we'll have to try and come to some kind of agreement. Only problem is this could take some time . . .'

At that very moment, Alex didn't think she had ever, *ever* in her entire life so badly wanted to murder someone.

Chapter 22

My love,

I know I'm probably the last person you want to hear from, but I just wanted to let you know how sorry I am. You have to know that I would never do anything to hurt you, at least not intentionally, but I made a big mistake, a huge mistake this time.

I realise there's no going back, and I'm not asking for that; I just wanted to let you know how much I regret what happened, and how I wish from the bottom of my heart it never happened, or that I hadn't caused it. But it did, and it's all my fault, and I would do anything to have the chance to go back and undo it all. But I can't.

I know I don't have any right to ask, but I hope you're OK? I'm really not sure what else to say. Just know that I never meant to hurt you, and I'm so very, very sorry.

Please forgive me.

Leonie sat by the windowsill, and tucked the letter into the envelope.

It was still driving her crazy trying to figure out what had happened with Nathan and Helena, and despite her and Alex's best attempts, they now seemed to have hit a real dead end in trying to find either of them. Despite herself, she'd been reluctant to read through any more of the letters once Alex had suggested that they should leave well enough alone, but at the same time, it was hard it resist.

Was her friend right? she wondered now. Should they just stay out of this whole situation and give up trying to reunite the couple?

After all, Leonie knew better than most that there were some situations that just couldn't be fixed, and some actions that couldn't be undone. And for the umpteenth time since it all happened, she wished she'd had the presence of mind to foresee what was coming down the line for her and Adam.

Especially when things really began to crumble . . .

Dublin: Nine months earlier

It was a late Thursday evening and Leonie was home later than usual, having decided to do a spot of late-night shopping in town.

Letting herself into the apartment, she was struck by how quiet things seemed. Although Adam was usually home from work well after her, she'd sent him a text earlier letting him know that she'd be a little bit later today, so he might need to start preparing dinner himself. But it seemed he hadn't returned yet as the living room blinds were still down and Leonie figured she must have forgotten to open them before she left this morning.

'Hi.' The voice came so unexpectedly she almost jumped out of her skin.

'Adam, yikes, you frightened the life out of me!' she said laughing, but almost immediately, realised that something wasn't right. Adam was sitting rigid on the sofa and staring into the distance, the room practically in darkness.

'Hey, what's wrong?' she said, opening the blinds and flooding the room with early evening light. It was only then that she saw his face.

'Adam?' she asked again, worried now. He looked terrible, his expression was ashen and his bright blue eyes were devoid of their usual sparkle. My God, Leonie thought, stricken with terror, was he ill or something?

'You didn't hear?' he replied, his tone flat and zombie-like.

'Hear what?' She stood rooted to the spot, afraid to move. 'What's going on, Adam, you're scaring me.'

'It was all over the news this evening, I thought you'd have heard.'

At this, Leonie felt a jolt of relief. Well, whatever the problem was, it couldn't be health-related. 'To be honest, work was a bit mad today, I had lunch at my desk and afterwards I went shopping, so—'

'It's Microtel,' he interjected, and then she heard the catch in his voice. 'They're gone.'

'What do you mean, "gone"?' she frowned. 'Gone where? Adam you're not making any sense.'

Adam's tone was wooden and the words came slowly. 'The company I've been with for the last seven years is going out of business. They called a meeting this morning to tell us that they're going into liquidation.' He turned to look at her, his face white. 'It's all over, Lee. As of this morning, I'm officially unemployed.'

'What?' Leonie was flabbergasted. It was probably the last thing she'd expected. 'But they can't just do that, surely? What about a redundancy package, or least some more notice to give you time to find something else . . .'

He shook his head. 'It doesn't work like that. They have no obligation to do anything for us now. It's over and that's all there is to it.'

Leonie looked at him, trying to take in the implications of what he was saying. He'd worked at the Microtel plant for years and as far as they were both concerned, probably would for life. His current engineer's position was a senior one and the pay was great. How had this happened?

'I don't get it . . .'

'I didn't either at first. But I've had all day to get used to it, and believe me, it's happening. I'm out of a job.'

She sat down beside him on the sofa and put her arms around him. 'Love, I'm so sorry. I wished you'd phoned to let me know—'

'I was in shock, Lee, we all were. You should have seen everyone's faces at the meeting this morning. We were stunned. Sales were up, so as far as we knew Microtel was solid. We never saw it coming.'

'I can't understand it,' she said. 'If sales were up then why . . . ?'

Adam ran a hand through his hair. 'I don't either. All I know is that for the first time in my life I have no job to go to. And it's not a nice feeling.'

'Oh Adam, don't think like that, you'll drive yourself crazy. Yes, this is an awful blow, a terrible blow, but we'll get through it. You'll find another job soon, I'm sure of it. You're very well qualified, and have so much experience—'

'Yeah, me and all the other engineers that were laid off this morning,' he said bitterly.

Leonie bit her lip. So it mightn't be that easy to find a position elsewhere that quickly, but at the moment there really was no point in Adam stressing about it. OK, so the timing couldn't be much worse, what with the mortgage on the new apartment and the expense of the wedding, but this was a just a setback, a major setback mind you, but nothing they couldn't deal with.

'Please don't let this get you down too much. Yes, it's a big shock, but it's not the end of the world. We'll be fine, I know we will.' While her salary was nowhere near the level Adam's had been, it would certainly tide them over for a couple of months at least. 'We'll just have to tighten our belts and cut down on a few things here and there until we get back on our feet, OK?'

Adam shook his head. 'I'm sorry, Lee, this isn't the way things should be.' He put his head in his hands 'God, I feel like such a loser.'

'Hey, you stop that right now,' she scolded him. 'None of this is your fault, it's just one of those things, and there's certainly no point torturing yourself about it. What you need to do now is take a bit of a breather, let it all sink in and then come back fighting.'

'I know.' Adam looked up, his expression so full of self-doubt and uncertainty that Leonie's heart went out to him. For as long as she'd known him he'd been so confident and sure of himself, and it was now hugely troubling seeing him vulnerable and afraid.

'What's done is done and we can't change it,' she told him as they talked about it some more over dinner. 'What we *can* do is control how we react to it.'

'I'm sorry for being such a wuss about all this,' he said. 'It's just I've never really had to worry about money or where it's coming from. I've had a job since I left college and was so sure things would just keep going as normal.'

'Maybe you were complacent, I suppose we both were. But try and look at the positives here. We've still got one good salary coming in, enough to cover the mortgage and our living expenses, for a while at least.' She set down her fork. 'But perhaps it might be no harm to consider postponing the wedding, at least for—'

'No way,' Adam interjected firmly, his mouth set in a hard line. 'I don't want that. It's six months away – I'll have another job by then, surely? I'll make bloody sure I do anyway. No, it would kill me to have to do that to you.'

Leonie was heartened by his determination, but at the same time they needed to be practical. 'Well, as long as you know that I have no problem with it being delayed a little longer if needs be. The here and now is what matters.'

'Thanks, Lee,' Adam said, reaching across the table for her hand, 'I don't know what I'd do without you.'

Afterwards, they sifted through their most recent bank and credit card statements, trying to ascertain where they could make some cutbacks.

'Well, at least the car is sorted,' Adam pointed out with some relief, having paid upfront for his Alfa Romeo two years before.

Leonie picked up their joint bank statement. 'I suppose I should cancel my *Heat* subscription and stop buying so many books . . .' The rest of her sentence trailed off as she realised something. 'Adam, what about Andrea's maintenance payments, and Suzanne's pocket money? We can hardly keep those up now, can we? Not now you've lost your job?'

Adam blanched. 'Oh God, I haven't even thought about that,' he said stricken once again. 'What am I going to do?'

'Well, you'll have to discuss this with Andrea, but the way I see it, she can't possibly expect us to keep paying out the same kind of money for maintenance. Suzanne's pocket money is a luxury we can no longer afford.'

Adam looked deeply ashamed and Leonie's heart went out to him.

'We'll all have to make some sacrifices, at least temporarily,' she said trying to choose her words carefully. She hoped Adam agreed with her because there was no way – no *way* they could continue to support two households at the same level now.

'I'm not really sure if we *can* stop her maintenance payments though,' Adam pointed out. 'What if she ends up taking me to court or something?' He ran a hand through his hair, and Leonie could see that he was becoming more and more distraught by the minute.

'Well, I'm not suggesting we stop paying maintenance completely, but if you and I have to cut back because of this situation, then surely it's only right that Andrea does too?' she argued, trying to be reasonable.

'I suppose. I just really don't know what to do . . .'

'Well I do,' she said firmly. 'Until you get sorted with something else, I'll be the only one bringing in a salary, and our first priority needs to be to ourselves, as a couple.'

Adam nodded. 'I know. I'll give her a call later to talk things through,' he said and Leonie was relieved he seemed to understand that there was no other choice.

'You've got to be joking, Adam!' Even sitting two feet away from him on the sofa, Leonie could hear Andrea's outraged squeals on the other end of the line.

'There's nothing I can do, Andi, you must have heard about it on the news.' Adam's gaze met Leonie's and he shook his head exasperated. 'I know, and I'm sorry but it means we'll all have to make some sacrifices – at least in the short term. It's not ideal but what can you do? Yes, of course we'll be able to contribute, just not at the same level and . . . what? Why?'

Moving the receiver away from his ear, he frowned and offered the phone to Leonie. 'She wants to talk to you.'

Leonie raised an eyebrow. What did Andrea want with her? 'Hello?' she said into the mouthpiece with some hesitation.

'This is totally unacceptable,' the other woman began in her usual whiny voice. 'It's an outrage in fact.'

Leonie was mildly surprised that Andrea seemed to be just as upset about the plant closure as they were. Perhaps she'd misjudged her after all. 'I know, it's shocking isn't it, but—'

'Well I'm telling you now I don't like it. I don't like the way you're trying to sideline Suzanne like this. I always expected it mind you, but—'

At this Leonie's eyes widened. So much for her understanding! 'Andrea, I have never once tried to sideline her, she's always been welcome here. But Adam lost his job today! Do you hold me responsible for that too?' At this, her fiancé's head snapped up angrily.

'I certainly think you're prepared to use the situation to your advantage. It's obvious you've always had a problem with us, and this is the perfect opportunity to rub our noses in it.'

Shaking with anger, Leonie let Adam take the phone from her. How dare she? To think that the silly wagon had the gall to try and blame *her* for this? Didn't she realise that if it wasn't for her salary she and her precious daughter would be getting nothing at all?

'That was totally out of order, Andrea . . .' Now Adam was back on the phone trying to appeal to his ex's better nature.

'I'm sorry,' he said afterwards, sounding utterly deflated. 'She's being completely unreasonable.' He put both hands up to his face. 'I'm so sorry I caused all this, Lee.'

'It's not your fault,' Leonie tried again to reassure him, but inwardly she was very worried indeed.

If Adam was finding all of this hard to handle now, how on earth would they get through it when times really got tough?

Chapter 23

My darling Helena,

I'm sorry but I just had to write to you again, as I badly need to reach out to someone now and you're the only one who might be able to understand.

It's getting tough here now, and sometimes I feel very lonely and incredibly afraid. It helps to think that there's someone out there, someone who understands me, although I guess you still haven't come to terms with what I've done or the decisions I've made. My love, I haven't come to terms with that either. And the worst part of it all is you were so right. This is a crazy place, a crazy situation and I really shouldn't be here – nobody should be here.

Just please try to understand that no matter where I am, or what I'm doing, I'm always thinking of you.

Please Forgive Me.
Nathan

Alex was on her way out for an early evening run, when she was waylaid by Seth, who was sitting on the bottom step outside the house.

'Hello there, stranger.'

'What are you doing here?' she asked warily. She didn't

want to talk to him, still found it hard to even *look* at him after that cheap trick he'd pulled with the car. Doug had advised that if Seth was planning to kick up a stink it was probably best for them to come to some kind of agreement about it, but the car was her baby and Alex wasn't going to give it up without a fight. So instead, she'd asked her lawyer to see if he could find some way round the shared asset situation, given that Seth had willingly bought it for her as a gift. Doug had told her he'd do what he could, but until this was sorted, Alex's divorce plans had once again ground to a halt.

Seth smiled as if reading her thoughts. 'Don't worry – it's nothing to do with us. I just found something today that I thought might be of interest to you.'

'Like what? And why not just use the phone?'

'I didn't think you'd pick up if you knew it was me,' he said, making a pretty good point. 'It's about that guy you and Leonie are looking for: Nathan.'

Coincidentally, Leonie had only that day shown her another one of his letters, but this – like the others – revealed little about where the guy was or what he was writing about, and she knew Leonie was becoming frustrated at the lack of progress.

'Well, I was just on my way out.' Alex indicated her running attire of shorts and trainers. 'But I'm sure Leonie would . . .'

'I checked. She's not in, and it's no problem – I could do with the exercise,' he said, falling into step alongside her. 'Fancy heading down by the Presidio?'

The popular city park bordering the Pacific was where they'd usually jogged back when they were together, and exactly where Alex had been heading. A huge playground of running trails, it was one of her favourite places for a run in the Bay Area.

'OK,' she agreed, naturally suspicious of his motives, but

at the same time interested to hear what he had to say. 'So what did you find out?'

'Well, you know I'm back working at the dive shop,' he said, jogging alongside her and Alex nodded. 'Well, I was down there yesterday looking through some of our PADI paperwork from last year, and I came across the name Nathan Abbott. I only noticed it because I heard you guys mention it recently, otherwise it wouldn't have meant anything.' When she didn't react, he went on. 'Assuming it's the same guy, it means he must have gone out on a dive with the company at some stage.'

'When was this?' she asked between breaths. 'I mean, what date was the paperwork?'

'Mid-March sometime last year. I thought it might help.'

'Good lead and I'll check it out, but chances are it's not our guy,' Alex said, explaining how they'd since learned that while Abbott was Helena's surname, it was likely that it wasn't Nathan's.

'Was she listed too by any chance?'

'Helena Abbott?' Seth frowned. 'Not that I noticed. I could check though.' He seemed uncommonly eager to please, she realised. Maybe he'd since recognised that the thing with the Mustang was a cheap shot.

'Thanks for that, it gives us something else to go on anyway. Leonie will be pleased.'

'What gives with her and those letters anyway?' Seth asked. 'She seems kind of fixated by them.'

'She is, and I can't say I understand why. It's just a bunch of letters after all. But I think she's a bit of a romantic at heart.'

Seth smiled. 'Whereas you, on the other hand, are a cynic.'

Alex kept running, the beginnings of a grin on her face. 'I guess I am.'

'You don't think this guy deserves another chance?'

'Well, I don't know what he's done, so how can I decide if he deserves another chance or not?'

'But it sounds like he really loves this girl though, doesn't it?'

'Well, maybe he should have thought of that before he did something stupid.' She looked sideways at him. 'Just checking we're still talking about Nathan here, right?'

Seth was all innocence. 'Of course.'

Stepping up the pace, they continued jogging in silence for a while as they made their way towards the park entrance via Lombard Street. It was a beautiful evening and the park was busy with families, dog-walkers and lots of tourists. As if by rote, Alex and Seth cut across Lincoln Boulevard and headed straight for the northern end of Crissy Field to the coastal trail, which offered sweeping vistas of the Pacific Ocean and the Marin Headlands.

'You know, I really missed this,' Seth said after a while, as up ahead the Golden Gate Bridge loomed. 'In Miami, most of the time it was too damn hot to run any great distance.'

'I can imagine.' Alex wasn't sure if she wanted to talk about what he did or didn't get up to in Miami, seeing as he hadn't bothered sharing any information about it up to now. 'Although I would have thought the whole laidback Caribbean lifestyle suited you perfectly.'

'It did for a while I guess. Still, I always knew I'd be back – this is practically home, after all.' Then, slowing his pace considerably, he grinned. 'But whatever about being out of practice, I think I'm also a little out of shape! Breather?'

'Sure.' Alex slowed alongside him beneath the bridge and they both paused for a moment listening in silence to the thud-thud of traffic overhead, while below whitecaps crashed against the shore. Then, once he'd got his breath back, they took off again, this time at a more leisurely pace.

'Leonie seems like a nice girl,' he said after a couple of minutes.

'She is.'

'So what's her story then?'

'Her story?'

'Yeah. I mean, I know that she moved here a couple of months back and works in a flower store, but what's she doing here in the first place? Clearly there's something else going on there, isn't there?'

'I don't know too much about it, to be honest.' It was interesting that Seth's conclusions were pretty much the same as hers, although Alex wasn't going to admit as much to him.

'Yeah, I mean how does an Irish girl wind up halfway across the world for no particular reason?'

'How does anyone wind up anywhere? There's nothing unusual about it as far as I'm concerned and even if there was, it's absolutely none of my business.'

'So you *do* think there's more to her than meets the eye!' he teased, and Alex cursed herself for being so easy to read. 'My guess is she's running from something.'

No shit Sherlock, she agreed silently. 'Probably a guy. It's nearly always a guy.'

'Of course it is,' Alex drawled. 'What else *could* it be? I mean, it's not as though our lives revolve around anything else, is it?'

'OK, OK, maybe that's a bit too simple. But when I was talking to her that time in Monterey, before you came along—'

'When you were flirting with her, you mean.'

Seth suppressed a smile. 'Anyway, I got the sense that she doesn't trust people too easily.'

'Or maybe she just proved herself immune to your charms?' Alex couldn't resist taunting him.

He shook his head. 'Gimme a break, Alex, I'm just telling you what I think, that's all. As I said, she's a nice girl and I think all this stuff with the letters is more than just a passing interest on her part.'

Alex was now genuinely interested in hearing his take on it too. 'What do you mean?'

'I just think they could have taken on some kind of extra significance where she's concerned. Maybe she identifies with what's going on with that couple because she's been through something similar herself.'

Alex thought about it and decided it made some sense. Leonie did seem uncommonly fixated on reuniting the couple in the letters, irrespective of knowing what actually happened between them. She recalled how disappointed she'd been when the Helena Abbott they'd encountered in Monterey didn't seem to be the woman they were looking for, and how determined she still was to find either one of the couple, despite Alex's advice to leave well enough alone.

'She's certainly taken with their story, I'll give you that,' she said to Seth. 'And she'll be over the moon if she can get to the bottom of this. But as for her going through something similar, I have no idea.' She resolved to try and broach the subject again with her sometime, assuming that Leonie wanted to talk about it of course. Chances were she'd run away to put her problems behind her rather than confront them head on.

'Well, either way, she certainly comes across as a romantic old soul,' Seth said. He gave her another sideways glance. 'And speaking of romance, how are things going with Doctor Love?'

Alex stiffened. 'Fine, thank you.'

'Only fine? That doesn't sound so great to me.'

'Seth, knock it off, OK? I don't want to talk to you about this now – or ever, for that matter.'

He flashed a wide grin. 'I'm sorry I just couldn't resist. Don't mind me, I think you guys make a great couple.'

She smiled, despite herself. 'Sure you do.'

'No, honestly, Alex, I really do. If you're happy, I'm happy.'

'Funny how you didn't seem to think about that before you disappeared down to Miami,' she said, the words out of her mouth before she could stop them. Damn it, she hadn't planned on the conversation taking that turn.

Seth drew up short, panting. 'It wasn't like that,' he said gently. 'Things were crazy, and we both needed space . . .'

'Well, you certainly gave me that,' she said, unable to keep the bitterness out of her voice.

'Alex . . .'

'Anyway, it'll all be over soon,' she said brightly, unwilling to discuss it any further.

'It will,' Seth agreed, but there was an edge to his tone that made her worry if he had something else up his sleeve.

Chapter 24

On Monday morning, Leonie was at Flower Power inputting credit card details into the store terminal when she got a call.

'It's for you,' Marcy said, handing her the cordless phone, 'some crazy woman from Ireland.'

Leonie frowned in confusion, wondering who on earth would be calling her here, and tentatively she held the receiver to her ear. 'Hello?'

'I'm coming to see you!' Grace said excitedly down the line. 'I have my ticket booked and everything.'

'What? Where?'

'To San Francisco, where do you think? I'm sick to the teeth of hearing about Alex and Marcy and all these people I know nothing about. And I miss you. So I said to Ray, forget the family holiday – honestly I think we'd be better off waiting until the kids are older and a bit less, well, mad, I suppose, but Ray knew I needed a break so he offered to stay home to mind them and suggested I go over to you for a long weekend instead. Can you believe that? If I didn't know better, I'd swear he got hit over the head or something but I'm not about to look a gift horse in the mouth, so I checked the website last night and got a flight out for the Thursday after next!'

Leonie, who'd been wondering if Grace would ever take a

breath, couldn't believe what she was hearing. Grace was coming to San Francisco! And soon!

'I can't believe it . . . I mean, this is fantastic! I don't know what to say. But Grace,' she added then, her tone softening, 'I know I sounded a bit down the last time we talked but please don't think I ever expected you to—'

'Feck it, Leonie, we've been friends for donkey's years, and friends are supposed to be there for each other in times of need, aren't they? Now, of course it wasn't *my* fault that you decided to up sticks and fly half way across the world, but like they say if Muhammad won't come to the mountain . . .'

Leonie felt tears in her eyes. She was unbelievably touched that Grace was prepared to come all this way just to be there for her. And in truth, the timing couldn't be better. She had been a bit down in the dumps over the last week or so, what with hitting a complete dead end with the letters, and for some reason starting to rethink and relive everything that had happened back home.

'How long will you be staying?'

'Just for a long weekend – until the Monday. I couldn't leave Ray with the twins for that long. Don't get me wrong, *I'd* love to, but he'd be up the walls for any more than a weekend and would probably have packed his own bags by the time I got back. So just the four days. But someone told me that staying in my own time zone will avoid the jetlag so if I do that I should be grand.'

Leonie had to smile at this. 'You do know that we're eight hours ahead here?'

'Exactly, it's ideal. I'll have no problem getting up at the crack of dawn whereas in reality it'll be like having an Irish lie-in. And I don't get too many of those either, I can tell you.'

'True.' Leonie smiled indulgently, deciding not to point

out that by the same reckoning, Grace would also be in bed by teatime.

'So is it OK if I stay with you? I know you said your place is small, but the ticket was pricey enough, without a hotel bankrupting me too—'

'Are you mad? I wouldn't *dream* of having you stay in a hotel! Yes, yes, of course you'll stay here – you can have the bedroom and I'll take the couch and—'

'Not at all, sure you know me, I'll throw myself down anywhere,' Grace said in her usual easy-going way, which merely reminded Leonie again how much she'd been missing her and how brilliant it would be to see her. 'Now, I'm not looking forward to ten hours on my own on the plane, but won't it be a bit of peace and quiet for once? And I've never been in America before so I'm dying to see what all the fuss is about, not to mention putting faces to the names of all the people you keep talking about.'

Leonie grinned. It would be fantastic to be able to introduce her to Alex and Marcy. And speaking of Marcy, when she got off the phone, she'd take a look at the roster to see how things were fixed here for the weekend of Grace's visit. She knew she was off that Friday but not so sure about Saturday. But as Flower Power closed on Sundays, even if she did have to work one day out of the weekend she'd still have loads of time to spend with her friend. And no better woman than Grace to entertain herself in any case.

'I still can't believe you're coming!' she told her, delighted. 'I can't wait to see you and we'll have such a brilliant time, I promise you.'

'I can't wait either,' Grace said, sounding just as enthusiastic. 'USA – here I come!'

The afternoon Grace was due to arrive, Leonie booked a

Lincoln town car to collect her from the airport. Although they were a cheap and a relatively common means of transport from the airport, she knew her friend would get a huge kick out of travelling to the city in a big plush American car and it would be a great start to her first visit to the States.

While waiting at arrivals, she thought she would burst with anticipation, she was so looking forward to seeing Grace. The last time she'd seen her, Leonie had been in a pretty fraught situation, so it would be wonderful to be together now in much happier circumstances.

After a few minutes Grace appeared through the crowd, laden down with luggage and grinning from ear to ear. Dropping her suitcases, she launched herself at Leonie, and the two hugged as if they hadn't seen one another in years.

'I can't believe you're actually here!' Leonie said, feeling more emotional than she'd anticipated. 'And you look fantastic, have you lost weight?' Typically, Grace had made no effort whatsoever with her appearance, her fair hair fell in heavy strings around her face and she wore not a scrap of make-up, but still she looked wonderful.

'Well, if I have, that flight alone would have accounted for a stone at least, what with the manky food they gave us,' she said rolling her eyes. 'And as for the drink . . . I was disgusted. Here I was planning to load up on freebies to help pass the time and then your woman puts her hand out looking to be paid.'

'So a good flight then?' Leonie grinned.

'A long flight, Lee, honestly I don't know how you do it. I was bored out of my skull watching that teeny little plane on the screen; it was like it wasn't moving at all.'

'Didn't you read or watch a film?'

'I thought I might, but to be honest I just was too excited to concentrate.' She looked around her trying to take it all in. 'America – I still can't believe I'm here!'

'Me neither, but um . . . how long did you say you were staying again?' Leonie asked, looking down at her two enormous suit-cases. 'No, wait let me guess, you brought the twins too?'

Grace winked. 'You know me,' she said. 'Always come prepared.'

She was full of chatter on the journey from the airport and brimming with great ideas on how to beat the jetlag.

'Staying on Irish time is definitely the way to go,' she assured Leonie. 'I didn't change my watch at all when we landed so if I keep that up I should be fine.'

'OK.' Leonie wasn't about to argue.

'And I want to see and do *everything* and . . . oh, is that the bridge?' she said, her face falling as she pointed out the window of the car. 'It's not very golden at all, is it? I suppose it's true what they say about these things not living up to your expectations.'

'Maybe because that's the *Bay* Bridge,' Leonie told her smiling. 'And don't worry, I doubt you'll be unimpressed when you see the Golden Gate.'

But after being 'disappointed' by her initial glimpse of San Francisco, Grace seemed to very quickly fall in love with everything else about the city. 'Oh my God – a cable car!' she shrieked, upon catching sight of the Powell-Mason car heading downtown, its bell clanging as it went. 'And look . . . lesbians! Oh, I can't wait to tell Ray all about this, he warned me they'd be everywhere!'

'Um, I don't actually think they're lesbians, Grace, just a couple of girls out shopping.'

'Oh.' Her disappointment was palpable. 'Well hopefully we might find a few later.'

'I'll do my best,' Leonie replied with a smile.

A few minutes later, the car dropped them off outside the house in Green Street.

'Oh wow,' Grace enthused, her eyes out on stalks as she got out. 'You live in one of these? But it's like a doll's house! God, I had no idea this place was so pretty, all the hills and the trees and these beautiful houses . . . it's almost like being on Wisteria Lane!'

Leonie smiled as she helped Grace carry her bags up the steps. 'I loved it when I first saw it too.'

Once inside the apartment Grace felt the need to open every door, look inside every cupboard and inspect every piece of furniture. And like Leonie, she was immediately drawn to her beloved bay window. 'Oh, you can see the sea from here and oh. My. God,' she gasped, enunciating the words extra slowly as she caught sight of San Francisco's most famous landmark, which at that moment looked vibrant and luminous against a gorgeous clear blue sky. '*That's* the bridge?'

'That's the bridge,' Leonie repeated, knowing Grace was experiencing the sense of spellbinding awe most people did when confronted in real life by such an iconic structure. 'We can head out and see it tomorrow if you'd like. And take a tour of Alcatraz too maybe, I haven't had a chance to go there myself yet.'

'Hmm, seeing as I've just escaped from my very own Alcatraz,' Grace murmured wryly, 'I just might give that one a miss if you don't mind.'

'Whatever you prefer,' Leonie laughed and switched on the kettle. 'Fancy a cuppa?'

'What – don't you have anything stronger? Or has all this wholesome California lifestyle got to you already?'

Leonie went to the fridge and took out a chilled bottle of Californian bubbly. 'Well, I was planning to wait till later, but what the hell? No time like the present.'

Grace rubbed her hands together like a small child when

Leonie popped the cork. 'This is just fantastic! I still can't believe I'm here – drinking bubbles with you in San Francisco! Oh, it really is beautiful in here, Leonie,' she said looking around. 'Is this your own stuff or was it like this when you moved in?'

'Most of it's my own, but I inherited a few things,' she said, immediately thinking of the letters. But she'd tell Grace about those some other time.

'I love the fireplace, and the ceiling and the floors . . . oh, everything is just fabulous!'

The two continued to chat and sip their drinks as they sat facing each other on the window seat, their backs to the wall while they stared at the sailboats entering and leaving the bay. Grace was completely entranced by the views and the way the city descended in almost higgledy-piggledy fashion towards the water.

'You'd pay a fortune for a view like this in Dublin – not that you'd get anything like this, with the bridge and all the gorgeous houses, and oh, can we try out one of the cable cars? They're probably old hat to you by now, but I'd just *love* to give it a go! And will you show me the flower shop where you work and—'

'Relax, I'll show you anything you want,' Leonie said, grinning at her enthusiasm.

'Good woman! So what'll we do tonight? Are you going to bring me out on the town? I'd love a good night on the tear. Anywhere but an Irish pub though,' she added with a firm shake of her head. 'I swore to myself that I wasn't going to come halfway across the world and then go to an Irish pub . . .'

'Are you sure you want to go out, though?' Leonie looked at her watch. 'It's after two in the morning at home now, and I thought you wanted to stay on your own time.'

Grace stared at her, suddenly realising her grand plan had just been shot to shreds.

'Ah, to hell with it,' she said. 'Don't I have the rest of my life to sleep? But I will tell you one thing – I'm absolutely ravenous after all that travelling. Is there anywhere close by we could go to for a good feed?'

Leonie smiled. 'I think I know just the place.'

Still slightly giggly from the champagne, the two spent the following couple of hours down at the Crab Shack chatting and bantering with Phil and Dan who (luckily) seemed amused with Grace's unbridled delight at them being a couple.

'I know it's San Francisco but, I don't know, I just didn't expect them to be *everywhere*,' she confessed, wide-eyed.

'Come off it, Grace – they're hardly everywhere! And it's not as though we don't get gay couples at home.' But she knew that Grace was just so delighted to be here that she was overstating everything while wholeheartedly throwing herself into the experience.

'So, tell me, how *are* you?' Grace asked meaningfully after the meal, when their chatter had calmed down considerably. She tried to stifle a yawn and despite her protests, Leonie knew that the time difference was gradually starting to get to her.

'I'm great,' she told her breezily. 'As you can probably tell, I love it here.'

'And?'

'And – what? That's about the sum of it really.'

'Oh, come off it, Leonie. This is *me* you're talking to now. You're making it sound like coming here was something that just happened on a whim! What about everything that happened back home – are you trying to tell me you're fine about that now too?'

'Actually, I am,' she replied, a bit uncomfortable about

having to confront this now. But it was the truth of sorts, as she'd been so engrossed in her new life here that she'd almost succeeded in pushing the worst of it to the back of her mind. 'What's the point in dwelling on it? What's done is done and there's nothing anyone can do to change that.'

Grace looked sceptical. 'So you're over it, is that what you're saying?'

'Pretty much, yes. As far as I'm concerned, Adam and I are over and done with and we've both moved on.' She fiddled with the straw in her water glass. 'So, have you heard anything from him recently?' she asked, unsure whether or not she wanted to know the answer.

'No, but then again, why would I? It's not as though I've ever been allowed to tell him anything.'

'Thanks for that, you know. I really do appreciate you not saying anything about where I am.'

Grace yawned again. 'Doesn't mean I agree with it though.'

'Well, then we'll just have to agree to disagree. You think I should have stayed and faced the music, whereas I know I had to go. We're just different that way, I suppose. Anyway, I'll tell you what,' Leonie continued gently, 'why don't we talk about it some other time. You've only just got here, and I'm thrilled that you are so let's not drag things down.'

'It's also part of the reason I'm here though,' Grace reminded her.

'I know and I really appreciate that, but for the moment at least, I think we should just concentrate on showing you a good time.'

Grace yawned again, before finally succumbing to the inevitable. 'Believe me, I'm all for that too. But Lee, do you think we could go home now? I feel like I haven't slept in *days*!'

Chapter 25

The next day was filled with a mixture of sightseeing and shopping. After a good night's sleep on the sofa, Grace was a bundle of energy and raring to go, and following a breakfast of fluffy blueberry pancakes from a deli close by, Leonie took her friend to Flower Power to say hello to Marcy.

'So *you're* the famous Marcy?' Grace said, pumping the older woman's arm enthusiastically. 'I've heard loads about you.'

'Likewise, sweetheart,' Marcy replied. 'Welcome to San Francisco. So how are your two little darlings?'

'Well, if you're calling them "darlings", I think Leonie's definitely been telling you lies!' she grinned. 'And according to what Ray told me on the phone this morning, they haven't changed much while I've been away.'

'I'm sure they're missing you all the same,' Marcy said smiling. 'So what have you two got planned for today then?'

'We thought we'd pop down to Union Square for a bit of shopping and then do some touristy stuff this afternoon,' Leonie said.

'Sounds good. Hard to see everything in such a short visit though. You'll have to come back and see us again sometime, Grace.'

'I'd only be too happy to! But if Leonie came home, then maybe I wouldn't have to,' she said pointedly.

Marcy cocked an eyebrow at Leonie. 'Hey, you're not thinking of running home and leaving me in the lurch now, are you?'

'Absolutely not!' she said shooting Grace a glare. 'You know I wouldn't dream of doing something like that.'

'Good, cos we'd all miss you round here,' Marcy said before adding archly, 'even if you're not so hot at flower arranging.'

'Well, *that* was sensible,' Leonie grimaced, when she and Grace left the shop.

'I know – I'm sorry, I really shouldn't have said that about you coming home. But she's so nice that, to be honest, I kind of forgot she's your boss.'

'She is lovely. But if you like Marcy then you'll really love Alex. She's coming out with us tonight, I think. She had something on with Jon – the guy she's seeing – but is going to try to postpone it.'

'Brilliant, I'm looking forward to that.'

To Grace's delight, they hopped on a cable car down to Union Square, where she went mad buying presents for Ray and the kids in all the shops.

'Oh look!' she gasped, stopping at a souvenir shop to pick up a toddler-size black-and-white striped 'Alcatraz inmate' outfit. 'God almighty, could this be *any* more perfect for my two?'

At around midday, Leonie took her down around Chinatown. As expected, Grace was enchanted by the area's famous Dragon Gate and Grant Avenue with its countless oriental-style buildings, fish markets, stores and restaurants. In Portsmouth Square, they stopped off to watch a session of Tai Chi, while all around elderly men were playing Chinese chess.

'I'm loving this!' Grace grinned. 'But is it just me, or are all these gorgeous smells making you hungry?'

'Well, we're in the right place for that,' Leonie replied, suspecting that if Grace already liked what she'd seen of Chinatown, she should really get a kick out of having dim sum for lunch.

Finding a table at a nearby eatery, she quickly explained the concept to Grace who was at first perplexed by the notion of choosing whatever took her fancy from the little carts of food wheeling past their table. 'So we just point out whatever we want and they give it to us?' she said faintly mystified by the array of grilled, baked or deep-fried meat and shrimp nestled in threes and fours on little bamboo dishes. 'But how do we know what we want?'

'I suppose that's the beauty of dim sum,' Leonie told her, pointing to a portion of what she knew was shrimp dumplings. Following her lead, Grace tentatively chose a dish of lettuce cups stuffed with barbecue pork. 'There's no menu, they'll bring out new stuff from the kitchen every few minutes. Don't worry, you can have as much or as little as you want, they just tot it all up at the end.'

'Wow, Ray would love this!' she said, her confidence growing with each new dish she tried. '*Especially* the idea of eating as much as he wanted – we'd have to lift him out with a crane!'

Leonie smiled at her. 'I'm glad you're enjoying yourself.'

'I'm *loving* it. Lee, I haven't been here twenty-four hours yet and already I'm having a ball! Although to be honest, I don't know if it's the city or just the novelty of actually being able to have an adult conversation.'

She gave a lopsided smile, and right then Leonie sensed that Grace may have felt her absence much more than she realised. It was strange because in recent years (and particularly after the twins were born) she'd always felt that *she* was the one more dependent on their friendship. Grace had always seemed so content and involved with her family that Leonie didn't think that moving away would affect her all that much.

'They're probably all missing you like mad. How is Ray getting on so far?' Grace's husband had phoned first thing that morning and was sending text updates on a regular basis, but Leonie didn't know if they were reassuring or frantic. Knowing Ray it was probably the latter.

'I don't think he knows what's hit him. He has Mammy Niland coming over this evening though, so that'll take the pressure off,' she said referring to Ray's mother. She rolled her eyes. 'The same one will be thrilled not having me around to watch her like a hawk.'

To say that Grace and her mother-in-law didn't get on was an understatement, and Leonie knew that the older woman had never been much help with the twins as she rarely offered to babysit or any other kind of assistance. It was a shame because Grace's own mother had died many years before, and like any new mum her friend craved a support network or someone to turn to.

Now, Leonie realised with some remorse, by moving here she was pretty much guilty of the same offence.

'It'll be good for Ray to know what you do day-in day-out though, won't it?' she said.

'Not that'll it make a blind bit of difference,' Grace said shaking her head fondly. 'But to be fair, it was his suggestion that I get away for a few days. I think he knew I was heading towards my wits' end.'

Leonie looked up, realising for the first time that perhaps there was considerably more to this visit than meets the eye. 'Oh Grace, I'm so sorry, I honestly had no idea you were finding things so tough,' she said, feeling somewhat of a heel.

237

'I know I haven't been much of a friend lately . . .'

'Will you go away out of that, it's nothing to do with you!' Grace wouldn't hear of it. 'I don't know, I suppose I just get a bit . . . and I thought I would never, *ever* say this after the huge effort we had in trying to have them, but sometimes I feel a bit . . . I don't know . . . constrained, maybe? Don't get me wrong, I love Rocky and Rosie to bits and I wouldn't be without them, but—'

'Grace, that's completely understandable and I'm *certain* you're not the first mother to feel that way – nor will you be the last,' Leonie reassured her. 'Having one child must be upheaval enough let alone two at once. And they take up so much of your time it's only natural you'd feel a little bit cut off.' But again, she felt deeply ashamed that she hadn't anticipated this, and was annoyed at herself for leaving Grace in the lurch.

'Ah, don't mind me, I think it's just being here, out on the town without a care in the world and now polishing off dim sum in this lovely city that's bringing this on,' she said dismissing her own concerns. 'You know, I never really did the travel thing when I was younger, so I suppose it's only now I'm seeing the attraction.'

'That's exactly it,' Leonie agreed, now more determined that ever to show her a great time. 'So let's be sure to make the most of it while you're here.'

Later that evening, the girls headed back to Green Street, having spent some of the afternoon at the Golden Gate Visitors' Centre, and the rest of it down by Fisherman's Wharf just people-watching and taking it easy.

At around seven, Alex called up to say hello to Grace, and to Leonie's delight the two seemed to click right from the off.

'Oh my God, Leonie didn't tell me you were like a *model*!' Grace exclaimed when they were first introduced. 'I'll tell you one thing, I'm glad my hubby's not here; I'd have to lock him away!'

'I doubt that very much,' Alex laughed, but Leonie could tell that she was instantly won over by Grace's forthrightness.

'She's married herself, anyway,' she informed her with a mischievous grin, and Alex gave her a look.

'Soon to be divorced though,' she clarified quickly, '*very* soon I hope.'

'Divorced . . . seriously?' Now Grace looked uncomfortable and Leonie realised that she hadn't actually told her anything about the Seth situation. 'Oh, I'm very sorry to hear that.'

'Hey, don't be – it's actually really good news,' Alex told her, but when Grace still looked perplexed she made some attempt to explain. 'It's a long story, but I'm seeing someone new now.'

'Not for long, if the husband has anything to do with it,' Leonie teased, referring to Seth's most recent behaviour, and Grace listened agog while Alex filled her in on the current state of affairs.

'Two men fighting over you – even better,' she said, before adding with mock relief, 'so my Ray wouldn't have had a look-in anyway!'

She and Alex laughed, and Leonie hoped it was the first of many a giggle the three would share that evening.

'So, where will we go tonight?' she asked, when they'd finished much of the initial getting-to-know-you stuff.

Alex shrugged. 'You guys choose – I'm cool with anything.'

She turned to look at Grace, who was now slumped on the sofa looking surprisingly listless. 'Grace? Do you fancy going out?'

Her friend tried to suppress a yawn. 'I'm sorry, I don't know what's wrong with me but at the moment I don't think I could move off this couch if there was a bomb under it.'

'The jet-lag hitting you again?'

She nodded sadly. 'I think so. So much for trying to beat it. I'm still starving though – no fear of me that way.'

'Well, why don't we just get take-out?' Alex suggested. 'I haven't eaten and there's this great place down the street.'

'Sounds like heaven. Would you mind, Lee?' Grace said mournfully. 'I'm sorry but I've no energy for anything else at the moment – at least not until I get some food into me.'

'Fine by me,' she said, thinking this sounded like a very good plan. 'And who knows – maybe you might buck up after a glass or two?'

As it turned out, it only took Grace one glass of wine to buck up, and once she did there was no stopping her. She, Leonie and Alex chatted happily over takeaway and after a few more glasses of Pinot Grigio, Grace got braver and grilled Alex some more about her relationship situation.

'So will you marry the doctor when you've divorced the other fella then?' she said, turning to Alex who was sitting on the sofa alongside her.

'Grace!' Leonie chided, hitting her with a cushion. 'You shouldn't ask personal questions like that.' But then she turned to Alex, curious. 'Will you?'

'Come on, it's too early to even think about something like that,' Alex told them defiantly. 'And anyway, I'm wary of jumping into anything so fast, not after before.'

'I don't know,' Grace said dubiously, taking another mouthful of wine, 'it sounds to me like the ex is still on your mind there somewhere.'

'That's *exactly* what I said!' Leonie agreed vehemently. 'But she won't hear a word of it.'

'Keep saying it all you want, Leonie. Seth is a loser, I told you that from day one.'

'Well, he might be a loser, but I for one wouldn't kick him out of bed for eating crisps,' she giggled, winking at Grace.

'Crisps?'

'Potato chips, sweetheart,' Grace quipped, and Alex looked mystified as the other two fell around laughing.

'You guys are hilarious, you know that?' she said, looking from one to the other. 'A real double act.'

Leonie straightened up. 'Seriously though, Grace, you should see Seth,' she insisted. 'Absolutely *unbelievable*.' Then she shrugged. 'But then again, I suppose Jon's not half bad either . . .'

'Thank you!' Alex exclaimed. 'I was just about to point that out!'

'Aw, do you have any photos?' Grace moaned. 'It's driving me mad not being able to picture who the two of ye are talking about.'

'Actually I do,' Alex said, standing up. 'I've got a picture of Jon and me taken not long ago. And I'm sure there's gotta be one of Seth knocking about somewhere too,' she added gruffly.

When Alex went downstairs to get the photos, Leonie and Grace topped up their respective glasses.

'She's lovely,' Grace said. 'I can see again why you've settled in so well here.'

'She is lovely and I'd be lost without her. But Grace,' she said, her tone growing serious, 'I haven't really told her anything about Adam, so I don't want—'

'Here we go,' Alex said coming back into the apartment. Photos in hand, she flopped back down on the couch beside them.

'Right, now don't tell me which one is which, OK?' Grace

warned. 'Just let me work out which one I'd go for myself.'

'Good idea,' Leonie agreed, giving Alex a knowing look.

Leaning across, she studied the photographs. The first was a beautiful shot of Alex and Jon taken that night at the Palace of Fine Arts, and the other was of her and Seth – looking suntanned and happy on a beach somewhere. Although Alex was smiling in both photos, Leonie was struck by how radiant she looked in the second one, and Seth seemed equally blissful. As she'd only ever witnessed the couple at each other's throats, seeing them so unashamedly happy together was an eye-opener.

'Bloody hell,' Grace was saying. 'The *two* of them are fine things . . . what is this – Melrose Place?' She shook her head, puzzled. 'I don't know, I certainly wouldn't be able to pick one from the other – not that I'd be ever be that lucky though. God almighty, why can't Irish men look like that?'

'Hey, don't say that, Ray is lovely too!' Leonie declared. She pointed to Grace's handbag on the other side of the room. 'Show her.'

'Oh, all right.' Grace grudgingly got up. 'But Alex, I have to warn you, wait until you see the big mucker head on him . . .'

Leonie didn't think she'd ever laughed as much in her life when a giggling Grace took out a photo of her husband and put it alongside the others.

With mussed-up hair and dressed in a too-tight Ireland rugby jersey that stretched over his burgeoning belly, poor Ray looked like he'd just got out of bed. The photo was obviously taken on a boozy night out, and was so utterly at odds with the smooth, tuxedoed Jon or the toned, tanned Seth that it was hilarious. And no one found it more so than Grace herself.

'I'm sorry, I shouldn't be showing you that one,' she

guffawed, when the three photos were lined up side by side. 'He's doesn't usually look that bad, but you have to admit, there is a hell of a difference . . .'

Leonie could tell that Alex found it bemusing that she and Grace found the whole thing so funny, and very graciously she kept quiet on the subject of a comparison.

'He looks like a lovely guy,' she told her. 'And you're really lucky to have someone you can rely on.'

Instantly Grace stopped laughing. 'I am, aren't I?' she said, picking up the photograph and looking at it again. Then she smiled. 'And you're right, he is a lovely guy.'

Watching her two friends, Leonie suddenly felt saddened, realising that by rights, there should be a photo of Adam in there to have a laugh over too. But there wasn't.

'Leonie, are you OK?' Alex asked, spotting her sudden change of mood.

'She's grand,' Grace supplied, an understanding glance passing between the two of them.

But Alex seemed to understand too. 'Goddamn men – why do we even bother?' she said, casting the photographs aside. Then, she picked up the half-empty bottle of wine. 'So, who needs a top-up?'

On Grace's third and final night, she and Leonie went out for dinner, just the two of them. They were in the Stinking Rose, a hugely popular Italian place on Columbus Avenue.

'I can't believe I'm going home tomorrow,' Grace complained, tucking into a starter of garlic-steamed clams. 'The days have just flown by.'

Leonie smiled. 'Well, I hope you enjoyed it.'

'I've loved every second. But Lee, you're not going to stay here for ever though, are you?' she asked. 'I mean, you have to think about coming home sometime.'

She knew this conversation had been brewing all weekend, but it was still difficult to talk about it. 'Maybe, but not now. I'm really enjoying life, Grace, it was the best decision I could have made.'

'Would you not at least tell Adam where you are, though?' she persisted. 'At least if he knew, then maybe—'

'I'd still rather he didn't,' Leonie interjected, pushing her chicken around the plate. Then she sighed. 'Look, I suppose it's hard to explain, and yes, maybe I should make contact or at least give him an idea of where I am, but then what? At least this way, I'm still in control of what happens – even if it's nothing. It was my choice to leave everything behind.'

Grace nodded. 'I think I know what you're saying. Surely you must still care a little bit about him, though?'

A little? Leonie smiled tightly. 'Of course I do, but I also know that after what happened things could never be the same again. There's no going back.'

'Yes, but—'

'Look, Grace. I know that you're only trying to help and I appreciate that, but there's nothing you can say that will change my mind. What happened happened, and no matter what way you look at it, it changed our relationship for ever. There was no way we could get married after all that. I know I couldn't forgive—'

'Yes, but I think *that's* part of the problem. This really isn't about Adam at all is it, Leonie? It's more about you and what you can't do. *You* can't move past it.'

'You're right, I can't,' she admitted honestly. 'So how could I possibly expect him to?' When Grace didn't reply she went on. 'Anyway, from what you're saying, he seems to have moved on just fine without me,' she continued, referring to the fact that Adam hadn't been in touch with Grace recently.

'I wonder how things panned out with Andrea in the end?' her friend mused. 'Do you think they're still—?'

'I don't care,' Leonie said shortly, feeling a physical pang at the mention of the woman's name. 'I'd imagine so or at least, I hope so – for Suzanne's sake, if nothing else.' Then she sighed. 'But I don't think we should ruin your last night by talking about that witch.'

Grace helped herself to another portion of garlic bread. 'So, there's really no talking to you then, is there?'

'Nope,' Leonie said determinedly. 'But,' she continued, deciding now was as good a time as any to broach the subject, 'seeing as you're here, I have a favour to ask.'

Chapter 26

Having seen off Grace at the airport on Monday morning, Leonie took a cab back to the city, her thoughts still full of the conversation they'd had the night before. It was interesting that her friend believed that she and Adam could still possibly have a future together, even with everything that had happened.

Looking back, she herself wished that she had spotted the signs, or recognised the coincidences before everything came to a head. But never in a million years could Leonie have anticipated what was about to happen, and for this she only had herself to blame.

Dublin – Six months earlier

A couple of months after the layoff from the factory, Adam still hadn't found a job. It wasn't for lack of trying; he'd applied to every organisation in the sector he could think of, and registered with every recruitment agency in the city, but to no avail. As a result, he was becoming more and more dejected by the day.

'I just feel so bloody useless,' he complained to Leonie, who by then was almost too tired to argue any different, not when she was coordinating all the evening events she could to claim more overtime and try and keep things going.

After much grumbling on Andrea's part, they'd eventually agreed a substantial reduction in maintenance for her, and had no choice but to put a stop to Suzanne's additional pocket money, something the teenager had been livid about. Even with these savings, things were still very tight indeed.

Adam had since taken over the majority of the housework and cooking (always insisting on washing up afterwards while Leonie tried to stay awake in front of the TV), but as the weeks went by, he gradually became more and more disillusioned, and started to neglect this part of his life, too.

'There was nothing in the fridge, so I thought we'd just get a takeaway,' he said one evening when Leonie came home to find him sprawled across the couch watching TV. The breakfast dishes she'd used that morning still lay unwashed on the countertop, and the living room was strewn with dirty coffee-cups and the remnants of Adam's lunch.

She'd had a busy day at work and was bone-tired, so discovering that he hadn't bothered to clean up, let alone even *attempt* to make dinner was the last straw.

'A takeaway?' she repeated disbelievingly. 'Adam, we can't afford to be wasting money on takeaways, not when I'm barely keeping our heads above water as it is!'

She hadn't meant to sound so bitter and accusatory but she was frustrated and downright annoyed at his lack of effort that she couldn't help it.

He looked at her, clearly wounded. 'So you keep reminding me.'

'Reminding you of what?'

'Of the fact that *you're* keeping our heads above water,' he clarified, and Leonie could have kicked herself for her choice of words. 'But you're the one lucky enough to have a job, aren't you?'

This was another change she'd noticed in him recently, a

growing tendency towards self-pity. It was inevitable, she supposed, but hardly helpful in the circumstances.

'That's not what I was saying,' she argued tiredly. 'I was merely pointing out that takeaways are a luxury we really can't afford at the moment.'

'Oh, come on,' he retorted. 'A couple of quid is hardly going to break the bank.'

She felt her irritation rise again. 'That's not the point, Adam, and you know it. There's no need for us to order in, not when one or either of us is perfectly capable of cooking dinner.' She was trying to choose her words carefully, but a side of her wanted to come right out and tell him to cop on.

'But there's nothing there to cook, I told you that.'

'Then why not go out and get something, Adam? Food doesn't automatically appear in the fridge, you know.'

'Oh, I see,' he said, wounded. 'So now I'm a selfish bastard as well as an unemployed one, is that it?'

'Oh, for goodness' sake!' Leonie exhaled deeply. 'I know you've had a tough time lately, and it must be hard trying to keep going when you've had so many knock-backs, but you have to understand that it's tough for me too. I hate seeing you like this, all depressed and full of negativity, but for both our sakes you have to snap out of it.'

'Snap out of it! Snap out of what exactly? What the hell do you expect me to do, Leonie?'

'Well, there are plenty of things you could be doing around here, like washing the dishes or making dinner, but lately you've decided to just sit around feeling sorry for yourself.' Leonie hated, *hated* berating him like this, but at this point it was a case of having to be cruel to be kind.

Adam stared at her, stung. 'I can't *believe* you think I'm lazy—'

But their discussion was temporarily (and perhaps

fortunately, Leonie thought) cut off by the sound of the telephone. As the handset was nearest to him, Adam answered, while she went through to the bedroom, and tried to calm herself down. Was she awful to talk to him like that? A takeaway would hardly have killed them, would it? But at the same time, he *was* being thoughtless, whether it was intentional or not. The place was in a heap and he hadn't done any housework in days. Not to mention that he didn't seem to truly understand the perilous state of their finances.

The bedroom door opened and Adam's head appeared around it. 'I have to go out,' he said gruffly.

'Oh, where to?'

'Down to Wicklow. That was Suzanne; there's a problem with her computer and she wants me to take a look at it. They were going to call out a repair guy but . . .'

But Andrea knew that this time she couldn't land us with the bill, Leonie finished silently, amazed at the fact that yet again his ex had managed to inveigle her way into their lives. And wasn't her timing just wonderful!

'You're going out now?' she said. 'What about dinner?'

'It's OK, they're having theirs later so Suzanne put my name in the pot,' he told her, before adding meaningfully, 'so no need to worry about me.'

Clearly not, Leonie thought, but despite herself couldn't help but feel very worried indeed.

After that, there followed a multitude of 'little jobs' at Andrea's. The chimney needed cleaning, the roof needed repairing and one time there was a complex issue with the washing machine, all of which required Adam's more frequent presence at his ex's house.

'See how she's manoeuvred this situation to her advantage?' Leonie complained to Grace. It was a Saturday morning and they were having coffee in her friend's kitchen, Adam having yet again been summoned to Andrea's rescue. 'We're no longer paying her usual king's ransom, so she's been forced into finding more imaginative ways to have Adam bow to her every whim.'

'I really don't like the sound of this,' Grace said worriedly. 'It's bad enough that you two aren't getting along at the moment, without *her* being stuck in the middle of it all too.'

Leonie bit her lip. 'I know, but there's nothing I can do to stop it, is there? I can't very well refuse to let Adam help her out – not when I was the one who suggested cutting her maintenance in the first place.'

Adam had said just that when Leonie had tentatively raised the subject of how many odd jobs suddenly needed doing at his ex's house.

'Well, she used to get tradesmen in before but she can't afford that now . . . ' he said, the implication left hanging in the air.

Leonie wanted to retort that for someone who was apparently so strapped for cash, Andrea seemed to have no problem acquiring the new Prada coat she'd been wearing last time she'd dropped Suzanne off, but she didn't want to start another argument. Now she wondered if curtailing Andrea's maintenance payments had been the biggest mistake of her life.

Suzanne had barely spoken to Leonie since they'd reduced her pocket money and, evidently taking her mother's lead, seemed determined to put all the blame on her.

'It's like, so embarrassing,' the teenager had whined during a recent visit. 'What am I supposed to do for clothes? The girls will think I'm such a loser on Saturdays if I don't buy loads in Bershka.'

'Primark has got some great, cutting-edge stuff these days,' Leonie had suggested, but by the murderous look on Suzanne's face she might as well have recommended she wear hand-me-downs. Like Grace, Leonie thought it would do Suzanne good to have to prioritise her spending for a while. The girl had absolutely no concept of the value of money as it was.

'I mean, in our day we were lucky to scrape together enough for a ticket to the pictures, let alone have our own DVD collection,' her friend said and Leonie had to laugh.

'In our day?'

'Well, you know what I mean. There's certainly no way I'll be mollycoddling my two like that. As soon as they're old enough, if they want money, then they'll just have to go out and get jobs for themselves.'

'I agree with you, but Andrea obviously thinks very differently to us. She sees it as Suzanne's due.'

'But that's what I don't understand. Adam's been more than good to them both over the years; it's not as though he has to make up for lost time or anything.'

'I know, but he's a very dedicated father.'

'Maybe more so than the father of my own two!' Grace laughed. 'But you're great for putting up with it too; I don't know if I could.'

Leonie made a face. 'Clearly I'm not so good any more. I don't know, Grace, maybe I shouldn't have been so insistent about cutting funds from the outset. Then Andrea wouldn't be calling on Adam so much now, which means he might have a better chance of finding another job.'

'Don't be silly,' Grace argued. 'There's no *way* you could be expected to keep two households going. What do they expect you to do – work twenty-four hours a day? But Adam should know better if you ask me. Doesn't he ever stop to think how difficult all this must be for you too? I mean, how would *he* feel if you'd lost your job and ended up spending all your free time at your ex-boyfriend's?'

Leonie's head shot up. 'You think there's more to it than meets the eye?' Obviously this was something she'd considered herself, but because they'd split up so long ago, and Andrea was supposedly in a relationship of her own, she really didn't think there was anything to worry about. Most of all, she loved and trusted Adam and firmly believed that he loved her too. OK, so they were going through a rough patch at the moment, but didn't all couples at one time or another?

'No, no, that's not what I meant.' Grace was quick to reassure her. 'I just feel that Adam's being very thoughtless really, considering you're the one who's under pressure to keep things afloat.'

Perhaps this was true, but Leonie was sure that this was just a temporary phase they were going through. What with Adam disillusioned with his work situation, and Leonie stressed out with hers, there were bound to be some pressures. But at the end of the day, what all of this boiled down to was money, which with any luck would be a temporary problem at best.

And, her and Adam's relationship was way too solid to be undermined by something as trivial as that, wasn't it?

A few weeks later, much to Leonie's relief, Adam found a job; a mechanical engineer's position in a firm based in Kildare. Although the salary was slightly lower than the one he'd got from Microtel, he was over the moon at being back in the workforce.

As a result, tensions between them lessened considerably and while Leonie still wasn't happy about all the time he'd been spending at Andrea's, there was no denying that keeping himself occupied had a positive effect on Adam's mental state.

'I suppose it was just nice to be able to do *something*,' he confessed to Leonie one evening over dinner, a meal he'd prepared himself from start to finish.

Upon her return from work that day, she'd found the apartment spotlessly clean, and Adam in the kitchen surrounded by newly bought groceries. 'I just felt like such a bloody waster all the time, whereas when I was there, I felt useful.'

Leonie smiled, trying her best to conceal her hurt that it had been his ex who had brought him out of himself, and made him feel better about everything.

'Well, in the beginning, I did suggest you do a few bits and pieces round here to try and keep your mind off things . . .' she began tentatively, not wanting to go over old ground.

'I know, and you were right. But I was so focused on finding another job that I just couldn't see the wood for the trees.' He reached across the table and took her hand in his. 'I'm sorry for being such a gobshite, Lee, and especially sorry for taking so much of it out on you.'

'Hey, that's what I'm here for,' she joked, pleased that he was back to himself.

'I know, but it wasn't until Andrea pointed out how much you were doing to keep things going . . .'

At this, Leonie raised an eyebrow. *Andrea* had pointed this out? Well, miracles would never cease! And to think that briefly, she'd worried if she might be in serious danger of losing Adam to her . . . Now it seemed she owed the woman a favour.

'I shouldn't have taken you for granted,' Adam was saying. 'I was an idiot.'

'Look, you didn't take me for granted; you just weren't yourself,' she reassured him. 'And while I'm glad we're back on track now, I really was worried about you. I'd never seen you like that before, so down and disheartened about everything.'

'Well, it wasn't much fun for me either,' he said with a wry smile, 'but thank God it's all over with now. I don't want to go through anything like that ever again.'

Neither do I, Leonie thought, silently thanking the heavens that the old Adam was back.

After that, things pretty much began getting back to normal.

Leonie and Adam re-established their wedding plans; deciding to have the ceremony in spring the following year. This would give Adam plenty of time to settle into his new job, and allow him to make the necessary arrangements with the new company to take time off for the honeymoon.

The two of them decided on a two-week trip to the US; Leonie eager to return to the land of her birth, and Adam just as eager to visit it for the very first time. 'I've always wanted to explore the Deep South,' he'd said when they were discussing their plans.

'New Orleans and Mississippi sound cool, well at least they do in Grisham novels.'

Leonie agreed but was also keen on heading over to the West Coast to California, one part of the country she'd never been, but which had always held a huge attraction for her. Either way, they had plenty of time to decide and thanks to Adam's new job were financially on track to cover both the honeymoon and the wedding.

And after three long months of 'roughing it', Andrea's generous maintenance was restored (albeit at a slightly reduced rate), as was Suzanne's pocket money. Leonie was surprised to find herself almost relieved about this; it meant that she might now leave her and Adam in peace, and allow them to get on with planning the rest of their lives.

But of course this was wishful thinking.

Barely a few weeks after Adam started the new job, and

just as he and Leonie were settling nicely back into a routine, there came yet another 'urgent' phone call.

'It's Suzanne,' Adam told Leonie, when he'd finished speaking to the girl's mother. 'Andrea is going away for a long weekend next Thursday, and she wants to know if we can take her. I told her it should be fine, but I'd ask you first. What do you think?'

Leonie groaned inwardly. A few days of the teenager moping and sulking around the place was all they needed, and as it was the school holidays, no doubt they'd see a great deal of her (equally moody) friends too. 'The weekend is fine, but as there's no school, how will we look after her when we're both at work?' she pointed out.

Adam grimaced. 'I hadn't thought of that.'

But surely Andrea had considered it, Leonie thought, and if so, she must have known that in the circumstances, Adam would hardly be able to take time off to babysit. Typical! 'And wait, isn't that the same weekend as your work thing?'

The new company had arranged a team-bonding weekend away.

'You're right,' Adam groaned. He picked up the phone again. 'I'd better tell her it doesn't suit.'

'No, wait, has she booked somewhere?' Leonie asked, thinking that it really wasn't all that long since that holiday in the Caribbean Andrea had 'so desperately' required. 'And how come Suzanne's not going with her?'

'I don't know, she didn't say. I suppose she's probably just going away with friends.'

Or perhaps the mysterious Billy, Leonie mused.

'What about Hugo? Who's going to mind him? Or is she bringing him too?'

'Again, I don't know, she didn't actually mention anything about Hugo . . .'

Leonie had to smile. Trust Adam to get the bare minimum of information! Not that it was really any of their business who Andrea was or wasn't with, but at the same time she couldn't help but be curious about it.

Nevertheless, the fact remained that someone needed to be around to look after Suzanne.

'I suppose I could do it,' she offered. 'I'm due time off from Xanadu as it is, and given all the extra hours I've done recently, getting a couple of days shouldn't be a problem.'

'You're sure? It won't affect your leave for the wedding?'

'Nope, as I said, I'm owed more than I've taken, so this'll be a good excuse as any to take advantage of it. This time of year is manic too so I won't mind getting away from it for a while.'

'Lee, you're an absolute star, you know that, don't you?' Adam said, coming across and sweeping her into his arms.

Leonie snuggled into his embrace. 'If you say so,' she grinned, deciding that if offering to keep an eye on Suzanne for a weekend made him this happy, she'd gladly do it for ever and a day.

As it turned out, looking after the teenager wasn't that much trouble at all. During the day, Leonie pretty much left Suzanne to her own devices as often as she could, encouraging her to meet with her friends or go shopping, whatever she preferred. She gave her lifts to wherever she wanted to go and as a result the girl spent most of her time hanging around town, or at her favourite haunt: Dundrum shopping centre. It seemed that Suzanne, like her mother, was content once her pockets were being refilled on a regular basis, and if that was what it took for the entire extended 'clan' to reach some form of equilibrium, then Leonie was happy too.

She was also making the most of her unplanned few days

off, the weather was dry and she was spending lots of time out for walks or curling up on the sofa catching up with her reading. The last couple of months had been tough, so a few days of taking it easy and doing pretty much nothing at all was welcome. But best of all, her offer to mind Suzanne had scored considerable Brownie points with Adam, and given their recent troubles this was an added bonus.

'I knew the pair of you would come through it,' Grace told her, when on Friday afternoon, she called over to her friend's house. Suzanne was out with her own friends somewhere but had reassured Leonie she'd be back in time for dinner. 'Adam is crazy about you, and the two of you are made for each other.'

Leonie grimaced. 'I don't know, it was touch and go there for a while. I was beginning to wonder if there was something going on with him and Andrea . . . '

'Not at all, I had a sneaky feeling you were blowing things out of proportion,' Grace teased, having none of it. 'And as I said before, if Adam had any interest in her, then why isn't he still with her?'

'I know, but when things weren't going so great with us, and they were spending so much time together . . . I don't know, men can be weird sometimes.'

'You can say that again,' Grace drawled. 'Sometimes I wonder what's going on in their heads at all. You know the way we're doing up the bathroom at the moment?' she asked and Leonie nodded. 'Well, Ray came home yesterday with a new shower tray. Apparently there was a choice between an "easy plumb" and a "non-easy plumb" and guess which one he came home with?'

Leonie grinned. 'Knowing Ray, I suspect the non-easy?'

'Yes! Now, why on earth would *anyone* . . . ?' she trailed off, shaking her blond head in bewilderment. 'Ah, never mind my eejit husband. Adam is great and I was full certain he wouldn't let you down.'

'Well, maybe if you'd seen Andrea, you might have had a few reservations. She's the mother of his child, remember, so there was always a huge amount of history there.'

'Exactly. It's *history*, so there's nothing to worry about. It was a rough patch but you got through it, and now all is hunky-dory again.'

Leonie smiled, feeling happier than she'd been in ages. Grace had been right as usual and despite her recent doubts, she really did have nothing to worry about where Adam and Andrea were concerned. OK, so his ex might be a *million* times better-looking than her with a great figure and the most amazing clothes, but Adam had his chance and he'd chosen to walk away. And, lucky for Leonie, now he was marrying her.

'So how come you got stuck with minding the little princess?' Grace asked with a wry smile. 'Is Mummy off on a saucy weekend?'

'That's what I was wondering,' Leonie replied. 'All Adam said was that she was going away somewhere. He didn't say where, or more importantly who with.'

'A bit of a coincidence that Adam's away too then, isn't it? Ha, maybe you were right after all,' she chuckled, obviously tickled by the notion. 'Oh give over!' she groaned, seeing Leonie's face. 'I was only joking.'

'I know, I know. Just don't be putting ideas in my head!' Leonie said laughing. 'I'm bad enough as it is.'

'Well, I've said it before and I'll say it again. You have *nothing* to worry about with Adam. Believe me he's just not that kind of guy.'

'Leonie, I like, really need a favour.'

'Sure, Suzanne, what's up?'

It was Saturday evening and Leonie was about to suggest to Adam's daughter that they order a takeaway. She'd cooked for them up until then, but tonight she fancied something different. The takeaway she and Adam used did a great vegetarian pad thai and as she knew Suzanne liked oriental food the idea should go down well.

'I need to go home.'

Leonie frowned. 'Home – to Wicklow you mean? Why?'

'I left something behind, something important.' The girl didn't elaborate and knowing Suzanne, Leonie thought, she didn't intend to.

'Something important,' she repeated levelly.

The teenager nodded.

'Well, is it really that urgent? You're going home tomorrow after all.'

'Please, I really, *really* need this.'

Leonie was taken aback at how genuinely worried the girl seemed to be; this time there was a complete absence of the usual whining and belligerence that so characterised her. Then again, perhaps she'd finally realised that such behaviour held no tack with her future stepmother. Even so, a drive all the way to Wicklow and back in pre-Christmas traffic . . .

'I don't know, Suzanne,' she exhaled apologetically. 'It's late, and the N11 is always so busy at this time of year . . . '

'It's my Pill,' the girl interjected, and Leonie's head snapped up.

Suzanne was staring at the floor, awkwardly clasping her hands together. 'I'm supposed to start on the new pack today after the seven-day break from the last one, but I forgot to bring it with me . . . '

Leonie stared at her, flabbergasted. The girl was barely fifteen years old! OK, so she'd always looked and behaved older than her years, but Leonie had (rather naively she thought now) always considered this to be a bit of a front. And despite her somewhat revealing clothes and wilful behaviour, she hadn't considered for a second that Suzanne would get up to . . . that. But clearly if she was so worried about missing a pill, she must be! Did Adam know about this?

'Dad doesn't know,' Suzanne said, as if reading her mind. 'Please don't tell him, Leonie, he'd kill me.' Her pleading sounded so immature and childlike, it made the whole situation even more distressing.

'It's not up to me to tell him, but I must admit I'm a little taken aback,' she told her gently. 'I suppose it's good that you're being responsible and everything, but at the same time, you're still very young to be . . . ' She looked at her. 'I take it you *are* . . . doing . . . that, seeing as continuing on the full course is so important to you?'

Bloody hell, this really was one very awkward conversation!

Suzanne wouldn't meet her gaze. 'Can we just go and get it?' she said, avoiding the questions and Leonie supposed she couldn't blame her. She wasn't her mother and had no right to be questioning her like this. But thinking of which . . .

'Does your mother know about this?' she asked. 'About you being on the Pill, I mean.'

Suzanne nodded emphatically. 'Yes, but she doesn't want Dad knowing either. He'd go ballistic.'

Leonie couldn't understand why Andrea would approve of this, but then again she hadn't a clue what raising a teenager was like, had she? 'OK then, we'll drive down to get it later. But let's get something to eat first, OK?'

'Thanks, Leonie, I really appreciate this.' The less belligerent Suzanne behaved, the younger she seemed.

While waiting for their food to be delivered, the two sat side by side on the sofa watching TV, Leonie trying her best to come to terms about what she'd just heard. Now that she knew about this she couldn't help but view Suzanne differently.

God, was she some kind of prude for being shocked by this? Well, no matter what she might think, Leonie wasn't going to be responsible for Suzanne missing her pill and getting into even greater strife because of it.

When they'd finished eating, they got in the car and headed off to Wicklow. Suzanne didn't say too much on the way and Leonie was just as happy to drive in silence, lost in her own thoughts.

She felt that Adam should really know this, but at the same time, it really wasn't any of her business, and it certainly wasn't up to her to tell him. Should she have a word with Andrea maybe, express her concerns? She could imagine the other woman's reaction, and in fairness Andrea would be right to tell her to go and get stuffed.

Leonie turned off the N11 at the Ashford exit and headed in the direction of the house. When they pulled up outside the door, she was surprised to see a car parked outside. It was an old, battered Volkswagen that looked to have seen better days.

'Whose car is that?' she asked Suzanne.

'Billy's,' the younger girl replied easily, getting out of the car.

Ah, Leonie mused, so she was right in thinking that Andrea had gone away with her boyfriend. Clearly the other woman preferred to travel in her own classier Audi, rather than that clapped-out banger of a thing. She was surprised; for a supposed devotee of the finer things in life, Leonie found it hard to reconcile Adam's ex with a man who drove a car like that. Then again, maybe it was just some run-around the guy used and, like that joke bumper sticker, his other car actually *was* a Mercedes?

'Do you want to come in?' Suzanne asked then. 'I won't be long, but like, seeing as you drove me all the way down here . . . '

Leonie nodded. 'I suppose I might as well stretch the legs.'

Suzanne used her key to open the front door and as they went inside, they were both struck by the sounds of a TV on somewhere in the house.

The two exchanged looks. 'Sounds like someone's here.'

Suzanne shrugged and headed in the direction of the sound. 'Maybe Mum's home early,' she said, opening the living-room door.

Leonie followed her with some considerable reluctance; the last thing she wanted was a face-to-face meeting with Andrea. But when she entered the room, she came face to face with someone completely different.

Sprawled on the sofa in front of the TV watching football and surrounded by beer cans, pizza boxes and the detritus of whatever he'd had for breakfast, was a tall, lithe and, from what Leonie could see of him, attractive man. Although he looked to be about the same age as Leonie, he was dressed in worn, faded denims, a cut-off T-shirt and sported a longish, grungy hairstyle which gave him a much more youthful look. He was so enthralled by the game that he didn't seem to have noticed them come in.

'Billy!' Suzanne exclaimed. 'What are you doing here?'

Ah, so this was the famous Billy, Leonie thought, with interest.

'Had to make the most of havin' the place to myself, didn't I?' he said, in a thick Dublin accent.

'But where's Mum, I thought you were going away with her.'

'To one of those bloody spa places? You've got to be kiddin'.'

'Oh right.' Suzanne seemed confused but at the same time

not particularly bothered about the situation. Clearly, Billy making himself at home in this house was a regular thing. 'This is Leonie, by the way,' she said, introducing her companion.

'Cheers, Leonie,' Billy replied, holding up a beer can in half-hearted salute, his eyes never leaving the screen.

But Leonie didn't return his greeting; she couldn't return it. As it was she'd barely heard it over the loud thumping of her heart, couldn't quite process it through the noisy ringing in her brain.

And as the room began to sway and the ground suddenly felt spongy beneath her feet, she couldn't do anything else but just stare at Billy; the full implications of his appearance almost too great for her to contemplate.

Chapter 27

Following some savvy legal work from Doug, Seth and Alex's dispute about the Mustang was eventually resolved in her favour, which meant that three long weeks later, Alex was once again free to lodge a fresh no-fault divorce petition against Seth. She expected some form of protest or dramatics and pleaded with him beforehand to be at home when the process server called. But to her amazement, her errant husband had allowed himself to be served, which meant that she and her lawyer were at least further along in submitting the petition to the courts.

Soon, she would finally be free of Seth, free of all the draw-backs of being married to him and most importantly, free to start her life all over again with Jon.

Well, at least she would be in a few months time once the completed documents winged their way through the courts.

'It shouldn't take too long,' Doug assured her. 'He's given up contesting and assuming there are no more disputes . . . '

Again, Alex almost expected something to go wrong at the last minute and for Seth to come up with some crazy excuse for a delay. But no, for once in his life he was being adult about something and had finally managed to see sense.

'Aren't you a bit sad, though?' Leonie asked when she

learned that Seth had finally agreed to go along with Alex's wishes.

'Are you crazy?' she retorted, although in truth it did feel a bit strange. Especially when Seth was back living here in San Francisco. When he was away it was pretty much a case of out of sight out of mind.

Almost.

But she was glad now for Jon's sake that her status was finally clarified. Not that he was angling for them to get married or anything, but just in case . . .

Anyway, Alex wasn't about to jump into marriage again so soon, not when she'd made such a mess of it the first time round. Although admittedly, it had been great right up until Seth messed up. But had she really expected anything different? She could never see her ex being a serious candidate for marriage – real marriage – with all the normal stresses and strains and ups and downs of everyday life. He didn't have the emotional intelligence for that; his recent behaviour towards her and Jon being a case in point!

Alex thought back now to one particular memory, an afternoon she and Seth had spent down at the Golden Gate Park a couple of summers back.

It was the fortieth anniversary of the famous Summer of Love in '67 and a massive reunion festival was taking place. Hippies filled the park in their thousands, gathering in the grass in front of a huge stage area where folk singers rehashed all the old sixties favourites.

The air was ripe with the smell of pot and barbecued food, and Alex and Seth were having lunch on a grass verge overlooking the main concert area, having picked up some food at one of the nearby outdoor food stalls.

As Alex waited to order Louisiana gumbo at the Cajun stall, while Seth chose something elsewhere, she got into conversation with one of the hippies, who like many of the others were wearing T-shirts adorned with the usual 'Peace & Love' slogans.

'See that guy?' he said to Alex, pointing at an old black-and-white photograph printed on the back of his T-shirt. A long-haired youth was pictured in a crowd atop someone's shoulders. 'That's me here, forty years ago,' he told her proudly.

Alex peered at the photograph. 'You haven't aged a day,' she joked, thinking that the man in front of her could easily be mistaken for a high-powered businessman or banker, if you overlooked the tie-dye bandana.

'Those were good times – no, *great* times,' he said wistfully and she had to smile. It must have been quite something to be part of a movement that was a real catalyst for social change back then. Although hippies had always been part of the culture in San Francisco, Alex didn't know too much about the height of the movement in the sixties other than what her folks had told her. But her mum and dad had only flirted with the lifestyle and the politics, not like some of the guys here.

And while her folks had eventually moved on to a more conventional life, she could tell that most of the people here today still embraced the same philosophy that so appealed to them forty years before. There was a great sense of belonging and a spirited carefree approach that appealed to Alex – although she really didn't think she could get used to all that pot.

'Look at that,' Seth said when he returned, pointing out an elderly couple strolling by hand-in-hand. Both had long grey hair tied back in a ponytail and were dressed in baggy, brightly coloured clothes. Alex had to look twice to confirm that the small animal they were walking on a lead alongside them really was a cat.

She chuckled. 'Yes, I can see how that whole free love concept would suit you,' she teased.

'That's not what I meant. I meant *that*,' he clarified, pointing to how the old couple were holding hands. 'That'll be you and me one day.'

Alex laughed. 'Minus the cat, I hope!'

She remembered being touched by that; his easy belief that they'd still be together holding hands in their old age. But she should have realised that this was nothing but naivety on Seth's part, in the same way that he'd once commented on a father and child playing ball together and talked about having a son so he could do the very same. What Seth didn't realise was that all of those things took commitment, maturity and a lot of hard work.

And in the end, she thought sadly, he was incapable of all three.

The phone was ringing when Leonie let herself into the apartment after work.

'Hello, could I speak to Leonie Hayes, please?' a male voice asked.

'This is Leonie speaking,' she said pleasantly.

'How do you do? I'm Gene Forrest, the owner of your apartment and I believe you wanted to speak with me.'

'That's right, yes, thank you for phoning me back.' Leonie was amazed that the rental agency had actually passed on the request for the landlord to contact her. It was such a long time ago that she'd almost forgotten about it.

'I'm sorry it took so long for me to call. I've been out of town for a while and am only catching up on messages now. So how can I help?'

'Well, I'm not sure if you can really . . .' Leonie went on to explain about the letters she'd found. 'I just wondered if

Helena Abbott might have left you a forwarding address when she moved?'

'I'm sorry, ma'am, I actually just bought the place the end of last year. I knew there were already tenants in place, but I have to tell you I don't have much to do with any of that – the agency does it for me. That's why I was surprised to get your message.'

'So ownership of the property recently changed hands?' Leonie asked, her brow furrowing.

'Yes. Now I don't know much of the details because it was an executor sale, and I think the previous owners may have lived there at one point, but I really couldn't say for sure. I know there was some furniture and stuff left behind, but as far as I was aware it had been moved . . . '

Leonie almost dropped the phone. An executor sale?

Was there a chance that Helena, *their* Helena had actually *owned* this apartment and some of the 'stuff' left behind included the box of letters?

In which case it had been a complete waste of time looking for a forwarding address or driving all the way down to Monterey to grill some poor woman who clearly couldn't be her.

Because Helena Abbott was most likely dead.

Her mind racing, she thought back on what Alex had said about there being a 'situation' with the couple who had lived here previously, the couple that they'd assumed were the Abbotts.

'Do you know how long it's been since the previous owner died?' she asked the landlord, her thoughts racing as things finally began slotting into place.

'I have no idea. My lawyer handled all the legalities and paperwork so I really don't know what else to tell you.'

'No, that's fine – you've been a great help actually.'

'You said there's some mail still coming? I guess it's probably best to just have it returned.'

'You're right, yes, of course. I'll do that.' Leonie didn't see any point in explaining that this was what she'd been trying to do for the last couple of months. 'Thank you so much again for calling.'

'My pleasure. I hope the apartment suits your needs, but if you have any problems let the agency know. I'd give you my cell, except I'm in and out of the country quite a lot so—'

'No, no, that won't be necessary. I won't need to bother you again.'

'All right then, Ms Hayes,' Gene Forrest said. 'You have a good day.'

'You too,' Leonie said, replacing the receiver.

'What? You're kidding me!' Downstairs, Alex seemed just as surprised at this news as Leonie. 'Although, now that I think about it, her being dead is probably the simplest explanation.'

'Remember you said there was some kind of fuss upstairs last year when that couple were moving out?' Leonie reminded her. 'A situation, I think you said. What was that?'

'I really can't say – it was just stuff I heard, gossip, I guess,' Alex replied, pulling her dark hair into a ponytail. 'Although I think someone said something about the police being called and—' she gasped, dropping her hands. 'You're not thinking . . . you really don't think that Helena could have been—'

'It's certainly worth a thought,' Leonie said. 'You said those two were always fighting. We know from at least one of the letters that Helena was already married and having an affair with Nathan. So maybe the husband found out.'

'And you're thinking he did something – out of jealousy?'

Leonie sighed jadedly. 'I don't know. I really don't know what to think anymore, Alex,' she said. 'We've been going around in circles with this thing for a while now. Maybe the husband found the letters and that's how he discovered the affair. And maybe he's the one who locked them away in the back of the wardrobe.'

'But they were still sealed when you found them,' Alex pointed out, 'so he couldn't have read them.'

'What if there were others before those though? If the husband knew who they were from and they kept coming, maybe he suspected that the affair was still going on.'

'Well, if the husband *was* intervening, it would also explain why Helena never replied,' Alex conceded.

Leonie shook her head in bewilderment. 'I just couldn't believe it when the landlord said it was an executor sale.'

She thought back to that first day she'd viewed the property with the guy from the agency, and how she'd sensed at the time that the apartment hadn't been lived in for some time, yet there were still belongings to be moved. Although thinking about it again, if it was an executor sale, and Helena and her husband both owned the property, then it must mean that the husband had died too.

'I wonder if that couple did actually own this place?' Alex pondered when Leonie put this to her. 'I guess it's a possibility as they were here when I moved in, but for some reason I always assumed the whole place was rented.'

'Is there any way we could find out?' Leonie wondered out loud. 'Or find out if there *was* any kind of . . . incident . . . upstairs.'

'I'm sure we could but does it really matter now? If Helena's gone, then we can't exactly forward the letters to her, can we? So what's the point? We might as well just throw them out and forget all about it.'

But Leonie was so involved now, and wanted so much to get to the bottom of their story, that she still found it hard to just discard the whole thing. Today's news had only added to the list of unanswered questions about this situation. Yet, as Alex pointed out, there was really no longer much of a mystery to be solved where the letters were concerned, was there? If Helena had died, then one way or the other—

Then suddenly the thought hit Leonie like a speeding train.

Just wondered if you ever got those other letters I sent you? I guess not.

She looked at Alex. 'Nathan doesn't know.'

'What? What are you talking about?'

'Helena – if she's dead, be it by natural causes or otherwise, he doesn't know it. The last letter came around Valentine's Day, remember?'

Alex's face changed. 'Wow. You're right.'

Poor Nathan. There he was still sending heartfelt, pleading letters to the love of his life, pouring his heart out and desperately hoping for a reply. Yet if what they now suspected about Helena were true, then no reply would ever be forthcoming.

'So no, I don't think we should give up looking for Nathan,' she said, feeling more sorry than ever for him. 'If anything, we should be trying even harder.'

Chapter 28

My darling,

I don't think I can take much more of this. Things are getting harder and crazier here now and I just don't know if I can cope any more. I know what you're thinking, that it's all my own fault for being here in the first place, but even I couldn't have imagined how tough it would be.

Again, you were right. There is no justification, no explanation for what is happening here and while I thought my intentions were pure, I realise now how stupid I was. I wish I'd listened to you more and understood what you were really trying to tell me. But we come from very different worlds you and I, and while I thought this wouldn't matter, and that we'd be together for ever, I realise now how truly naive I really was. I had no right to ask to you to wait for me, and no right to ask you to change your mind.

So I guess it's payback time in a way. I was stupid, and you were right and now we both have to live with the consequences.

Please Forgive Me.
Nathan

Nathan marked a page of the book he was reading and set it aside. It was a good book, decent enough, but he wasn't in the mood for reading. To be honest, he was tired of reading, tired of watching TV and sleeping which was just about all he seemed to do these days.

Although he hadn't slept all that much the night before, which was likely the very reason he felt so antsy, but then again, this place would make anyone feel that way.

'What's up with you, Nate?' Frank had asked him over breakfast that morning but Nathan knew he didn't really care. He was really just going through the motions, same as everyone around here. No, that was lousy, Frank was a decent guy and he in particular had gone out of his way to help Nathan settle in when he first got here.

He looked around the room, although you could hardly call it a room. More like a coffin. Although maybe that was unfair, the place was OK from time to time and Nathan gradually got used to it over the last while, but still he liked his freedom. Who didn't?

A lot of the others were OK too, although some of them were a bit too loopy for his liking. Nathan preferred to stay away from the loopy ones, just in case it was catchin'. He gave a wan smile. He shouldn't be so grouchy really; this place wasn't the worst. Anyway, he had a pretty good idea why he'd been so antsy lately and it was all his own fault.

He should have known better than to open up old wounds by deciding to write to Helena. What did he think he'd achieve? She couldn't care less about him now, much less give a damn about what he thought. Most likely, she'd forgotten him completely. Nathan was annoyed with himself for daring to hope – at least for a while – that Helena would read it and maybe try and make contact.

Idiot. That was before he realised that even if she did get it and by some long shot wanted to reach him, he hadn't thought to tell her how to go about it. Man, he was stupid!

Oh well, Nathan thought, picking up his book again. What was done was done and it was own fault for getting carried away by crazy dreams and nostalgia, the kind of stuff that had been getting him into trouble for most of his life.

So yeah, today, Nathan felt annoyed, stupid and frustrated, but perhaps more than anything else, he felt lonely.

It was Monday morning and Leonie meandered slowly through the crowds on Fisherman's Wharf. She had a day off from Flower Power and was heading for the pier to do something she'd wanted to do since her arrival, but for various reasons had just never got round to. She'd thought that she and Grace might do it during her friend's trip that time, but Grace hadn't been in the least bit interested . . .

But more importantly, she felt she needed a diversion. While she'd absolutely loved having her here, Grace's visit had somehow brought into sharp focus everything that had happened back home.

This, coupled with the frustration of being so helpless in trying to uncover the truth behind Nathan's letters, was starting to wear her down and she didn't want that. She wanted to feel as liberated and optimistic as she had when she first arrived in San Francisco four months ago, confident that she was leaving all the bad stuff behind. Chances were this was also partly the reason she'd become so absorbed with pursuing the letters in the first place; it had kept her focused and her mind occupied, and not only that, but there was also the possibility that she might be able to do some good. And Leonie needed that.

Even Marcy had noticed her recent change of form. 'Geez, what's gotten into you lately?' her boss had asked on Saturday, when Leonie was less talkative than usual.

'To be honest, I don't really know,' she'd told her. 'I think I'm probably just missing Grace.'

But was it Grace she was missing, or Adam? Leonie swore she wouldn't think about it, had promised herself that no good would come of going back over it again, but still she wished she'd done things differently, that she hadn't been so rash in the decisions she had made. Who knows what way things might have turned out then?

'Maybe I've been working you too hard,' Marcy ventured. 'I can be a tough old broad sometimes, but don't think I don't already know that.'

Leonie smiled. 'Don't be silly! Of course you haven't!'

'Well, even so, I think you need a day off. But don't just sit at home staring out the window – do something with it. You're living in one of the greatest cities in the US of A, sweetheart. Go and enjoy it!'

Which was how today Leonie found herself taking her place behind a long queue of tourists snaking all the way along Pier 33, waiting to board the ferry. Standing at the back of the line, she shivered lightly, glad that she'd heeded Alex's advice and brought a sweater.

'The boat's chilly on the way over and it can be just as cold on the Rock,' her friend advised when Leonie told her where she was headed. 'And for more reasons than one too, that place creeps me out,' she added with a shudder.

Leonie had to smile at the idea of Alex getting the heebie-jeebies over an old abandoned prison; especially when hardly anything fazed her as a rule. And while she herself would have preferred some company on the trip, there was also something nice about getting out and about in the city on her own; something she hadn't really done since she'd met Alex. She'd have been lost without her the last few months, Leonie thought, as the queue gradually began to disperse and everyone boarded the boat. But even if Alex hadn't been working today, it was unlikely she would have come along given her reaction to Leonie's plans.

She took the stairs to the top deck, and headed for a seat on the right-hand side, again taking Alex's informed advice. 'Much better for views on the approach to the island. Sit towards the back if you can though, the front gets *very* windy.'

The journey across the bay took about fifteen minutes, and when the ferry docked on the rear of Alcatraz island, it was met by a ranger who gave the tour group a brief orientation and history of the place, before leading them up a series of steep slopes towards the cell house.

Leonie was held rapt by the man's colourful accounts of the prison's history and the details of so many unsuccessful escape attempts over the years. Looking back across the bay to the city skyline, which to the naked eye looked deceptively close, Leonie could see why escapees – misled by the true swimming distance – had drowned or died of hypothermia in the ice-cold waters before reaching shore.

But today the island looked beautiful, and the crumbly old buildings juxtaposed against a sleek, glistening city skyline and cloudless blue sky was breathtaking.

At the entrance to the prison block, all visitors were given headphones for an audio tour of the cell house. Leonie ambled through the old, dusty, concrete building, mesmerised by the narrow, empty cells and their extraordinarily stark appearance. The tour narrator's voice and accompanying sound effects of cell doors clanging and prisoners shouting gave a spooky and disconcertingly vivid sense of what it must have been like to be banged up in a place like this.

As she listened through the headphones to an ex-prison guard give an account of how the cell block operated, she just couldn't imagine being locked up in such a cold, windowless and impossibly tiny space, little bigger than a shoebox.

And it must have been doubly difficult here, Leonie realised, because the breeze carried sounds from the city across the water; people going about their daily business, laughing, working and enjoying themselves – a cruel reminder of the freedom the prisoners themselves had forfeited.

She shuddered, listening to the guard give a detailed account of a highly regimented prison life at Alcatraz: how inmates were only allowed to talk during meals and recreation, how receiving and sending letters had to be approved by the warden, and visitation rights had to be earned.

She wandered slowly from place to place – the visitors' area, recreation ground, library and solitary confinement cells – each just as eerily creepy as the last. Alex was right, this place gave you the willies and Leonie wished she hadn't been so offhand about coming here on her own.

By the time she reached the dining area – a large sunlit room surrounded by high barred windows – the voice in the headphones had changed to that of an ex-Alcatraz inmate recounting his time here.

As she listened to the man's deceptively ordinary and rather harmless-sounding voice, Leonie tried to remind herself that this guy had likely committed a terrible crime to have ended up in here in the first place. Still, it was incredibly difficult not to feel sorry for him. Who knew what circumstances led people to this cold, miserable hunk of rock surrounded by water? She smiled, knowing that if Adam were here, he would no doubt be amused by this sort of thinking, and while she was no liberal, she did wonder if . . .

Leonie stopped short as something the prisoner had said suddenly caught her attention.

'*It's like time stands still here, yet life goes on all around . . .*'

She stood rooted to the spot, almost afraid to move, as in her brain the gears slowly began to click into place.

Time stands still here. She'd heard that very same expression somewhere before, hadn't she? Sometime very recently. But where?

Leonie looked out the window, where a single seagull drifted along in the wind, the perfect metaphor for the freedom such a place denied.

This place . . .

Suddenly it hit her. Yes, the expression was familiar but she hadn't heard it, she'd *read* it, or at least a slightly different version of it.

In this place, sometimes time almost seems to stand still.

And with a burst of comprehension that made her dizzy, suddenly Leonie knew exactly where to look for Nathan.

'You're not seriously suggesting . . . ' Alex didn't know what to say.

On her return from Alcatraz, Leonie launched herself off the ferry and back on to dry land, eager to return to Green Street and read through every one of Nathan's letters again, this time with a completely fresh eye and taking into account her suspicions.

And having done that, she was more convinced than ever that she was right.

'Don't you see? It all makes so much sense now,' she tried to persuade Alex when her friend returned home from work that evening. 'All those references to "this crazy place" and "feeling scared and lonely" . . . I assumed he must have been talking about the break up from Helena, but that wasn't it at all! And we always thought that it seemed odd that he never once talked about coming to see her, or tried to arrange a meeting with her. Because he couldn't!'

Alex studied the letters all laid out on Leonie's coffee table. 'I don't know, it's still a hell of a reach . . .'

'No, it isn't.' Leonie swung her legs beneath her on the sofa. 'It's exactly what we thought before. He kept writing to her at this address because he had no way of knowing that she'd died. Oh, Alex, I don't know why we didn't figure this out before!'

She was beside herself with excitement.

But everything fitted. The heartfelt, reminiscent approach, the apologetic tone. And as for the plea for forgiveness . . . well it made *complete* sense now, didn't it?

'It would certainly explain the federal-type postmark,' Alex admitted grudgingly, as she tried to weigh up what Leonie was suggesting. 'Not that I know much about these things, but I'd have thought it would be clearer on the envelope where they were coming from.'

'Not necessarily. I'm sure there must be some privacy issues with things like that, surely?'

'Maybe, but assuming for a second that this is what you think it is, then how does it change anything?'

'It changes *everything*, Alex!' Leonie couldn't believe she even had to ask. 'For one thing, it's more important than ever that we find him now. Think about it, the poor guy languishing in a place like that—'

'Um, Leonie, I wouldn't be so quick to sympathise. Who knows who we're dealing with here? These guys are experts at manipulating people and now that I think about it, this may be exactly what's going on with these letters.'

'Oh, come on.' Leonie couldn't believe her attitude.

'I'm serious! Admit it; you were taken in by this guy from the off.' She shook her head incredulously. 'Talk about "you had me at hello"!'

Well, she might have a point there, Leonie conceded; from

day one Nathan's words had made a huge impression on her, and she supposed she should try and look at things a bit more cynically, but if anything, what she'd recently discovered made her more determined than ever to let him know why his letters remained unanswered.

'Look, none of us know why he's there, so there's no point in speculating,' she said. 'But at least now that we have an idea *where* he is, we can send the letters back and maybe include one of our own telling him the news about Helena.'

'Are you serious?'

'Of course. Isn't that what we've been trying to do all along?'

'I don't know.' Alex looked uncomfortable. 'I'm really not sure we should get involved in this kind of thing.'

'But we're already involved, how can we just turn our backs on it now? Not when we finally know where to find him—'

'I wouldn't hold my breath about that; we've got nothing but a first name . . . in reality, Leonie, we've still got very little at all.'

'Yes, but there must be records we could check, or people who could help point us in the right direction . . . '

Alex looked to be in two minds. 'Well, there is this guy from work, he works with the crime reporters,' she murmured. 'I suppose I could ask him to check the fed databases tomorrow.'

'Could you?' Leonie could barely contain her delight. 'That's fantastic!'

'Don't get too excited; like I said we don't even have a surname. But from the postmark, I guess we can assume the facility is in California so that narrows it down somewhat . . . ' She trailed off, deep in thought, and Leonie could tell she'd now slipped into investigative mode. While Alex had been content to give up the search after discovering Helena had likely passed away, this new information had renewed her interest in the letters and the mystery surrounding them.

'Is there anything I can do?' she asked.

'I guess you could go through these again with a fine-tooth comb, and with this in mind, see if you can figure out anything else that might point us in the right direction. But Leonie,' she added, a distinct warning in her tone, 'we've got to be very careful here. If we do find this guy, we can't just go rushing in there without knowing exactly who we're dealing with.'

'I know.' Leonie was duly chastened.

'Nathan might be looking for forgiveness, but like I've said all along, who says he deserves it? And if he is where we think he is, then a judge has already decided that maybe he doesn't.'

Chapter 29

Dear Helena,

You don't know how much I've enjoyed writing these letters and thinking back over our time together. Although I think I can safely assume you haven't especially enjoyed receiving them.

In which case you'll be happy to learn that this will be my last letter to you. Things have gotten so bad lately I'm not sure how long I have left, so I thought it best to finish this thing on my own terms while I still can.

In any case, I think it's time I let you go once and for all. In this crazy place, sometimes I wonder if I've wasted my life, if I've ever done anything good. Most of the time, I just feel so alone and scared of what tomorrow will bring.

So, my love, I guess this is it. Through my own stupid fault, I never got a chance to tell you face to face that you mean more to me than anyone I've ever met. And while they say a man shouldn't waste time and energy on regrets, this man knows for sure he messed up when he didn't grab the chance with both hands to be with you for ever.

I'm sorry for chickening out, and for making the wrong decision.

But sorry doesn't do justice to how I feel about not being able to see your smile one last time.

Please forgive me,
Nathan

Days later Leonie and Alex were still knee-deep in the search for Nathan's whereabouts. Despite Alex's colleague's best attempts, they still had no luck locating him in any of the federal prisons' databases. Granted, without a surname they knew it was a long shot, but even despite this, Leonie had been quietly confident they'd find something eventually.

Once the initial excitement of figuring out that he might actually be in prison had worn off, Leonie had started to think seriously about what his crime was. She couldn't imagine it was anything terribly serious like murder, chances were his offence would be more of the white-collar variety. Maybe insurance fraud?

Anyway, it didn't especially matter what Nathan was there for, what was really crucial now was to locate the facility he was being held in.

For her part, she'd trawled through old news stories on the Internet looking for a mention of his name in connection with a crime of some sort, and had read back through the letters dozens more times in the hope of finding something, anything, that could give them a clue to his whereabouts.

It was strange, but she still sensed that there was something else they were missing about this whole situation, something important that could very well hold the key to the entire mystery.

'Did you notice that he mentioned something in this last one about "chickening out"?' Alex said holding up one particular letter. 'I think that's the first time he's made any direct reference to what he might have done.'

'I wonder what he did do?' Leonie asked, swinging her legs off the end of the window seat. It was Thursday evening and while she and Alex had decided to have a quiet night in with a movie and a takeaway at Leonie's, neither of them could resist going through the letters one more time.

'I know,' she said to Alex. 'It's funny how when you read these again, knowing what you do now, they take on a totally different significance. When I read that one initially, I actually thought that "chickening out" might refer to something about Helena. That maybe she'd decided to leave the husband to be with Nathan, but he got cold feet and took off? Yet somehow I couldn't see him having cold feet about wanting to be with her full-time.'

'So what did he chicken out of then?' Alex mused. 'Something to do with the crime, I suppose. Maybe he gave himself up?'

'I have no idea, and it's driving me crazy that we can't find out,' Leonie said, frustrated. 'All we know is that no matter what he might have done to end up in there, the poor guy still thinks Helena refused to forgive him, without realising that she probably never even got the chance to decide.' She looked at Alex. 'Talk about forgiveness, Alex, I don't think I could ever forgive *myself* if we don't find him now.'

'Well, I think I need a break,' her friend replied, shoving the sheaf of letters aside and stretching languorously on the sofa. As she did she knocked over the wooden box containing the empty envelopes, and they fell to the floor.

'I'll get those,' Leonie said as Alex reached down to pick them up. 'There's Coke in the fridge if you want it.'

'No offence, but I'm think I'm more in the mood for something stronger. I've got a couple of beers in the fridge downstairs. Fancy one?'

'Good idea,' Leonie agreed and while Alex popped downstairs to her own place, she picked up the envelopes and began loading them back into the box.

And as she did she noticed something. Something strange. Her heart sped up as the significance of what she was seeing struck her, and she stared at it almost immobile for the few minutes before Alex returned.

'Here you go . . . what is it?' the other girl asked, seeing her frozen expression.

'The first envelope,' Leonie said uneasily, handing the envelope to Alex. 'It's different.'

Her friend frowned and set the bottles of Corona down on the coffee table. 'Different in what way?'

'Take a look at the front of it.'

It was the letter she'd opened by mistake around Valentine's Day, Nathan's first (or in reality his most recent) letter. She didn't know why she hadn't noticed it before – possibly because at the time she'd been so rough with the envelope it was difficult to spot, but now that she had realised the difference, and more importantly, what it could mean – it sent a shiver down her spine.

'There's no postmark on this one,' Alex said, seeing it immediately.

'I know.'

'So it didn't come through the mail?'

'Exactly.'

'Shit.' Leonie could tell by her expression that Alex had come to the same conclusion.

'So he's out?'

Leonie's thoughts whirled. 'I don't know. I don't know what to think at all now.'

The most recent letter was markedly different to the others in that it had no postmark on the envelope, and Helena Abbott's name and apartment number was written on the front of it. Which could only mean that someone had dropped it off by hand.

'Looking back, I suppose that first letter was always that little bit different to the others, but once I'd opened them all

I never really noticed it. It was only a short note, whereas the others were longer and more detailed . . . '

'None of that really matters now,' Alex said quickly. 'What matters is where this guy is. All this week we thought he was in prison, which I'll admit at first I thought was a long shot, but like you said it fit.'

'It did. And reading through them again, I'm still convinced that's the case. But—'

'But people in prison can't put notes through letterboxes, Leonie.'

'I know. But maybe he could have had someone else drop it off—'

Alex shook her head. 'There are far too many maybes here,' she interjected, exasperated. 'Maybe Helena's dead, maybe she's not, maybe Nathan's in prison, maybe he's not!' She threw up her hands in despair. 'I don't know and to be honest, I'm not sure if I even *care* anymore. We're tying ourselves up in knots with this thing.' She looked at Leonie. 'I'm sorry and I know this means a lot to you, but all this is turning out to be a complete waste of time. We don't know what the story is behind these letters, and if you ask me we'll never know.'

'No, we can't just give up,' Leonie argued, although she too was thrown by this most recent discovery. She'd been so sure . . . but then again as Alex kept pointing out, they really couldn't be sure of anything, could they?

'But what else are we supposed to do? We've already tried everything we can think of to locate either one of them. It's not as though we can go around state penitentiaries asking if they have any inmates called Nathan, or keep grilling every person called Helena Abbott to see if it's her. She could very well be dead, and we don't even know his surname!' Alex was just about at the end of her tether.

'I know.' Leonie shook her head at the hopelessness of it. 'I know what you're saying and I've racked my brains too. I don't want to give up but it's hard to see what else we can do to find them now, short of taking out a full-page ad in a newspaper or—what?' She stopped short when Alex gave her an odd look.

'That's it!' the other girl exclaimed, wide-eyed.

'What?'

Alex slapped a hand to her forehead. 'Why the hell didn't I think of it before?' she groaned, while Leonie just sat there, waiting to hear what she had in mind. Alex took a notebook out of her handbag and began writing furiously. 'Up to now we've been trying to pick out a needle in haystack,' she said, 'when all along we should have been using a damn magnet.'

The following morning Alex pitched to Sylvester her grand idea for a potential *Today by the Bay* slot.

Deciding it would be best not to betray her connection to the origins of the story, she began by telling her boss that some interesting letters had been sent by a member of the public to the station. The truth, or indeed any other explanation, would have greatly lessened the likelihood of his allowing her to run it.

'I think it's right up our street,' she told him. 'The guy has been sending love letters to this girl who no longer lives at the address, yet they can't be returned. I think whoever sent them to us thought they were too important to ignore, and while they couldn't find the guy, maybe we could.'

'I think I like it,' Sylvester said, after some thought. 'And the public will go crazy over it.'

The thinking behind the TV piece was that they'd run a heart-warming story about undelivered mail from a man called Nathan searching for his lost love Helena and with such exposure, maybe somebody who knew (or had known) either one of them would see it, realise the significance and arrange to contact the station.

'We should use some of these,' Sylvester said, flicking through the letters that Alex showed him. 'The fancy handwriting's good – it'll fit with the slushy theme. They'll have to be subtitled though.'

'Wouldn't we need to get copyright permission to do that?'

'How can we, if there's no return address? Anyway, for all we know, it could have been the guy himself who sent those letters to us in the hope that we'd put them on TV. If you're worried, I'll talk to the lawyers about it, but as the letters were sent to us, I'm pretty sure it's legal,' he went on, and Alex gulped.

Having got the go-ahead from Sylvester, the piece was due to go out the following week. While Leonie had reservations about how much personal information they should disclose, she and Alex had both agreed that getting some form of result was more important.

'We'll only use first names and leave out the Green Street address too,' Alex agreed with her, while putting the piece together in its early stages. She also agreed to leave out of the piece (and in the initial pitch to Sylvester) their suspicions that Nathan may have been writing the letters from a prison cell.

'It's the sort of thing that will bring all kinds of wackos out of the woodwork,' Alex told Leonie. 'And not only that but it runs the risk of alienating the public or frightening either one of them away too.'

'Do you really think there's a chance they might see it?' Leonie couldn't contain her excitement. Alex knew her remark about putting out a full-page ad came more from desperation than anything else, so when she'd come up with the idea of appealing for them on TV, Leonie too couldn't believe they hadn't thought of it before.

'Who knows?' Alex replied. But it was the last throw of the dice as far as she was concerned and if nothing else, it would make damn good TV.

The following Thursday evening Leonie sat glued to the telly, waiting for the six o'clock news to hurry up and finish, so that the *Today by the Bay* slot could air. But even better, and much to her delight, all throughout the lead-up SFTV news kept running teaser spots about the upcoming story, which meant that by the time the piece about the letters did appear, there was an even greater likelihood of a captive audience.

Alex had explained that there was a possibility the station would do this, but she couldn't be sure. 'It depends on how much of an impact they expect it to make,' she'd told Leonie when the slot was recorded and the finishing touches were being put to it. 'And, of course, whether or not it gets bumped for some wacko with a shot of a UFO hovering over the Golden Gate,' she added drily.

But it was obviously a quiet day for the wackos, as before every ad break during the news the station ran the teaser preview of the upcoming *Today by the Bay* piece, which they'd entitled 'Please Forgive Me'.

'It's coming up soon, so stay tuned to SFTV News,' the news anchor repeated for the umpteenth time. Leonie still found it hard to get to grips with the way the TV stations seemed to assume that all viewers had the attention span of a goldfish. Why else did they feel the need to bombard people with teasers and practically beg them to 'stay tuned'?

It was frustrating, because she had to sit through almost a full hour of irrelevant guff before the *Today by the Bay* slot finally appeared.

Leonie hugged herself and felt a shiver up her spine as the piece began with a gentle female voiceover against a background of tear-jerking, Oprah-style piano music.

'With today's dependence on email, cellphones and all kinds of quick-fix modern communications technology, it's heartening to find that some of the old-fashioned methods of reaching someone still exist.'

The voice paused for a moment, while the music cranked up and on screen a blurry montage of faceless people in the physical act of writing letters was displayed. Leonie smiled, amused at the idea of Alex being associated with something so utterly devoid of subtlety. Yet she knew it would be compelling to anyone watching; hell the piece was compelling to her and she already knew every last detail!

'But this old-fashioned and very simple act of writing letters might just be the final act in one particular love story,' she continued, and at this, Leonie felt a lump in her throat.

'Meet Nathan,' the breathy voice intoned, as one of his letters appeared on screen, the distinctive ink handwriting immediately recognisable to Leonie, but illegible to most other people – which was why his words were helpfully subtitled underneath.

In my head I can still see your smile, hear your laugh and feel your arms around me . . . It's driving me crazy to think that I might never see you again. I'm so sorry for what I did . . . I never meant to hurt you. Please forgive me.

'Touching words, I'm sure you'll agree. But the problem?' the voice paused for dramatic effect. 'None of the letters have actually reached the person they're addressed to. It's kind of like a modern-day version of that old Elvis classic, except these letters weren't returned to sender, they were sent to us here at SFTV.'

Leonie realised she was holding her breath as the voice went on to explain how there were in fact ten letters, all addressed to a woman called Helena, whose whereabouts appeared unknown.

'So, how she can forgive Nathan if she doesn't know he wants her to?' The speaker paused so viewers could consider this very important question. 'Well, we at *Today by the Bay* think this man deserves another chance. So, Helena, if you're out there and you recognise Nathan's handwriting, or maybe even his words, get in touch with us at this number.' An 1-800 number flashed across the bottom of the screen. 'We've got a pile of love letters just for you.'

The brief, but Leonie had to admit, very moving piece cut back to the studio, where the presenters were both wearing 'aw shucks' smiles.

'Well, I don't know about you, Ken, but I've forgiven him already,' the blonde co-anchor commented to her colleague.

'Yes, he certainly sounds like a keeper, Megan. Let's just hope she gets in touch before it's too late.'

Chapter 30

A day later and the response to the slot could only be described as overwhelming. Telephone calls and emails to the station were coming in by the bucket load, the majority of which were from women claiming to be Helena and declaring everlasting love for Nathan 'no matter what'.

Others were from viewers who insisted that if Helena wouldn't forgive him then they would, and one woman even asked that SFTV News put forward a marriage proposal to him. Almost everyone had been touched by the letters and especially moved by Nathan's fruitless pleas for forgiveness.

A few responses also came from men who insisted the letters belonged to them and who were planning to sue the station for broadcasting them without permission. While Alex had known in advance that they were likely to get some unusual and downright wacky responses, she was now especially glad that they'd withheld the fact that they didn't have Nathan's permission to run this piece, to say nothing of letting them know where they suspected his location to be.

Unlike Leonie, she was sceptical that either one of the couple would see it (personally believing that Helena had, in fact, died), but at the same time, was content to go through the motions. Which was why Alex spent much of the following morning at the station returning calls to the various women claiming to be Helena. She'd also forwarded some emails to her personal email account so that she and Leonie could go through them in their own time, and weed out the time wasters from those who looked promising.

Midway through that morning, she got a surprise call from Seth.

'Interesting piece yesterday,' he said, without preamble. 'Did you find your guy then?'

'Not quite,' she said, filling him in on their suspicions about Nathan's whereabouts.

His reaction was predictable, which was exactly why Alex had mentioned it. 'You've got to be kidding me! The guy could be a freakin' psycho for all you know!' Seth exclaimed horrified, and she smiled, absurdly pleased she'd got a rise out of him.

'Seth, remind me again why this is any of your business?'

'Because I don't want you involved in that kind of trouble! If the guy's banged up, then who knows what you're getting into?'

'How touching. But like I said before, this is none of your business, so keep out of it.'

'It is when my wife is getting herself mixed up with a bunch of cons—'

'*Ex*-wife,' Alex retorted through gritted teeth. 'Despite what you think I don't actually need a piece of paper to tell me that.' Unfortunately, she did of course need that, but she wasn't going to admit as much to him.

'Just remember, that this is classic con stuff, Alex, you know – manipulating people to feel sorry for them . . . '

'And what would you know about it?'

'I just know what these kinda guys are capable of. How else do you think they get where they are?'

'Again, I'm touched by your concern but we're doing just fine, thanks.'

'Alex, just be serious for a second, OK? You're right, this *isn't* any of my business, but I still can't help but worry about you – and Leonie. You two really don't know what you're getting into.'

'Seth, like I said, butt out.'

'How can I butt out when my wife is getting involved with dangerous stuff like—'

'For the last time, Seth, I am *not* your *wife*!' Alex cried, exasperated. Where did he get off patronising her like this? 'Don't you get it? You and me are *over*, the divorce is going through as we speak, and there are no more last-minute stunts for you to pull.'

'Really.' Seth's tone was flat.

'Yes, really. You lost, Seth, deal with it!' Then Alex put her hand over the mouthpiece when out of the corner of her eye she could see one of the girls in the office waving frantically at her. 'What?' she asked Jill.

'There's a woman on line three who says she wants to talk to someone about the letters, and this one sounds like she really knows what she's talking about.'

'How so?'

'She passed not one but *two* of the checks you gave us,' Jill said eagerly, referring to the criteria Alex had set down for separating the crank calls from potentially genuine ones. 'A surname called Abbott and an address on Green Street.'

What? Alex wanted to whoop for joy. The TV slot hadn't given out either piece of information so this sounded *very* promising. 'Seth, gotta go. I don't have time for any more of your games just now, OK?' she muttered into the phone and without waiting for his reply, immediately hit the flashing button for line three.

'Hello?' she said, trying not to sound too eager. The majority of crank callers could smell desperation a mile off.

The voice on the other end sounded small and nervous. 'Hello, um, I saw the piece on TV about the letters to Helena from Nathan. I used to know a man called Nathan, you see and I just wondered . . .' she sounded almost apologetic.

'I'm sorry, ma'am, but is it OK if I ask you your name? Mine's Alex,' she added warmly, trying to put the woman at ease.

'Oh yes, I'm so sorry.' Unfortunately this seemed to have the opposite effect and now she sounded flustered. 'Silly me, of course I should have said so before. It's Helena Freeman here, although Nathan would have known me as Helena Abbott.'

Alex's dark eyes widened. Helena Abbott? Was she still alive? Well, if this woman on the phone was who she said she was then . . .

'Nice talking to you, Ms Freeman. And how can I help you today?' Then she frowned, remembering that she and Leonie had deduced from the letters that Helena's *married* name was Abbott? So where on earth did Freeman come from? Unless, Alex wondered, her mind scrambling to try and put the pieces together, the woman had since got divorced and reverted to her maiden name? No wonder they'd had no luck finding her!

'Well, it's *Mrs* Freeman actually,' she corrected, sending Alex's assumptions flying all over again. 'Like I said, I thought I recognised some of those letters you showed. At least, I thought I recognised the handwriting . . .'

Alex was perplexed. 'You mentioned to reception something about Green Street?'

'That's right, yes. It's the family home – well it was, we sold it recently after my mother died and—'

At this Alex's ears pricked up. The family home? And recently sold too – the executor sale the landlord told Leonie about. So if this woman was in fact Helena, then it was not her but her *mother* who had died. Alex's mind was doing cartwheels now.

Could this finally be the Helena Abbott they were looking for? Not dead, not living in Green Street anymore but still alive and well in—

'Mrs Freeman, do you still happen to live in the Bay Area?'

'No, I'm in Santa Barbara now. Why do you ask?'

'Well, I think we should meet up and talk some more.' She smiled, knowing that Leonie would be over the moon with this development. 'And if you are who you say are, then I believe we have some things that belong to you.'

'I still can't believe we actually found her!' As expected, Leonie was beside herself with excitement when later that evening she and Alex met up after work at the Crab Shack to discuss the day's developments.

Having spoken to her on the phone for a while longer, Helena Abbott had agreed to travel to the city to meet with Alex on Monday, and collect the letters in person.

'I don't want to hand them over until I'm a hundred per cent sure it is her, although from what she told me over the phone, I'm pretty confident.'

Their conversation had indeed convinced her; who else would have known the details about Green Street or that the letters were addressed to not just Helena but Helena Abbott?

'So, did she say anything else about Nathan, or have any idea about where he might be now?' Leonie asked.

Alex shook her head. 'I got the impression that they haven't been in contact for some time and it sounds like she's married to someone else.'

Alex sensed Leonie was somewhat disappointed on Nathan's behalf. 'So what will you say when you do meet her?' her friend mused then. 'Are you going to tell her where we think Nathan is, or . . . '

'I don't know, Leonie. If we do establish it is in fact the right Helena, then it's not really any of our business after that. We just pass on the letters that are rightfully hers and then it's really up to her what she wants to do with them, don't you think?'

She knew Leonie couldn't figure out how she could be so blasé about it all, considering all the effort they'd put into finding the couple, whereas Alex knew that for her part Leonie was simply *dying* to find out what Nathan had done. Well, it had always been more her baby than Alex's, for reasons that were still unknown. Why had she been so dogged about this all along? Was Seth right, had something similar happened to Leonie, something she was projecting on to this situation?

Thinking of Seth, Alex now felt a little bad about the way she'd spoken to him that morning. It was kinda out of line, given that he'd sounded so concerned about her, and she probably shouldn't have said some of those things. Then again, she mused, annoyed with herself for worrying about it, chances were most of it would have just bounced off Seth, he had such a damn thick skin . . .

A few minutes later, she and Leonie paid the check and headed back towards Green Street, their conversation still full of Helena Abbott and what she would be like.

'Well, I really think I should come along on Monday too,' Leonie said firmly. 'Just in case you're not sure if it is her; at least if we're both there we can decide for sure, as the last thing we want to do is give the letters to the wrong person.'

'Yes, I kind of guessed you would.' At this stage, Alex couldn't really care less who they gave the letters to, she was that tired of the whole thing. 'Which is why I told her there'd probably be two of us—'

'Who's that?' Leonie asked, cutting her off. They'd turned on to Green Street and were approaching the house when something or actually *someone* standing on the steps outside their place caught their attention.

'I don't know,' Alex said, and as she tried to make out the solemn-looking figure standing on the sidewalk, she suddenly felt an inexplicable shudder. And when she looked further down and spotted the flashing lights of an SFPD cruiser parked alongside the curb, she realised that she was right.

Something was wrong.

'What's going on?' Leonie asked, seeing it too.

Quickening her pace, Alex approached the figure, which they could now plainly see was a uniformed police officer.

'Are you a resident of this building, ma'am?' he asked, without preamble.

'Yes,' she replied, suspiciously.

He looked down at his notebook. 'I'm looking for Alex . . . ?'

'That's me,' she said, understanding immediately that whatever was going on, it was bad.

'You're listed here as spouse and next of kin for Mr Seth Rogers?'

Alex tried to force air into her lungs, and stop the ground from moving beneath her feet. 'I'm his . . . wife, yes,' she spluttered, barely able to keep her composure.

'What's happened?' Leonie managed to utter the words she couldn't, and for this Alex was grateful.

'I'm afraid I have some bad news, ma'am. Earlier this afternoon, Mr Rogers was airlifted from the waters beneath the Golden Gate Bridge.'

'Airlifted . . . ? Why? How?'

'We're not sure of the full details yet, but witnesses reported seeing him leap off the bridge.'

'*What?*' Alex gasped, hearing Leonie's sharp intake of breath alongside her. People jumped off the bridge all the time, it was one of the most popular spots in the whole country for . . . that kind of thing . . . but it couldn't be . . . Seth *wouldn't* . . . ? Again, Alex remembered her last words to him, something about the divorce being inevitable and no more stunts for him to pull, but surely he didn't think she meant *anything* like . . . ? Oh no, hell no, he couldn't be . . . *couldn't* have . . .

'He was taken downtown to Memorial and straight into surgery. I understand he's pretty banged up, so you might want to get on down there.'

Alex didn't know what to make of this, and the relief she'd felt upon hearing Seth was in hospital and not in the morgue was immediately undermined by what he'd said afterwards. Did it mean he'd be OK, or was in trouble . . . what?

Her fingers trembling, Alex quickly unlocked the garage and took out the Mustang. She made the trip to the hospital with Leonie in a complete daze, her mind fraught with the various possibilities. What had Seth been trying to do? What was he trying to prove? Alex's emotions seemed to suddenly swing from terror to distress and finally to anger. What the *hell* had he been thinking?

'There could be another explanation,' Leonie was saying from the passenger seat. 'I don't know Seth as well as you, but I *do* know that's not him. He wouldn't do something like that, Alex.'

'I don't know,' she replied, her mouth set in a hard line. 'I don't know anything anymore. I don't know what's going on with him. Since he came back he's been so weird and completely unpredictable. Not in that way but . . . oh my God, if something happens to him . . . '

'Don't think like that,' Leonie reassured her. 'We'll be there soon and we'll see what's going on then. In the meantime, just try and stay calm and think happy thoughts.'

Think happy thoughts! This conversation was so surreal it was almost funny, and despite herself, Alex forced a brief smile. Good old Leonie for always looking on the bright side of things; what would she do without her?

But when they reached the hospital, she soon realised that she would have to do without her – temporarily at least – as Seth was in theatre and the medical staff would only allow family access to the waiting area.

'That's OK. I'll wait here,' Leonie insisted, and Alex didn't have the energy to argue.

'What's going on?' she asked the nurse who accompanied her down to theatre. 'Will he be OK?'

'It's difficult to say at this time,' the nurse said evasively and Alex felt frustrated, knowing it was a complete non-answer.

She quickly took out her cellphone and dialled.

'Sweetheart, calm down, OK?' Jon said when Alex explained what had happened. 'I'll be there as soon as I can.'

True to his word, Jon made it to down the hospital in record time and following a frank conversation with one of the nurses he managed to extract the true nature of Seth's condition.

'Honey, I'm not going to sugar coat this for you,' he told Alex gravely. 'He's critical, he has multiple broken bones and fractures, and possibly some injury of the spine.'

'But what does that mean? Will he be OK or—'

'All I can tell you is he's got good people in there working on him. I know Richard Harrison, he's one of the best.'

'Oh God, Jon – this is all my fault!' Alex confessed. 'He phoned me at work today and I was horrible to him . . . ' She still couldn't believe that Seth would have reacted so badly to it, or maybe he'd just decided that her behaviour was the last straw and enough was enough. Maybe he'd finally realised that she really meant what she'd said and wasn't coming back to him.

Seth had after all, always been a man of extremes . . .

'Don't be crazy, of course it wasn't your fault. Maybe it was an accident.'

But Alex knew he was only trying to make her feel better. People generally didn't fall off a 250-foot bridge by accident. This couldn't be just another one of Seth's silly tricks to obstruct the divorce; anyone who went off that bridge did it for one reason and one reason alone.

Oh, my God, Seth what have you done?

Leonie was still waiting outside when Jon and Alex re-emerged a while later. Jon had convinced Alex that there was no point in her waiting around, especially as it looked as though Seth would be in surgery until the early hours.

'You should go home and get some sleep,' Alex urged her friend, when she'd updated her on what little they knew about his condition.

'So should you,' Jon pointed out when Leonie, reluctantly, left, but there was no way Alex was going anywhere while Seth's life still hung in the balance. 'There's nothing you can do here.'

'No, I've done more than enough already,' she said grimly.

'Alex come on – don't do this to yourself.'

'Jon, he could only have done something like this because of me – because of *us*!' she cried distraught. 'He's been trying so hard to stop the divorce, which I always thought was just out of sheer pigheadedness. But what if it wasn't? What if he really thought there was a chance that I'd change my mind?'

'Alex—'

'And if he dies, it'll be all my fault for never taking him seriously enough, for never trusting him and always assuming he's up to no good! That's what happened you know,' she said, not sure if she was saying it to Jon or herself. 'With our marriage. I never believed a word he said.'

'But with good reason, remember?' Jon said gently. 'Honey, from what you told me he wasn't exactly a man you could trust.'

'Don't talk about him like he's dead!'

'I'm not, I'm just saying . . . look, sweetheart, none of this is doing you or Seth any good. What you need to do is to go home and get a good night's sleep, and then tomorrow when Seth's had time to recover from the surgery . . . '

'But what if he doesn't recover?' Alex whispered. 'What if the injuries are too bad? I know well what kind of damage a fall like that can do, Jon; we covered this stuff at work one time.'

Nine times out of ten a fall from the bridge resulted in – if not immediate death – then certainly a very slow and painful one. The surviving one in ten generally had injuries and suffering beyond words.

So even if by some miracle Seth did manage to come through this, what kind of life could he look forward to anyway? He could be paralysed or for ever incapacitated . . . and all because she'd never bothered to listen or take him seriously.

'Look, let's just wait and see, OK? I'll ask the nurses to call us immediately when he gets out. Then I'll phone Richard and find out how things look.'

Alex couldn't help but wonder what would have happened if Jon had been the surgeon on call when Seth was brought in. She wasn't sure how she'd feel if that had been the case.

The man she now loved trying to save the life of the one she was still married to?

It was a crazy and pointless thought, and Alex didn't know why she'd even considered it. Jon would have worked as hard as the next guy to try and save Seth; she knew that without question. And she just hoped that whoever was working on him now would do everything possible to make him pull through.

He had to pull through, didn't he? For as long as she'd known him Seth had thrived on danger and thrills, hell, the guy would face death every day of his life if he could!

She smiled faintly, thinking again of him flopping around on top of that bull at the rodeo. He was so happy . . . so spirited and dynamic; surely someone who practically *gorged* on living life to the full couldn't be snuffed out just like that?

Jon was still trying to convince her. 'Alex, please, let me take you home.'

'No,' she said, heading straight back down the hallway toward the operating theatre. 'I'm not going anywhere.'

Chapter 31

Two days later Seth was still unconscious.

According to Jon, the doctors had done pretty much all they could during surgery, and while thankfully none of Seth's vital organs had sustained major damage from the fall, until he regained consciousness they couldn't be certain of the outlook.

'For now, we just have to wait and see,' the doctor said. Leonie could only imagine how difficult such a thing was for Alex.

That first night, Alex had reluctantly called Seth's family to break the bad news, and spent the whole weekend pacing the floors outside the ICU, hoping and praying that he'd pull through, and Leonie knew, still blaming herself for what happened.

And she also knew that today's planned meeting with Helena Abbott was the last thing her friend wanted to do, but it wasn't something they could postpone, not when the woman was travelling up from Santa Barbara to meet them.

'I could just go by myself to meet her,' Leonie suggested. 'You really don't need this now on top of everything that's going on.'

Alex shook her head. 'Doesn't matter; I can't do anything but sit on my hands and wait for his folks to get here. Hell, if nothing else, it might help take my mind off this goddamned situation for a little while.'

'As long as you're sure.'

Knowing her friend, Leonie could appreciate why Alex would need a distraction. She was a woman of action – someone who always needed to be in control – and all this waiting around for news was driving her crazy.

Alex had agreed to meet Helena at Union Square at three, suggesting the outdoor café bar located at the edge of the plaza, but because the cable cars heading down there were busier than expected, they ended up being a little late.

'Keep an eye out for a woman wearing a light pink jacket and a purple neck scarf,' Alex told Leonie, as they hurried up the steps towards the plaza. When setting up the meeting, Helena had given these details as a means of identifying her while Alex in turn had told her to look for a tall brunette and a redhead carrying a wooden storage box.

Leonie scanned the packed tables outside the café bar. It was a beautiful afternoon and the place was thronged with people. 'I don't see anyone sitting alone here,' she said to Alex.

'Maybe she had to share a table; it's very busy here just now.'

'I still can't see anyone fitting the description.' Leonie was at a loss.

'Well, if she's here, I'm sure she'll find us. Take the box out of the shopping bag so she can see it.'

Leonie did so, and they wandered up and down the plaza in front of the café, hoping that some woman would come forward and identify herself as the person they were meeting. To their dismay, no one did.

'Maybe she had second thoughts, or got cold feet?' Leonie suggested, her disappointment almost palpable.

'It's possible, I guess. Or it could be that she just couldn't get a table and is waiting somewhere else.' Alex looked further along the plaza to where throngs of people were gathered along the steps, but there was still no sign of any woman fitting the description Helena had given. Alex shrugged, not particularly concerned one way or another. 'She could just be running late.'

'I suppose.'

But another ten minutes passed by and there was still no sign.

Leonie gave a long frustrated sigh. To think that they'd come so close to getting answers, only for Helena not to turn up! But why wouldn't she have come? If she was interested enough to call the TV station and agree to meet with Alex then why change her mind? Unless something had happened in the meantime . . .

'Excuse me?' said a voice from behind them. Both girls whirled around, but Leonie was disappointed to see a much older woman smiling sweetly at them. Probably just a tourist looking for directions or something.

'Hi there,' replied Alex in a kindly voice.

'I'm so sorry to disturb you,' the woman went on and it was only then that Leonie realised, her heart pounding, that the same woman was wearing a pink coat and purple head-scarf – 'but you wouldn't happen to be Alex, would you?'

'Yes, can I help you?'

Oh. My. God. Leonie could only look on in amazement as the woman, who had to be sixty if she was a day, extended a hand and introduced herself. 'I'm Helena. It's very nice to meet you.'

To her credit, Alex didn't bat an eyelid. 'You're the lady I spoke with on the phone?'

'Yes, I was sitting over there, and I wasn't sure if it was you, but when I saw the two of you with the box I thought I'd better come over and introduce myself.'

Leonie couldn't say anything, she was so disappointed. Why didn't Alex think to ask the woman what age she was beforehand? This had been a complete waste of time! On any other day it might have been funny but she'd been so looking forward to finding out once and for all, what or who they'd been searching for all these months. Surely this woman, God love her, wasn't the Helena they were looking for?

Alex was doing her best to rescue the situation. 'I'm sorry,' she began, casting a surreptitious but meaningful glance at Leonie, 'but I'm afraid there's been a mistake.'

'What do you mean?' the woman said uncertainly.

'It's my fault. I should have thought to ask if you were . . . I mean, I couldn't tell from your voice that . . .'

'Yes?' she prompted, clearly not having a clue that anything was amiss. She didn't strike Leonie as one of those weirdos that Alex had been warning against, but you could never tell with these things, could you? If anything this Helena just seemed like a nice old dear who'd come along out of curiosity, or maybe in her day she had indeed gone out with a man called Nathan, hence the mix-up. Still, she was surprised at Alex for not checking her out fully on Friday.

'Ma'am, I appreciate you coming all the way here to meet with us, but I'm afraid you're not the person we're looking for,' she said gently.

'I don't understand?' Now she looked mightily frazzled and Leonie's heart went out to her. 'You seemed pretty certain the other day on the phone, so what's changed? I'm Helena Abbott, or at least I was once.' She smiled at Leonie. 'It only feels like yesterday, but time passes so quickly these days.'

Leonie returned the smile automatically.

'So, are those my letters?' she said, indicating at the box. 'Poor old Nathan Reed, I really can't imagine why he's writing to me. All that was such a long time ago, we were only kids really . . . ' she said wistfully.

Such a long time ago? Leonie looked at her stunned. *Was* there a chance they had got it all wrong, that they'd just assumed . . .

'Helena,' Alex began, and by her tone Leonie knew she was thinking along the very same lines. 'When was the last time you heard from Nathan?'

'Well, let me see . . . ' she said looking thoughtful. 'I would think it was round about the time of the Be-In.'

Leonie was clueless. 'Be-In?'

'You mean the Human Be-In, that famous anti-war protest in Golden Gate Park?' Alex supplied.

'Yes,' Helena confirmed, while Leonie tried to pick her jaw up off the ground. 'So thinking back, it would have to be, I'd say sixty-seven.'

'*Nineteen* sixty-seven?' she repeated, flabbergasted.

'Yes,' sixty-odd-year old Helena Abbott confirmed innocently. 'Why do you ask?'

The three women found a table nearby where they could talk over coffee – much to Leonie's relief, as she didn't think her legs would be able to hold her up for much longer.

To think that they'd assumed all along that Nathan and Helena were younger and that the relationship had been a recent one. Then again, why *wouldn't* they have assumed it when Nathan's letters gave that impression?

'This is all very strange,' Helena said, staring at the box of letters Leonie was still holding in her lap. She still didn't want to part with them until she and Alex were *absolutely* sure they had the right woman.

'I'm sure it is,' Alex said, taking the lead. 'Helena, as I explained to you over the phone, we needed to open all the letters to see if we could find information about either one of you.'

'What do they say? I can't understand why Nathan Reed would be writing to me after all these years. Don't get me wrong, I'm very pleased but . . . what do they say?' she asked again.

Leonie looked at Alex, willing her to ask more questions. She couldn't contemplate handing the letters over and not finding out the history and background behind them. She was in too deep for that.

'You mentioned his surname was Reed?' Alex said. 'It's just he never included this information in the letters. The thing is, he didn't include any contact details in them at all which was one of the reasons we made the appeal.'

'One of the reasons?'

'Yes.' She indicated the box. 'Helena, these letters are yours and I'm sure you'd like to go through them in your own time. Clearly some of them are very personal and again, I'm sorry that we invaded your privacy by reading them. But we felt it was necessary to help find either one of you guys because . . .' She paused slightly. 'Well, you'll see yourself from the letters but . . . '

'But what?'

'We'll get to that,' Alex said quickly, and Leonie sensed that she didn't want to upset the woman by rushing straight in with any unfounded suspicions. 'But first, I get the impression that the two of you haven't been in touch for some time?'

'No, I haven't heard from him since . . . well, since before he went away.'

Went away? Leonie repeated silently. *Was* it possible that Helena knew that Nathan was in jail? If so, he must have done something pretty terrible to be in there for so long! What kind of people were they dealing with here?

Alex kept talking. 'And do you have any idea where he is now, and why he might be writing to you?'

'I have no idea. To be honest, I really wasn't sure if he was alive or . . . ' She looked away sadly and Leonie realised then that no, Helena didn't seem to be aware of anything untoward. 'I moved away from the Bay Area a long time ago. Nathan used to live down by Pacific Drive. He adored being near the ocean.'

'So you two never actually lived at Green Street.'

'Lived . . . together?' She gave a little laugh. 'No, that would never have happened. We used to spend a lot of time there though,' she said blushing a little. 'It was my mum and dad's place. I still had a key and used to go there sometimes when I knew they weren't there. You see, my dad kicked me out right after I married my college boyfriend—'

'So you and Nathan *were* having an affair then?' Leonie blurted before she could stop herself and Alex gave her a look. OK, so accusing a sixty-year-old woman of infidelity probably was a bit tactless!

Helena nodded bashfully. 'I suppose you could say that. But you must understand, at the time . . . well, I guess it's difficult to explain to young people these days, but back then it wasn't so strange, not for us anyway. And Eddie was no angel either. He knew what was going on of course, but I guess he didn't really understand just how serious this one was.'

O – K. Leonie was finding it difficult and a little weird to reconcile the older woman sitting in front of her as someone who had an open marriage. But what did she know?

Helena seemed to sense her reaction. 'Things were different back then, you see. I was a silly young girl and thought I could change the world, that *we* could change the world,' she added, and as neither she nor Alex seemed to understand what she was talking about now, they decided to just let her talk. 'When I was growing up, the world was changing so fast and everything seemed so pointless and out of control. Our governments were corrupt – not that much has changed there – but it felt as though no one understood or even cared.' Then she smiled, which made her face seem much more youthful. 'But when I went to college, I discovered that there were lots of people who, like me, cared very much about what was going on in the world, thousands of like-minded people, and many of them were drawn here.'

Bloody hell, Leonie realised suddenly; the laidback marriage to the college boyfriend was suddenly making a whole lot more sense, Helena Abbott had been a bona fide hippie!! She looked at Alex to try and gauge her reaction but her friend seemed too engrossed in what Helena was saying.

'All of us decided to turn our backs on that world and create a new one, a kinder, more compassionate, freer world. At the time we really thought it *was* a revolution but I guess we were deluding ourselves,' she said with a shake of her head. 'It was what Nathan had been trying to tell me all along but of course I wouldn't listen. I was too immersed in this ideal of a brave new world, that somehow if we cared enough, we could change history.'

Leonie recalled how in the letters Nathan's words had always sounded similarly touchy-feely and expressive, not at all what you'd expect from your typical macho male. But again, she supposed this made sense for someone who too must have been part of the hippie movement.

'He was a very gentle soul,' Helena said wistfully, echoing Leonie's long-held impression of him. 'A real romantic and we were besotted with one another. I suppose you could say it was love at first sight for me.'

For him, too, she thought, but didn't want to admit to the woman that she knew too many intimate details about their love affair.

'So, as I say, I was married but at the time, that didn't matter. Fidelity was another thing most of us eschewed in those days. Although, in truth, Eddie and I were crazy for marrying back then. We were still in college and still finding our place in the world. I'd always been a worry to my parents, so marrying some beatnik liberal with no prospects was just another way of rebelling, I suppose.' She shook her head. 'As I say I was foolish, headstrong, and completely immersed in the cause.'

'The cause,' Alex repeated. 'You mean the civil rights movement?'

Helena sighed, as if such things still weighed heavily on her. 'That and many others, any righteous cause we could think of really. But the big one, particularly round about sixty-six, sixty-seven was the war.'

'Vietnam,' Alex said, understanding.

'But what about Nathan?' Leonie asked then. Helena and her causes were all very well but she wanted to find out what had happened to the couple. Why was he writing to his old girlfriend now? What had happened since that had caused him to get in touch with her at their old love-nest?

'When I met Nathan Reed I discovered what real love and real passion was like,' the older woman said, her cheeks reddening slightly. 'He was completely different to Eddie, different to any other man I'd ever met really. Intelligent, loving, compassionate . . . I adored him.'

'So what went wrong then?' Leonie persisted, seriously puzzled. 'It's obvious from the letters that Nathan loved you as much as you loved him.' *And possibly still does.*

At this Helena looked pained, and Alex gave Leonie another warning glance.

'Again, you must understand how important, how all-consuming our hatred for this war was. Half a million Americans sent across the world to fight for something that few supported.' She gave a short laugh. 'Things don't really change, do they?'

OK, Leonie thought, we didn't come here for a lecture. What did the Vietnam War have to do with anything?

'I guess I should have been more understanding. Goodness knows, Nathan never really had much of a choice, especially coming from a family like that.'

'Much of a choice . . . ?'

'I'm sorry, I'm not making much sense here, am I?' Helena apologised. 'Like I said, Nathan Reed was one of the gentlest, most compassionate men I've ever known. So to think that he could even *consider* going off to a place like that . . . '

A place like that.

All of sudden, Leonie's heart sped up and took off like a galloping racehorse. And her thoughts whirled in a thousand different directions, as just like that, she got it.

In this place . . . sometimes I wonder if I've wasted my life, if I've ever done anything good. Sometimes I feel so alone, and scared of what tomorrow will bring . . . Sorry doesn't do justice to not being able to see your smile one last time . . .

And she understood that right from the beginning, she and Alex had been completely mistaken in their assumptions about Nathan's whereabouts, they'd been completely mistaken about *everything*!

Those letters hadn't, as they'd suspected, been written recently from a prison cell. Instead they'd been written from somewhere very different, another part of the world, and in a completely different time.

'Nathan was a soldier in the Vietnam War?' she gasped, and Alex looked from her to the older woman, shocked.

Leonie could guess what she was thinking. The letters certainly didn't look that old, indeed they didn't look aged at all, the way you'd expect forty-odd-year-old documents to look, apart from the old-fashioned ink handwriting. But she recalled now, they'd also been wrapped in cellophane and carefully tucked away in the back of a dark, dusty cupboard, hidden away from the world and from the elements for who knows how long . . .

Helena nodded. 'We came from opposite ends of the spectrum. He'd not long enlisted when we first met, although he didn't tell me that for some time. His family was military so it was expected. It was so hard to reconcile, you see. My kind, gentle Nathan going to a place like that and becoming involved in such terrible things . . . I went crazy when I found out. I just couldn't understand why he would want to do such a thing, but the truth was he didn't really understand.'

Things are getting harder and crazier here now and I just don't know if I can cope any more . . .

Leonie was finding it hard to square lovely gentle-sounding Nathan Reed as a soldier.

'What do you mean "he didn't really understand"?'

'Well, he wasn't one of us, but I think he was still respectful of what we were trying to achieve. The problem was that he felt the complete opposite to me. He truly believed that in the end the war would be a good thing for us all, felt that we needed to take a stand – against communism,' she added for Leonie's benefit, correctly guessing that she wasn't terribly clued-in about that time. 'As I said his family was military, still are.' She looked away. 'It's very hard to explain the way we felt back then. We were both so headstrong and so sure in our beliefs . . . you don't get that so much these days. Not to mention we were young, foolish and most of the time, completely scared to death.'

Leonie was still trying to get her head around such conviction. She knew that in those days many social movements had been hugely powerful forces for change, but it was still incredibly difficult to comprehend. How could a couple who seemed to be so completely in love with one another be driven apart by simple ideology?

'So what happened?' she asked.

Helena looked pained at the memory. 'I tried everything I could to talk him out of it, to try and bring him round to my way of thinking. But I couldn't do it. I only found out about his enlisting when he admitted he'd been called for a tour. He was an intelligent, educated man with the world at his feet and a great future ahead of him. I begged him not to go, to stay here in San Francisco with me, with *us*, but it was no good. He had to go, felt he was letting his country down if he didn't. "I'm no draft dodger," he said, when of course most of my male friends were burning their draft cards in public.'

'You said Nathan enlisted but what about your husband?' Alex asked. 'Wouldn't he have been drafted?'

Helena smiled, sadly aware of the irony. 'Eddie, like most of our kind, was a college student and exempt. Like I said, we were all so idealistic, thought we were all so brave and courageous, when really we didn't have a clue. It took me a very long time to realise that guys like Nathan were actually the brave ones.'

Just please try to understand that no matter where I am, or what I'm doing, I'm always thinking of you.

'So you two broke up when he went away,' Leonie said then, guessing that this was the most likely scenario. But clearly, given the letters, the break-up had borne heavily on Nathan's mind.

And the worst part of it all is you were so right. This is a crazy place, a crazy situation and I really shouldn't be here – nobody should be here.

'Right beforehand. Once I knew what he was and what he stood for – and I mean that as a reflection of my state of mind at the time, not now – I just couldn't be around him anymore. I loved him of course, but I couldn't approve of what he was doing, I didn't want to approve. I guess that idea appealed to me too, the whole tortured love affair idea,' she added with a self-effacing smile. 'Like I said, back then I was a very foolish girl. He tried so hard to talk me round, told me he'd do one tour and then come back, asked me to wait for him, but I just wouldn't listen. I'll remember the very last thing he said to me though,' she continued, the beginning of tears in her eyes, 'and it was that, more than anything else that makes me certain those letters are mine.'

Leonie didn't even need to ask what that was. 'And have you?' she said, meeting the older woman's gaze.

Helena nodded. 'Of course I have,' she said sadly. 'I forgave him a very long time ago.'

'But Nathan doesn't know that,' she replied, 'and clearly this is something he regretted very deeply, perhaps still does.'

'But it was almost forty years ago! I would have thought it was long forgotten by now. It certainly is by me anyway.'

Although by the look on her face, Leonie knew Helena wasn't quite telling the truth. Nathan was obviously someone she had loved very deeply, and forty years or not, it still hurt. How incredible that feelings should run so deep even after all this time and – no, hold on, she thought, as something struck her. Nathan might have written the ones in the box all those years ago, but he'd sent another only four months ago, the one Leonie had opened by mistake! Why?

Alex was circumspect. 'Well, Helena, I guess we've done our duty by returning these letters to their rightful owner,' she said before draining her coffee. 'What you do with them now is entirely up to you.'

'No!' Leonie exclaimed, momentarily forgetting herself. 'I'm sorry, I mean, yes of course it is up to you what you want to do, but as you've already admitted you've forgiven Nathan, don't you think you should tell him that?'

'Leonie . . . ' Alex warned.

'I'm sorry, but this is important. The guy is still writing to her for goodness' sake!' She was shocked at her own depth of feeling about this but all this time she'd sympathised with Nathan, for more reasons than one. She quickly explained to Helena about the most recent letter.

'He's still writing to me?' Helena repeated, shocked.

'Yes, and we still don't know where he is, although we have a good idea—'

'Well, we don't actually know for certain,' Alex interjected with a sharp glance at Leonie. 'In fact, we don't know what the hell we're talking about, and we've already got it wrong on so many other counts . . . ' she added pointedly.

'I suppose so,' Leonie admitted crestfallen and more than a little ashamed now. She turned to the older woman. 'I'm sorry, I didn't meant to be so pushy, it's just . . . well, we've been trying so hard to find you two that it feels wrong to give up now.'

It broke Leonie's heart to think that they couldn't pursue this to the end and find Nathan, now that they knew the truth about his letters to Helena. And so hard to believe that the ones in the box were forty years old, as never in a million years would she have guessed this from their appearance. But then, she had wondered how they'd come to be stowed away like that.

'You said the apartment in Green Street was your parents' place?' she asked Helena. 'How come the letters never made their way to you?'

Helena looked away sadly. 'My parents . . . well, my father anyway, disowned me after I got involved in so much trouble. So perhaps my mom kept them for me. She died last year actually,' she said, tears now brimming in her eyes. 'Dad is a while gone now too. The moved out east and the years just went by, and somehow we never did manage to reconcile.'

'She died recently?' At this, Leonie's ears pricked up. 'So did your parents still own the Green Street place then?'

'Yes, when I heard they moved I figured they'd sold it, but then when Mom died, I discovered that it was still in the family. As the only child, it was left to me.'

Which explained the recent executor's sale and the reason the letters never managed to reach Helena, Leonie mused. Had Nathan just taken the chance with his most recent letter on the off-chance that Helena still lived there?

She didn't know. And as Alex pointed out, it really was none of her business now – not that it ever had been.

'Anyway,' she said to Helena, trying to heed her friend's advice, 'Alex is right – it is up to you what to do now, and I suppose contacting Nathan could be nigh on impossible in any case so—'

'It might not be that hard at all actually,' Helena interjected. 'In fact, there's someone who – one way or the other – should be able to tell us exactly where he is.'

Chapter 32

That 'someone' turned out to be David Reed, a high-powered and highly decorated local senator who had served his time in both Vietnam and Korea, and who also happened to be Nathan's brother. The Reeds were a very well-known and respected political family in the Bay Area. Alex recalled how Helena had mentioned that in view of his military background, Nathan could have done little else.

'I think I recognise the surname,' she said when Helena told them about Nathan's family, who she planned to contact as soon as she'd read the letters, and perhaps felt ready to hear the truth.

Some years after Nathan's departure she had divorced the beatnik boyfriend, moved to Santa Barbara and got married again to a man called Bob Freeman, hence the surname. But the second husband had died some six years before.

'I'll admit I kept tabs on how the Reeds were doing over the years now and again,' she said. 'Newspaper articles, things like that.' But ominously, she revealed, Nathan hadn't been mentioned.

Leonie was held rapt by the woman's story and Alex wondered again why all of this seemed to mean so much to her. She herself would have been just as happy to deliver the box of letters to Helena and having learnt their story, left it at that and got on with her own worries. But for Leonie, it all seemed to run so much deeper.

When they said goodbye to Helena in Union Square and returned to Green Street, Alex decided to broach the subject once and for all.

'Seeing as we're uncovering old stories, are you ever going to tell me yours?' she asked, when they'd finished discussing Helena and whether or not the couple would ever be reunited. 'I mean, I know you've had something else on your mind all this time, something other than those letters.'

Her friend looked at her and Alex momentarily felt guilty for raising the subject, particularly after what had been a particularly emotional few days for everyone. But it seemed that this time, Leonie was prepared to lower her guard.

She looked away. 'I don't know where to start . . . and I honestly don't know if you'll believe me.'

'Try the very beginning,' Alex said. 'After everything that's come to light lately, I really don't think anything would surprise me.'

Dublin: Six months earlier

Following her shock at finding Billy in Andrea's house, Leonie drove back to Dublin in a zombie-like trance, almost unable to contemplate what she'd discovered. And it *was* a discovery, not just a suspicion, because almost as soon as she'd walked into that room and seen Billy there . . .

There was only one conclusion to come to.

The guy hadn't even noticed her lack of response, had barely acknowledged her presence. He was so immersed in the football there could have been an earthquake going off beneath him and he wouldn't have realised.

'Come on, mate, you don't know what you're doing!' he'd

remonstrated, arm out to the TV, the cigarette still dangling from his lips.

Leonie had slowly left the room then, there didn't seem any point in staying. Instead she went back outside and waited in the car for Suzanne. Clearly he wasn't too concerned about anything other than the football, and looked to be right at home in Andrea's front room. What was it that Suzanne had said?

'He's Mum's boyfriend, but . . . they're always fighting.'

She gave a sideways glance at Suzanne, who was listening to her iPod, not a care in the world. Did *she* know about this? Highly unlikely, as she would surely have said something before . . .

Leonie felt nauseous as she drove along the N11, the beautiful blue sky and warm evening sunshine making a mockery of her dark thoughts.

But was she absolutely sure? She wondered now, trying to be rational for a second. Had her imagination *really* run away with her this time? After all, it would be crazy to just launch straight in with accusations if she wasn't one hundred per cent sure. So for argument's sake, and especially before she confronted Adam, she needed to put the pieces together.

She tried to figure it out, tried to think back on everything Adam had told her about his and Andrea's previous relationship. OK, so according to him, they were together in the very early days of Suzanne's life but split up for good when she was still a young baby. That was the version she'd been given anyway, and as far as she was concerned there was no more to it. So what about Billy, she wondered, her thoughts going right back to the root of all this. Where and when did he come into it?

'So where does Billy live, then?' she asked Suzanne, when they'd returned to the apartment.

The teenager was on the sofa watching TV and drinking a Coke. She'd been quiet and rather subdued since their discussion earlier, and Leonie sensed that she was staying in to keep in her future stepmum's good books, and especially in the hope that she wouldn't tell tales to her dad. But Leonie wasn't concerned about that now. She had much bigger fish to fry.

Suzanne shrugged. 'Some place in Wicklow town. I don't know; I've never been there.'

'But he stays at your house a lot too.' He certainly seemed at home there anyway, despite the fact that the place was unoccupied.

'Sometimes. But he goes away with his band a lot.'

His band? Leonie raised an eyebrow. That certainly accounted for the scruffy, juvenile dress sense and dodgy hair!

'He's in a band? How exciting.' She hated coaxing information out of the teenager like this; it seemed underhand somehow, but she needed to get an idea of what was going on in order to try and get her head around it.

'I don't think they're very good though,' Suzanne said, finishing her Coke. 'They've been around for ever and you never, like, see them on MTV or anything.' She rolled her eyes. 'And Billy's *always* broke.'

Leonie stood still, almost afraid to move. 'Really?' she said, wanting to draw out this particular line of conversation further.

'Yeah.' Suzanne picked up a cushion and plumped it up, before setting it down again. 'It drives Mum crazy.'

'I guess that's not very helpful when she has to buy stuff for Hugo – and you, of course.'

'I know, especially when he's always borrowing money off her too. He, like, *never* has money for anything. That's how I know the band is rubbish,' she finished, confident in this pronouncement.

Again, Leonie's heart began to race. 'Your poor mum; she must get tired of that sometimes,' she said, trying to choose her words carefully.

'She hates it, and they're like, always fighting about it. I don't know why she puts up with him really. I wouldn't let a guy treat me like that.'

'Like what?'

'Like never taking her out to dinner or giving her nice things or anything. And sometimes he goes on tour with the band for ages without telling her, and doesn't, like, phone when he's away.' She rolled her eyes again. 'But I guess she loves him, although I honestly don't know why.'

Leonie was getting a strange depiction of Andrea here, one totally at odds with the one she'd been familiar with up to now.

'But you get on well with him all the same?'

She shrugged. 'He's OK. I hate the way he always smells of smoke though, that's really gross. And sometimes he gets drunk and acts, like, totally brainless, kinda like some of the guys I know, even though he's got no excuse cos he's supposed to be an adult.'

'I hate the smell of smoke too,' Leonie said distractedly, her heart sinking afresh as this entire situation gradually became clearer. Billy sounded like a complete and utter waster. He had no real job, drank and smoked like a trooper and was continuously cadging money off Andrea. Hardly the ideal father figure.

'He's a good dad to Hugo, I'd imagine though?' She let the question hang in the air for a while.

'I guess. He doesn't really take care of him though, not the way my dad takes care of me.' She turned to look at Leonie, her expression so innocent and devoid of guile it was almost as if she'd morphed into a different person. 'I know I'm really lucky he's so nice to me, and I guess I don't really show it all that much.'

Leonie tried to smile. 'It's OK, he knows you love him.'

But once they'd moved on to the subject of Adam, she knew she'd have to put a stop to the conversation and soon. She couldn't talk or even think about her fiancé at the moment.

Not when her suspicions were being confirmed more and more as time went on.

As expected Grace too was horrified. 'Oh my goodness, are you absolutely sure about this?' she said, white-faced when Leonie told her what she was thinking. 'Because you need to be absolutely, one *hundred* per cent sure before you say anything. I mean, if you just come right out and—'

'Well, it's impossible to be absolutely sure, but I'm about as sure as I can be,' Leonie admitted, jadedly.

It was mid-morning on Sunday, and they'd met up for brunch in a café on South Anne Street. After a full night spent tossing and turning and trying to figure out what to do next, Leonie was desperate to talk things through with someone before Adam returned later in the afternoon. Suzanne was again out meeting friends, so she'd phoned Grace for crisis talks.

As it was a gloriously sunny day, they managed to bag an outside table under the heat lamps, and now Leonie stared unseeingly at passers-by as they strolled along the streets, enjoying a crisp, bright Sunday morning, seemingly without a care in the world.

'And he's in a band, Suzanne said?' Grace said referring to Billy.

'Yep, although not a very successful one if he keeps coming back to Andrea for handouts.' She went on to recount every-thing else Suzanne had told her about the thus-far enigmatic

Billy. 'Lucky for them that Adam's so generous, isn't it?'

'But what was he like?' Grace asked, taking a bite out of her breakfast bagel. 'I mean, apart from . . . Did he have any reaction to you being there or . . . ?'

'Are you mad? He barely even realised we were there, what with the football and the thick haze of smoke around the place. God only knows what he was smoking either,' she added.

'But will he say anything to Andrea about you?' she said, and Leonie realised what her friend was getting at.

'I don't think so. I doubt he even copped who I was, probably assumed I was just some friend of Suzanne's. So no, I doubt he's given her anything to worry about. Although I understand now why she was so keen before to keep him under wraps.'

'Is it that obvious?' Grace said sadly.

Leonie sniffed, her eyes glittering. 'Unfortunately, yes. I knew it as soon as I walked in the door. There's no doubt in my mind that I'm right, Grace.'

'Well, you have to be, don't you?'

'I just feel so stupid that I didn't suspect anything before,' she admitted to her friend, trying to bite back tears.

'But how would you? You only knew as much as Adam had told you, and naturally enough you took that as gospel. Anyone would.'

Leonie gulped back her coffee. 'I know but with Andrea, I always knew there was something not quite right, something I just couldn't put my finger on. It didn't help that I disliked her on sight – well, even before that actually – and especially hated the way she had Adam wrapped around her little finger. And still has, obviously,' she finished with some bitterness.

'So what are you going to do?' Grace asked the question

that Leonie had spent the night asking herself over and over. 'How are you going to approach this?'

'I don't know yet,' she said in a low voice. 'Obviously I can't let Andrea—'

'This isn't just about Andrea though, is it?' Grace pointed out. 'That's what you have to consider.'

'I know.'

Pausing briefly to eat their food, they were both silent for a few moments, while Leonie considered the enormity of everything she'd learned over the last twenty-four hours. And just when she and Adam were supposedly back on track and she'd turned some kind of corner with Suzanne . . .

'To be honest, I'm still reeling over Suzanne's admission about her being on the Pill,' she said to Grace. 'It just seems so sad to me, and I can't figure out how any mother could allow—'

'Ah, Leonie, come off it,' Grace interjected in a no-nonsense tone. 'I don't think any mother actually *allows* something like that. Suzanne might seem too young in our eyes but she's big and bold enough to be responsible for her own actions, and in fairness to Andrea, wagon or not,' she added sardonically, 'at least she's making sure the girl is being responsible about it. I know she's barely fifteen, and believe me, I'd hate to think that my two would be up to divilment at that age, but if they are, then there's not a whole lot I can do about it other than encourage them to be responsible too.'

'She's hardly a great role model herself, is she?' Leonie said dourly. 'Considering.'

'Clearly not, but—'

'Ah, don't tell me you're sticking up for her.'

'I'm not sticking up for her at all. To be honest, I think she's an absolute *bitch*, but at the end of the day she's also a mother.' Grace picked at the remains of her bagel. 'And like any of us, maybe she was only trying to do her best for her kids.'

Leonie's mouth dropped open. 'I can't believe I'm hearing this! Now you're trying to *justify* her behaviour?'

This wasn't what she'd expected at all, especially not from Grace, who knew almost as much about the Adam and Andrea situation as Leonie herself. How could she even think about defending her in this situation? And even worse, how could she not be completely *horrified* by Andrea's behaviour?

'Of course I'm not trying to justify it,' Grace said. 'Believe me, I'm just as appalled as you are. A woman who could do something like that . . .' She shook her head in bewilderment. 'It's disgusting, no matter what the circumstances. But I suppose I'm also just trying to play devil's advocate. This is a dangerous situation, Leonie, and you need to be *very* sure you have your facts right before you go shooting your mouth off to Adam. Have you made up your mind about what to say to him?'

Leonie's heart sank at the mention of his name. 'Not really.' She gave a watery smile. 'There's a small side of me that wonders if I should just carry on and say nothing, but I know I can't do that.'

'But you do realise that whatever you do say is going to have enormous repercussions on the two of you, don't you?'

'I know.'

Leonie knew exactly what Grace meant. After this, her and Adam's relationship – if there was one after all this – would never be the same again. But at the same time, she also knew that she had to do what she believed was the right thing.

Regardless of the consequences.

'Adam, I need to talk to you about something.'

It was late that same afternoon, and Adam was just home

from his team-building weekend away. He'd arrived back at the apartment in great form, full of chat about it all, and when soon afterwards, Andrea called to pick up Suzanne and the two were once again alone, Leonie decided she couldn't put this off any longer.

'Sure, what's up?' he said easily, his mouth full of chocolate M&Ms. 'God, I'm starving. Will we order in tonight or, hey, what's the matter?'

Leonie kneaded her hands together, and perched herself alongside him on the armrest of the sofa. 'Look, before we start, I want you to know that I've thought long and hard about this,' she began, her mouth drying up all of a sudden. 'You're my fiancé and I love you but—'

'Hey, hey, what's all this about?' he asked again, his carefree expression vanishing as he realised she was being serious. 'What's going on, Lee? Did something happen while I was away?'

'No, no, it's nothing like that. Suzanne was fine.' She was quick to reassure him. 'It's just that . . . ' Now that she'd started, she wasn't sure of the best way to approach this. Should she just come right out and say it? No, she couldn't do that, not with something like this. 'Can I just ask you a couple of questions first?' she asked. 'Just so I can get a few things straight in my head.'

Adam looked perplexed. 'What kind of questions?' he said, sitting forward. 'Leonie, you're kind of freaking me out here, to be honest.'

'I'm sorry, I don't mean to – it's just . . . well, I just wanted to ask a couple of things about you and Andrea. I mean, I know you told me all about it before but—'

'Is *that* what this is?' he interjected, his blue eyes twinkling with amusement. 'Are you jealous of Andrea? OK so I might have spent a lot of time down in Wicklow recently, and I

wouldn't blame you for feeling a little peeved about that in
the circumstances. I know what you women are like and
Andrea did say . . . '

'Say what?' Leonie asked shortly, wrong-footed. What had
the conniving little wagon been saying behind her back?
Bloody hell, was there no end to her scheming?

'You really can't stand her, can you?' he said. 'OK, I know
dealing with her isn't exactly a bed of roses but—'

'I don't hate Andrea,' Leonie assured him, lying through
her teeth. 'And despite what you think I'm not jealous of her
either. This is about something else entirely.'

Adam frowned in confusion, but she could tell she had his
full attention. 'Go on.'

But by now, Leonie was no longer sure whether she *should*
go on. 'I'm sorry,' she said backing off, 'I just wanted to clear
up a couple of things in my head, that's all.'

She walked away from him towards the kitchen.

'About me and Andrea?'

'Yes, but it doesn't matter,' she said with a carefree wave
of her arm. 'We'll talk about it some other time. Do you fancy
a cuppa?'

'No, it *does* matter, Lee.' He stood up and followed her
into the kitchen. 'I want to know what's bothering you about
Andrea and what I can do to set it right. Look, I'll admit I
was very much into her way back when. But I was twenty
years old, Leonie, and it didn't take me that long to get over
her – especially when I moved to London.' He shook his head
and smiled. 'But then, when I found out she was pregnant –
with my baby – well my first reaction was complete and utter
shock.'

'And how *did* you find out about the pregnancy?' Leonie
asked him. 'You never told me that.'

Adam leaned against the countertop. 'Andrea got in touch.

She'd heard through a few friends that I was back home for the weekend, and she phoned me up and arranged a meeting. She was quite a way gone at that stage, so as you can imagine, I was a bit, – well, floored.' He looked at her. 'But look, as I said, that was years ago, a lifetime ago almost. Even though we got back together, there really was nothing between me and Andrea back then, and there isn't anything now either. It's all about Suzanne.'

Of course it is, Leonie reflected.

'I believe you,' she said in the most neutral tone she could muster. 'But was there any particular reason why she hadn't let you know about the pregnancy before then?'

'Well, because she couldn't, I suppose,' he said shrugging. 'I moved to London shortly after we split up, and we hadn't kept in contact. So she moved on with her life and I with mine until . . .'

'And hadn't she started seeing someone else in the meantime?' Leonie asked, relieved that Adam had now more or less taken the lead in the conversation. 'When you found out about Suzanne, I mean?'

'As far as I remember, yes, she'd taken up with Billy again not long after I left.' Leonie nodded. She took out a mug and put a teabag in it. 'So were you surprised when she told you about Suzanne?'

'Well that's a weird question – of course I was! Imagine someone telling you out of the blue that you're going to be a father! I felt pretty damn guilty too, I can tell you. Look, where is all this going?' he asked again, sounding more than a tad impatient now. 'Is this about maintenance again? I guess I thought we'd worked all that out . . .'

'I'm just curious that's all,' Leonie said.

'Yeah, it was a strange time, but now I wouldn't have it any other way.' He smiled. 'Suzanne's one of the best things that has ever happened to me, Lee; the best thing I've ever done in my life.'

And right then Leonie realised that she couldn't do it. She couldn't continue down the road she was headed, she decided, a lump coming to her throat. It wasn't right and it wasn't fair. She loved Adam and he didn't deserve this.

She was about to tell him that he was a great father, when all of a sudden, he seemed to tense up and his body became ramrod straight.

'Oh my God,' Adam said, enunciating the words slowly and painstakingly. 'Oh my God. I can't believe that you . . . ' His gaze bored into hers, and Leonie was horrified by the hard glint in his eyes and the white pallor of his skin. 'I know what you're suggesting,' he whispered, looking at her like she'd just crawled out from under a rock. 'At least, I know what you're *trying* to suggest, and I can't believe you would even consider it.' He turned away and ran a hand through his hair. 'I can't believe that someone who's supposed to love me, who I'm supposed to *marry*, for God's sake, would knowingly try be so spiteful!'

Now Leonie was pale too. 'Adam . . . ' she pleaded reaching for him, although she realised now that it was too late. She'd gone too far, and while she'd thought she had pulled herself back from the brink, she hadn't done it in time.

'Don't touch me!' he gasped, in a voice that Leonie had never heard him use before and which sounded dangerously close to that of a wounded animal.

'Please, I wasn't trying to do anything, I was just . . . '

'I know what you were trying to do,' he barked hoarsely, 'or more exactly, what you're trying to *say*.'

'Adam, you don't understand.' As a desperate last-ditch measure, Leonie tried to explain herself. 'Yesterday I drove Suzanne down to Wicklow and I saw Billy. OK, I'll admit I was going to talk to you about it, but then I realised I couldn't do it. I couldn't hurt you.' Her bottom lip wobbled. 'But for your own sake, you must at least consider the possibility that—'

'Don't say it, Leonie, don't even *think* it!' Adam warned her murderously. He picked up his jacket and marched towards the door.

But she knew she had to try and save this situation, it was her only chance of saving their relationship. 'You don't understand, Adam, I'm not making things up! The resemblance is incredible, there's just no way that . . .'

By now, Leonie was in tears, and she could see that Adam was dangerously close to them too. 'I'm sorry, Adam, but Andrea lied,' she sobbed, before finally getting the words out. 'Suzanne can't possibly be your daughter – she looks exactly like Billy.'

Chapter 33

On Tuesday morning, Alex stopped by the station to check in with Sylvester and arrange to take some more time off, when she got the long-awaited call from the hospital telling her that Seth had regained consciousness. His folks who had been abroad when she called were due to fly in that same afternoon and Alex prayed she'd have good news for them.

'Does this mean he's OK?' she cried with a burst of relief. 'How is he?'

'The doctor is examining him now, so I'm afraid that's all I can tell you,' the nurse replied.

Alex raced down to the hospital in quick time, calling Leonie at work to tell her the (hopefully) good news.

'I'm just not sure what to expect,' she admitted fearfully, before promising to call her again later for an update. 'What if he's paralysed, or doesn't want to see me or—?'

'Just see what the doctors have to say first, OK?' Leonie soothed. 'Is Jon with you?'

'No, he was working last night, so he's gone home to get some rest,' Alex said cursing the timing. It would have been nice to have Jon here to translate what (if anything) the doctors had to say about Seth's condition.

But on the other hand, it was probably better that she go to see him on her own. Especially if . . .

When Alex reached the ICU and saw Seth lying in traction on the hospital bed, drips, bandages and machines all over, she almost threw up. He looked so shattered, so *broken* and it was all because of her.

'Mr Rogers, your wife is here,' the nurse said, leaning over him and to Alex's amazement and immense relief, Seth opened his eyes and . . . what the hell, was he *grinning* at her?

'Hey, darlin',' he greeted her hoarsely, and his behaviour was so unexpected and so normal, yet completely out of place given the circumstances, that Alex wasn't sure she'd heard right.

But then, she thought with considerable relief, it meant that he couldn't be that upset at her. Why else would he be grinning? Especially when he was in so much pain? Suddenly, all the heartache and worry of the last few days came tumbling out in a combination of relief, frustration and downright confusion.

'What's going on, Seth?' Alex cried, unable to control her emotions. 'What the *hell* were you doing jumping off the Golden Gate Bridge? It's a two hundred and fifty-foot drop!' As the nurse left the room, she seemed to give a sideways glance at Alex's decidedly non-sympathetic tone. Well, she didn't feel all that sympathetic at the moment. After all she'd been through the last few days and now Seth was *laughing* at her, for Christ's sake!

'Yeah. I know how big a drop it is,' he replied, grimacing.

'So what the hell were you *doing*? Was it some kind of dare or . . . ? Jesus, Seth, you scared the hell out of me! Your folks will be here soon, but I really didn't know what to say to them on the phone. All this time, I thought it was . . . that you'd—'

He looked at her, understanding what she was getting at. 'That I was trying to sign out, or something?' he finished, his breath coming thick and heavy. 'Come on, Alex, I thought you knew me better than that.'

'Well why would I think otherwise, when the cops told me you were seen jumping off the bridge?' For some reason, tears were now rolling down Alex's cheeks – especially weird when she felt so damned angry. But there was no denying she was unbelievably relieved too.

'I'm sorry, I thought you knew,' he gasped grimacing, and despite his bravado, there was no denying he was in considerable pain. 'I told the cops when I woke up.'

'Told them what?'

'There was this kid . . . ' Again he paused for breath and licked his lips. 'Hey, any chance you could . . . get me some water?'

'Sure.' Alex filled a glass from the nightstand and held it gingerly to his lips, her emotions dissipating somewhat. He really was in a bad way, and now that she knew her worst fears about his motives were unfounded, she wondered what the extent of his injuries actually was. Severe internal and external fractures, the doctors had said. What did that mean? Then almost without realising it, she reached down and took his heavily bandaged hand in hers.

Seth beamed. 'Why honey . . . I didn't know you . . . cared!' he teased, and Alex instantly let it fall. 'Hey, I'm only kidding,' he added with a slight wince. 'I'm glad you're here, Alex. For a while there I thought I . . . really was a goner.'

So did I, she said silently. 'Just tell me what happened – and start at the beginning.'

Through painful fits and starts, Seth explained that on Friday afternoon he'd been jogging across the Golden Gate Bridge when he noticed a group of teenagers near the south tower. 'They'd been drinking beer and . . . making fun of this smaller guy, daring him to climb out on to the . . . ledge,' he told her, his hand shaking uncontrollably as he tried to hold the glass of water. Alex quickly took it from him and held it to his lips, her heart breaking to see him so helpless. After a pause, Seth continued. 'Poor kid looked terrified, and the others just . . . watched and laughed so . . . ' Grimacing, he stopped mid-sentence.

'Hey, slow down,' Alex soothed, mopping his damp brow.

'I guess I figured they were . . . bullying him. I went over and tried to break it up, told them I'd call security if they didn't.'

'There was no security around?'

'Not that I could see. Believe me, if there was, I wouldn't . . . be in this situation now, would I?'

Alex nodded. Point taken.

'I stepped over the barrier to try and help the kid off the ledge, but a couple of the bigger guys turned on me and told me to . . . mind my own business. There was a bit of a scuffle and I guess I must have lost my footing.' He shook his head. 'Before I knew it, I'd gone off the ledge and . . . into the water.'

'For Christ's sake, Seth!' Alex was so horrified she couldn't contain herself. 'Why would you go and get involved in something like that? It wasn't exactly one of your crazy bungee jumps, was it?'

Still, she couldn't help but feel impressed and oddly proud that he had intervened. But now comprehending the magnitude of it all, and how weak and helpless he was as a result, all of a sudden she started blubbering.

'Hey, it's . . . OK,' Seth whispered, reaching for her hand again. 'Someone must have seen it all because the rescue choppers were there within minutes. They got me out, although I don't know how the . . . kid fared afterwards. Do you . . . think you could find out?'

'For God's sake, I don't give a damn how the stupid kid is!' Alex exclaimed. 'You could have *died*!'

Seth looked away. 'I know, and if I'd given half a thought to what might happen, I would have minded my own business and just kept going,' he said solemnly.

'Hitting that surface . . . it was like every bone in my body started to vibrate all at once.' He bit down hard on his lip, as if just thinking about it unleashed a fresh wave of pain.

'Oh God, Seth . . . ' Alex couldn't stand it. 'What the hell possessed you to butt in like that?'

When he didn't immediately reply, she stood up and adjusted the blinds, just for something to do.

Recollecting himself, Seth sighed. 'Oh, I don't . . . know. I guess that thing you said about Doctor Love always saving people got to me somehow.'

She whirled around, incredulous. '*What?*'

'Gotcha,' he chuckled (with considerably difficulty) through his bandages. 'Hell, I don't know, Alex . . . I just saw the poor little guy looking . . . scared so I stood up for him. I didn't really think about the consequences.'

And what were the consequences? she wondered now, as Seth lay flat on his back, his body battered and broken. He might be trying to talk a good game, but it was easy for Alex to see past the bravado. He was in serious pain and very, very scared.

Again there was a heavy silence in the room, until eventually Seth spoke again.

'I know what you're . . . thinking, and you're right,' he said solemnly, and Alex reached for his hand and squeezed it, preparing to console him. But instead his face broke into a mischievous grin. 'I guess I *am* one hard . . . son of a bitch to get rid of.'

Chapter 34

Despite his bluster Seth wasn't out of the woods just yet. He would have to remain under close observation in the ICU over the next few weeks, and while the damage to his spine didn't appear as grievous as the doctors first suspected, they still needed to keep an eye on his internal injuries. He would be confined to a wheelchair for a while and needed extensive physiotherapy, so it would be a long time before he was back on his feet. In the meantime, his parents had arrived and although they were as warm as ever, and seemed thrilled to see her, Alex still felt somewhat uncomfortable around them, given the divorce.

This was the information she gave Leonie when later that day she called to update her on the situation, and the not-so-insignificant fact that Seth hadn't been trying to hurt himself.

'That's fantastic news!' Leonie said, relieved. 'I'm thrilled he'll be OK.'

'Well, we don't know for sure yet, but at least he didn't . . . ' Alex still couldn't even say the words.

'I know, and see? I told you he wasn't like that.'

'I can't believe he almost died trying to stand up for some stupid kid,' she continued, still shell-shocked not only by Seth's actions, but perhaps also, Leonie deduced, by the thought of losing him. Despite her friend's relentless protests to the contrary, Leonie suspected that Alex still had some feelings for Seth. Her reaction to his accident, and her subsequent vigil at his bedside had proved that. OK, so he may have misbehaved in the past, but any fool could see he was still head over heels in love with his wife. Who knew what the future might hold for them?

She'd intended on going down to see him at the hospital later, but according to Alex, visits were, for the moment, strictly limited to family only. 'Which just means me and his folks, I guess.'

'Hmm, lucky they're still married then, isn't it?' Marcy said archly, when Leonie told her this.

She smiled at the irony. 'I know, I thought the very same thing. But I still wouldn't go pointing that out to Alex if I were you!'

For her part, she was glad that she'd taken Alex into her confidence and told her the circumstances surrounding her and Adam's break up and her reasons for leaving Ireland.

'I'm beginning to understand why you were so obsessed with those letters,' Alex said shrewdly when Leonie had finished recounting her sorry tale. 'And why you identified so much with Nathan's pleas for forgiveness. But correct me if I'm wrong, in this situation I don't think Adam alone can grant you that,' she continued, echoing what Grace had said before. 'You need to be able to forgive yourself first.'

'How can I? I ruined Adam's life by uncovering the truth about Suzanne,' Leonie argued. 'He loved that girl with all his heart. As far as he was concerned she was his daughter and he never had any reason to think otherwise.'

'Yes, but you weren't the one who pulled the wool over his eyes, were you?'

That might have been so, but at the end of the day, Leonie

knew it was her meddling that brought the truth to light and while she doubted that Adam (much less herself) would ever be able to forgive that, she hoped that someday, he might at least be able to understand.

If anything, Nathan's letters had taught her that this was as much – if not more important.

And although she loved San Francisco and her new life here, she couldn't get away from the fact that she loved Adam a hundred times more and still missed him desperately. So many times she wanted to pick up the phone and tell him again how sorry she was, but she just couldn't summon the courage do so.

'Well, I think you should just bite the bullet and talk to him,' Alex said when Leonie tried to explain this. 'OK, so he was mad at the time, but what about afterwards when things calmed down?'

'There's no point,' Leonie reiterated. 'How could he ever respect or trust me again after what I did? I effectively took his daughter away from him; there is no coming back from that.'

'But shouldn't he be the judge of that? From what you told me, he sounds like a pretty decent guy. And I'm sure if you two just talked things over—'

'It doesn't matter now,' Leonie said, thinking Alex sounded exactly like Grace.

But they hadn't seen the expression on Adam's face that day.

Forgiveness just wasn't an option, not in this case. Anyway, that really wasn't the point. She didn't want forgiveness. All Leonie ever wanted was for Adam to know that she'd never meant to hurt him, and if she managed that, it would be enough.

*

It was two weeks since Seth's accident and Alex still wasn't sure how to feel. She didn't think she'd ever been so scared as when that cop appeared on her doorstep and she'd known instinctively it was about Seth.

Granted, she didn't think she'd ever come across anyone so frustrating and downright infuriating, but in that split second she got a glimpse of how it would feel if she lost him for ever. And Alex was frightened of how that had felt, and of the way she felt when she came in to the hospital every day and saw him lying in the bed, alone, injured and still very scared about what was to come.

Satisfied that he was over the worst, his folks had returned to Texas.

'I know I couldn't be leaving him in better hands,' Sally Rogers had said, giving Alex a gentle hug. 'Whatever's going on between you two is none of my business, but whatever happens just remember you'll always be like a daughter to me.'

'Be sure to come down and visit us again on the ranch sometime,' Bud added, and Alex was deeply touched by their graciousness towards her.

She also had to admire the gracious way their son was dealing with his own situation, not to mention his bravery in landing himself in it in the first place. But she'd spent so much time with Seth since the accident that Jon had recently taken her to task about it.

'What's really going on here, Alex?' he'd asked, after she'd postponed yet another night out with him in favour of visiting the hospital.

'It's hard to explain, but I guess I kind of feel responsible for him,' she told him. 'His folks couldn't stay on here indefinitely, and he doesn't really have anybody else . . . '

'Why on earth do you feel responsible?' Jon was unimpressed.

'Alex, the guy cheated on you, and left you high and dry—'

'I know.' Alex really didn't need reminding. She and Seth were over, she knew that, but she couldn't turn her back on him just yet, especially when he was still in such a fragile state.

But she also knew she didn't need this kind of pressure from Jon, not now, not when her thoughts and emotions were in turmoil. 'Look, I get what you're saying, and you're right, maybe I shouldn't feel obligated, but I do and I can't help it.'

'Well, I'm sorry but I think you should know I'm not happy about it. Not happy at all.'

'I know.' Alex sighed and took his hand. 'Look, Jon, maybe it might be better if the two of us took some time out from each other for a while.'

He looked at her. 'Time out?'

'Yes, I know you're upset with all the time I'm spending at the hospital and you've every right to be, but you have to understand why I'm doing it. He's had a tough time of it lately and with the divorce coming through soon too . . . I just think maybe things will be easier once all that's over with.'

Jon was silent for a while, and then he exhaled deeply. 'I guess I should have seen this coming. OK, so maybe I can appreciate you needing some time. I just don't know why you're wasting it on that—'

'Thank you, Jon, I really appreciate that, and once the divorce comes through, I promise you all of this will be sorted out once and for all.'

That had been a few days ago and, for everyone's sake, Alex hoped this was true. Now in the hospital, she turned to look at Seth.

'I almost forgot to tell you, we finally found Nathan,' she said, having spoken briefly to Helena that evening before heading to the hospital. The older woman had phoned to let the girls know that she'd been in contact with the Reed family who'd told her Nathan was now based in San José, and she was making arrangements to pay him a visit as soon as it could be arranged.

Upon reading the letters, Helena had been overjoyed and heartbroken in equal measures. Understandably, she'd also been taken aback by the depth of Nathan's sincerity.

'I had absolutely no idea he felt this way,' she confided to Alex. 'I'd always assumed he just forgot all about me, and got on with the rest of life. It's terrible to think that it all got to him so much. And with all those terrible things he was going through . . . '

Thinking now about the older couple's impending reunion, Alex found herself oddly envious of Nathan and Helena. Would she ever find someone whose love for her dominated his thoughts for almost half a century? Hardly likely, she thought with a wan smile, when she couldn't even dominate her own husband's thoughts for half a year!

'That's great. I'm sure Leonie's pleased,' her ex replied, his voice still dry and raspy.

'Oh, she certainly is.' Upon hearing Helena's update, Leonie had been over the moon at the prospect of their reunion.

'It's kind of awe-inspiring though, isn't it?' Seth said. 'To think that after all these years his love letters will finally be answered . . . '

'Yeah, well, who knows how it'll go – give them a few days in each other's company and maybe they'll end up killing each other,' Alex countered, unable to help herself.

Seth looked at her. 'Was what I did so bad that it made you that cynical?' he asked, his voice tinged with sadness, and Alex could have guessed that the conversation would inevitably come round to this.

'Seth, let's not do this now, OK?' she said, wishing he'd go back to making stupid jokes about his situation. But no such luck.

'I'm sorry,' he said, almost out of the blue. 'About back then, I mean.'

'I know what you meant,' she replied in a quiet voice.

'I just didn't know what to do. I didn't come home that night because you were so angry with me, yet it was the wrong thing to do because no matter how much I tried to convince you I hadn't done anything wrong, you just wouldn't believe me.'

'Seth,' Alex began tiredly. 'Why can't you just admit once and for all that you cheated on me? Why keep insisting otherwise?'

'Because I'd be lying.'

He stared right at her then and with a start, Alex wondered if he might actually be sincere. They'd talked a lot in this room over the last while, *really* talked and once Seth gradually dropped the cocky bravado act, she began to remember exactly why she'd fallen in love with him back then. Now, her heart began to hammer against her chest.

'What?' she whispered.

'I never cheated on you, Alex. I swear on my life, my family, the Mustang, everything I hold dear that nothing happened with that girl. Sure, we were fooling around when you walked in to the bar but it was just stupid flirting and nothing was ever going to come of it. Look,' he continued solemnly. 'At the time, you and I were only just married and I guess I didn't properly understand what that meant, I was just being my usual dumb, immature—'

'Don't forget selfish and pigheaded.'

'If you say so, yeah,' he said sheepishly. 'I'll admit I was selfish and stupid and crazy, all the things I wish I wasn't. But it was only when you'd kicked me out that I realised how serious it was, but by then you wouldn't even let me explain.'

'Because to me there *was* no explanation,' Alex countered. 'You lied to me about where you were going that night, so why on earth did you think I'd believe you about anything else. It's not like life is like some big game, and you can make up your own rules! OK, maybe I believe you when you say you made a mistake but—'

'Alex, my biggest mistake was lying to you about where I'd been. But that was my *only* mistake, I swear to you.'

'No . . . ' she protested unable to take this in. 'That doesn't make sense. You must have done something. Why else would you have stayed out all night, or moved out when I asked you to? Why would you let me believe—'

'Alex, my dad always told me that when you come up against an immoveable object, eventually you've got to stop pushing.'

She was so stunned she couldn't think of anything to say.

'And boy, were you immoveable!' Seth smiled and shook his head, but Alex could see in his eyes that he too had been wounded by what had happened back then. 'All that stuff about you never being able to trust me, and how you'd expected it all along. How was I supposed to deal with that? The more I denied it, the angrier you became, so eventually I figured I'd just leave you be for a while, that maybe when we'd spent some time apart and you calmed down I could convince you that you had it all wrong. But then, a few weeks later you hit me with the divorce thing and—'

'You decided to take off.'

He shrugged. 'I couldn't think of anything else to do. You wouldn't talk to me . . . , wouldn't even see me . . .'

Alex laughed humourlessly. 'Well, you and Leonie sure have a lot in common,' she said. 'When did running away ever solve anything?'

Seth gave her a studied look. 'It might not have solved anything, but it kept us married, didn't it?'

She felt a lump in her throat. 'Seth . . . '

'Look, Alex, you know I don't want us to get divorced – I never did. That's mostly the reason I made sure you couldn't find me.'

'But a whole year . . . '

'I know. I never planned to stay away that long, believe me. It's just . . . well it was good just being home on the ranch for a while and out in the open with the horses. Then when one of the guys told me he was heading on down to Florida for the summer, I figured I'd tag along and maybe stay for a couple of weeks tops, but that turned into longer than I planned. I knew I'd have to make my way back eventually though. And that's what I was doing when I bumped into you in Monterey.' He shook his head. 'I'm sorry, I know I shouldn't have let things go on for so long,' he went on, and Alex pretended not to have heard the catch in his voice. 'All I know is that I love you like crazy, and this last year has been hell without you.'

There was a long silence that neither one of them seemed to want to fill.

Then Seth met her gaze. 'You said something before about my not being a saint down in Miami? Well, you were wrong.'

She gave him a sceptical look.

'Believe what you like but I wasn't interested. Thinking back, I wasn't in the least bit interested in *her* either, but she was coming on strong and it was almost like I was on autopilot—'

'OK, I don't think I need to hear the details,' Alex interjected quickly. But she was floored by the idea that Seth hadn't been screwing around in Miami, and he seemed so sincere and determined that she almost believed him.

'So I guess what I'm saying is, I never broke that marriage vow,' he added his voice wavering. 'Never.'

But, Alex realised with a start, *I did*.

Seth seemed to read her thoughts. 'Is he worth it?'

She didn't reply – not knowing what to say or even think.

'Hell, Alex, I know you, and I also know that you and Mr Stuffed-Shirt aren't right together. He's just some guy who takes you out, buys you things and makes you feel good. But he won't make you happy in the long run.'

'And you can?'

'Damn right I can! And I will, if you'd just give me another chance.'

Alex gulped. No, he was wrong about Jon. She'd only ever held back on sleeping with him because she kept telling herself she couldn't do it when she was still married to Seth. But had it been less about principles and maybe more about getting even? Nevertheless, if Seth was telling the truth then in the end it was *she* who had ended up breaking their marriage vows.

And Alex didn't know how she felt about that.

'This is all such a mess,' she said, her voice breaking. Her feelings about Jon notwithstanding, there could simply be no going back with Seth, because if she allowed herself to even contemplate trying again and moving on, the infidelity – *her* infidelity would always be there in the background like some huge blot on a page.

'I'm sorry,' she said, her eyes filling with tears, as she studied her ex, bruised and broken on the bed. 'This is just too hard. I don't know what to say, or what to think now. For what it's worth . . . I think I believe you when you say that you didn't cheat on me, but Seth, it's too late.'

'We could call the lawyers—'

'That's not what I meant. So much has happened . . . everything's a mess. We can't go back, not now. And then there's Jon . . . '

'I know,' he said wearily and Alex realised that he understood her dilemma more than she realised.

The two again remained silent for a long time, both lost in their own thoughts, until eventually he spoke again. 'I guess you could say we both messed up then, didn't we?'

She nodded, not trusting herself to speak.

Seth sighed and looked away. 'Well, if you really want to end this marriage,' he finished, sounding well and truly defeated, 'then this time, I promise I won't stop you.'

Chapter 35

The following day at Flower Power was a busy one. It was almost June, Mother's Day was just around the corner and hordes of customers were getting their bouquet orders in early.

Marcy had put Leonie in charge of taking in the new stock out back while she served up front, which meant that she could only relate to her boss in snippets all that had happened over the last few days.

While she was thrilled that she'd uncovered the truth behind the letters and a reunion between Helena and Nathan was now on the cards, in all honesty, she now felt oddly bereft that the situation was by all accounts finished with. This . . . quest (or whatever it was) had kept her so occupied over the last few months that she wasn't sure what to do with her time now.

Although she really shouldn't complain considering that poor Alex had plenty to contend with at the moment, what with trying to juggle her obligations towards Seth throughout his recuperation, and trying to get to grips with her feelings for Jon. Leonie thought it had been very generous and mature of him to give Alex the headspace she needed until the divorce came through and . . .

'Leonie, can you take a call?' Marcy called from out front.

'Sure.' Probably Alex, or maybe even Grace, she thought, wiping her hands on a cloth. She'd called her friend from home first thing that morning but hadn't got a reply.

But it seemed not. 'Some guy about an order,' her boss said handing her the phone. 'Asked for the redhead he was speaking to before, so I guess that must be you,' she stated blithely before going on to serve another customer.

Leonie picked up the phone; faintly disappointed it wasn't Grace. 'Hello?'

'Hi, I'm sorry, I can't quite remember your name, is it Laura or Leah, something like that?' The voice was low, and to Leonie, sounded a bit muffled although it could just be a bad line. 'I spoke to you the other day.'

'It's Leonie,' she said pleasantly. 'How can I help you?'

'Well, this is a bit embarrassing,' the man began, his voice hesitant, and she deduced that he was speaking quietly for fear of being overheard. 'I was looking for some advice on a bouquet for my fiancée.'

'Sure.' Leonie couldn't remember speaking specifically to this person, but then again why would she? She spoke to lots of different customers every day. 'What would you like?'

'Um, well it's sort of complicated,' he said, and again the voice was so low it almost sounded like he was speaking through a gag or something.

'Complicated.'

'Yes. You know the way flowers have meanings? Well, I want to pass on a particular message but I'm not sure what flowers to use.'

'Oh, I get it.' Poor guy, he was obviously trying to arrange something special for this woman. A proposal perhaps? Although he had already mentioned that she was his fiancée so . . . 'Yes, some flowers do have symbolic meanings, but I would say the majority of people only know the usual ones, like red roses for love, or lilies for sympathy, that kind of thing. What message were you hoping to get across?'

'Forgiveness, actually,' he replied and at this, Leonie had to smile. Wow, there must be something in the air! But she probably should have suspected as much given that according to Marcy the two main reasons men sent flowers were to either impress or apologise!

She thought hard, trying to recall from memory the flower symbolising forgiveness – wasn't it something purple; violets or lilac, maybe? While she'd learned a lot about flowers over the last few months, she really couldn't be certain about this, so she thought she'd better ask Marcy.

'Hold on a moment and I'll check,' she said, putting her hand over the mouthpiece. Luckily her boss was free, having just finished with her customer. 'Marcy, what's the forgiveness flower – you know, the one that means I'm sorry?'

'Purple hyacinth,' her boss replied without even having to think about it, which made Leonie suspect she'd come across this particular request more than once!

Still smiling, she spoke into the receiver. 'It's purple hyacinth,' she told the caller. 'Would you like us to incorporate it into a bouquet with some other complimentary flowers, or just a simple hyacinth arrangement with perhaps a few greens?'

'I'm not sure. Whatever is most likely to get the message across, really.'

'Don't worry,' Leonie tried to reassure him. 'I'm sure your fiancée will accept your apology no matter what way you send them. And if she's not sure of the symbolism, you can always put the message on the card.'

'No, no, I don't want to apologise to *her*,' the man disputed, and this time Leonie got the faintest hint of an accent, was it Irish? 'That's not what I meant.'

'I'm sorry, I'm not sure I understand. The flowers aren't intended to make up with someone?'

'They are, but it's for something *she*'s done, not me.' Suddenly the voice was no longer stifled and was now coming through clear as day. And right then Leonie understood why it had been disguised from the very beginning. 'I was upset for a while, but I want to let her know that I'm over it now, and everything is OK.'

Her heart began pounding like a racehorse and the receiver shook in her hand.

'What?' she breathed into the mouthpiece, not daring to believe what she was hearing, or more importantly, whom she was talking to.

'I got the letter. I know she didn't mean to hurt me, and the flowers are to let her know in turn that I forgive her.'

Leonie closed her eyes, trying to get a hold of herself. Could this really be . . . ? Noticing her change of mood, or more likely her shell-shocked expression, Marcy came over. 'Everything all right?' she asked.

Leonie nodded wordlessly.

Adam's voice was now clearly audible over the line and she couldn't understand why she hadn't recognised it immediately. 'So, do you understand what I'm trying to say?'

'Yes,' she breathed, as tears pricked at the corner of her eyes.

By now, Marcy was staring at her, perplexed. 'What's going on?'

And suddenly before Leonie's watery eyes, Adam himself appeared out front, mobile phone in hand and smiling at her through the glass.

For a second, she wondered if she might be dreaming, but then just as quickly and almost certainly instinctively, Leonie bolted out the door and practically launched herself at the love of her life.

They held on to each another for a long time, Leonie hugging him to her as if he might disappear as easily as he'd materialised, before she finally drew back and looked at him. 'What are you doing here?'

'What do you think I'm doing?' he laughed. It had been so long since she'd seen that smile and she wanted to kiss every inch of it. 'Didn't you get all that on the phone? Or do I really need to send a bouquet?'

'But when did you . . . ? I mean, how did you . . . ?' Then she understood, and her lips pursed in automatic disapproval. 'Grace.'

'Now, before you jump to any conclusions, she said absolutely nothing of her own free will. Not that you'd do anything like that – jump to conclusions, I mean,' he teased and Leonie turned pink. 'But before we get into this, I think it's only fair you put your woman there out of her misery,' he added, looking past her shoulder to where Marcy was watching, open-mouthed.

Going back inside, Leonie quickly made introductions, and a rather half-hearted attempt at an explanation.

'Hey, I recognise you,' Marcy said eyeing Adam suspiciously. 'You were here yesterday, weren't you?'

Adam shrugged and looked at Leonie. 'I thought you might be working, but she said it was your day off.'

'And you didn't think to mention it?' she gasped at Marcy.

'I just assumed he was a customer. Hey, this is a florist's, not a dating service!' she said feigning irritation but Leonie could see a smile working its way across her lips. 'Now, get the hell on out of here. Clearly you and this guy have some stuff to sort out.'

Leonie grabbed her things, not needing to be told twice.

'Charming,' Adam said, when they went outside.

'Don't mind Marcy, her bark is worse than her bite, and she's been brilliant to me this last while.'

'So – a florist's?' he queried, raising his eyebrows. 'How did that come about?

Leonie shrugged. 'She was looking for staff and I needed a job. Anyway, forget about how I ended up here, how on earth did *you*? How did you find me?'

'I'll tell you all when my teeth stop chattering,' Adam said, and she noticed for the first time that he was only wearing a T-shirt. 'Bloody hell, so much for California being warm and sunny. It's like bloody Siberia!'

'You get used to it,' she said thinking back on how she too had found the climate difficult at first. 'But maybe we should go for a coffee somewhere and help warm you up.'

They stopped off at a café nearby, and as she sat at the table as Adam paid for their coffees, Leonie was tempted to pinch herself. Adam was here in San Francisco, and he had forgiven her! She couldn't believe it and was dying to find out what was going on, or more importantly how he had found her. It had to be Grace, of course.

'It was Suzanne, actually,' Adam admitted once the coffee had warmed him up.

'What?' Leonie didn't know what to make of this and once again, she shifted uncomfortably at the memory. 'Adam, I can't tell you how sorry I am for all of that, and especially for my part in it. I should never have—'

'I know – I got your letter.'

She looked away, feeling kind of silly all over again. Inspired by Nathan's letters to Helena, a while back she'd written one of her own.

*I know I'm probably the last person you want to hear from,
but I just wanted to let you know how sorry I am. You have
to know that I would never do anything to hurt you, at least
not intentionally, but I made a big mistake, a huge mistake
this time.*

*I realise there's no going back, and I'm not asking for that;
I just wanted to let you to know how much I regret what
happened, and how I wish from the bottom of my heart it
never happened, or that I hadn't caused it. But it did, and
it's all my fault, and I would do anything to have the chance
to go back and undo it all.*

But I can't.

I know I don't have any right to ask, but I hope you're OK?

*I'm really not sure what else to say. Just know that I never
meant to hurt you, and I'm so very, very sorry.*

Please forgive me.
Leonie

Having once again sworn her friend to secrecy, she'd given
it to Grace during her visit here and asked her to send it on
to Adam.

'Although I'm sure he couldn't care less now one way or
the other,' she'd told her at the time.

'I'll make sure it gets to him anyway,' Grace promised.

That was weeks ago, when she and Alex were still in the
midst of trying to find Helena and, like Nathan, Leonie felt
that she needed to do something to atone for her own behaviour. She had no idea what Adam would make of it, but it
had certainly made her feel a bit better, temporarily at least.

'I'm so sorry,' she repeated now, tears in her eyes.

'Hey, as I said before, it's OK,' Adam insisted. 'Yes, I was
angry at the time, actually livid would probably be a better

description, and very hurt too, but . . . ' He swallowed hard, and Leonie knew that whatever about the anger, the hurt certainly hadn't gone away. 'Anyway, as I said I've sort of come to terms with it.'

'Well, I know it's probably none of my business, but do you mind me asking what happened after you . . . I mean when you . . . I'm sorry, I'm not really sure what I'm trying to say.'

'You're wondering if I took your suspicions any further? Well of course I did.'

He went on to explain how, following weeks of denial and downright anger, most of which was directed at the by-now absent Leonie, he eventually plucked up the courage to confront Andrea.

'She vehemently denied it at first, until I started threatening her with DNA tests and legal action,' he said, his jaw tightening. 'Then she caved. Said she wasn't quite sure herself at the time, because she and Billy had been on a break when we got together, so she'd just assumed . . . ' He exhaled deeply. 'But as you say, you'd want to have been an idiot not to notice the resemblance. In her defence, she says that it was only when Suzanne got older that she realised she'd made a mistake. But by then of course I was already paying maintenance and Suze and I had a close relationship, so what could she do? I try to keep telling myself that she genuinely didn't set out to hoodwink me, but at the same time I just can't say for sure.'

'I'm so sorry, Adam. I should never have even suggested anything, especially when I know how much you love Suzanne. I opened a can of worms that should never have been touched, I know that now, but at the time, all I could think about was how she'd deceived you and I was angry about that. I was so caught up in the immorality of it all that I didn't stop to think how the truth coming out would affect you or Suzanne or any of us really.'

'I know that, but I don't mind admitting that for a long time, I swung wildly from directing my fury from you to Andrea and back again. It was like you'd both let me down. And caught in the middle of it all was Suzanne, this poor confused and innocent little kid who knew nothing about what was going on.'

Leonie had tears in her eyes. 'The poor thing, I can only imagine.' And it was all her fault.

'But as I said, once I'd calmed down and tried to put things in perspective, I realised that to all intents and purposes she *is* my daughter, Leonie. And I love her very much. I've been caring for her and about her for the last fifteen years, and I couldn't give that up overnight just because the DNA wasn't right.'

'I know, and that night, the night it . . . all came out,' she said reddening, 'I realised that too. Problem was I realised it too late, as I'd already led you so far down that path . . . it was almost like a runaway train, and I couldn't stop it.'

'That was something I only realised afterwards too. You didn't actually say anything about Billy that night, did you? You just suggested it.'

She nodded. 'Suggesting it was bad enough. It was none of my business and I had no right.'

'Well, I can't say I'm glad that it happened, or that I don't feel a complete idiot for being taken to the cleaners by Andrea after all this time. Rest assured that that extra maintenance she was so fond of has been completely choked off now and she was lucky I didn't choke her with it.' He gave a wan smile. 'But at the end of the day, I don't regret it either because it helped her raise Suzanne into the young lady she is today.'

'So what happened?' Leonie asked, recalling what Grace

had said about Suzanne moving in with Adam. 'Did you tell Suzanne the truth?'

Adam gave her a strange smile. 'Actually no, because as far as I'm concerned she *is* my daughter. As for Billy, apparently he hasn't a clue one way or another, and I doubt he'd care either way. You were right; he is bad news and a very bad role model for a girl her age. So having talked it out, Andrea and I eventually came to an agreement not to say anything. Of course, she's happy enough to keep it quiet, as she knows there'd be ructions if it all came out now. Maybe we will tell Suzanne one day, but now is not the time, not at such a fragile age.'

Leonie nodded, understanding. While for Adam's sake she was horrified at the scenario, and not entirely in agreement about the ongoing deception, it wasn't really up to her to decide. And Adam was right: landing such a bombshell on Suzanne wasn't in the teenager's best interests, at least not for the moment.

'So, I didn't see her for a while, but as this happened to coincide with your leaving, she assumed it was because I was heartbroken.'

Leonie smiled. 'Well, I'm glad I did something right!'

'She wasn't wrong, you know,' he said, his tone growing serious. 'Yes, I was angry about what had happened, but when the dust settled, I realised I'd taken it out on you when it wasn't your fault. But by then you had disappeared into thin air and I had no idea you'd left the city, let alone the country! For a while I just assumed you'd gone abroad to stay with either of your folks to lay low for a while and let me get it all out of my system.'

'I guess I should have at least let you know what I was doing. But the truth was, Adam, I wasn't quite sure myself and I didn't honestly think you'd care. I just wanted to get away from what I'd done, I wasn't even sure where and somehow I just ended up here.' She blushed. 'It's stupid, I know, but I've always found it easier to just get away and put all the bad stuff behind me. Anyway, you never answered my question. How did you find me? It couldn't have been the letter . . . you mentioned something about Suzanne?'

'Yes. Well, as I said, when I eventually came to my senses, she insisted on coming to stay with me for a while, so she could try and help take my mind off my broken heart.' He laughed. 'But she could see first-hand how miserable I was – especially after getting that letter – and when she asked what had happened I told her that we'd had an argument about the wedding, and that you'd left me. She'd cottoned on to the fact we'd gone through a rough patch when I lost my job, and she put two and two together and decided that it was all her fault for asking for too much money.' At this Leonie's eyes widened. 'I don't know, I guess she's more clued-up than we gave her credit for. Anyway, it took me ages to convince her that it wasn't about that, but she wouldn't listen. After that I think she made it a bit of a mission to try and get us back together. But in order to do that, she had to do what I couldn't – find you. So to cut a long story short, one day in town, she bumped into Ray – she knew him from that time he and Grace came to dinner, remember? Well, he revealed that he was minding the twins while Grace had gone to San Francisco.'

'But Grace never said a word!' she exclaimed, thinking that surely her friend would have given her some kind of warning.

'To be perfectly honest, I doubt Grace even has a clue that Ray let it slip. As I said Suzanne can be very persuasive, and through some combination of guile and trickery, she also managed to get out of him that you worked in something to do with a florist's or gardening. Don't ask me how she did it; clearly she learned a few tricks from her mother – she certainly didn't get it from me anyway,' he joked, but still Leonie could see the pain in his eyes.

'I don't believe it! How could she have possibly got that much information out of him?' But Ray could be a bit naive, and Suzanne was indeed very persuasive.

'Come on, it's Suzanne we're talking about here? You know as well as I do that she can be a demon for getting her own way! But however she managed it, she managed it, and after that it was only a matter of googling every florist or nursery in the entire city, and then phoning them up to find out if an Irish girl called Leonie worked there. She did that herself, and found you within a few days.' He shook his head, a mixture of pride and disbelief in his eyes.

'And you came all the way over here to find me? Why not just phone?'

'Because I know what you're like, and I knew from the letter that you'd blamed yourself for everything that had happened. I wanted to tell you personally that everything was OK. And hell, I fancied the trip, as we never got to go on that honeymoon. But mostly, because Suzanne insisted upon it.'

'She made you come all the way out here?'

'She said you'd been very good to her recently,' he said, a question in his eyes and Leonie deduced that Suzanne must have been grateful she hadn't grilled her too heavily about being on the Pill, or told her father about it. She smiled, pleased that Suzanne thought highly enough of her to help try and get her and Adam back together. 'And she reckoned it was the only way I could convince you to come back. But I suppose there was a side of her that fancied the trip too so we waited a few weeks until she could get the time off school.'

Leonie blinked. 'You mean she's here with you?'

'Yep. We're staying in some hotel down by Fisherman's Wharf. And while I've spent the last few days staking out Flower Power in the hope you'll be there, she's been going mad buying stuff in Gap, and has me eating in all these mad places like Forrest Gump . . . '

'You mean *Bubba* Gumps,' Leonie corrected laughingly. 'I can't believe you and Suzanne came all the way out here to find me!'

'And hopefully bring you back too,' Adam said gently and she looked up.

'Do you really mean that?' she said, her heart singing.

She wanted more than anything in the world to go back to him and the life they'd had before. Of course she'd miss this city, her job and especially Alex and Marcy, but being with Adam was much more important. OK, so Marcy would probably be a bit miffed about leaving her in the lurch, but she was sure Alex would be fine. Anyway, she was certain they would all keep in touch, and they could always come and visit . . .

Adam reached for her hand. 'Why else do you think I came all the way out here? It wasn't for the sunshine, let me tell you.'

'Well, I wasn't sure, I thought maybe you might have just wanted to tell me how things panned out, just you know . . . so I wouldn't have to worry about it anymore.'

Adam shook his head fondly. 'Maybe back there I should have made things clearer by asking for a bouquet of red tulips.'

'Why red tulips?'

He gave her a disappointed look. 'What – you don't know? Some florist you are.'

'Honestly, I don't know,' Leonie insisted, trying to rack her

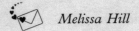

brains once again. Red roses yes, but red tulips? 'What do they signify?'

'Well, seeing as you're the one who likes to solve mysteries,' Adam said with a mischievous smile, 'I guess you're just going to have to figure that one out for yourself.'

Chapter 36

September

The morning mail plopped on to the mat, and Alex padded barefoot into the hallway to retrieve it.

She was expecting a few things this week; in particular a wedding invitation. Leonie was back in Ireland and back with Adam, and while she missed her friend, she knew she was insanely happy.

Aha, there it was!

Going back into the kitchen, Alex opened the first envelope, immediately recognising Leonie's distinctive handwriting.

Removing the contents, she had to smile at the sickeningly sentimental, but at the same time unashamedly romantic inscriptions on the invite. The theme on the day would be 'everlasting love' which apparently had something to do with red tulips, as there were pictures of them dotted all over the invite! It was – as the girl herself might describe it – 'pure Leonie'. Clearly she hadn't changed.

Alex was really looking forward to travelling to Dublin for the wedding at the end of the year. She hadn't been to the Emerald Isle before, and it was supposed to be a pretty cool place. It would be nice to see her and Adam too; they'd met a few months back when Leonie's fiancé had come to the city to whisk her off her feet and bring her back to Dublin, and he seemed like a really sweet guy. Not to mention it would be good to catch up with Grace too.

By the sound of things, this wedding would be one hell of a celebration.

Then Alex's gaze shifted towards the second, more official-looking piece of mail. Her eyes widened when she saw the postmark. Could this finally be it?

She took a deep breath, and turning it over, opened the flap before gently sliding a single piece of paper out of the envelope.

She felt a mix of emotions as she unfolded the document and examined it properly.

State of California Divorce Decree

The bonds of matrimony now existing between the Plaintiff and the Defendant are dissolved on the grounds of irreconcilable differences, and the Plaintiff is awarded an absolute decree of divorce from the Defendant.

So that was that.

Her marriage to Seth was finally over. There were no more delays, intentional mistakes and most importantly, no more disagreements. After their long conversation at the hospital, he finally understood what Alex wanted – what she *needed* – and for once he'd agreed with her, and complied with her wishes.

'I guess you're right,' he admitted sadly, when she'd managed to convince him that there was no other way. 'It is worthless. We made a mockery of our vows.'

She knew that Jon too was relieved to have the situation finally clarified.

Having made a fresh pot of coffee, she put the single sheaf

of paper signifying the end of her marriage under her arm and returned to the bedroom.

'Anything interesting?' her companion asked.

'Mmm, maybe,' she teased, before happily dangling the piece of paper in front of his face.

'Well it's about time!' he exclaimed, sounding just as pleased as she was.

Getting back into bed, Alex slid beneath the covers alongside him while together they both studied the divorce decree, each keenly aware of its significance.

'So, I guess, that's that then,' she said, resting her head against his bare chest. 'As of today that marriage is done, over with, history.'

'And thank the Lord for that too,' Seth chuckled, reaching down and gently kissing his ex-wife on the head. 'We've got that blank page you wanted, so now we get to start over.'

Epilogue

Nathan was alone in the day room by the window, reading the latest Grisham novel. He liked Grisham; the guy wrote in great detail about skulduggery amongst the upper echelons of politics and power and by Nathan's reckoning, always got it pretty much spot on. Nathan had more experience than he'd like with that kind of thing, but he was never really cut out for politics. His brother, on the other hand, had exactly the right personality for mixing with the wheelers and dealers, which was probably why David was still out there fighting the great fight, while Nathan was stuck here doing – well, doing nothing really . . .

He paused mid-thought, as he heard the sound of footsteps outside in the hallway and Frank's loud booming tones getting closer.

'I should warn you that he can be a cantankerous old goat sometimes, but don't take it personally,' the other man joked, stopping outside Nathan's room. 'Yo, Nate my man,' he called in, 'you've got a visitor today so be nice.'

Visitor? What visitor? Nathan had never had a visitor here before.

'Must be some mistake,' he muttered gruffly, turning to look, but Frank had already taken off back down the hallway, whistling as he went. 'I don't know about any . . .'

But then his gaze alighted on the solitary figure standing in the doorway, and his old ticker gave a little somersault.

It couldn't be . . . could it?

And right then time seemed to slow down, as incredibly, Nathan came face to face with the woman he had loved for most of his life, yet never expected to see again.

'Helena . . . ?' he said croakily, unable to believe his eyes.

'Hello, Nathan,' the woman said, moving tentatively towards him, her hands shaking. Even though he could see she was old, as old as he was, the years just seemed to melt away and in his mind, she was forever twenty-two and he would be forever twenty-four.

Helena . . .

'I'm hallucinating, I must be,' he whispered softly, unable to take his eyes off her. 'Frank must have upped my meds this morning.'

'It's no hallucination, Nathan,' she replied with a nervous laugh. 'But I must say I'm glad you recognise me after all this time.'

'How could I not when you're still as beautiful as ever? Oh my Lord, is it really you?' he said, his voice cracking with emotion, as he went to get up out of his chair.

'It's really me,' she said, approaching slowly. 'I talked to your brother a while back and he told me you were here, so I thought it was time I paid you a visit.'

'Never thought you'd see me in a place like this, did you?' he said suddenly self-conscious about his surroundings. All this must look pathetic to her.

'Nothing wrong with being looked after, Nathan,' she replied gently. 'After all you've been through.'

'Ah, the only thing wrong with me is laziness,' he told her lightly, 'that and a pesky old ticker, which means I have to let these clowns push me around and tell me what to do.'

'It's a very pretty place and that aide seems nice too.'

'Yeah, Frank's OK,' Nathan agreed. 'But this is an open patient facility you know, I can get out of here whenever I like. I just don't bother all that much.'

It was the only reason he'd agreed to residential care; if Cypress Gardens had been a closed facility Nathan would have run a mile.

Well, he would have tried anyway.

'So that's how you delivered that last letter.' Helena said, as if talking to herself, and Nathan's head snapped up.

'You mean you got my sympathy note? I wasn't sure if you were still living at Green Street, but when I read about your mom in the obits in the *Chronicle*, I thought I'd drop by to pass on my condolences next time I was in town. I couldn't bring myself to ring the bell though . . . '

'I haven't lived there for forty years, Nathan. Actually, I haven't set foot inside the place since . . . well, since the last time you and I . . . ' She trailed off, bashful. 'So I'm sorry but I never got those other letters you sent either. At least not until recently.'

'The other ones . . . ' he repeated frowning, 'you mean the ones from—'

'Yes. I didn't get them way back then, you see. I moved away, and Mom must have kept them for me, and it was only when . . . oh, it's such a long story.'

She was close now, so close that Nathan was almost afraid to touch her in case it was really all a dream and she would dissolve in front of his eyes. 'Well, as you can probably tell, I've got all the time in the world to hear it,' he murmured, tentatively reaching for her hand.

'I'm so sorry, I should never have made you choose like that.' Helena was moved to tears as the emotion of it all overwhelmed her too. 'It's me who should be asking for forgiveness, I should never have . . . '

'Shush, it's OK,' he interjected gently and closed his eyes as his precious Helena rested her head on his shoulder. 'None of that means anything now, and I don't care how long those letters took to find you. All that matters is that they did and you're here.'

Then, Helena gently wrapped her arms around him, and for the first time since returning to his country thirty-eight years before, Nathan felt like he'd finally come home.

before
I forget

melissa hill

Abbie's memories are her most precious thing.

Even though they're sometimes painful, she can't stop
herself looking back, reliving the love of her life.

Until a freak accident means that she could lose it all:
every memory and experience she has ever had.

Abby can't believe it's true. She feels fine.
How could she possibly forget all those moments
that make her who she is?

Determined to fight it, Abby makes a list
of things she's always wanted to do. She's going
to save her memory by having the most
unforgettable year of her life.

HODDER

wishful thinking
melissa hill

Louise wishes she could be slim, pretty, and popular.
So she can't believe it when it seems her wish is coming
true. If only it didn't all cost so much . . .

Dara wishes she could go back in time, and change
everything. But she's married now, and nothing can
change that. Can it?

Rosie wishes she knew how to make her children happy.
Even though they're both grown up with their own lives,
they seem to need her more than ever.

Three very different women, about to make a journey
that will change their lives forever.
You should be careful what you wish for . . .

HODDER

the last to
know

melissa hill

Eve knows what she wants.
After nine good years and two lovely children together,
it's about time Liam made an honest woman of her.
After all, they're as good as married anyway.

Eve's sister Sam knows more than she should.
Sam has always thought that Eve's too good for Liam.
And she can't help but be suspicious about the
long business trips to Australia that take him
away from his family all too often.

Meanwhile, on the other side of the world,
Brooke knows nothing.
Then a mysterious delivery arrives and promises
to change her life forever. It seems someone doesn't
want Brooke to be the last to know . . .

HODDER